THE OFFSIDE CORONER

THE OFFSIDE CORONER

BOOK EIGHT OF THE
FENWAY STEVENSON MYSTERIES

PAUL AUSTIN ARDOIN

THE OFFSIDE CORONER
Copyright © 2020 by Paul Austin Ardoin
Published by Pax Ardsen Books

ISBN 978-1-949082-39-5
First Edition: September 2022

For information please visit:
www.paulaustinardoin.com

Edited by Max Christian Hansen and Jess Reynolds,

Cover design by Ziad Ezzat of Feral Creative Colony
www.feralcreativecolony.com

10 9 8 7 6 5 4 3 2 1

In memory of Katie

TABLE OF CONTENTS

PART 1

THURSDAY

CHAPTER ONE

Shadows from the candles danced on the white tablecloth. In the dim light, Fenway Stevenson looked across the table at Craig McVie, who smiled easily as he took a sip of wine. Fenway returned her gaze to the two women at the table about ten feet behind his left shoulder.

He set the wineglass down and searched her face. "What's going on?"

McVie cleaned up good, as her mother would have said. His tailored suit fit his muscular body well, the blue in his tie pulling out the color of his eyes. His freckles gave his face a boyish quality, but it was a good look.

Both women were in profile, sitting across from each other, as the server set salads in front of them.

"I know you think I won't attract as much attention as you," Fenway said, "but I still think you should be on this side of the table."

"I had to slip the maître-d' fifty bucks to sit us here," McVie murmured, leaning forward. "I'm not screwing it up by looking like a creepy guy taking pictures of two famous women."

Fenway gasped.

McVie's eyes went wide. "What? What happened?"

"Annabel." Fenway leaned forward conspiratorially and whispered, "She ate a bite of salad."

McVie's shoulders slumped, and he shook his head, the corners of his mouth curving up slightly. "Fine, I deserved that." He took out his phone, tapped the screen, and handed it to Fenway from across the table. "But we still have a job to do."

Fenway glanced at the screen: the camera app. Of course. "This is so gauche," Fenway said, forcing a smile as she held up the phone.

"People come to Maxime's for special occasions all the time. They're fine with pictures."

Fenway pointed the camera phone slightly above her smiling boyfriend's right shoulder, zooming in on the two women at the table behind him.

She checked the photo on the screen. It was a clear, in-focus shot of two casually-dressed women having dinner at a nice restaurant. The woman on the left was in her mid-thirties and had high cheekbones and a smooth, luminous complexion, with skin dark enough that she, like Fenway, might also be half-Black. Even sitting, the woman looked tall—possibly even taller than Fenway.

"Well?"

"They're eating," Fenway said in a low voice. "Not staring longingly into each other's eyes, not making kissy-faces—"

"Take a couple more," McVie said.

Fenway raised the phone and tapped the screen again.

The young woman on the right looked to be in her early twenties, with brown hair brushing the tops of her shoulders, large green eyes, and a pale, freckled complexion. She wore dark jeans and a billowy cream-colored blouse. But with folded arms, her demeanor, unlike her dinner companion's, was hardly relaxed.

Fenway handed the phone back to McVie and spoke in low tones.

"If Annabel and Maggie *are* having an affair, they're having a fight." She glanced quickly at the younger woman, who pursed her lips while looking across the table.

"A lovers' quarrel?"

"Maybe." Fenway squinted. "Mathilda could be wrong, you know. This might just be a fight about their soccer team."

McVie chuckled. "And how can you tell the difference?"

"I don't know. The start of training camp can be tough. Annabel's at the end of her career. Maggie's the next big thing. Maybe Annabel's trying to give Maggie the benefit of her experience and Maggie's being an arrogant prick."

"More photos," McVie said, handing the phone back.

Fenway cocked her head, a smile playing on her lips.

"Please," McVie finished.

"Sure." Fenway took the phone and snapped another photo. She always enjoyed any excuse to eat at Maxime's, but the specter of McVie's assignment hung oppressively over the table. Why did Mathilda Montague hire McVie, anyway? She'd read the "50 Most Powerful Women" articles—surely Montague had a security detail to follow her wife around.

McVie cocked his head. "Is there *anything* suggesting they're involved?" He was tenacious; that much was clear. And perhaps that's what Mathilda Montague wanted: a bulldog private eye Annabel wouldn't recognize so she'd let her guard down.

"They're two athletes going out to dinner." Fenway handed the phone back. "Even if they *are* sleeping together, they probably know better than to show it in a place like this."

McVie placed the phone above Fenway's place setting. "Why don't you hang onto this? If they do anything—"

"Unless she wants thirty pictures of her wife eating lettuce, there's nothing to see."

"Not yet, maybe." McVie leaned back. "I wish I could hear their conversation."

"They're not talking," Fenway said. She leaned forward and smiled. "We could use this time to pretend that you and I are on an actual date."

McVie grinned. "Of course."

Fenway sat back in her chair. "You know, we haven't done a whole lot since I—since I got back from L.A." She ran a hand over her head; her hair was finally starting to grow back. "Dinner every so often, and I stay over a lot, but we haven't even been to a movie or gone out dancing."

"We went to Magic Mountain for the weekend." McVie chuckled. "And you like roller coasters way more than I do." His face pinched slightly. "But I know what you mean. I've been swamped with the demands of the business." He looked up at her. "And I figured you needed the break. You do look more rested since you got back."

Fenway scoffed. "After what I went through? There was only one way to go." And even before she'd been accused of murder in L.A.: the car bomb that had almost killed her, her father jumping in front of a bullet meant for her—Fenway looked down at the table.

"I just meant," McVie said quickly, "that it's good to see you happier." He motioned to the table behind him with his head. "Maybe I could whisk you away to Vegas and take you to a Neons game."

"Also on your client's dime?" Fenway picked up her fork and examined it, then set it back down. "Have you heard any rumors about the Neons?"

McVie sat up straight. "Like what?"

"Like—if they're for sale?"

He picked up his wineglass and took a small sip. "Are you suggesting my client might want to buy the Neons, and that's why she's having me—"

"Not her," Fenway said. "Dad."

McVie set his glass down. "Nathaniel Ferris—buying the Las Vegas Neons?"

Fenway cleared her throat. "Okay—my dad has been asking me about owning a sports team." She leaned forward. "At first, I just laughed—I mean, he's rich, but all the baseball and basketball teams are way out of his price range. But now—well, with the Neons holding training camp here, I realized he might be talking about a team in the AFF."

"He wants to *own* a women's soccer team?"

Fenway shrugged. "Ever since Ferris Energy sold, he hasn't had a lot to do. I think he's romanticizing team ownership, but I understand the appeal." Fenway gave McVie a half-smile. "He likes being a big fish in a small pond. If he bought the Vegas Neons, he'd be the biggest fish in the league."

The server brought their entrees, a large steak for McVie and seared scallops for Fenway, who widened her eyes as the dish was placed in front of her.

"Lovely," Fenway murmured.

"I'm glad you finally figured out Maxime's has other things on the menu besides pheasant."

"Perhaps one day," Fenway said, a wry smile crossing her face as she picked up her fork and knife, "I'll be adventurous as you are."

McVie stared at his bone-in ribeye. "Are you saying—"

"You get the same steak every time we come here? Yes." Fenway put a scallop in her mouth and chewed. Buttery, garlicky, fantastic.

McVie picked up his fork. "Besides your dad's sudden interest in women's soccer, have you heard anything else that makes you think the Neons are for sale?"

Fenway swallowed. "No. But after Sandra Christchurch's husband passed away, there's been talk that her heart isn't in it anymore." She lifted a forkful of potato to her mouth. "Plus, with those two behind you on the team—this is the year to sell high. Annabel Shedd is still on cereal boxes."

Fenway ate a few more bites as she kept one eye on the table behind McVie. Maggie Erskine was withdrawing more and more into herself. She hadn't taken a bite of food in several minutes. Annabel leaned forward, talking, but Maggie crossed her arms and didn't meet Annabel's eyes. Hmm—maybe this *was* a conversation about their relationship.

"What's going on?" McVie asked in a low voice.

"It looks like Annabel is telling Maggie something she doesn't want to hear," Fenway said. "Maybe Maggie *is* being an asshole."

Annabel stopped talking, set her fork down with a sigh, and got up from the table.

"Oh—she's leaving the table."

"Who? Maggie or—"

"Shh!" Fenway hushed sharply. Annabel walked quickly past their table, her footsteps solid, shoulders tense as she ran a hand over her face and exhaled slowly.

"Excuse me," Fenway said, shoving another scallop into her mouth. Ooh—it was delicious. Maybe even better than the pheasant. "I need to go to the restroom."

McVie reached across the table and took Fenway's hand. "Don't make it obvious you're following her."

Fenway gave McVie a sly smile. "It'll look like I want her autograph." She pushed her chair back and stood. She hated to leave at the beginning of the meal—hopefully her food wouldn't be cold when she got back.

She wound her way between the tables to the back, where she ducked into a hallway with a subtle and elegant "Rest Rooms" sign. Annabel stood halfway down the hall with her back to Fenway, about ten steps past the door to the women's restroom.

"I swear, if you don't do something about Maggie and that

monster, I will," Annabel hissed into her cell phone. Fenway barely heard Annabel's words, but fortunately, the hallway's plush carpet deadened the noise coming from the dining room. She walked as slowly as she dared toward the women's restroom, then opened the door quietly. She didn't think Annabel noticed—and that was good. She wouldn't have to pretend to be a fan who followed her into the restroom.

Once inside, Fenway paused, listening carefully. The door was too thick to make out anything Annabel was saying in the hallway. She turned the corner, finding a large, comfortable area with marble sinks with elegant brass fixtures on the right side and a row of stalls with dark wooden doors on the left.

Fenway had left her purse on her chair: a rookie mistake. She couldn't pretend to be fixing her makeup. She took a deep breath and turned to the mirror.

McVie was right: In the two months since Fenway had cleared her name, she looked happier. Less exhausted, anyway. The bags under her eyes were almost completely gone. Of course, it helped that her workload had been light for the last eight weeks.

And she and McVie were having fun—and maybe more than that. They'd gone away for the weekend—yes, only to Magic Mountain for a couple of days, but she hadn't gone on a vacation with a boyfriend for—well, she couldn't say for sure she'd *ever* done it. She smiled at her reflection. Her hair, finally getting long enough to style a little, was behaving exceptionally well. She hoped McVie wouldn't have his mind on his client too much tonight.

The door opened.

Fenway stepped forward to the sink and washed her hands as Annabel walked in. Fenway stole a glance as the soccer star stood next to her, lips pursed, her eyes staring daggers at her own reflection.

Fenway cleared her throat. "Hey, I'm sorry, I know you're out to dinner and all, but—you're Annabel Shedd, aren't you?"

Shedd startled and seemed to notice Fenway for the first time. "Oh—uh, yes."

"I watched you score the winning goal in the World Cup. You're fantastic."

A tired smile crossed Shedd's face. "Thanks."

"Not often we get celebrities all the way up in Estancia."

"Sure," Shedd said easily. "The Neons have their training camp over at the university this year."

"Oh, Nidever University, right? I think I remember reading about that." Fenway gave Shedd what she hoped was a warm smile, then went for the kill. "This is such a romantic restaurant, isn't it?"

Annabel furrowed her brow. "Is it?"

"Well—I'm here with my boyfriend. Hasn't taken me anywhere in a while, so I think a place like this is his way of making it up to me."

"I hope you're enjoying your night. Always nice to meet a fan." She turned and went into a stall, signaling the end of the conversation.

Fenway took a paper towel and dried her hands. She'd been hoping to get some kind of reaction with the romantic restaurant comment. Maybe Annabel would be startled that dinner with Maggie might be seen as romance. But no, Annabel hadn't been flustered at all. No information.

Perhaps Annabel was thinking of something else: *If you don't do something about Maggie and that monster, I will.*

It's possible that Maggie had a problematic ex, or maybe a stalker. Or maybe Annabel was trying to convince Maggie to get out of an abusive relationship. Fenway's shoulders were tight as she walked out of the restroom.

She walked back through the main dining room. Maggie slumped forward with her elbows on the table, not touching her food. Fenway sat and looked at McVie's plate; his enormous steak was half-eaten.

Fenway scooted in and ate another scallop. It was, fortunately, still warm.

"Well?"

Fenway chewed and swallowed, then leaned forward, her voice low. "Annabel was on the phone. She said something about keeping Maggie away from 'that monster,' and said she'd do it herself if she had to."

McVie pursed his lips. "Not exactly a smoking gun for their affair."

"No." Fenway took another bite. "And when Annabel came into the bathroom, I gushed about Maxime's being a romantic restaurant. Hoping to get some sort of indication one way or the other."

"Like a guilty reaction?"

"Right. I was hoping she'd react like she'd been caught cheating with Maggie." Fenway crinkled her nose. "But that was a no-go. She acted surprised that it was considered romantic, then wished me a good evening."

McVie scratched his chin. "That doesn't help either way. I don't know—Matilda is convinced Annabel is having an affair."

Fenway frowned. "Does she think Annabel is cheating on her with Maggie specifically, or was it a feeling she was sleeping with someone else?"

"She mentioned Maggie specifically."

"If Annabel is trying to get Maggie out of a bad situation," Fenway said, "I can see how it might look like an affair. How a spouse hundreds of miles away might get the wrong idea." Fenway put another bite of food on her fork and stared at it for a moment. She used to be like Montague too, she was sure. Jealous. Insecure about all the relationships she'd ever been in, even friendships. For a long time, it had been Fenway and her mom against the world, and Fenway didn't trust anyone to look out for her.

"Maybe Annabel is trying to convince Maggie to leave her current relationship because she wants Maggie all to herself."

Fenway furrowed her brow.

McVie shrugged. "I've seen a lot of cheating spouses in the last few months. It's never all about the sex. There's always something that looks innocent at first. A friend helping you through a tough time. Two work colleagues blowing off a little steam at a bar. These things never come out of the blue."

Fenway was silent.

"You okay?"

Fenway looked up at McVie. "Just thinking about the *monster* comment."

McVie straightened up and shot Fenway a warning glance. A moment later, Annabel crossed in front of their table and sat back down with Maggie.

"We can talk shop afterward," McVie said. "Let's enjoy this dinner since it's delicious."

"And since it's going on the expense account."

"Which makes it taste a little better, yes."

Fenway batted her eyelashes. "Maybe I'll get a second glass of wine."

Ten minutes later, Fenway was done with her meal. McVie had made a sizable dent in the second half of his steak. Fenway picked up her wineglass, a single sip left.

"Do you want to stick around, Craig? Another glass, or maybe dessert?"

"We should get the check. Follow them back to the team hotel, make sure they're not headed anywhere they shouldn't be. Then we can go back to my place, and I can type up my notes."

"We could." She leaned forward and ran her finger around the rim of her glass. "Or my place."

"All my stuff for the case is at my place."

Fenway emptied her glass. They'd been spending most nights at his place lately, mostly with this same excuse: he'd had to go out on an investigation at some point in the evening, and he had to type up his notes.

Then it hit her: they'd spent every night for the past two weeks together. She hadn't planned it, and she'd seen other friends. She'd gone out for drinks at Winfrey's with her staff. She'd eaten dinner with Sarah a couple of times—McVie only wanted to eat at Dos Milagros once a week, and Sarah was a more-than-willing partner in crime. But after dinner with Sarah, she'd driven to McVie's, arriving moments after he'd returned from staking out another possibly-cheating spouse.

After the excitement of the last year—wow, had it almost been a year since she'd moved to Estancia?—she was glad to have a few boring days when no one was shooting at her or framing her for murder or trying to stab her in her kitchen. She was all for the adrenaline rush of investigating a case, of working it until something clicked. But she was glad to fall asleep in McVie's arms every night.

Rising voices pulled her out of her reverie.

"I'm not trying to control you, Maggie—" Annabel snapped.

"You don't understand," Maggie retorted, pushing her chair back from the table. She grabbed the short olive-green jacket from the back of the chair. "He's the one who believed in me."

"It's not just him! You could be the starting goalie on half the teams in this league."

"You think I can just go to Minneapolis or Tampa, and they'll build the team around me?"

"I bet a few teams would be happy to—"

"You don't get it," Maggie said, slurring her words. "This league wasn't even around when you came up. You had to scrape and fight for everything." She looked Annabel in the face straight on. "And don't get me wrong, I appreciate it."

Annabel's jaw tightened. "You're better than you give yourself credit for—"

"He plays to my strengths," Maggie said.

"That's what coaches do." Annabel leaned forward. "More than a starter in the league—you'll compete for keeper in the next World Cup. I know what it's like—"

"You don't know what I have to go through."

Annabel sat back in her chair as if stung. "I don't know?"

"I'm going home," Maggie said, getting unsteadily to her feet. "Back to the hotel, I mean. I gotta be ready for tomorrow afternoon."

"I'm only looking out for you."

"Stop trying to control me!"

"Come on, sit down. I'll drive you back to the hotel. You've had a lot to drink."

"I can get an Uber." Maggie turned on her heel, eyes not quite focused completely, and veered toward the front door.

"Maggie—" Annabel grabbed her purse and yanked out a credit card.

"Follow her," McVie hissed.

CHAPTER TWO

Fenway crinkled her nose in confusion. "I thought you wanted to follow Annabel, not Maggie—"

"Where do you think Annabel is going after she pays her bill?" McVie whispered. "Out to see Maggie. And I have to close out, too."

"I can't just go out and stand next to Maggie. She'll know something's up."

McVie dug his wallet out of his pocket and held out the valet slip. "Get the car if you need an excuse. Now go."

Fenway grabbed her purse off the back of the chair and hurried outside. She pushed open the heavy front door and walked onto the carpeted area of the sidewalk, under the awning.

Maggie was standing about thirty feet down the sidewalk, past the valet stand, wobbling slightly. She held her cell phone and tapped on the screen.

Fenway froze. Her mind raced—there had to be some way for her to figure out what was going on. Maggie was drunk—that might get her to loosen her tongue.

The door opened again, and Annabel stormed out of Maxime's,

right past Fenway without giving her a second glance. "Maggie —come on."

"I'm going back to the Broadmere," Maggie said, pulling her olive jacket tightly around her. "I'll see you on the field tomorrow."

"I gave you a ride here," Annabel said.

"I don't need a ride back."

"You're drunk."

Maggie held up the phone. "Not too drunk to get an Uber. Go. Finish dessert. I bet there's another rookie on the team who'd love to be *mentored*."

"If you'd just let me explain—" Annabel said, and then looked at the valet stand. A man in a bright blue coat stood there, doing his best to pretend he wasn't hearing the conversation.

"Explain *what?*" Maggie said, mocking Annabel. "Whatcha talking about, superstar?" She spread her arms, then dropped them at her sides. "Whatever you have against him is *your* problem. Maybe you don't need him on your side. But I do." She turned her back on Annabel and walked another few paces down the sidewalk.

Annabel opened her mouth to say something, then appeared to think better of it and clamped her mouth shut. She took two steps backward, then turned and walked back inside as McVie came out.

"Anything?" he asked softly.

"Not yet."

McVie's phone rang, and he pulled it out of his pocket. He looked at the screen and frowned.

"What is it?"

"It's Amy." He glanced at Fenway. "I'm sorry, I have to take this."

Fenway nodded. As much as Fenway disliked Amy, she and McVie were still co-parenting Megan. Fenway didn't like the two of them talking, but she understood—

Fenway grabbed McVie's forearm as he answered.

"Hi, Amy—hang on just a second." McVie looked into Fenway's eyes. "You got an idea?"

Fenway glanced up at McVie and winked. "You know what?" she said loudly enough for Maggie to hear. "Get your own damn car." She shoved the valet ticket into McVie's hand. "We are on a *date*. You talk to your ex on your own time." She turned on her heel and clomped down the sidewalk toward Maggie.

"You okay?" Maggie said to Fenway in a low voice once she got close enough.

"My boyfriend is a dickhead," Fenway said, pulling out her phone. "I fly into town and find out he promised his ex-wife he'd help her install cabinets tomorrow."

Maggie shifted her weight from foot to foot.

"And before you say anything," Fenway said, holding up a finger, "he told her he'd go over there *after* he knew I was coming. I hope there's an Uber available."

She unlocked her phone and tapped a message to McVie.

Sorry it was the first thing that popped into my head
Trying to share an Uber with Maggie back to their hotel

"You're not texting your boyfriend, are you?" Maggie said. "Quickest backslide ever."

"Of course not," Fenway said. "It's one of my friends back home." She sighed melodramatically. "She *told* me he was an asshole. She warned me not to fly down." She frowned as the message showed *Delivered* next to it. She tapped the phone again. "Oh no," she said. "I don't have connectivity. Shit."

"Really?" Maggie said. "Weird. I got five bars."

"I could use a bar, for sure. A full bar." Fenway looked toward the door. "Maybe I can ask them to call me a taxi. How much do you think it would cost for a taxi to take me to the Broadmere Hotel?"

"The Broadmere? That's where I'm staying." Maggie appraised Fenway, leaning too far to one side and nearly losing her balance. Fenway caught her elbow.

"Whoopsie," Fenway said, then internally rolled her eyes. *Whoopsie?*

"I'm frine. Frine. Umm. I'm *fine*. The cocktails hit me a little hard, is all." Maggie pointed at Fenway. "If your man is being an asshole, I bet you could use a drink. And not one of these two-hundred-dollar cabernets, either. Like, a real drink. Like a vodka martini." She enunciated *martini* slowly and carefully.

"Or scotch?"

Maggie pushed her lightly on the shoulder. "Yes! Like scotch. Listen, come share the Uber with me. It's stupid not to when we're both headed to the same place."

"You don't mind?"

Maggie shrugged, then lifted her eyes toward the front door of Maxime's.

Fenway followed her gaze. "You have relationship problems too?"

"What, her?" Maggie laughed. "I'm straight, and she's married. You don't recognize her?"

It was almost a denial—but Fenway had interrogated too many people who'd attempted to mislead her. "I guess I didn't see her very well."

"She *only* scored the winning goal in the World Cup last year." Maggie crinkled her face, and a horrible British accent came out: "Best not forget that."

"Oh, of course—Annabel Shedd. I thought she looked familiar." Fenway cocked her head. "You two are on the women's soccer team in town for training camp, aren't you?"

Maggie raised her hand. "Guilty as charged." She dropped her arm, and her face fell. "I know she's been in the league twelve years longer. I appreciate that, you know?"

"Sure."

"But this is *my* career, not hers. You know? She needs to mind her own business."

"I hear that."

"Yes." Maggie enthusiastically smacked Fenway on the shoulder. "You get it." Her eyes lost focus again. "You know we don't even have a collective bargaining agreement? Everyone says I'm a big deal, and I'm barely making minimum wage." She pointed back at the restaurant. "But Annabel, she gets the makeup ads and the big contracts—"

"And the cereal boxes," Fenway said.

Maggie thumped her upper chest twice, almost at her collarbones. "Nothing is guaranteed for me—*nothing*." She let her hand fall to her side and looked at the ground. "I hope the hotel has some good scotch."

A late-model SUV pulled up to the curb. The window rolled down. "Maggie?" the driver asked.

"That's me," Maggie said, walking around to the other side of the car.

Maggie's defenses were down—maybe Fenway could get her to open up during the ride. Fenway got in.

They rode in silence for a moment, then Fenway piped up. "Thanks for the ride, Maggie."

"You're welcome." She turned to Fenway, her eyes glassy. "What's your name?"

"Joanne." The fake name Fenway always used. It came easily to her lips.

"Sorry, I talk a lot. You said what? You flew here to spend the weekend with your boyfriend? And he's spending it with his ex?"

"I don't mind if he has a decent friendship with her," Fenway said quickly, thinking of McVie's real ex-wife. "I mean, he treats her okay even though she cheated on him, which means he's not a creep. But I took vacation from work. I spent my money to fly here for the weekend. And I'll be stuck in his apartment all day tomorrow while he helps her with her cabinets." She sighed. "Serves me right for going out with him before the divorce was final."

Maggie sank into her seat and was silent.

"So what team are you on again?"

"Oh—the Vegas Neons."

"Really? Didn't you win the league championship last year?"

"Lost in the final."

"And you're a player?"

"Yes."

"What position?" Fenway asked, opening her eyes wide.

"Goalkeeper."

"Oh. Wow. A professional goalie—that's awesome."

"Thanks," Maggie said, but her green eyes darkened.

They pulled up in front of the hotel a few minutes later. Floor-to-ceiling windows were part of the block-long façade of the hotel on Broadway, and the hardwood floors of the lobby were stately and warm. The bar was on the other side of the lobby from reception, probably to minimize noise. Maggie made a beeline for the bar and sat down on an empty stool. The crowd was lively for a Thursday night.

"What can I get you ladies?" the bartender said.

"Scotch," Maggie said, putting her elbows on the bar.

"The same," Fenway said, sitting down next to Maggie. She looked around appreciatively at the fancy décor. "I thought I read an article saying everyone in women's soccer had to share rooms at cheap roadside motels."

"Yeah," Maggie said. "We stayed in some real dumps last year. But this year, Coach Flash is really pulling out all the stops."

"Coach Flash?"

"Oh," Maggie said, "our head coach. Everyone calls him Coach Flash."

"A grown man called Flash? Like Flash Gordon?"

Maggie's eyes glittered. "It's kinda cute, I guess." Her smile dropped. "But man, he works the shit out of us."

"Really?" Fenway leaned forward.

"I mean, the number of times we had two-a-days?" Maggie blew a raspberry. "And he's always on me for everything." She looked up at Fenway and plastered a smile onto her face.

"So ask for a trade."

Maggie shook her head. "He believes in me. He traded Gabby this winter."

"Who's Gabby?"

"You never heard of Gabriela Fortuna?"

"No." A lie—Fenway had read the Neons' media kit—but Maggie barreled on.

"Last year's starter. So now it's on me."

The bartender set down two glasses with an inch of scotch in each. They both picked up their glasses, and Fenway took a drink. Huh—not too bad for a well whisky. She appraised Maggie, who was staring at the scotch glass in her hand. "Fancy place for two team-mates to go out to dinner."

Maggie blinked. "What—that place?" She giggled. "No. Annabel's just too hoity-toity to eat at regular places."

"Ah." Fenway swirled the scotch in her glass, then tried a more direct question—maybe Maggie's tipsiness lowered her guard. "So were the two of you on a date?"

Maggie turned to look at Fenway. "A date? I'm *straight*. Didn't I say that?" She giggled again. "Plus, she's almost fifteen years older than me."

Fenway blinked hard—yes, that was about the same age difference between her and McVie, but that wasn't exactly a denial from Maggie, either. She set her glass down. "You said Coach Flash was pulling out all the stops."

"Yeah. It's been nice. He's treating the team pretty good so far."

What did Coach Flash have to do with the choice of the hotel? "Isn't the owner the one who decides where you stay?"

"Ms. Christchurch might have the checkbook," Maggie said, "but Coach Flash persway—persway—uh, *convinced* her to open it." She flexed her bicep and grinned. "We gotta be well-rested for the season." She took a swig of her scotch. "I shouldn't drink this much. But what the hell—I don't have to be on the field till one."

"Maybe you can sleep late and hydrate."

"This is so stupid, you know?" Maggie's eyes watered, and she blinked quickly. "So stupid."

"What's stupid?"

Maggie gestured vaguely to the bar. "I'm not trying to do anything bad."

Fenway hesitated—maybe this was her chance to get Maggie to open up about her relationship with Annabel. McVie's words ran through her head: *It's never all about the sex. There's always something that looks innocent at first. A friend helping you through a tough time.*

She chose her words carefully. "People don't know the whole situation," Fenway said, looking into Maggie's face. "Some people might judge you, say you're doing a bad thing, but they don't know the whole story, do they?"

Maggie turned to Fenway, and after a brief moment, their eyes locked. "You know what, Jane? You're all right."

Fenway's stomach dropped; Maggie wasn't going to spill her guts. She sighed and didn't bother correcting her fake name. "Maybe this should be your last one."

Maggie stuck her tongue out at Fenway. "I'm here to help a fellow woman get over her boyfriend being a crap bag," she said. "I'm not cutting out after just one drink."

Maybe there was hope yet. Fenway clinked glasses with Maggie and took another sip of scotch.

A tall, trim man in a black sportscoat and a light blue Oxford shirt appeared behind them. He wore a salt-and-pepper beard, and his close-cropped hair was gray where he hadn't yet gone bald. "Good evening, Maggie," he said. "Celebrating your last night of freedom, I see." He turned to Fenway. "You're not with the team."

"This is my friend Jane," Maggie said, reaching out to put her hand on the man's shoulder; she missed, and her hand caught his elbow instead. "Speak of the devil! Jane, this is Coach Flash. You have him to thank for me staying at the same hotel as you."

Flash nodded at Fenway. "Lovely to meet you," he said evenly, in a tone suggesting otherwise. Turning to Maggie, he lowered his voice. "First day of practice tomorrow, Maggie. I might want to work everyone hard. I've put my reputation on the line for you. You want to be on top of your game."

Maggie dropped her eyes.

Flash turned his back on Fenway and clasped Maggie's hand, leaning forward and whispering into Maggie's ear. Then he took a step to the side as Maggie hastily shoved her hand into the pocket of her olive jacket. "I hope to see you again, Jane," he said to Fenway. "Maggie, have a wonderful evening."

Fenway watched him walk away. "He's kind of strict."

"He has to be. Four championships." Maggie wiggled four fingers in front of Fenway's face. "I could be the starting goalie for the team hoisting the Pickering Trophy this year."

"Is this his first year coaching the Neons?"

"Second. He drafted me last year."

"Oh—so when you said he believed in you—"

"He was my coach before," Maggie said, slurring her words. "I was goalie on the championship team at Shellmont U." Her eyes lost focus again. "I'm lucky. He was there for two years when he took a break from the pros."

Fenway took another sip.

"You know how many people started following me on Photoxio after the finals?" Maggie pushed the drink away and stood. "A hundred thousand."

"That's a lot."

Maggie turned toward the elevator, staring for a moment, then glanced back at Fenway. "I know I said I wouldn't be a party pooper."

"You're leaving me? We just got here!"

Maggie leaned forward and spoke in a stage whisper. "Coach Flash. Can't be out late."

"I understand. Thanks for sharing the Uber." Fenway nodded at the bartender. "I'll pick up the tab. Least I can do."

"You're all right, Jane." Maggie hopped off the barstool, then rocked for a moment.

"Need help?"

"I'm frine." She giggled. "Really, I'm frine." She began walking toward the elevator, then spun and pointed to Fenway. "Strength, girl. Don't let that man put his ex over you."

"Thanks, Maggie."

Fenway pulled out her phone. Messages from McVie showed on the screen.

Let me know whats going on
Im outside Broadmere − followd Shedd here

She texted back.

I'm at the Broadmere too − I'll come out after I pay

She flagged down the bartender. "I'm ready for the check."

He smiled. "It's been taken care of."

Fenway raised her eyebrows, then scanned the bar for Coach Flash, finding him sitting at a table on the other side of the room. He checked his watch and then stood and strode to the elevator, not giving Fenway a second glance.

When Coach Flash got into the elevator, Fenway stood from her stool and walked through the lobby and out the front door. She spied McVie's beige Toyota Highlander across the street, about half a block down, and hurried over. McVie was looking at his phone, so she rapped on the passenger window with her knuckles. McVie unlocked the car, and Fenway got in.

"Quick thinking," McVie said.

"Thanks." Fenway stared out the front window as McVie started the engine. "I thought I might have scared Shedd off after I talked to her in the bathroom."

"Amy heard you, though."

Fenway winced. "Oh—sorry. Did you have some explaining to do?"

McVie shrugged and put his seatbelt on, letting the engine idle. "I'm not sure she believed me, but it doesn't matter." He leaned forward slightly in his seat. "Did you get anything we can use?"

She shook her head. "I thought I could get Maggie to talk to me about Annabel. She was pretty drunk. But she just complained that Annabel wanted to lecture her."

"Doesn't mean they're not—"

"I know, Craig."

"But you talked to Maggie? What did she say?"

"First, she said she was straight."

McVie tilted his head. "Because no one has ever lied about their sexual orientation before."

"But she never actually *said* they weren't involved—she just said she was straight." Fenway shifted in her seat. "And secondly, the Neons' head coach gave Maggie his hotel room key while we were talking, and he left for the elevator almost immediately after she did."

"What?" McVie's jaw dropped.

"Now that I think about it, I suppose it didn't necessarily have to be *his* room key. And it's entirely possible Maggie didn't go into his hotel room after she got on the elevator." She steepled her fingers and stared at her hands. "Of course, it's possible Maggie is involved with both the coach *and* Annabel." Fenway turned to McVie. "What happened with Annabel?"

"She drove into the hotel parking garage. A minute or two later, I saw her through the window, crossing the hotel lobby."

"Do you think she saw me talking to Maggie at the bar?"

McVie shook his head. "I don't think so. She had her eyes on the floor the whole time, like she was depressed about something."

"I think," Fenway said, "Annabel was trying to convince Maggie that Coach Flash was a bad guy. Maybe she was trying to convince Maggie to break it off with him and have an affair with her instead. Or maybe I'm way off base and she was just looking out for Maggie."

"I don't know," McVie said, stroking his chin thoughtfully. "You've been right a lot before."

"I've been wrong a lot before, too."

McVie sighed. "I don't think Mathilda Montague will like my report, but I better get home and type up the notes."

Fenway reached over gently and put her hand on McVie's knee. "Maybe you can write out just a skeleton of the notes and then we can —you know, spend a little more time together tonight."

McVie smiled, then leaned over the center console. Fenway kissed McVie softly on the lips, then again.

"I hope you don't have to work early tomorrow."

"I think I'm old enough to decide if I want to stay up late." Fenway smiled. "Now *your* boss, on the other hand, is wholly unreasonable about your working hours."

"He is a cruel, cruel man," McVie agreed, settling back into the driver's seat.

"I say you tell him you'll finish the report tomorrow morning because your girlfriend is demanding some quality time."

McVie smiled. "One of these days, Fenway, your conniving ways won't work on me."

Fenway grinned—then the words were out of her mouth before she could stop them. "Speaking of conniving ways, what did Amy want?"

McVie straightened up in his seat. "She wants to sell the house."

"The big mansion?"

"She says it reminds her too much of Rick."

Oof. Had it only been three months since the death of Amy's second husband? Fenway nodded. "I guess I can understand that. That's one reason I sold Mom's house after she passed—I couldn't look anywhere without thinking of her."

"I get it." The corners of McVie's mouth turned down. "But I'm not sure what her plan is."

"What about Megan? Isn't she going to be a senior in the fall?"

"Yes—assuming she passes all her classes. Which right now is a pretty big *if.*"

Fenway narrowed her eyes. "I hope Amy stays in the same district. If I were Megan, I'd hate to leave all my friends and go to a new school my senior year."

"Yeah, well, Megan and her boyfriend just broke up, so that might not be as important."

"Maybe Megan could move in with you until she finishes high school?"

"She and I haven't talked about it." McVie frowned. "Come to think of it, we haven't talked much in the last month or so."

"She did cancel the last two weekends with you." Fenway looked up into McVie's eyes. "Is everything okay with her?"

"Besides her grades and her boyfriend? The two biggest things in a teenager's life?"

"Yeah." Fenway paused. "But you're supposed to see her this weekend too, right?"

McVie nodded. "I'll talk to her. Who knows—maybe she'll even give me more than one-word answers." He put the car in gear and drove out of the parking lot.

Fenway settled in the passenger seat for the drive back to McVie's apartment.

PART 2

FRIDAY

CHAPTER THREE

"Morning, Sarah."

"Morning, Fenway." Sarah Summerfield stood and handed Fenway a stack of paper. "These forms came in from the M.E. for your signature, and I've printed out a few résumés."

"Anyone look good?"

"Migs is leaving some big shoes to fill, but with some training, the woman I put on top might work out. Got her associate's only last year, but she has a bunch of awards and volunteer programs. I think she'll be a good fit."

"Thanks," said Fenway, glancing at the topmost résumé. She walked into her office and set the stack of papers down on her desk. Sitting in her leather chair, she plugged her laptop into the docking station. She'd forgotten to grab coffee before she sat down; now she was wondering if maybe this was a Java Jim's day instead of coffee out of the office carafe. But when she heard and smelled the machine finishing its work—Sarah had brewed a fresh batch just for her—she decided to stay in. A minute later, she was at her desk again with a steaming mug.

She was working through her email when Sarah came in with another printout.

"Hey," Fenway said. "Something else?"

Sarah shut the door behind her.

Fenway's head snapped up. "You better not be quitting."

"No, no." Sarah smiled. "But you'd been asking about the Vegas Neons. The women's soccer team."

Had Fenway said too much to Sarah a few days before and jeopardized McVie's investigation? Mathilda Montague might be a pain in the neck, but she was a *rich* pain in the neck, and McVie's business could use the cash. "What about the Neons?"

Sarah placed the printout in front of Fenway.

Neons Coach Levinson Fired on Sex Abuse Charges

The Las Vegas Neons fired coach Paul "Flash" Levinson on Thursday after multiple allegations of sexual misconduct, harassment, and inappropriate relations with players came to light in a report obtained by the *Las Vegas Gazette*. The report alleges the misconduct, which includes sexual coercion, goes back more than a decade, and refers to evidence from when Levinson coached his former team, the St. Louis Gateways, as well as his time at Shellmont University in North Carolina.

Neons owner Sandra Christchurch called a press conference at 8 a.m. Friday morning to make the announcement. "The Neons organization has no tolerance for the appalling behavior exhibited by former Coach Levinson. Those who have come forward are heroes and should be treated as such." The women who made the allegations have not been identified.

AFF Commissioner Bartholomew Yates said via a prepared statement that the league is cooperating with the investigation. Yates provided no further response about the allegations.

Levinson took the Shellmont program to prominence, including a college championship, in his two-year head coaching stint between the Gateways and the Neons. He is often credited with discovering goalkeeper Maggie Erskine, whom the Neons selected in the first round of last year's AFF draft, and who was announced as the starting goalkeeper for the upcoming season.

Levinson could not be reached for comment.

Fenway felt the bile rise in her throat, and she squeezed her eyes shut. Suddenly she was back in her first year at Western Washington. Her Russian Lit professor. Her face pressed against his office carpet. He grunted as he pushed her dress up.

Fenway opened her eyes, her mouth dry. Her heart was pounding.

Okay, breathe. It's just a news story.

But she saw Paul Levinson, in her mind's eye, slip something—a card, maybe his hotel room key—into Maggie's hand. And the look on Maggie's face. Resignation? Duty?

Fear?

Levinson could not be reached for comment.

Had Levinson known about his imminent firing when he'd whispered into Maggie Erskine's ear the night before?

And suddenly Annabel's relationship with Maggie seemed much less like an affair.

"Where—" Fenway's voice broke, and she coughed to cover it up. "Where did you get this? It's not even 8:30 yet."

"Got the news alert on my phone." Sarah looked at her watch. "Must have been a short news conference. I thought it might be useful."

"I appreciate you keeping your eyes open." Fenway stood and looked out her office's glass wall at Dez Roubideaux's empty desk. "Have you seen Dez?"

"She was called out just before you got here. Death at a hotel—I'll check to see which one."

As Sarah left her office, Fenway tried to read another email. But the mention of a hotel nagged at her. *Please don't be the Broadmere.* Just thinking about the place made her feel stupid. She didn't want to go there, where the Neons would be crowding the lobby to talk about the coach's firing. She'd talked to Annabel like a fan and then, to Maggie, pretended she knew nothing about soccer. If she ran into the two of them together, it could get awkward.

She told herself to relax. There were other hotels than the Broadmere, and anyway, if the death was something routine, like a heart attack or a stroke, Dez would handle it. There'd be no reason for Fenway to go.

She turned her attention back to her inbox. Things had calmed down in Estancia in the last month or so, so there was nothing too pressing. But the bad feeling about the hotel lingered, and she deleted an email she'd meant to file. Just as she was about to undelete it, Sarah's voice called out.

"It's the Broadmere."

Fenway ran her tongue over her teeth and inhaled deeply.

"Any information on the decedent?"

"White male in his fifties."

Levinson could not be reached for comment.

She thought about all the people in management positions in sports organizations—coaches, athletic directors, team owners—who'd been caught in sex scandals, or stealing money, or worse. Sometimes they had no comment, but most often they strongly denied the accusations, then slunk away, saying they didn't want to become a "distraction" for their team. And went on with their lives. Had this one felt enough shame to take his own life?

Fenway's phone buzzed, and she took it out of her purse. A text from Dez.

Get over to the Broadmere NOW

Her stomach dropped. She grabbed her purse and hurried out of her office.

———

Fenway parked on the street in front of the Broadmere and hurried through the small front lot to the entrance. To Fenway's relief, she saw neither Annabel nor Maggie on her way through the mostly empty hotel lobby to the elevators.

On the ninth floor, a uniformed deputy lifted the police tape to let her into the suite.

The door opened into a penthouse apartment-style room: a sleek, modern living area with high ceilings, painted in elegant earth tones. On the right: a sofa, two leather benches, a coffee table, and a large television mounted on the wall above the fireplace. On the left: a desk, dining table and chairs, all made from dark wood. Straight ahead: a red sliding door, possibly leading to the bedroom, and a door on the left which Fenway assumed was the bathroom.

The man's body, splayed out on his stomach, lay between the coffee table and the television. Fenway was struck by the similar hues of the burgundy of the bedroom door and the pool of blood underneath his head. Right arm up at an acute angle, left arm awkwardly positioned with his hand by his hip. He wore black-and-gold sweatpants and a white T-shirt stained with blood, a large splotch between his shoulder blades. His feet were bare. His face was turned toward the television—it was Coach Flash. She cursed under her breath—this could get complicated.

Fenway's paper overshoes crinkled as she walked around the coffee table. "Thanks for calling me, Dez."

Dez was a few inches shorter than Fenway, her eyes boring into the body, taking in all the details. Her hair was dark, short, and tightly curled, and she motioned toward the body with her head. "Figured you'd need to see this one for yourself. Victim's name is Paul Levinson. He's the head coach of a Las Vegas-based soccer team."

"The Neons." Fenway crouched next to the body. "CSI coming?"

"Melissa de la Garza is on her way."

"Who found the body?"

Dez took out her notebook. "An assistant coach who gave his name as Rocky Portello. His ID shows his given name as Roger."

"Does everyone in this organization have a nickname? First *Flash*, then *Rocky*."

"Flash?"

"Yeah, the decedent. Everyone called him 'Coach Flash.'"

Dez harrumphed. "Wasn't fast enough to get out of the way, I guess."

Fenway narrowed her eyes at Dez.

Dez cleared her throat and shuffled her feet. "I understand they were here for their training camp." She tapped the notebook. "You follow soccer?"

"Enough to know what the offside rule is, anyway." Fenway gave Dez a small smile. "My dad's been interested in—uh, talking to the Neons' ownership. I've done a little digging." She looked around the room to avoid Dez's eyes—no need to mention McVie until it was relevant—but also to understand the layout of the crime scene.

The living room's two benches and sofa were covered in sumptuous leather. The wallpaper design was a jumble of randomly sized circles, each full of smaller, concentric circles, predominantly cream and brown, matching the brown hardwood and cream rugs. Fenway suspected the designer's target was thoughtful elegance, but it looked fake instead. When she looked at the red sliding wooden door near the back of the living room, Dez said, "Bedroom."

Fenway pointed at the other door. "Bathroom? Or closet?"

"Bathroom. One door from the living room, one door into the bedroom."

Fenway knelt beside the dead man's head.

The red door into the bedroom slid open, and Officer Celeste Salvador stuck her head out. "Sergeant? Can we get a bottle of water?"

"I got it," the deputy at the door said, and closed the door as he exited.

Fenway angled her head toward the bedroom and gave Dez a questioning look.

"A young lady is in there. Asleep when Coach Rocky made the 9-1-1 call."

Not Maggie Erskine, please. If it was, Fenway might be a witness for sure. She was already in a gray area. "What's her name?"

"She's still fairly out of it. Quite a hangover, or at least she's pretending to have a hangover." Dez flipped a page in her notebook. "Margaret Lynn Erskine."

Oh no. Fenway would have to disclose what she knew—at least, as much as she could without jeopardizing McVie's investigation. "You know Coach Flash was fired this morning?"

Dez shook her head. "Like I said, I don't really follow the league."

"He was accused of sexual misconduct with his players. And Margaret—she goes by Maggie—is one of his players. Star goalkeeper. The organization fired him after a report came out."

Dez pursed her lips. "She's a person of interest. Maybe a suspect."

Fenway held up her hands. "Maybe you shouldn't tell me anything more. I was here last night. I saw our decedent talk to Maggie Erskine."

"You were *here* last night?"

"At the bar in the hotel." Should she say she'd shared an Uber with Maggie?

"Did you see them enter?"

"Yes, but they entered separately. Maggie was sitting at the bar. When Coach Flash came in, he spoke with her about being ready for tomorrow's practice. Then it looked to me like he slipped something into her hand. Whispered something in her ear, then took a seat across the bar."

"So, they didn't enter together, and they didn't sit together?" Dez blinked. "Did they argue? Did she get mad after he told her what to do?"

"No, nothing like that."

"What did the coach slip into Miss Erskine's hand?"

"The way they both acted, I suspected it was the coach's room key."

"Why?"

Fenway crossed her arms. She wasn't used to being grilled. "Because they didn't acknowledge they'd touched hands. No 'excuse me' or anything. It was the way you'd act if you wanted to pass something off but didn't want anyone to know."

"And you thought it was a room key?"

"Yes."

"Did you *see* a room key?"

Fenway shut her eyes and thought. It definitely looked like Coach Flash had pressed something into Maggie's hand. But she didn't see anything pass between them.

"No."

"So, you saw the two of them talk. You saw them touch hands? Like, holding hands, or a high-five, or what?"

Fenway shook her head. "Nothing so specific."

"Did they leave together?"

"No. A minute or two after the coach talked to Maggie, she left. She took the elevator upstairs."

"And the coach was still in the bar?"

"Yes. He had a drink, then he left a couple minutes later."

Dez took a step back. "What were you doing here last night?"

Fenway considered. She could say it was none of Dez's business, but that wouldn't be helpful. She hated to mention McVie, but telling a half-truth about him seemed best just now. "After that drink with Maggie, Craig met me here."

Half-truth. Okay, maybe one-third.

A quarter, at least.

Dez rubbed her chin. "I don't think you saw anything either the prosecution or defense would want you to state in court."

Fenway inwardly bristled. Dez had twenty years on her, but Fenway was still the boss. "I'm aware of the conflict-of-interest guidelines, Sergeant." Her voice was gentle but firm.

Dez closed her notebook. "You know what I mean, Fenway."

"Yes." Fenway bent down to examine the body, then straightened up again. "I believe Maggie Erskine was drunk when she left. She was slurring her words and could barely walk. I don't know if that'll make any difference."

Dez frowned. "I don't know either. Did you want to sit in when I question Maggie?"

Fenway shook her head. "She might recognize me from the bar. I sat at the stool next to her." She didn't say they had talked. Or shared an Uber. "After I examine the deceased, I'll question the coach who found Levinson's body."

"He's next door."

"Any reason you didn't keep him in here? It's unusual to let the person who found the body leave the scene."

Dez hooked her thumb over her shoulder in the direction of the bedroom. "With Maggie Erskine in there, I didn't think it was a good idea to let anyone besides the investigation team stay in the room."

"Makes sense."

Fenway turned back to the prone form of Paul Levinson and studied the body for a few moments. His head was turned slightly to the right, a bloody mass near the crown of his skull. "Wound appears to be in the parietal bone, roughly ten centimeters from the coronal suture." She looked up at Dez. "Blunt force trauma. Lots of blood. Consistent with a massive head wound."

"I figured."

Fenway leaned in closer. "Hmm. Shape of the wound suggests something... oval in shape? Not a baseball bat. The angle is wrong. And it's too thick to be a fireplace poker. Well—'thick' is the wrong word. Maybe flat on—" She looked up. "Oh, of course. A golf club. Probably a driver."

Dez nodded. "Set of golf clubs in the hall closet—and you're right, the driver's missing. Guess what we found in the shower?"

"Ah. Someone tried to wash all the blood off it?"

"That's what it looks like. CSI will probably find some."

"Why is it still in the shower? You'd think someone would try to get rid of it."

Dez scratched her temple. "Do you know what *else* we found in the shower?"

"What?"

"All of Maggie's clothes."

Fenway rested her elbows on her knees. "Her clothes?"

"Stained with blood," Dez said. "It looks like most of it's been washed out. It was all in a big wet puddle on the floor of the shower."

"And—the police found Maggie in bed when they came in?"

"She was asleep. Coach Rocky calling 9-1-1 didn't wake her up."

Fenway stood and took a step back from the body. "So, what do you think happened, Dez?"

"I'll tell you what it looks like from what I can see. But this is preliminary."

"Of course."

"It looks like Miss Erskine hit Mr. Levinson over the head with the golf club and tried to wash the murder weapon off in the shower. But then realized there was blood all over her as well. She took all her clothes off and tried to wash the blood off them, too." She pointed at the bedroom. "Then, in her drunken stupor, she figured she'd deal with it in the morning, and she passed out on the bed."

"Ah. It's open-and-shut in your mind?"

Dez shook her head. "Not at all. That's a first glance. The girl's steady and strong enough to clobber a man to death and then can't stay awake ten more minutes?"

"Odd." Fenway tilted her head. "You mean someone wants us to *think* it was Maggie?" Fenway flashed onto the name *Mathilda Montague*, who thought Maggie was sleeping with her wife. It would be a long way to go for someone to commit murder just to frame their spouse's supposed mistress, though.

"Not impossible, but it doesn't feel right. Let me sit with it for another half hour and maybe I'll see it different."

"And of course we haven't questioned her yet."

Dez was quiet.

"Have you been in the room with Maggie?" Fenway asked.

"I brought her some clothes when she wanted to know where hers were. I'd like to bring her down to the station to question her. Things might not line up perfect, but she's still the prime suspect." Dez set her mouth in a line. "And I hate to say it, but if the coach is accused of sexual misconduct with his players, there's even more of a reason to think Maggie is involved."

Fenway nodded soberly.

"I don't think it's a good idea to bring Maggie out past the body until we cover it, and I don't want to cover the body until Melissa gives her okay."

Fenway looked at the closed door. "Does she even know he's dead?"

"Yeah, but not that his skull's bashed in."

"What did she say about the golf club and the clothes in the shower?"

"We closed the shower curtain before we let her into the bathroom to get dressed."

"How do we know she didn't see anything?"

"Celeste kept an eye on her." Dez shrugged. "Only so much we can do. We either let her into the bathroom where she might see the murder weapon, or we lead her through the crime scene before we interview her. Neither is ideal."

Fenway nodded grimly. "Probably the right call—but she's been shut in the bedroom since she woke up? Kid must be miserable."

"We're getting her some ibuprofen, and room service is bringing a little breakfast. Not much else we can do."

"Take her statement in the bedroom. If she's guilty, she's got nothing but time to think of explanations to make herself look innocent. The more time you give her, the more convincing the lie will be."

"Okay," Dez said, "let's both go do it."

"We? No, Dez, I sat at the bar with her—"

"Let's see how foggy her memory is. If she recognizes you but pretends she doesn't remember anything from last night—"

"It won't mean much." Fenway pointed to an empty tequila bottle on the coffee table. "Coach may have gotten her twice as drunk as when I saw her."

Dez went quiet for a moment, then looked sideways at Fenway. "You don't think she did it."

"What? Uh—I'm trying not to assume too much. Based on what

we've learned about this guy, the hotel may be crawling with women who hated him. Men too, in all likelihood."

"But you think Levinson got her even more drunk and—"

"Yes. Maggie wasn't sober enough to give consent." Fenway blinked. She tasted copper in her mouth.

"Are you implying," Dez said slowly, "that she did it in self-defense? Or that it was justifiable?"

Fenway paused. "I'm not ruling out the possibility. Maybe she was sober enough to—" She shook her head. "No, I'm not saying anything else. Let's get her statement."

Dez leaned in close to Fenway and lowered her voice. "Celeste Mirandized her when I got here. Real smooth, too, like it was for her protection, in the middle of a conversation about her role on the team this year."

"She didn't ask for a lawyer?"

"Not yet." Dez took a step back. "Celeste is going for the detective's exam, you know."

"I heard."

Dez shifted her weight from foot to foot. She opened her mouth, but Fenway spoke first.

"Yes, yes, Dez, I know. Mark hasn't put in his retirement paperwork yet, but if he does, and Celeste passes her exam, you know I'll consider her."

"All right, as long as you know what I think." Dez stepped over to the door and slid it open. Maggie sat on the king-size bed with her back against the headboard. The young goalkeeper wore a gold-and-black T-shirt with the Neons logo on the front, paired with gray sweatpants.

Maggie looked up at Fenway. "I'm ready to talk."

CHAPTER FOUR

MAGGIE'S EYES SHOWED NO RECOGNITION OF FENWAY, ONLY HOPE that someone might get her out of this situation.

"Can you give us a minute, Officer Salvador?" Dez murmured.

"Certainly. Door closed behind me?"

"Thank you." Dez turned to Maggie and motioned to Fenway as Officer Salvador left the room. "This is my associate, Fenway Stevenson. She's my boss, and we're here to take your statement about what happened yesterday evening." Dez studied Maggie's face, then sat on the foot of the bed as Fenway took a seat in an overstuffed armchair in the corner.

"I was at the bar with you last night, Maggie," Fenway said. "Are you still okay if I question you?"

"You were at the bar?" Maggie said groggily. She pressed a hand to her temple. "I'm sorry. I was really drunk."

"What *do* you remember from last night?"

The heat rose to Maggie's cheeks. "Annabel took me out to dinner. I thought it was like a striker-goalie bonding session, you know? But—but then, she started telling me she knows about Coach Flash and all the stuff he's—uh... I think her words were 'the stuff he's done to you.'"

"What did she mean?" Dez asked.

Maggie pulled her feet up onto the bed and sat cross-legged. "Somehow she knew he's been—been asking me to do things for him."

"Running errands?" Dez asked gently. "Getting coffee? Picking up his kids from school?"

"No," Maggie mumbled.

"What kind of things?"

"Personal things." Maggie stared down at her hands. "Mostly, um, sexual things."

"Ah." Dez nodded and motioned her head toward Fenway.

"You were—having an affair?" Fenway asked.

Maggie curled her mouth down into a frown. "Ugh. No. Well—I guess technically. But no."

"What was it, then?"

"I mean, it was usually after he'd yelled at me for fucking up on the field, you know? Screaming when I let a rebound in, or for misplaying a back pass. He'd bring me up to his hotel room after the game or after practice and give me a thorough dressing-down, you know? And then—" Her voice hitched. "I don't really know what happened after. I don't know how it happened the first time."

Fenway was itching to ask her when it started, how long it had been, to make her make sense of this. She'd seen this before, up in Seattle in the E.R. There were five girls from the same high school field hockey team. They came in together and insisted Fenway do a rape kit on their teammate and friend. She remembered the scared look on the girl's face, the reports of how he'd twisted her words, how he'd turned her noes into yeses and how the shame burned her.

Fenway had thought she'd be called as a witness at his trial, but last she heard, the coach had taken a plea agreement.

The shame on Maggie's face was the same look the field hockey player had given her.

Fenway wondered if she'd had that look of shame after her Russian Lit professor... She had to pull her attention back to the present.

"He—he thinks I'm talented," Maggie said in a halting voice, "but says I don't work hard enough. I'm not dedicated enough to the team. I don't jell with his coaching style."

There was silence for a moment.

"Keep telling me about last night," Fenway said. "Annabel talked to you about what Coach Levinson was doing."

Maggie looked at the ceiling, tears welling in her eyes. "He was my coach in college. We won a championship together and—I mean, he took me under his wing, you know? He's—he's one of the only people who believed in me. Who honestly thought I could take it to the next level." She swallowed hard.

Fenway squinted at Maggie; she had a hard time wrapping her brain around the fact that Maggie thought her rapist "believed" in her. But she knew that all kinds of things were possible when someone like Coach Levinson had power over someone young and impressionable. And he'd gotten away with it for years. "So you argued with Annabel?"

Maggie's face changed, her eyes narrowing as she leaned forward. "I'm not getting any special treatment from him, okay?"

"I didn't say—"

"If anything, he works me harder than anyone else." Maggie's eyes flashed. "This is for the team. Don't you get that?"

Fenway looked at Dez, who rubbed her forehead.

"Maybe we should take a break," Dez said.

Maggie sat back on the bed, her eyes wide with fear. "I'm sorry. My head hurts."

"Do you need some water?"

"Maybe the bathroom."

Fenway shot a look at Dez. "We okay with that?"

Dez's face held no expression—the bathroom was probably still a better option than walking Maggie through the crime scene before she'd finished her initial statement. "Sure."

Maggie went into the bathroom, closed the door, and the sound of the modesty fan came on.

"Anger," Dez said.

"Hungover," Fenway said. "And think of what she's been through."

Dez stood and paced around the side of the bed. "I don't know how to say this, but I think you're putting the murder victim on trial."

Fenway blinked. "I'm trying to figure out what happened."

Dez cocked her head. "I remember seeing those pictures from your professor's office, Fenway. I know this must be—difficult."

Fenway inhaled sharply, then ran a hand over her short hair. "I'm fine. This doesn't have anything to do with that."

Dez studied Fenway's face for a moment.

A knock at the front door. "Room service."

Dez walked out of the room, then came back in with a large glass full of thick green liquid and a small pill bottle. "Ibuprofen and breakfast. Just what the doctor ordered."

"I hope that's a hangover cure."

Dez shrugged. "It's what she said she wanted. Some sort of kale smoothie."

The door opened, and Maggie came back out. Her cheeks were stained with tears, but she was in control. She pointed at the bottle. "Is that Advil?"

"Yep." Fenway forced a small smile onto her face.

"And that's the smoothie I ordered?"

"Right."

Dez shook two pills out onto Maggie's hand, and the young woman washed them down with the green smoothie. There was silence for a moment as Maggie drank.

"You were telling us," Dez said, "about what you did after your dinner with Annabel."

"I went to the hotel."

"How did you get back here?" Dez asked.

"Uh... I'm not too clear on that part." She closed her eyes. "I remember walking out of the restaurant."

"What restaurant was this?" Dez asked.

"The French place. It had a fancy awning in front. Gustine's or something."

"Maxime's?" Dez suggested.

"Yes. Maxime's."

Dez shot a look at Fenway, who nodded—she wasn't quite sure what she was nodding for, exactly, but whatever question was in Dez's mind, the answer was probably *yes*.

"How did you get there?"

"Annabel drove me from the hotel. She borrowed one of the team cars."

"Did you flag down a taxi when you left the restaurant?"

"Um—" She leaned backward and reached for the bedside table before flopping back. "Oh, right. You guys took my phone."

"Covering our bases," Dez said. "Why did you want your phone?"

"I probably got an Uber. I thought I'd check my app."

"We can check it."

"Okay. So the answer is, I don't remember how I got to the hotel."

"But you remember getting to the hotel."

"I remember," Maggie said, then bit her lip. "Oh—I ordered a drink from the bartender. And one for the woman sitting next to me. Was it a bourbon? I don't really remember."

Dez shot another look at Fenway, who nodded again.

"Then Coach Flash came into the bar too, and he told me I needed to be ready for the afternoon practice." She looked at the clock on the bedside table. "This won't take all day, will it? Because practice..." Her voice trailed off. "Practice is still on, isn't it?"

Fenway shook her head. "I don't know, but this is important, Maggie. Think. What else did Coach Levinson do? Tell you to stop drinking and go to bed?"

Maggie looked back down at her hands.

"He gave you something, didn't he?" Fenway pressed.

"His hotel room key," Maggie whispered. "But—it wasn't—it wasn't like I wanted to have sex with him. I didn't want him to be too hard on the team the first day."

Fenway cocked her head. "What do you mean?"

"Well—" Maggie looked like she wanted to crawl under the covers and never come out. "When he's in a bad mood, he makes the team do this whole exercise series—the Seven Summits. It's grueling. Sometimes we have two or three players throw up afterward."

"That doesn't sound good."

"One time he had us run up the steps of the bleachers holding a six-foot-long pole in the middle with buckets full of rocks hung from each end. If the buckets fell, we had to start all over."

Fenway tried to picture that in her mind—and immediately knew she'd be unable to balance heavy buckets on either end of a pole while running stairs. "How about when he's in a good mood?"

"He'll still work us hard, but nobody's puking, you know?"

"Did he tell you what he needed you to do to put him in a good mood so the team wouldn't have to do the Seven Summits?"

Maggie shrugged. "It's kind of something I picked up. If I wanted to be responsible for the team having a rough workout like that—on our first day of camp, no less—I'd go to my room and get a good night's sleep. If I wanted the team to have a decent day of practice—well, I knew what I had to do."

Fenway cleared her throat. "So you came up to this room."

"Yes."

"What did you do when you arrived?"

"I—" Maggie screwed up her face. "I took off my clothes and waited for him on the sofa out in the living room."

"Do you remember him coming into the hotel suite?"

Maggie tensed. "Yes."

Fenway looked at Dez, who shook her head slightly.

Fenway opened her mouth to speak, but nothing came out.

"It went like it usually goes," Maggie said evenly. "He brought me into the bedroom after—after a while."

"What time did he—did he come back to the suite?" Fenway asked.

"I don't know."

"Did he..." Fenway bit her lip. She didn't know how to phrase it.

"We had sex," Maggie said. "He opened the door, saw me on the sofa, and we had sex on the table. Then he took me into the bedroom and we—" Maggie squinted. "He gave me more to drink after we..." She blinked. "Sorry. It's a blur. I know he woke me up and had sex with me again. I don't know what time. Then I went back to sleep, and I woke up when the paramedics were here."

"You didn't get up at any time during the night?"

"No." Maggie shifted her weight on the bed. "At least, not that I can remember."

Dez leaned toward Fenway's ear and spoke in a low voice. "Melissa de la Garza just got here with the CSI team."

Fenway nodded, never taking her eyes off Maggie. "You didn't put your clothes back on?"

Maggie shot Fenway a confused look. "Of course not. And I don't know where my clothes from last night are, either."

Fenway was quiet for a moment. She glanced at Dez, who clasped her hands together but said nothing.

"Did you know," Fenway began, "Coach Levinson was fired by the team this morning?"

"What?" Maggie's eyes went wide.

"Yes. Allegations of sexual misconduct."

"But—but I never said anything!" Her face hardened. "Did Annabel say something? Because she doesn't—"

"Multiple allegations," Fenway said.

Fenway and Dez were quiet for a moment, then a look of realization crept over Maggie's face. "Oh my God," Maggie said, then her face crumpled into anguish. "Oh my God. I'm so stupid. I'm so, so stupid."

Maggie began to shake, and Fenway sat on the bed next to her as the quaking turned into sobs and Maggie's body folded.

———

A few minutes later, Maggie stopped sobbing and sat up, glassy-eyed, leaning her back against the headboard of the bed.

"Are you okay to continue?" Fenway asked.

Maggie shook her head. "I need a few minutes." She looked up. "How did you know Coach Flash was fired?"

"Sandra Christchurch held a press conference this morning. Only five minutes or so before the paramedics arrived."

"Do you know who reported it? Who else he's been doing this with?" Maggie's brow was creased, her shoulders tight.

"I don't," Fenway said, "but let's keep focused on last night."

"I've told you everything I know."

"After the last time—the last time he, uh, woke you up, did you hear anything? Maybe came out of sleep for just a moment, thought you were dreaming?"

Maggie shook her head. "Nothing like that."

"Did you see Coach Levinson before he came into the bar?"

Maggie shook her head. "Not that day. In fact, not for a couple of months. We spoke on the phone a couple of times during the off-season." She paused. "Oh—and I flew out to Vegas to see him when they made the decision to trade Gabby to Boston."

"Gabby?" Dez asked.

"Gabriela Fortuna," Fenway said. "The starting goalie last year."

"And a backup on the World Cup team," Maggie added. "The coach wanted to inform me in person that I was the starting keeper going forward. I think he wanted to assess my mental state."

"When was this?"

"Right after New Year's," Maggie said. "Nice time of the year to come to Vegas, I guess."

"Did he—" Fenway began.

Maggie averted her eyes. "I was in town for three nights. He and I had afternoon meetings and workouts all three nights."

"And where did he stay?"

Maggie was quiet.

"All right," Dez said. "Let's say another team finds out about the coach sleeping with you. And they accuse you of this being a quid-pro-quo kind of thing. What would you say?"

Maggie hung her head. "It wasn't like that. It wasn't anything like him saying *if you let me screw you, you'll become the starting goalie.* It was like I needed to show him I was grateful. I knew no one else would..." Her voice broke. "I'm so *stupid.*"

Fenway turned her head toward Dez. "I think we can move to a different—"

"Were you angry at him?" Dez asked.

"I wasn't. No, we didn't really have anything between us," Maggie said. "He's been my coach for years. Since first year of college. He and I have been working together for... well, it's been a long time."

"And how long has he been—" Dez's phone dinged. She looked at the screen briefly, then took a breath. "How long has he been asking you to, uh, show him you were grateful? Or get the rest of the team out of the Seven Summits?"

Maggie blinked. "I don't know. Years."

"As long as he's been your coach?"

Maggie nodded curtly.

"Okay, we'll take a break," Dez said.

They walked out of the bedroom and into the living room, closing the pocket door behind them. Fenway leaned toward Dez and lowered her voice. "You're getting into some dangerous water. This was sexual coercion. Let's not make it sound like we're blaming her."

"There's a dead man lying on the floor, Fenway," Dez whispered back. "If she killed him to get away from him, whether it was justified or not, we need to know. She's not on trial. I'm trying to get information."

"How much more time does Melissa need before we can cover up the body?"

Dez held up her phone. "That was Melissa texting me. She's taking a break. We can cover the body and get Maggie out of here."

"Let's have Celeste drive Maggie to the station," Fenway said firmly. "Our witness could use a break." She opened the door into the hallway. "I'll talk to the one who found the body."

Deputy Brian Callahan walked up to Fenway and Dez.

Dez frowned. "Deputy, you're supposed to be guarding the door to Coach Portello's room."

"I am—but I need to tell you that the woman at the end of the hall reported a theft."

"I'm sorry—a theft?" Fenway asked.

Dez motioned down the hall. "That's Sandra Christchurch's room."

Callahan nodded.

"What was stolen?" Fenway asked.

"A diamond tennis bracelet," Callahan said. "She'd put it in the room safe."

CHAPTER FIVE

"A DIAMOND TENNIS BRACELET?" DEZ LOOKED AT FENWAY. "THOSE are expensive."

"Let's be clear about this," Fenway said to Callahan. "We've got a murder scene back through there. That's more important than missing jewelry, no matter how expensive it is."

Dez crossed her arms. "Unless the theft is related to the murder."

Fenway blinked. "That's true. We'll talk to Ms. Christchurch soon."

"You want me to take her statement now?" Dez asked. "Or drive Maggie to the sheriff's office?"

"Sheriff's office." Fenway turned to Callahan and gestured to the door of Rocky Portello's hotel suite. "No one in or out?"

"No, ma'am." Callahan's eyes darted quickly down the hall to Christchurch's room, then back to her face. "Coach Portello's been in here since he left the crime scene."

Fenway walked the few steps to the door, took a deep breath and exhaled, then reached her hand forward and knocked.

It was opened a moment later by a trim, athletic white man, about six feet tall, with a walrus mustache and eyes that crinkled at the corners. At first glance, he looked to be in his early thirties, but his laugh lines and the hint of gray hair peeking out from beneath his Neons baseball cap suggested a man closer to his late forties. He wore a black-and-gold T-shirt with the Vegas Neons logo along with gray sweatpants and wore only black athletic socks on his feet.

"Yes, ma'am?"

Fenway showed him her badge. "I'm the county coroner. Are you Mr. Portello?"

"Please," he said, giving her a slight smile only half-visible under his mustache, "call me Rocky. Everyone else does." He stepped aside and held the door as Fenway walked in. The suite was a mirror image of Paul Levinson's room, but the dominant color was a cadet blue, not red; the wallpaper even had the same pattern. "The officer said someone would be here to take my statement. Is that you?"

"Correct." Fenway motioned for Rocky to sit on the sofa.

"You're the coroner and you're taking my statement?"

"In Dominguez County, my office investigates all deaths outside of a hospital or hospice center." She gave him a reassuring smile. "In the case of homicides, I lead the investigation."

Rocky sat and breathed out in a long exhale. "I'm a little nervous about finding the, uh—about finding Flash. I—I've never seen a dead body before. Except my dad, when he passed away in the hospital. Ashes to dust, right? But this was a lot different."

"I understand."

"I've never seen—there was so much blood everywhere. I've been coaching a long time, you know, so I've seen my share of injuries. And there were some nasty ones. One player got tangled up with another player when I was coaching at Western Rockies. I tell you, once you see a bone sticking out of a leg, your perspective on everything changes."

"I suppose it does."

"You said you were a coroner, didn't you? I'm sure you've seen much worse. And here I am blathering on about one dead body making me jump out of my skin."

"It's not an unusual reaction, Mr. Portello—"

"Rocky."

"Right, Rocky. It's common for people to react like that to dead bodies." Fenway managed a small laugh. "Sometimes I think I'm the one who's a little abnormal."

"I get it, I get it," Rocky said. "So anyway—you wanted to take my statement. I've never done this before. Do I just start talking? And where do you want me to begin?"

"Let's start with this morning."

"Right. Of course. Well—I woke up, I guess around five fifteen."

"*Around* five fifteen? You didn't wake up with an alarm?"

"As a matter of fact, I did. So it was *exactly* five fifteen." Rocky pointed a finger at Fenway. "You don't miss much."

"Why were you up so early?"

"It's the first day of training camp."

"But I heard the players didn't have to report until this afternoon."

Rocky took off his cap with one hand and smoothed his hair back with the other. "True enough, true enough. But we had to get everything ready for the players. We've been prepping for a while, of course, the field and the equipment and the locker rooms and eck-setter"—Fenway inwardly cringed at the mispronunciation of *et cetera* —"but we had some roster changes in the last couple of days. Soukita Manivong announced her retirement last week. Kind of expected, but we still had a roster spot to fill."

"So you were doing what?"

"Discussing some strategic shifts. We were thinking of changing from last year's 3-4-3 to a 3-4-2-1, but then I know Flash was thinking about dropping four defenders to the back line with a young keeper."

"Maggie Erskine."

Rocky nodded. "I think he'd made up his mind to do it. It's one of the reasons we traded for Darcy Nishimura."

Fenway tapped her chin. "Would Maggie think moving to four defenders was an insult?"

Rocky tilted his head. "Maybe so. Don't get me wrong—Maggie plays the game intelligently. A great keeper in college, for sure—I was an assistant on the championship Shellmont team. But the pro game is faster. Early last year, when we got her into some games, she was timid. She got better as the year went on, but she's playing against some international superstars, even though the European leagues are stealing more of the AFF players away. But it's no insult—half the teams in the league play four defenders on the back line."

"Did Mr. Levinson—uh, Coach Flash—tell Maggie about the switch to four defenders?"

"Sure. I mean, he had no reason to keep it from her. It's not like she wouldn't have noticed when we went out onto the field this afternoon." He chuckled. "We went to the Pickering Trophy game last year, and if we can make a deep playoff run this year with a young goalkeeper, I might've had my pick of open head coaching jobs next year. Now with Coach Flash, uh, passing, my future is up in the breeze. We were supposed to have everything together this year. And then Flash goes and does all this."

"Does all what?"

Portello looked up at Fenway. "Uh—gets himself killed. Sorry, I might sound a little harsh, but believe me, the owners in this league won't care about my sob story when I'm hunting for a head coaching job."

"I've read up a little on you, Coach Portello. You've been Coach Levinson's right-hand man for over a decade. You don't think you'll have the opportunity to step into the head coaching job now? Especially since training camp has already started."

Portello shifted in his seat. "I suppose. Flash put a succession plan in place, and I was supposed to take over from him at some point. But something like this—it could change everything."

Fenway noticed Portello's eyes light up. He talked a good game, but he thought he'd get the head coaching position, even after Coach Levinson's death. Still, Fenway couldn't fault him for playing down his chances of getting the job.

Fenway raised her head and found Portello looking at her expectantly. "I'm sorry, Rocky, but I think we've gotten off track. You said you woke up at five fifteen. What did you do after you got up?"

"Maybe it was closer to five thirty."

Fenway tilted her head. "I thought you said you got up with your alarm."

"What? Oh—you know, the snooze button."

"Ah."

"Anyway, I showered and got dressed, then I went downstairs and got coffee at the Java Jim's in the lobby. I got one for Coach Flash, too."

"You usually get him a coffee?"

"No, I don't, but he was running late, so I thought I'd save some time."

"What time was this?"

"I was supposed to meet him the lobby at six fifteen, then we'd head to the practice facility. He said he wanted to get the coaches' review session started by six forty-five, maybe seven."

"Anyone else meeting you for the coaches' session?"

"The other assistant coach—Lorraine Sunday."

"I remember her from the World Cup."

Portello scoffed. "Been milking her two shutouts for all they're worth—and then some."

"So how long did you wait for Coach Levinson?"

Rocky smoothed his mustache. "You have to understand, Coach

Flash is methodical. He's almost never late, and when he is, he has a damn good reason for it. Well—I may not always think it's a good reason, but he does."

"I'm not sure I follow."

"Let's say it this way: no one else can be late for his schedule, or there's hell to pay. But if he's the one who's late and you point it out, there's still hell to pay."

"He didn't like when others pointed out his mistakes."

"I mean," Portello said hurriedly, "it's not always a mistake. Sometimes, he's late for a good reason. Something he's doing for the team. And he took the Neons to the finals last year, so, you know, if it ain't broke, don't fix it, am I right?"

Fenway nodded.

"So I got his coffee, and I waited."

"Then you stopped waiting. And you unlocked his door and went inside?"

"Yeah."

"Why did you have his key?"

"Why did I—" Portello blinked. "He and I always take copies of each other's keys in hotels like this, you know, in case one of us gets locked out, so we don't have to bug the people downstairs. We stayed in a hotel last year that had an automated check-in. Flash locked himself out of his room, and it was like pulling teeth to get a human to show up to open it. Ever since, he and I have copies of each other's keys."

It was a long explanation. Fenway waited, but nothing else was forthcoming. She looked at his face; was he nervous? Or was he just off-kilter, expecting a first day of training camp but instead finding his head coach dead? "What time did you go back upstairs?"

"Well, I'd finished my coffee. I figured maybe he'd want to skip the review session because maybe he'd made his decision last night and didn't tell me about it. He's done it before. Or, you know, first day excitement, maybe he'd set his alarm wrong. But I don't know the exact time when I went upstairs."

"They probably have it on camera."

Rocky blinked. "On camera? What do you mean?"

"They always have cameras in hotels nowadays. We'll figure out what time you went upstairs."

Rocky nodded, frowning. "Then you must have the killer on camera. Entering the room."

"We might. Sometimes they don't have cameras in each of the hallways. It's becoming more common, though." Fenway leaned forward. "This might be difficult, but can you take me through what you saw when you came into Mr. Levinson's hotel room after you decided to come upstairs?"

Rocky swallowed. "I knocked first. I waited a little bit, but I probably tried the key before I should have. I didn't want to be any later than we already were, you understand."

"Sure."

"So—I opened the door, and I called him. He didn't answer, so I came in and shut the door behind me. And then I saw him on the floor." He shook his head. "There was blood everywhere. A big—I don't know—gash, I guess, on the back of his head. I couldn't believe it was real, you know? It almost looked fake, like a movie set or something."

"Yeah. I hear that a lot. Did you go anywhere else in the hotel room?"

"Uh—no. I was frozen in place for a few minutes. I don't know. What are you supposed to do? Should I have checked for a pulse? I know CPR. Maybe I should have done CPR. There was so much blood, and the big gash in his head—he was obviously dead, right?"

"I suspect so. We'll know more after I get some preliminary information from the CSI team."

"Anyway, I called 9-1-1. I don't know how long I stood there. The paramedics came, and then the Asian lady."

"Asian lady?"

"The, uh, police officer."

Oh—he was referring to Deputy Salvador.

Rocky ran a hand over his face. "The officer told me to leave the hotel room, but I thought someone should stay with the body. I mean, should I have stayed?"

"You were right to leave when Deputy Salvador asked you to."

"I was in the room next door," he continued. "When I heard the paramedics get here, I came out and used the key to open the room again. Was that okay?"

"I'm sure it was a confusing time, Rocky. You were doing what you thought best."

"And I don't know if I should mention this, but I must have stepped in the pool of blood while I decided what the hell to do. I don't really remember it, but I—I got blood all over my shoes. I guess I tracked it onto the carpet in the hallway and in this room, too. I hope this doesn't count against our cleaning deposit."

Fenway glanced up at Rocky.

His eyes went wide. "Oh, shit, what a horrible thing to say. My mind's going in a thousand directions. I apologize."

"No need to worry," Fenway said, as soothingly as she could. "But I'll need to bag up those shoes."

"I understand. I've got another pair, so it's okay."

"Did you notice if anyone else was in the hotel room?"

Rocky sat up straight. "There was someone else in the hotel room?"

"I'm asking you," Fenway said, "if you noticed anyone else there."

"No, of course not. I think I would have—" Rocky paused. "I didn't go into the bedroom. Or the bathroom." He grimaced. "Was there another body in there? Oh no." He groaned. "Was it one of the players?"

"Why would you say that?"

"Well, because—" Rocky screwed up his mouth. "I hate to speak ill of the dead, but there were rumors Flash wasn't completely faithful to his wife. And some players may have been, uh, involved with him."

"Rumors, Rocky? Wouldn't you be in the best position to know what went on with him?"

He shook his head. "Flash and I were friends, Coroner, but some things he didn't share with me."

Fenway nodded. "In my experience, if there's malfeasance by one person in an organization, other people are usually doing shady things, too."

"But I—"

Fenway held up her hand. "I'm not accusing you of doing what he did, but our investigation into Coach Levinson's murder might unearth some uncomfortable truths. Some of them you might not think are relevant. Some of them might put your relationships in jeopardy or mess with your future job prospects if they came out in certain ways. So I'd encourage you, if you know any secrets at all about Coach Levinson, you tell me about them now. Don't wait until we find it on our own—or worse, the media finds it before we do."

Rocky's face creased in concentration. "I mean," he mumbled, "maybe this is dumb, but I heard the owner had found out Flash was screwing around with players. I thought she might discipline him."

Fenway tilted her head. "Did you not hear about the press conference this morning?"

Rocky raised his eyebrows.

"Sandra Christchurch announced Paul Levinson was fired as the coach of the Vegas Neons at about eight o'clock," Fenway said.

Rocky's shoulders slumped. "So it's true." He covered his face with his hands. "I didn't think it would get so bad. I mean, other coaches have weathered far worse."

"It's a different time," Fenway said.

"And we have a female owner," Rocky said. "I told—" Then Rocky clamped his mouth shut.

"You told Coach Levinson something?"

Rocky sighed. "I told him she wouldn't put up with his bullshit."

"So you knew." Fenway felt her heart speed up. She tried slowing down her breaths to stay calm.

"I mean, he never out-and-out told me what he was doing. But when I referred to his bullshit, he knew exactly what I meant."

"So, would you say you were angry with him for what he was doing with the players?"

Rocky flopped back on the sofa. "I didn't really—I don't know. I figured he was cheating on his wife. Beyond that, I didn't know much."

"Coach Levinson was fired for sexual assault, Mr. Portello."

Portello leaned back in his seat and smoothed down the sides of his walrus mustache. "I didn't know."

"You didn't know? I find that hard to believe. The owner calls a press conference to fire the head coach and doesn't tell his staff?"

Portello chuckled. "Sandra Christchurch might be a lot of things, but she's not that heartless. I got a text this morning around six o'clock asking the staff to come down to the ballroom. She probably told everyone then."

"And you didn't make it?"

"I must have been in the shower. I didn't notice the message until after I found—after I came back here."

Fenway flipped the pages in her notebook. "I thought you were getting coffee at Java Jim's in the lobby before you went to meet Coach Flash at six fifteen. That would put you at the coffee stand at about six, wouldn't it?"

Portello frowned. "I'm sorry, Coroner, it's been a crazy morning. Yeah, I was probably standing in line for coffee when the text came through."

"And you didn't see it."

"Like I said, no. Not till after."

"So," Fenway said slowly, "what would you have done if you had known Coach Levinson had gotten fired?"

"I guess I would have been angry."

"At who? The owner? Coach Flash?"

"I don't know." Portello looked at the floor. "It's not like a new head coach will keep me on. He was rolling the dice not only with his job but with mine, too. And for what? Some girl less than half his age who never got her daddy's approval?"

Fenway sat up.

"Sorry—sorry. I didn't mean to be so harsh." Portello exhaled loudly. "I walked through my friend's blood a couple of hours ago, and now I find out his cheating got him fired on the first day of training camp? It's a little much."

Fenway paused for a moment. She wanted to call Rocky out—this wasn't "cheating," it was sexual assault. But putting him on the defensive would shut him down. Was there anything else she could get from him? Oh—the bracelet. "Just one more thing. Did you see a diamond tennis bracelet anywhere?"

Portello frowned. "A diamond tennis bracelet? The only person I know who has one is Sandra."

Fenway nodded. "Did you see her with it last night?"

"Come to think of it, no." He smoothed his mustache. "Lorraine is always complimenting her on it, but I don't think Sandra had it on at last night's coaches' meeting."

"What do you mean, Lorraine always compliments her on it?"

"I don't know—Lorraine said it looks nice, that she always wanted one like that. The usual stuff."

Fenway scratched her temple. "How often did Coach Sunday compliment Ms. Christchurch on her bracelet?"

"Uh—I don't know. I didn't keep track or anything."

"What happened in the coaches' meeting?"

"We went over our goals for training camp. The players who were fighting for spots on the team, what we needed to accomplish this first week, any concerns with players we might need to cut for salary reasons, that kind of thing. Not much had changed from the last meeting, to be honest."

"No inkling that Coach Levinson would be fired the next morning?"

Portello shrugged. "Nothing."

"How was Sandra Christchurch acting?"

"Acting?"

"Nervous, maybe? Like she had something to hide?"

"I didn't notice."

Fenway rubbed her forehead. "When you left the coaches' meeting, did you see anything unusual? Or hear anything?"

"I don't think so."

"Did you see Coach Flash last night at the bar?"

"No. I was here, studying film of a couple of our new players. I finished dinner around six in the hotel restaurant—"

"Anyone with you?"

"Just the waiter and my laptop. After the coaches' meeting, I came up here and studied until about ten. I was asleep by ten thirty, easy."

"Any noises you might remember? You're right next door to him."

"I'm a heavy sleeper. I have a white noise machine I bring with me, too. It's a godsend to have it when we're staying in some of those downtown hotels when we're on the road. So no, I didn't hear anything after I went to bed."

Fenway stood and handed him her card. "Let me know if you think of anything else. We'll have someone come bag up those shoes."

"Are we stuck in the hotel, or can we hold practice? The bus is taking the players to Nidever in a few hours."

Fenway considered. "I'll talk it over with my sergeant."

———

Fenway walked back down the ninth-floor hallway to Paul Levinson's hotel room and stepped inside. A sheet had been placed over the body. Melissa de la Garza knelt next to the coffee table, brushing fingerprint dust onto the bottle of tequila.

"Good to see you, Melissa."

"Hey, Fenway. Nice to see you too. Though it would be great if we ever met under less morbid circumstances."

"How's life with Donald?"

"I can tell he's never lived with a woman before." Melissa chuckled. "Of course, I've never lived with a man, either, so I guess there are some compromises we both need to make."

"Sure." Fenway had never lived with a man, either, and for a brief moment wondered what sharing an apartment with McVie would be like. "What have you found so far?"

"I've shipped off the golf club and the wet clothing to the lab," Melissa said. "No usable fingerprints."

"That's disappointing. Not that much of a surprise, I guess."

Melissa shrugged. "Sometimes criminals will touch something after they wipe it down. It's not unheard of. I thought we might get lucky."

"What else?"

"The woman who was in here earlier is your prime suspect, right?"

"Maggie Erskine. Right. She was found sleeping in the king bed in there, and those were her clothes soaking wet on the floor of the shower."

"Right next to the murder weapon," Melissa said.

"Correct. Erskine admits to being here last night, starting around ten o'clock, and says she didn't leave. She admits to having sex with Levinson, and I believe she was coerced into it."

"Coerced?"

"Yes. He'd promise to ease up on hard training exercises or guilt her into agreeing. She told us he'd been doing this since her first year in college."

"He was her coach in college, too? Shellmont University in North Carolina, right?"

"Correct."

Melissa frowned. "Sexual coercion—tough to prove."

"It is." Fenway paused. "And that means"—Fenway spoke haltingly—"it's possible that she didn't think he would ever stop. Maybe she couldn't convince anyone what he was doing was wrong."

Melissa nodded slowly. "Gives her motive to kill him."

Fenway pursed her lips. "When we spoke to her, it seemed like she was blaming herself, or maybe that sex was even consensual on her part." She scratched her scalp. "But if she was acting—or even if she wasn't—the nature of their relationship gives her motive. Maybe she'd finally had enough." Fenway blinked—

—and suddenly she was back on the Western Washington campus, walking in a daze through the sleet on her way to her Russian Lit class the morning after it happened, the anger and confusion and fear coursing through her veins.

"Battered woman syndrome?"

Fenway swallowed hard, coming back to the present. "What?"

Melissa tilted her head. "Are you all right, Fenway?"

Fenway waved her hand. "Yes, yes, fine. It—it's just me thinking about different angles of the case. What did you say?"

"Battered woman syndrome. That's not the medical term for it, but it is the legal defense. I mean, it's sort of old school, but it might still work."

"It's possible," Fenway said. "The owner of the Vegas Neons found out what he'd been doing and fired him. Don't you think she'd have let him know before the press conference?"

Melissa shrugged. "I don't know what goes through the owner's head."

"If the owner didn't tell him, I have to believe he knew he was on thin ice."

"Yeah, that makes sense."

"And yet," Fenway said, balling her hands into fists, "he still brings her to his hotel room and coerces her into sex."

"Like he's flaunting it." Melissa paused. "I might have snapped if I'd been her."

"She says she was drunk and asleep. But she might be lying about remembering what she did."

"What if it *is* battered woman's syndrome? Some kind of psychotic break?"

Fenway arched an eyebrow. "She's been through emotional trauma, so I suppose it's technically possible, but the chances are astronomical that Erskine had some sort of episode."

"Still," Melissa said, "it's hard to be too sympathetic for the murder victim." She stood and opened the door to the bedroom, then pointed to the bathroom. "How many bath towels are usually in the bathroom of a hotel like this?"

Fenway shrugged. "I'd have to check with housekeeping, but I think a top-tier hotel like the Broadmere usually provides guests with four of each."

Melissa walked around the bed and switched the bathroom light on with a gloved hand. "There are four hand towels and four wash-cloths, but only two bath towels."

"You're suggesting two bath towels are missing?"

"The most sensible thing to use to clean up a crime scene," Melissa said. "You'll want to keep an eye out for two blood-soaked bath towels."

CHAPTER SIX

Melissa walked back to the body, which was still covered with the sheet. "We'll do a little role play here. I'm the killer. I got really angry at Levinson, grabbed his golf club, and whacked him on the back of the head."

"Okay."

"The first blow likely killed him," Melissa said. "He was also struck twice in the shoulders and three times in the upper back."

"Someone was pissed off," Fenway said.

"I'd use the word *rage*," Melissa said.

"Can you tell anything about the killer? Height, maybe?"

Melissa shook her head. "Too many variables. We might be able to narrow things down a little when we run some computer scenarios, but I doubt we'll get a height or weight. And with the length of the club, a deadly blow could have been struck by anyone—male, female, even a preteen." Melissa glanced at Fenway. "I believe the killer used their right hand to deliver the blow, however."

"So probably right-handed."

Melissa stood with her hand raised as if she were holding a stick.

"So I'm standing here. I've just killed Levinson with a golf club—and then whacked him a few more times for good measure. He's lying in front of me. He's dead. Is the golf club still in my hand?"

"Yes."

"Do I drop it on the floor, or do I go clean it off?"

"Since it was in the shower, I assume the killer went to clean it off."

Melissa pointed to a dark smudge on the carpet. "There's a smudge on the carpet consistent with the head of the golf club here."

"Ah," Fenway said, nodding. "So the killer *did* drop it—perhaps in shock."

"Okay," Melissa said. "You're the killer. You dropped the golf club. What's going through your head?"

The hotel room door opened, and Dez stuck her head in. "Maggie is on her way to the station."

"So," Fenway said, "we let the rest of the team continue about their business? Or are we confining them to the hotel?"

Dez shrugged. "That's your call."

"But I'm asking your advice."

"We can't hold thirty people here at the hotel," Dez said. "You have any other strong suspects besides Maggie?"

"Not yet."

"Then I'd say the answer is pretty clear."

Fenway nodded, taking out her phone. "They'll be glad they can go to practice." She texted Deputy Callahan to relay the news to the team.

"We're walking through the scene," Melissa said. "Seeing if we can find explanations for the physical evidence."

"What did you find?" Dez asked.

"So far," Melissa said, "we've got the killer dropping the golf club on the carpet"—she pointed to the smudge on the rug—"after killing our victim."

Fenway put her phone away and pointed to the body. "Melissa found several locations on the body where it had been struck, not only the obvious head wound."

Melissa took a step forward. "Right now, I think the body blows were administered after the initial cranial hit."

"Right-handed perp?" Fenway asked.

Melissa nodded.

Dez screwed up her face. "Maggie's right-handed."

"Along with ninety percent of the population," Melissa said.

"Let's keep going," Fenway suggested.

"Right." Melissa pointed at herself. "I lost my temper and beat the coach to death. I dropped the murder weapon. So now what do I do?"

"Clean up," Fenway said.

"You're covered in blood," Dez said. "That kind of spray would have gotten all over the killer."

Melissa pointed to a few drops of blood on the wall and the high ceiling. "And the backswing of the golf club flung some blood around, too."

"So," Dez said, "you'd try to get to a place where you can wash up, right? Without tracking the blood everywhere."

"Okay," Melissa said, "so you walk to the bathroom. Through the entrance from the bedroom or the sitting room?" She pointed at the carpet in the sitting room between the corpse and the bathroom door. "I'd expect quite a bit of blood tracked there. I see a light spatter of blood I believe is from the initial flurry of blows, and there are a few drips between the body and the bathroom, but not enough to be consistent with someone walking through the room with blood on their shoes, or dripping from their clothes." She pointed at the sliding door into the bedroom. "And nothing on the door handle, either."

"Does this mean the killer walked to the bathroom or not?"

Melissa furrowed her brow. "The murderer might have had something to use to wipe a lot of the blood off before going into the bathroom."

"Hence your comment about two bath towels going missing," said Fenway.

"Blood dries quickly when exposed to air," Dez mused. "If Maggie —sorry, if the *killer*—had been standing over the body, being indecisive, might the blood have dried enough not to drip?"

"In order to dry enough not to drip, we're talking about hours, not minutes," Melissa answered.

"So—hold on, Melissa. You mean not enough blood dripped between the body and anywhere else in the room?"

"Correct. We'll get in here with Luminol in a couple of hours. But I'm surprised there are so few visible drips of blood."

"Does that make sense?" Fenway asked. "Do we really think Maggie, who was so drunk she was slurring her words and barely able to walk, hit her coach a bunch of times with his golf driver, then had the presence of mind to—to do *something* to stop from dripping on the carpet between his dead body and the bathroom?"

"If Erskine and Levinson had sex earlier in the evening," Melissa said, "I'll wager she wasn't wearing shoes. In fact, she may not have been wearing much at all. Maybe he wanted to go for round two or three and that was too much for her."

"According to Maggie, they first had sex on the table," Fenway said. "They moved into the bedroom later."

"Then it's possible her clothes were piled on the floor. She wipes herself off with her shirt, which might explain why there are no drips on the carpet." Melissa walked across the sitting room to the bathroom door. "And if this was open, she might have gone directly into the shower, washed herself off, ruined a couple of bath towels in the process, left her clothes in the bottom of the shower, and then realized her fingerprints were all over the golf club too. She comes out, grabs the murder weapon, dumps it in the shower, maybe washes it off with soap, then collapses, exhausted, into the bed, where she's found in the morning."

"After she just killed someone?" Fenway asked. "Wouldn't the adrenaline make that difficult? And in that scenario, when did she get rid of the two bath towels?"

"Maybe they dried out," Dez said.

Fenway shook her head. "No. They'd still be in the room, and they're not. The other two towels in the bathroom haven't been touched."

"I'll put a couple of deputies to search for two bloody towels in the hotel," Dez said. "But I just want to point out that everything you've said so far—except the towels—fits with a theory that Maggie is the killer. I don't like it, and I might think Coach Flasher—"

"Flash," Fenway mumbled.

"—got what was coming to him, but we're not here to argue a justifiable homicide defense. We're here to figure out what happened. Let's assume for the moment an explanation for the missing towels—assuming there were four in here to begin with—is forthcoming. Are there any other alternate theories either of you have?"

"Someone else," Fenway said, "could have come in and done exactly what you've suggested. If Maggie's clothes were in a heap in the siting room, the killer could have wiped off the blood, cleaned up and toweled off in the bathroom, then left the room, taking the towels with them."

"And wouldn't even see Maggie," Melissa muttered.

"Someone else would need a key," Dez said.

Fenway shook her head. "Not if Coach Levinson knew the killer. He answers the door, the killer comes in, they argue, and *whack!*"

Dez nodded. "Before I came up, I asked hotel security to get their recordings for us to review. They've gathered video footage and readied a viewing station. A little cramped, but it'll do."

"Excellent. If Levinson had another visitor last night, maybe it was caught on the recording. Maggie could have slept through every-thing." Fenway turned to Melissa. "Do you have a preliminary time of death?"

"From rigor and liver temperature, I'd say some time between eleven and two."

"Only three hours of footage to watch, Dez."

"I can't wait." Dez opened the hotel suite door.

———

The security footage station was a cramped room with slate gray walls and three banks of small monitors. A Black man wearing a charcoal security uniform nearly matching the color of the walls squeezed in with Dez and Fenway.

"I'll run the machines," he said, pointing to his nametag, which read *Ezekiel Washington*. "Y'all let me know if you want to go back or forward." He had an accent Fenway couldn't immediately place, consonants forward on his tongue. Maybe from Georgia, although it didn't sound cosmopolitan enough to be Atlanta.

"Are there cameras on each floor?" Fenway asked.

Washington shook his head. "Not in the hallways. Elevators, lobby, restaurant. Oh—and two cameras in the parking garage."

"So, Mr. Washington—"

"Mr. Washington is my father," he said. "Call me Ezekiel."

"Of course—Ezekiel. Could someone enter via the stairs and not be seen?"

"Can't use the stairs for mobility between floors," Ezekiel said. "The doors lock from the outside. Security issue." He stroked his chin. "Could maybe *exit* without being seen by the cameras. But not enter."

"What if someone propped the door open?"

"We've got sensors on each door. If someone props it open, it'll beep, and then about thirty seconds later, an alarm will sound."

"Pretty serious about security?"

"Our guests think it's important."

Fenway nodded. "Let's start the video when Maggie came into the bar last night—right around ten."

They sat in silence for a moment as Ezekiel found the spot in the recording.

"You and Maggie walked in together," Dez murmured to Fenway.

"Yes. She was pretty drunk. She offered to get a round of scotches."

"Any reason for her generosity?"

Fenway shrugged. "Like I said, she was pretty drunk."

On the screen, Levinson came in and spoke to Maggie, who stood. Levinson pressed something into Maggie's hand—that would be the hotel room key. He went to sit down at the other side of the room, giving his order to the server. A minute later, Maggie stood and carefully walked to the elevator.

"What room was Maggie assigned?" Fenway asked.

"612," Dez replied. "But hold on; I want to see what Levinson does."

Fenway pointed to the screen. "Look, there I am, trying to pay for both drinks."

"But the bartender doesn't take your card."

"No. He said it was taken care of. I think Levinson got it."

"Hmm." Dez looked at Fenway out of the corner of her eye and lowered her voice. "I'm pretty sure there's something you're not telling me."

Fenway hesitated.

"Is this about one of McVie's investigations?"

"Yes." Fenway motioned with her head toward the door.

"Excuse us for a moment, Mr. Washington," Dez said.

When they were out in the empty hallway, Dez closed the door softly behind them. "All right, what is it?"

"Craig's client is Annabel Shedd's wife."

"Her *wife?* Isn't Shedd married to some big casino mogul?"

"Mathilda Montague. She thinks Annabel is cheating on her."

"With who?"

"With Maggie Erskine."

"So—wait, is that why you and McVie were at Maxime's?"

"Right. I was helping out on his investigation."

"Stalking Annabel? And that's why you were sitting next to Maggie in the bar?"

Fenway grimaced. "Well—yeah. Maggie stormed out of the restaurant. She and Annabel had an argument."

"An argument? Like a lovers' quarrel?"

"More like—like when your friend says she doesn't like the person you're dating."

Dez brought her hand to her chin and tapped her fingers, one at a time. "So you're eating dinner with McVie, eavesdropping on dinner conversation between Annabel and Maggie. They have an argument, Maggie leaves, and you—follow her?"

Fenway rubbed her hands together nervously. "I pretended that I was having a fight with Craig, and Maggie and I both got in an Uber and went to the Broadmere."

Dez pressed her lips together. "Did you discuss Paul Levinson?"

Fenway shook her head. "Only when she mentioned that he was the coach. I was trying to figure out if Maggie and Annabel were having an affair. I didn't care who else Maggie slept with."

Dez rubbed her temples with both hands. "Had you ever met Maggie before?"

"No. We didn't talk about anything that would affect evidence collection. Or that would get grounds for appeal."

Dez studied Fenway's face for a moment. "Hmph. All right." She opened the door, and Fenway followed her in, where Ezekiel was sitting in front of the monitor, the same paused image of the bar on the screen.

"Everything all right?" Ezekiel asked.

"Perfectly fine," Dez said. "Shall we pick up where we left off?"

Fenway pointed at the monitor. "It's been two or three minutes since Maggie left the bar and got in the elevator. Look at Levinson— right here. He gets up and goes to the elevator too. Doesn't even settle his bar tab." Then she stopped.

"So he obviously planned to follow Maggie upstairs," Dez said, then glanced at Fenway. "What is it?"

"They had a coaches' meeting just a couple of hours before this," Fenway mused. "Rocky Portello said Christchurch gave no hint that she'd be firing Levinson the next morning."

"Some people are really good about hiding stuff like that."

Fenway shook her head. "I think something happened last night that changed the owner's mind." She kept one eye on the monitor, which showed the bar's half-full seating area.

Dez cocked an eyebrow. "Sandra Christchurch found out her diamond tennis bracelet was stolen. I wonder if that had anything to do with Levinson's firing." She turned to Ezekiel. "She held the press conference here, right?"

"In the ballroom," Ezekiel said. "It was arranged fast—it wasn't on the calendar."

"There's Annabel," Fenway said. On the screen, Annabel appeared in the bar. She was walking, staring at her phone, then she looked up and craned her neck as if searching for someone.

"Who's she looking for?" Dez asked. "Maggie?"

"I think so." Fenway watched Annabel walk slowly to the elevator, and get in. A moment later, Fenway got up and walked out.

Dez leaned over Ezekiel's shoulder. "You can speed up."

"Yes, ma'am," Ezekiel said, turning a dial on the controller. The digital recording sped up, but the faces, entrances, and exits were still clear. "We're at ten o'clock now."

Dez and Fenway leaned forward slightly and took in the bar scene, but no one else of interest—no one Fenway or Dez recognized, at any rate—entered or left.

"We'll need to identify any of the players or staff who were in the bar," Fenway said. "Log their in and out times, and what floor they exited on if they went into the elevator."

Dez nodded.

"One of the assistant coaches can identify all the Neons staff and players," Ezekiel said.

"Fine," Fenway said. "Can we look at the cameras for the elevators now?"

For the next hour, Fenway and Dez watched the whole night again in fast forward, this time with the monitors showing the elevators. As they suspected, Maggie Erskine exited on the ninth floor where the coaches and the owner had their rooms. A few minutes later, Paul Levinson entered the elevator and also got off on the ninth floor.

Several players from the team, including Annabel, got on the elevator, all getting off on the fifth or sixth floors. They continued watching, asking Ezekiel to scan to the moments of people entering and exiting the elevator.

A Black woman entered the elevator, her neat black braids hanging just to the top of her shoulders. She looked tall in the elevator and wore a tracksuit the telltale black and gold of the Vegas Neons. "Lorraine Sunday," Fenway murmured. "She's the other assistant coach."

"Does she have a history with Paul Levinson?" Dez asked.

"A history with the World Cup, for sure. Not sure about Levinson."

"Wait—she's a coach?"

"I know. Looks younger than some of the players, doesn't she? I think she's forty-five or so." Fenway took out her notebook and wrote Lorraine Sunday's name. "Coach Portello said she was always complimenting Christchurch on her tennis bracelet. What's the time stamp?"

"11:32," Ezekiel replied.

"We're now in the window of time when Paul Levinson could have been killed," Fenway said, "at least according to our preliminary estimates."

"Who else has a room on this floor?" Dez asked.

Ezekiel tapped on the keyboard in front of him, and a spreadsheet appeared on another screen. He squinted and placed his finger on the monitor.

"Sandra Christchurch. Paul Levinson. Roger Portello. Lorraine Sunday."

"So the owner, the head coach, and the two assistant coaches," Fenway mused. To Ezekiel, she said, "No one else was on the ninth floor? It was all the management of the Vegas Neons?"

"That's everyone," Ezekiel said.

"I haven't seen Sandra Christchurch on the elevator yet. Or Rocky Portello, for that matter."

"The video's start time was ten o'clock," Dez pointed out. "It's the day before training camp. The owner might, wonder of wonders, be responsible and is either working or getting a good night's sleep."

Fenway rubbed her chin. "If Sandra Christchurch was prepping for an eight o'clock press conference where she was announcing the firing of her head coach for sexual misconduct, she was probably on the phone with a team of lawyers or with a P.R. firm specializing in, uh, what do they call it—reputation management."

Dez squinted at the screen, fast forwarding through video of the empty elevator. "It's twelve fifteen on the recording now. Looks pretty quiet."

A flash of light in the screen. "Wait," Fenway said.

The red number above the elevator buttons read 6, and Annabel Shedd, dressed in the Neons' black-and-gold tracksuit, hair pulled back into a ponytail, entered the carriage.

"What do you think she's doing?" Fenway whispered.

Annabel frowned and shot her hand out.

She pushed 9.

CHAPTER SEVEN

"She's headed to Paul Levinson's hotel room," Dez said.

"But she didn't end up there," Fenway said. "Did she?"

"As far as I know, she was back in her room after Levinson's body was found."

"Maybe she went to bang on the door and demand that Levinson let Maggie out of his room," Fenway said. "We heard Maggie say Annabel was nagging her to stop letting Coach Levinson get in her head."

If you don't do something about Maggie and that monster, I will.

"Let's see how long she's gone."

Ezekiel slowed the playback down to normal speed.

"What time did she exit the elevator?" Fenway asked.

"12:18 A.M.," Dez said.

"If she knocked on the coach's door and he didn't answer, she should be back in a couple of minutes."

Dez and Fenway waited, leaning forward slightly, as the seconds ticked by on the video timecode.

"Four minutes," Dez said. "He must have answered the door."

"We don't know if she went to see Coach Levinson," Fenway said. "Maybe she went to the Neons' owner to complain about him."

"Or it might not be related," Dez said. "She could have met with one of the assistant coaches to—I don't know, ask about a soccer strategy or something."

"We'll interview her," Fenway said, "but I like to know the answers to the questions before I ask."

The corners of Dez's mouth tugged upward. "Six minutes."

"Want me to fast forward?" Ezekiel asked. He placed his hand on the dial and twisted it clockwise. The recording went forward ten minutes, then fifteen. The elevator picked up a man in a suit on the ground floor and deposited him on the third floor. Two players from the team entered on the ground floor and exited on the sixth floor.

"Annabel's been on the ninth floor a long time," Dez said.

The time code read 1:37 A.M., almost an hour and a half after Annabel had gotten off the elevator on the ninth floor. The elevator dipped to the ground floor again—

—and Annabel Shedd entered the elevator.

Fenway looked at Dez. "What just happened?"

"Did we miss Annabel getting on the elevator on the ninth floor?"

"No, ma'am," Ezekiel said. "I was here watching it like a hawk, same as you. I can tell you without a doubt she did not get on the elevator in the last hour and a half."

"Let's watch it again."

But the results were the same. Annabel never got back on the elevator on the ninth floor.

"The stairs," Fenway said. "She had to have left via the stairs."

Ezekiel frowned. "But the stairs don't open into any of the other floors. You can get into the stairwell from any of the floors, but you can only exit the stairs from the ground floor."

"Where's the exit for the stairwell? The lobby?"

"The parking garage. There's a walkway connecting Broadway and San Ysidro," Ezekiel said.

"Any cameras down there?"

"Two. They focus on the vehicle lanes, though."

Fenway shook her head. "Are there trash cans in the side alley? Maybe a dumpster?"

"Trash cans in the parking garage for sure."

Fenway put her hands on her hips. "We don't have a suspect pool limited to the people on the ninth floor anymore. Any of them could have exited via the stairs, or held the door to the stairwell open from the inside."

"Not for more than thirty seconds, remember," Ezekiel said.

"Right," replied Fenway. "And without camera coverage in the hallways or on the outside door, we can't be sure who was on the ninth floor or not."

Dez folded her arms. "I'm afraid you've got a point."

Fenway paced in a small circle. "Dez, can you keep going here?"

"Uh, sure," Dez said. "You coming back?"

"I don't know—I'm going to clear my head. See if there's another way I can look at this." Fenway opened the door and left the small video room.

She walked into the narrow hallway, then turned and was out the front door. The driveway for the parking lot emptied out onto Broadway. She strode across the small lot and turned right onto the sidewalk, not sure where she was going.

She pulled out her phone and dialed McVie.

"McVie Investigations."

"Hi, Craig. You've heard the news?"

"About Coach Flash's firing? Yeah, Mathilda Montague was on the phone with me as soon as the press conference was over. She's harping on me to figure out what it means for Annabel."

"Not only his firing." Fenway sucked in air through her teeth.

"Craig, I had to disclose what we did last night—your investigation into Annabel, what we were doing at Maxime's, and my little adventure in the Uber with Maggie."

"What? That could ruin the investigation. Who did you tell?"

"Dez, for one. I didn't have a choice. There's been a murder."

"A—a murder?"

"Yes. And it's Coach Levinson."

McVie paused. "The victim? Or the murderer?"

"The victim."

He breathed out long and slow.

"I'm sorry, Craig—I know I used to tell you details when you were sheriff, but now I can't."

"Yeah, I know how it is."

"I can't guarantee I can keep Mathilda Montague out of this, either," Fenway said. "I'll try, but we might have some questions for her—"

"I wish you could avoid that," McVie said.

"I really don't want to get you in the middle of this, Craig. I know how much business Montague could bring in."

"You go solve the murder," McVie said. "Now if you'll excuse me, I need to make a call."

Fenway looked up. She was walking fast and found herself six blocks past the hotel, heading down Broadway toward the heart of downtown. She'd be at the coroner's office building in another four or five blocks.

She hoped the Neons wouldn't close ranks—she hoped to interview them to get evidence. As it was, even if Maggie or Annabel had dealt Levinson the fatal blow, the video could be used to provide reasonable doubt for both of them. Fenway sighed. Without more physical evidence, it would be tough to attain an indictment against either Maggie or Annabel—never mind a conviction.

The mid-morning was overcast, and Fenway shivered. She only

had a thin blazer, and while this weather would have been balmy in a Seattle March, she'd started to get used to the milder weather of the California coast.

The sun broke through the clouds. She lifted her hand to her forehead to shield her eyes—she'd left her sunglasses at home. She stopped walking and let the sunlight wash over her.

The sun went back behind a cloud a moment later, and a breeze started, gentle at first, then strengthening until a few blossoms from a birch tree fluttered off a branch. If Fenway's hair had been as long as it had been a few months ago, it would have been over her face.

She would need to widen the net she was casting for suspects. Yes, Maggie was the lead suspect right now. Perhaps she'd had so much to drink that she finally got angry enough at Coach Levinson's coercion to kill him. And perhaps she'd been so drunk she tossed her bloody clothes in the shower along with the golf club and passed out in the king bed in the coach's bedroom.

Means, motive, opportunity.

Levinson could have opened the door for anyone—players, other coaches, the owner, even hotel staff. And he was killed with a golf club that was within easy reach.

As for motive—it would be easier finding someone who *didn't* have a reason to hate him.

So Fenway would have to think laterally. Get evidence she didn't yet have.

Like the two missing towels.

The staircase as a means of exiting the hotel without getting on camera. Garbage cans in the parking garage or outside a nearby fast-food place or mini-mart.

Then it struck her—the tennis bracelet.

She wasn't sure if it had anything to do with the murder, but Dez had been right to point out that the theft of the tennis bracelet might be related to Levinson's firing.

She needed to go back to the hotel.

Several minutes later, Fenway walked up the driveway of the Broadmere and entered the lobby. The light twinkled off a crystal vase on an end table.

She walked into the elevator, went up to the ninth floor, and knocked on the door to Sandra Christchurch's suite.

Nothing.

She knocked again, a little louder, but was greeted with only silence. Fenway listened carefully; nothing from inside at all. No sound of the television or music, no footsteps.

She stepped back, her shoulders slightly slumped, and went back to the elevator.

When she exited into the lobby, she took her badge out of her purse and made a beeline for the reception desk. The clerk looked up with large, watery eyes behind a pair of thick glasses. "May I help you?"

Fenway held up her badge. "Have you seen Sandra Christchurch leave the hotel? She's not in her room."

The clerk pointed to the restaurant. "She went in there about fifteen minutes ago." He tilted his head. "You're Fenway Stevenson, aren't you?"

She nodded, her ears getting hot.

"Your father is Nathaniel Ferris, right? He's in there too. I believe they had a business meeting."

Oh—of course. Who better to get information from on how to successfully run a women's soccer team than a woman who'd done it herself?

It might not be polite to interrupt their meeting, but this was a murder investigation. She straightened her blazer and walked into the posh restaurant adjoining the Broadmere. Her dad was sitting at a table with Sandra Christchurch, two flutes of mimosas between them.

In the mid-morning on a Friday, Nathaniel Ferris and Sandra Christchurch were the only ones in the dining room. Ferris leaned forward, elbows on the table, looking attentively at Christchurch. Fenway thought it was the most engaged she'd seen her father in a long time. Certainly the most enthusiastic he'd been since selling his oil company.

Fenway felt her shoulders lighten. Getting into a new type of business would be good for Nathaniel Ferris—if it was the *right* kind of business. It would certainly keep his mind off the demanding physical therapy he needed.

Making sure to keep her stride casual, Fenway walked up to the table. "Hi, Dad."

Nathaniel Ferris looked up and blinked. "Oh, Fenway, good morning." He motioned to Sandra Christchurch. "Have you met the owner of the Las Vegas Neons?"

The woman across from Nathaniel Ferris was petite but broad-shouldered, with white-blonde hair, a small nose, a strong jawline, and piercing gray eyes. Fenway shook her head.

"May I introduce you, then?" Ferris asked. "Sandra Christchurch, I'm delighted to introduce my daughter, Dominguez County Coroner Fenway Stevenson."

"Pleasure," Christchurch said.

"Ms. Christchurch," she said. "Of course, I know you by reputation, but we haven't formally met."

Ferris turned to Fenway. "I've noticed a lot of police activity at the hotel," Ferris said. "Did something happen?"

Fenway nodded. "Yes. We had a death reported this morning." She tilted her head at Christchurch. "Actually, that's why I'm here. Your hotel suite is on the same floor as the decedent's hotel room."

"Yes." Christchurch folded her hands and stared down at the table, her voice calm and even. "I heard Coach Levinson was found this morning. I do indeed have a suite on the same floor as his."

Ferris sat up straight in his chair. "And you still agreed to this meeting?"

Christchurch raised her head. "I don't wish to dwell on what I can't control. Work is something I can focus on. I can be productive, even in a dark time like this."

"If you're sure—"

Christchurch waved her hand at Ferris, almost dismissive.

Fenway leaned over the table slightly. "We've been attempting to interview everyone on the ninth floor before they left their rooms."

"Well, as you most likely know," Sandra Christchurch said, "I had a press conference this morning in the Pacific Crest Ballroom, across the lobby."

"Did you hear or see anything when you left your room this morning?"

"No." She cast her eyes down. "I think the topic of my press conference may have had some direct bearing on Coach Levinson's unfortunate passing."

"When did you return to your room?"

"I haven't been back. I've been right here since the press conference. I felt certain the police wouldn't want me to leave the hotel—especially since I reported a theft this morning."

Ferris's jaw dropped open. "A theft?"

"The bracelet Warren gave me two years ago."

"Oh, no," Ferris said. "You didn't leave it back home?"

"I wear it all the time. It means a lot to me."

"I'm sure it does."

Christchurch turned back to Fenway. "And as I had a meeting with Mr. Ferris this morning, I thought it would be wise to move the location of the meeting from his house to this restaurant." She gestured at the room, empty but for the three of them and the wait-staff. "Seems like we're about as alone here as we would have been at his house." She narrowed her eyes. "Except for you, of course, Miss Stevenson."

Fenway heard the slight bite to Christchurch's tone.

Ferris chuckled. "Well, Sandra, not only is Fenway Stevenson the county coroner, but she's also proven herself to be a trusted advisor in several of my business ventures." He glanced at Fenway; pride flashed briefly in his eyes. "She did quite well several months ago when she found herself in the precarious position of advising my company when I was out of commission. She identified potential risks, managed the public face of the business, and facilitated what became an extremely lucrative sale of my energy company."

Fenway felt her ears burn.

Ferris put his hands flat on the table. "Any scenario in which I become a majority owner of any team—existing or expansion—I would consult with Fenway extensively before making a final decision."

Sandra Christchurch's eyebrows raised, then her face softened. "I know how valuable it is to have someone you trust in matters of business." She glanced at Fenway. "I suppose I'm heartened that you appreciate what a big decision this is, even for somebody with your resources, Nathaniel. However, no matter your daughter's experience, she shouldn't be the only one to have a say."

"I have lawyers."

"And I have some questions for you," Fenway said to Christchurch.

"Of course." Christchurch looked up at Fenway. "Well, then, if you don't mind terribly, Nathaniel, let me have a conversation with Miss Stevenson about the tragedy of Coach Levinson's suicide, and then we'll continue the less pressing matters of team ownership."

Suicide? Fenway tried to keep her face impassive.

Christchurch turned to the server standing next to the bar and raised her empty coffee cup. The server nodded and walked briskly to the coffee station.

Ferris stood and held on to the table for support. For a moment, he quavered before standing up straight. "I know it's before noon, but I believe I shall avail myself of a libation or two at the bar." He winked at Fenway. "The joys of being completely retired. At least for a little while." He took a few small steps toward the bar, adjusted his sportscoat, and began to take another step.

Fenway stopped him with a hand on his back and leaned forward, lowering her voice. "Dad," she said, "where is your cane?"

"It's in the car," Nathaniel Ferris said. "I am *not* meeting with the most visible and powerful owner in the AFF looking like some kind of invalid."

Fenway's mouth turned down. "Come on, Dad."

"I'm sorry if it's an offensive thing to say, but that's business. I can't look weak. It puts me in a bad negotiating position."

Fenway shook her head. "It is *much* too soon for you to be walking without support. At least grab onto my arm. I'll accompany you over to the bar like a good daughter."

"You're being ridiculous." A bead of sweat appeared on Nathaniel Ferris's forehead.

Fenway took her father's arm and began to walk with him. "I think you're the one being ridiculous if you keep insisting you can do everything by yourself. You'll be able to again—I know it. But for now, you need a cane."

"It looks silly."

"You have the money to make it bad-ass. Get some sort of jewel-encrusted sword disguised as a cane so it, uh, *enhances* your presence."

Ferris managed a smile. "That would look pretty cool."

"Besides," Fenway said, "what would *really* give you a bad negotiating position is falling over, smacking your head on the corner of a table, and ending up on the floor with your head split open."

Nathaniel Ferris grunted.

"Picture this instead, Dad. Imagine yourself showing up with a crystal walking stick that makes you look like a wizard. Or some highly polished titanium high-tech cane that makes everyone think you're a British spy."

Ferris chuckled. "I appreciate your insight into my character, Fenway."

"Here we go, now."

They arrived at the bar, and Ferris sat down heavily on a stool, exhaling loudly. "I promise you, I'm fine. I'll have a Bloody Mary."

"The mimosa wasn't enough?"

"It's just orange juice, Fenway. Maybe I'll have a little appetizer to give myself some strength."

"No carpaccio."

He patted her hand. "I'll have a boring selection of crudités and you can report to Charlotte what a good boy I've been."

"All right, Dad, fine. Get whatever you want." Fenway looked over her shoulder; Sandra Christchurch leaned forward in her chair and stared at her.

Fenway clapped her father on the shoulder, plastered a determined look on her face, and strode toward the table.

CHAPTER EIGHT

"I APPRECIATE YOU INTERRUPTING YOUR BUSINESS MEETING FOR this." Fenway pulled her father's chair out. "Do you mind if I take a seat?"

"Not at all," Christchurch said. "Will you be starting with the theft, or with the death of Coach Levinson?"

Fenway blinked at her. She'd never worked a robbery before, but she'd seen her sergeants do it. She took her notebook from her purse and flipped it open to an empty page, then glanced up at Christchurch. How did she want to play this? If Christchurch thought Levinson's death was a murder, she might be less than forthcoming. But there was another card Fenway could play.

"Let's start with your missing tennis bracelet."

"It was stolen from my hotel room safe." Christchurch set her jaw. "I don't travel with a lot of expensive jewelry, but Warren gave me that bracelet on our anniversary before—before he passed."

Fenway wrote in the notebook, then looked up at Christchurch. "I'm sorry. Do you have a picture of the bracelet? Or a description?"

Christchurch took her phone out of her purse, tapped on the

screen, then showed the phone to Fenway. It was a picture of a tennis bracelet on the Dresden & Diadem website.

"This is what he got you?" Fenway winced at the price—it cost more than her car.

"Inscribed, too. 'To my beloved Sandra.'"

"That'll make it easier to track."

Christchurch gave Fenway a tight smile. "Is that supposed to give me some hope of finding it?"

"I—I couldn't say, Ms. Christchurch."

Christchurch pressed her lips together and exhaled through her nose. "Yes, yes, that's right. You're the county coroner. Shouldn't the sheriff be asking these questions? Don't you just do autopsies?"

"I'm at the hotel because the coroner's office investigates all deaths in the county that are"—Fenway counted each word off on her fingers—"unnatural, unexpected, unexplained, or unattended. I have two detective sergeants on my team, but I often lead investigations."

"So the theft of my bracelet isn't your first priority."

Fenway shifted in her chair. "We have the fingerprint team here. I'll ask to have them fingerprint the safe. See if there are any matches in our database."

"And then?"

"Someone from our robbery division will come in." Fenway paused. "When was the last time you saw the bracelet?"

"Just after I arrived last night."

Fenway nodded. "You put it in the safe..."

"Roughly eight o'clock."

"Anyone in or out of your room?"

"A brief meeting with the coaches. That was in the sitting room area of the suite, but they were gone by eight thirty."

"And did you check the safe after that?"

"Certainly not. None of the coaches would steal from me."

Fenway cocked her head. "None of them? You were about to fire

Coach Levinson, and from what I understand, that will put the others' jobs in jeopardy."

"We didn't discuss anything pertaining to their employment."

"You informed the team ninety minutes before the press conference—yet you didn't think to bring it up in the coaches' meeting the night before."

Christchurch narrowed her eyes. "That's correct, Coroner. How I run my team is my business."

Fenway flipped a page in her notebook—there was something Christchurch wasn't telling her, but it would do no good to press her. Not now, anyway. "If you don't believe any of the coaches took the bracelet, do you have any idea who *would* steal from you?"

Christchurch pressed her lips together. "Perhaps a hotel staff member. I left my room to attend the press conference."

"And what time did you leave your hotel room?"

Christchurch tapped her chin. "I didn't look at the clock before I left. It must have been around five thirty, or perhaps five forty-five."

"For an eight o'clock press conference?"

"As sudden as this decision was, I wanted to make sure to communicate with the players and the staff before the press conference. I wanted as few people as possible to find out during, or God forbid, *after* the press conference. So I sent an email and a direct message to all the staff and players to meet me in the small conference room at six thirty."

"Short notice."

"Coach Levinson's behavior didn't leave me with much choice."

Fenway opened her mouth, but then decided to take a different tack. "Was your impromptu conference well attended?"

Christchurch tapped her chin. "Perhaps half the players and staff came. Not ideal, but certainly more than I would have expected at six thirty. I'm sure many of them were asleep or in the shower."

"Who was there?"

"Lorraine Sunday, but not Rocky Portello. Darcy Nishimura and Aissa Oumar, but not Annabel Shedd or Maggie Erskine. I'm sorry, I wasn't taking attendance."

"Was that the first time you left your hotel room after you came back from dinner?"

"I had so many calls, I certainly didn't have any opportunity to go down until the morning." Christchurch smiled. "Are we still discussing the theft?"

"Yes." Fenway turned back a few pages in her notebook. "I wonder why you don't think any of the coaches took your bracelet. Your head coach would be fired twelve hours later. You don't think he suspected anything?"

"No."

Fenway closed her notebook and set it down on the table. "I don't understand how you—"

Christchurch raised a finger in front of her face. "I do not take the decision of firing one of the most successful coaches in the league lightly. There had been talk, a few players making statements, but I discovered additional allegations."

"When?"

"Within the last few—" Christchurch stopped, blinked, then continued. "Within the last week."

"A week? These are serious allegations—how did you not fire him then?" Fenway's throat burned. Just like her professor had a history of complaints—but the people in charge did nothing.

"With our litigious society, I must exercise caution."

You'll exercise caution about your head coach suing you, but not about your head coach sexually assaulting your players. Fenway wrote "Exercising caution" in her notebook, the pen ripping the paper slightly on the last *n*.

"I was conducting my own investigation," Christchurch contin-ued, "and I was made aware of evidence which convinced me the allegations against Coach Levinson were true and remediation needed to occur."

Hold on—Christchurch had hesitated when asked about the time frame. Fenway shifted in her seat. "Evidence you uncovered between the coaches' meeting and the press conference?"

Christchurch shook her head. "I'm not at liberty to say."

"You just alluded to that information a few minutes ago," Fenway said. "You said that it might have directly affected Coach Levinson's —his death."

"Revealing protected information, even in the course of a police investigation, may be illegal for me to do without a subpoena."

Fenway rubbed her chin and decided to change the subject. "Why don't you take me through what happened yesterday evening?"

"What would you like to know?"

"Let's start with what time you entered your hotel room."

Christchurch nodded. "I'd eaten dinner by the time I got to the hotel, so I would say I arrived about eight o'clock. I didn't check the exact time."

"You drove?"

"I hired a car to bring me to the hotel from the airport. Cypress Car Service."

Fenway wrote the name in her notebook.

"I checked into the hotel, went up to my room, put my bracelet in the safe, and set up my laptop," Christchurch continued.

"Sorry to interrupt," Fenway said, "but is this the kind of safe where you pick your own combination?"

"Of course."

"Did you pick something that many people might guess? Your birthday, for example?"

"I don't use my—" Christchurch snapped her mouth shut. "I see. Perhaps it was too easy to guess."

"Is there a particular group of people who might be familiar with the code? If they know a date you might have used?"

Christchurch exhaled slowly through her nose, pursing her lips as she did so. "Now that I think about it, the number would be easy for any member of the public to guess."

Fenway nodded. "You may want to change—"

Christchurch waved her hand dismissively. "Yes, yes. I'll make sure to do so. Carry on with your questions."

"You say you got your laptop next."

"Yes. I signed into my email and discovered I'd received a communication from my investigator discussing his findings."

"What were those findings?"

Christchurch smiled. "I'm not comfortable discussing anything further before I talk to my attorney."

Fenway nodded. "Then what did you do?"

"The coaches arrived for their meeting—Coach Levinson, Coach Portello, and Coach Sunday. We discussed final roster moves before the start of training, and they left about fifteen minutes later."

"Did anyone leave the meeting?"

"Before it ended? No, of course not."

"I mean leave the room, even for a moment or two."

Christchurch frowned. "Perhaps to use the restroom."

"All three coaches left your suite at the same time?"

"That's correct."

"Then what did you do?"

"I immediately called my lawyer to discuss my options and the legal repercussions thereof." Christchurch chose her words carefully, and Fenway scribbled her notes: *Contacted lawyer – discussed options.*

"About what time was that?" Fenway asked.

Christchurch took her phone off the table and began scrolling. "I called at 8:34 P.M. The call lasted for twenty-seven minutes and thirty-one seconds." She held out the screen toward Fenway. "As the call was with my lawyer, I'm afraid I won't be able to tell you what we discussed or provide any further details of the call."

Fenway screwed up her mouth. She'd had to talk to people who were well versed in the legal system before. But Christchurch seemed to have an extra dollop of paranoia on top of it.

There could be a valid reason for her reticence—especially when a coach whom she had hired was accused of sexual misconduct and then had been found dead. Fenway tapped her pen on the table. "You ended the call with your lawyer at about nine o'clock. What did you do next?"

Sandra scrolled again. "Approximately five minutes later, I contacted a person in the Las Vegas Neons' public relations department. She and I were on the phone for"—she tapped her phone and glanced at the screen—"one hour and forty-three minutes." She smiled at Fenway.

"And what did—"

"I realize, of course, our conversation is *not* protected by attorney-client privilege. However, it was of a confidential nature essential to the successful operations of the Las Vegas Neons. As such, I do not wish to volunteer the contents of our conversation without a warrant or a subpoena."

Fenway smiled. The verbal contortions were almost ridiculous, but the woman knew her rights. Fenway thought she knew the answer to her next question, but she asked it anyway. "When you ended the conversation with your PR department, had you decided to fire Coach Levinson?"

Sandra Christchurch smiled, showing no teeth. "Terminating Coach Levinson's employment was one of several possibilities I contemplated."

Fenway tried not to roll her eyes. "Did your PR department begin to set up the press conference immediately after you ended your call?"

Christchurch chuckled. "Very clever, Miss Stevenson. The press conference was set up after my call with them. I'm sure their records will show that."

Getting any information out of her was painful. Fenway took a slow, deep breath. "To the best of your knowledge, did Coach Levinson know about the investigation you were conducting?"

Sandra Christchurch shook her head. "If he found out about it, it wasn't because of me."

"I understand, but that doesn't answer my question. Did he know about your investigation?"

Christchurch paused, turning the gold band on her ring finger around a few times. "I don't know for certain he was aware of the investigation. I tried to run it as quietly as I could. But I have heard from other owners how difficult it is to keep the topic of these kinds of investigations under wraps."

"So you wouldn't be surprised if he knew?"

"On the contrary. I'd be quite surprised. But I allow for a slim chance it may have gotten out."

Fenway cocked her head. "Earlier, you said Coach Levinson had died by suicide—which would lead me to believe he knew not only about the investigation, but about your findings as well. If he didn't know about the investigation, what motive would he have for suicide?"

Christchurch furrowed her brow. "Just because I came to that conclusion, Miss Stevenson, does not mean I believe he had discovered the investigation was ongoing."

"What other—"

"His wife might have discovered his extracurricular activities, for one thing," Christchurch said. "Or perhaps a third party knew about his affairs and attempted blackmail he could ill afford."

Fenway straightened up on the chair. She couldn't catch the Neons owner in a lie or with contradictory statements.

Christchurch chose her words—even her body language—with precision.

Just the facts, then.

"Oh," Fenway said, holding up her index finger, "I didn't ask you what time you went to bed last night."

Sandra Christchurch leaned forward. "You already know I didn't hear or see anything unusual when I was in my room. Why is it important what time I went to bed?"

"It's a simple enough question, Ms. Christchurch."

Christchurch folded her arms.

"You said you didn't hear or see anything unusual, and you and he were on the same floor. As coroner, I'm responsible for signing off on the time of death. It's more likely you didn't hear anything if you were asleep."

Christchurch was silent.

"Ms. Christchurch, I must establish what went on in Coach Levinson's room and who was where on the night he died."

Sandra Christchurch placed her elbows on the table. "If I'm understanding you correctly, Miss Stevenson, from your phrasing, it appears you do *not* believe Coach Levinson died by his own hand."

Fenway smiled. "I asked you what time you went to bed."

Christchurch set her mouth in a line. "Unfortunately, Miss Stevenson, I didn't pay attention to the time. It may have been eleven P.M.; it may have been three A.M. I needed to relax after having stressful conversations with both my lawyer and our public relations department. I did some breathing exercises. I listened to some music. I eventually fell asleep, but I did not look at the clock. I only know when my alarm went off at five fifteen, I began getting ready for the day. And I began preparing myself for the press conference. I'm sure you have records of me at the press conference where over a dozen people can attest to my whereabouts."

Fenway scribbled in her notebook, then tapped her pen on the paper. Christchurch wasn't telling her everything—and not just the information she'd said she wouldn't give unless subpoenaed. But being evasive about her ritual before bed meant something happened.

"Before you went to bed," Fenway said, "did you hear any suspicious noises?"

"You mean like a gunshot or people arguing? No."

Fenway narrowed her eyes. "But you did hear *something*."

"Nothing I haven't heard in hotel rooms all around the world. Televisions from the next room. Footsteps in the hall."

"Footsteps?" Fenway's ears perked up—maybe Christchurch had heard Annabel and could tell her which way she went when she originally got out of the elevator.

"Yes, of course."

"But—your suite is the last room at the end of the hall," Fenway said. "There's nothing between your door and the stairwell. When did you—"

"I didn't make any notice of the time."

Fenway looked into Christchurch's eyes, and the Neons' owner stared back at her. Fenway needed to know about what happened in the ninth-floor hallway when Annabel got off the elevator. But no, Christchurch wouldn't talk.

She closed her notebook and stood. "Thank you for your time, Ms. Christchurch. I'll let you get back to your business discussion with my father." She took a step away from the table, gave a small bow with her head, and plastered what she hoped was a friendly half-smile on her face.

Christchurch gave her a curt nod.

Fenway walked to the bar, where her father was eating the last half of a deviled egg. The empty plate in front of him sat forlornly next to a Bloody Mary glass with only an inch of liquid in the bottom.

"So much for the crudités," Fenway said.

"Indeed." Nathaniel Ferris got down carefully from the stool and laced his right arm around Fenway's left elbow. Have you finished your interview?"

"Yes, you can go back to your business discussion." Fenway leaned closer to him and lowered her voice. "This woman owns one of the best, most successful teams in the AFF."

Ferris harrumphed. "I know. I do my homework."

"Be careful with how much of your plans you reveal."

His eyes twinkled. "You assume I have plans. Maybe this is just an exploratory meeting."

Fenway gave her father a skeptical look.

"Okay, fine. It's more than an exploratory meeting."

"Just to say, Dad—if you become an owner of a team in the league, you'll have to contend with people just like her." Fenway glanced over at Christchurch, who was busy scrolling on her phone. "She's savvy, she's smart, and she knows what she's doing."

"You forget—because you weren't around—but I didn't know the oil industry when I started Ferris Energy, either. I'm a quick study." Ferris brushed his hands off over his plate. "And besides, if I become an owner, it may be precisely because I *won't* have to contend with Sandra Christchurch."

Fenway furrowed her brow. "Why wouldn't you have to—" Then her eyes widened. "The rumors are true? Christchurch wants to sell the team?"

"Keep your voice down."

"Why would she want to sell? She's running one of the most successful franchises in the league. They're the favorites to win the Pickering Trophy this year."

"She bought low and she's selling high."

"I figured you'd take one of the underperforming teams and move them out to California. Or get awarded an expansion team."

Ferris shrugged. "What good is a private jet if I don't use it? Las

Vegas is only four hundred miles away. Besides, Charlotte and I have friends there."

"It's a high-profile team, Dad. No one would be upset if you moved a struggling team like Firecrackers FC out to a city like San Jose where people might actually *come* to their games." Fenway paused.

"New team identities are expensive."

"The Neons are probably the *most* expensive team in the AFF. Certainly the highest profile. Don't be one of those owners who embarrass yourself and embarrass the league. If you think this is just for fun and not a serious business venture, the other owners will eat you up and spit you out."

"I'm fully aware I'm playing with live ammo, Fenway."

Fenway paused. Maybe that was why Christchurch was being cagey: the conversations with her lawyers might have been about the team sale.

A head coach under investigation for sexual assault would lower the value of the team, for sure. And if Christchurch had decided to confront Coach Levinson, maybe things had gotten out of hand. It would certainly explain her vague answers about time.

Fenway forced her attention back to her father.

"I appreciate the help you gave Charlotte running the company while I was in the hospital," Ferris continued, "but it doesn't mean I've lost my sense of business." Ferris cocked his head. "You got scared off by a fifteen-minute interview with Sandra Christchurch?"

"If by 'scared off' you mean 'fed a healthy dose of pragmatism,' then yes, I did." Fenway patted her father's arm. "Now I'll accompany you back to the table."

"Thank you."

Fenway elbowed Ferris lightly in the ribs. "And I'll call Charlotte and make sure she buys a jewel-encrusted spy cane and brings it to you before this meeting is over."

CHAPTER NINE

THE ELEVATOR BELL DINGED FOR THE NINTH FLOOR. FENWAY stepped out into the hallway and took a quick step to the side as the two officers carrying the body bag on the gurney moved past her onto the elevator. Behind the gurney, Melissa strode forward.

Fenway caught her eye. "You'll let me know when Dr. Yasuda's ready to do the autopsy?"

"We have an opening—we can do it this afternoon. Dr. Yasuda wants to get Levinson in and out before the media knows what's happening."

"Smart." Fenway pointed to the open door of Levinson's hotel room. "Is Dez still in there?"

Melissa nodded.

Fenway stepped over the threshold of the hotel room.

With the body gone, Fenway noticed the short-pile wall-to-wall carpet looked plush but had very little give. Between the kitchen table and the wall next to the door was a large brown asymmetrical bloodstain, about eighteen inches at its longest.

Dez crouched on the floor in the middle of the seating area, staring at the bloodstain with a frown on her face.

"Everything okay?" Fenway put a pair of bright blue polyethylene booties over her flats.

Dez wrinkled her nose. "We don't have a lot to go on. This is a weird situation."

"Oh, come on, Dez. Who wants a boring, straightforward case where it's obvious it was the butler with the candlestick in the library?"

Dez sighed.

"I know, I know, I watch too many cop shows." Fenway took a pair of blue nitrile gloves from her purse and snapped them on. "I just spoke with Sandra Christchurch about both the bracelet theft and Levinson's death. She didn't see or hear anything, but anyone on the floor could have visited Levinson's room during the window of the murder. And we're missing two bath towels." Fenway gestured to the bathroom. "Melissa and I suspect they were used to clean up, then taken by the killer."

Dez stood, her back cracking. "And right now, Maggie's the prime suspect. She was here when Paul Levinson was killed, her clothes were in the shower, and there's no evidence to prove anyone else was here."

Fenway stepped to the hall closet door and opened it. A black sportscoat, two Las Vegas Neons windbreakers, and a woman's short olive-green jacket—the same one Maggie wore the night before. "Annabel got off on the ninth floor after midnight, and she had plenty of time to commit the murder, go down the stairs to throw away the bath towels, and come back inside. But then, you could say that about anyone else on this floor, too."

"It's a great story for the defense to establish reasonable doubt, but it sure doesn't help us." Dez shook her head. "We have evidence of a spray of blood. Is there any blood on Annabel's clothes when we see her re-enter the hotel? She wore the same clothes in the elevator both times we saw her—no blood spatter. Is it possible Annabel committed this murder? Yes. Would we be able to convict with what we have now? Absolutely not."

"We can't convict Maggie with what we have now, either," Fenway pointed out.

"I'm trying to put together the facts of the case." Dez stood and sighed. "It would be much more helpful if Maggie could remember what happened."

"If it was Maggie, how did she get rid of the towels? Did she take them out into the hallway? She wouldn't have been wearing anything —all her clothes were in the shower, soaking wet." Fenway crossed her arms.

"Maybe she took a hotel robe and went out into the hall." Dez's eyes sparked. "Or maybe Annabel came to the door—after Maggie had killed the coach. Maybe they were in on it together, so Shedd took the towels and dumped them. It could explain why Shedd took the stairs—maybe the towels are in a trash can in the parking garage."

"I'll check," Fenway said. "But wouldn't Annabel have worked with Maggie to put her in a better situation than waking up in the murder victim's bed?"

"She—" Dez thought for a moment. "Probably. Maybe there's something we didn't take into account."

"But your comment about Annabel coming to the door is a valid one. It means we have to consider other scenarios. Maybe Annabel was the one who killed him."

Dez gave Fenway a curt nod. "It's time for us to go to the station and continue our interview of Maggie."

Fenway stepped toward the door. "Besides Rocky Portello and Sandra Christchurch, who else was on this floor?"

Dez flipped open her notebook. "Lorraine Sunday, the other assistant coach. I heard she works with the goalkeepers. The general manager is back in Vegas. And as for other hotel guests, it's the off-season. The team has three floors all to themselves."

They walked out of the room into the hallway, and Fenway's phone buzzed in her purse. It was a text from Sarah.

You didn't sign the forms before you left

"Ah, crap."

"What?" Dez asked.

"I have to sign a bunch of forms that sre due today."

"It's only a few blocks to the office. We're going back there anyway."

Fenway stopped in front of the elevator, staring blankly at the buttons.

"What is it?" Dez asked.

"So we saw Annabel come up to the ninth floor, *not* take the elevator down, then walk in the front door of the hotel."

"Right."

"Hmm." Fenway texted Sarah back.

Can you bring the forms to the Broadmere? I'll meet you here and sign them

Fenway put her phone in her purse. "So it's possible the killer used the stairwell to avoid the cameras and get rid of evidence. Like those towels."

"Or get away, full stop," Dez said, scratching the back of her neck.

"So we need to examine the stairwell."

"I already had Deputy Salvador walk down all nine flights of stairs. She didn't find any blood anywhere. No trash cans, either—not in the stairwell. Two trash cans on the first floor of the parking garage."

"Did they examine the doors?"

"They took fingerprints."

"What about blood transfer? Luminol?"

Dez crinkled her nose. "I'm not sure—we can check. And there are no cameras in the stairwell—but there *are* cameras in the parking garage. If anyone left by the stairs, they could've been recorded."

"Good thinking," Fenway said. "Can you go to the security office and ask Ezekiel to show you the parking garage video?" Fenway reached out to push the button for the elevator.

"What are you going to do?"

Fenway scratched her temple. "I want to know how that stairwell —well, *works,* for lack of a better term. How long it takes to go between floors. How noisy it is, maybe. Even how the doors open and close. Something's bothering me about the stairwell, and I think I need to see it with my own eyes to figure out what it is."

"Don't you have forms to sign?"

"Like you said, Dez, we're only a few blocks away from the office. I asked Sarah to meet me here."

The elevator dinged, and Dez got in. "Have fun," she said, an amused smile playing on her lips as the doors slid shut.

Fenway turned and walked down the hallway toward the exit stairs. She took out another pair of blue nitrile gloves, even though CSI had already dusted the handles and the rails of the stairs for prints.

The sign on the beige door said *Exit Stair* in red block lettering. Fenway checked both sides of the door, looking for a different sign saying *Emergency Exit Only, Alarm Will Sound.* Nothing. She turned the handle and pushed open the door.

It opened with a solid click. Fenway turned the handle and examined the latch. Angled at the end, it slipped easily in and out of the mortise plate with each turn of the handle. It was a solid mechanism. She felt for anything out of place around the latch, but it was clean: no lubricant, no glue or adhesives, nothing.

She opened the door a little further and looked up. There, in the center of the top of the door jamb, was a metal plate.

She reached up and felt the top of the door. In the exact same spot that would align with the plate was a long indentation and what felt like a glass ball, its diameter nearly the thickness of the door.

Fenway pulled the door almost completely shut and heard a faint clicking noise. She pushed the door open again, not turning the handle.

So it was possible to fool the door sensor into thinking the door was latched closed.

Fenway stepped into the stairwell and let the door shut just until she heard the click—but before the latch engaged. It looked closed—unless you examined the door closely. And she pulled the door open easily.

She examined the latch again. Nothing—there was no tape, no sign of anything being tampered with. She held the door open and felt the hinges. Nothing there, either. She ran her gloved hand around the door jamb, then the edges of the door itself—still nothing. As she stood up, the door slipped out of her hand and slammed shut.

Great.

She reached for the handle, but it wouldn't turn.

She walked down to the eighth floor, her shoes clanking on the metal of the stairs. The door at the landing of level eight said *No Entry*. And sure enough, like the ninth floor, this handle also refused to turn when Fenway tried it.

Ezekiel had been correct: the stairwell was designed to be *entered* from any floor but only *exited* through the ground floor.

After descending another seven flights of steps, Fenway pushed open the exit door and found herself in the small parking garage. The first floor only had room for perhaps thirty cars. The vehicle ramps leading to the second floor were steep.

A buzz from her purse: Sarah.

OK I'm here where r u

Fenway texted back.

Parking garage

About five feet from the door, a gray trash can sat next to a concrete pillar. A heavy black plastic bag rested inside the can; it was less than a quarter full. No towels, nor any bag or box big enough for a bath towel. No help there.

The door from the hotel opened, and Sarah Summerfield walked into the garage. She was almost Fenway's height, with soft blonde curls cascading to her shoulders. Wearing a blue dress with small white flowers and a light blue sweater, Sarah held a thick manila folder under her arm.

Fenway pointed to the folder. "The forms I was supposed to sign this morning?"

Sarah nodded and pulled a pen out of her purse.

The parking lot was about a third full; most of the overnight guests were probably out and about. Fenway made a beeline for a white Corolla across from the stairwell. Sarah followed, setting the folder on the trunk and handing Fenway the pen.

"Las Vegas Neons, huh?" Sarah said, as Fenway signed the first form.

"Right. You remember the press release you gave me this morning where the head coach was fired."

"Not your case—I was talking about this car." Sarah gestured to the Corolla. "It's got a parking sticker and a license plate frame that both say *Las Vegas Neons.*"

"Oh. This must belong to one of the assistant coaches or the players."

"Probably." Sarah turned the page. "You've got to initial at the top, too."

"Right, sorry." Fenway scrawled her initials, then moved to the next form.

Sarah looked more closely at the Corolla. "Do the Neons have a team car?"

"I don't know. Why?"

"If they do, this is probably it."

"Why do you say that?"

"There's nothing personal in it *but* Neons stickers. And it's all very corporate, very professional." She tapped the top of the next form, and Fenway initialed. "Looks like it's taken care of in, well, a certain way. Like a rental car."

Fenway nodded. "I know what you mean." She raised her head and pointed with her chin. "Now *that* is a personal car."

A red Italian sports car was parked across two spots in the corner, almost invisible in the shadows despite the design of the vehicle.

"Looks fast even standing still," Sarah said.

The low-slung rocket had a candy-apple-red exterior. Its Nevada plates read *FLASHEEE.*

Fenway twirled the pen in her hand. "Our victim's car."

Sarah squinted. "Wait—is that the head coach? Flash? The press release said he got fired this morning, right?"

"Right." Fenway pointed Sarah's pen at the Italian sports car. "I guess he lived large. I didn't realize women's soccer paid well enough for a coach to afford a car that, uh, flashy."

"The money sure isn't going to the players," Sarah said, flipping another page. "Three places to sign on this one."

"Hang on." Fenway pulled out her phone.

"I know you don't like to do the paperwork, Fenway—"

"I'm texting Melissa de la Garza that Coach Levinson's car is in the parking garage. Maybe they know already, but it doesn't hurt to double-check."

"Yeah, okay."

Fenway hit *Send*, then put her phone back in her purse.

Sarah pushed the form in front of Fenway, and she signed it. "Four more, then we're done."

"You're like my mother telling me to eat my vegetables."

"I'd make a choo-choo noise if I thought it would get you to sign these before leaving the office. You missed an initial at the top."

"Right." Fenway made an F, then a big swoosh for the S.

Sarah clicked her tongue in approval. "See? With the right attitude, this can be delightful." She flipped the page. "What are you doing in the parking garage, anyway?"

"Officially, I guess I'm looking for some evidence I think was thrown away. But really, I'm trying to figure out what's bugging me. Something doesn't fit, and I can't figure out what it is."

"You missed a signature line on this one." Sarah tapped the page.

Fenway signed.

"That was the last one." Sarah gathered the papers together and stacked them back in the folder. "See you back at the office?"

"Maybe soon." Fenway looked around the garage. "I see a camera at the entrance. Do you see any more?"

"One at the exit." Sarah looked around the parking garage, then turned and pointed to a breezeway, encased in shadow, in the back wall of the garage. "I bet you could walk from the exit that you came out of all the way to that breezeway and the cameras wouldn't pick you up."

Fenway looked at her out of the corner of her eye. "How are you able to see all this?"

Sarah smiled, but it didn't reach her eyes. "I had to," she said simply. "I didn't always—you know, I had to be careful with who could see me."

Fenway nodded, kicking herself mentally. "Sure—yeah, I think I get it." Her phone buzzed, and she took it out of her purse. The message was from Dez.

> *Housekeeping confirmed 4 bath towels were in Levinson's room yesterday afternoon*
> *Both the daily inventory and the housekeeping sheet confirm*

So, two towels were definitely missing. Fenway looked toward the breezeway. "Do you have a minute?"

"I really should get these forms back to the office."

Fenway grimaced. "I could use your help. I keep getting distracted. I should have noticed the white Corolla—all those Neons stickers."

Sarah hesitated. "What do you need?"

"We think the killer might have used two hotel towels to clean up."

"Then thrown them away somewhere other than the hotel?"

"That's right. And I could use your insight."

Sarah pressed her lips together. "If it were me," she said, "I'd avoid the cameras and go through to the back street."

Fenway looked at the entrance of the parking garage, then followed the concrete walkway with her eyes all the way to the breezeway out the rear. "Okay—come on."

As they entered the breezeway, the wind whipped through the narrow space, blowing Fenway's blazer open and forcing her to pull it tight around her body.

The walkway emptied out onto a side street with a mix of residential houses and apartment buildings.

"Where are we?" Fenway said.

"San Ysidro Street." Sarah pointed to the left, where a small market stood, diagonally opposite an AutoQuest parts store. "That's Fourth Street."

"Lots of apartment buildings," Fenway said. "Lots of dumpsters behind those buildings."

"Was your suspect in a hurry? Did they know the area?"

"Probably in a hurry, yes. And I doubt they were familiar with the area." Fenway took a few steps forward onto San Ysidro Street. "I bet the towels are in one of these—"

Sarah stopped. "Fenway, what are you doing?"

"I'm—" Fenway bit her lip. "This could be the key piece of physical evidence we need."

Sarah shook her head. "You have *people* for this. You can't spend the next few hours digging through the trash behind apartment buildings."

Fenway pointed. "What about the mini-mart? Or the auto parts store? At least—"

"I'll call Sheriff Donnelly when we get back to the office. She can have four or five deputies searching the area." Sarah folded her arms. "Isn't Dez interviewing your main suspect right now?"

Fenway paused, then nodded.

The sun tried and failed to break through the clouds. They walked back down San Ysidro Street, then entered the Broadmere Hotel's parking garage through the narrow breezeway.

"I'm sorry," Fenway said. "My brain's going a thousand directions today."

"Don't worry about it," Sarah said. As she walked toward the breezeway, the clicking of her high heels echoed through the parking garage. "If the killer came down the hotel stairway with a trash bag full of bloody towels, you assume they left on foot and tried to conceal the evidence."

"That seems the likeliest scenario."

"And you assumed the killer would pick a trash can or a dumpster, far enough away from the hotel to make it difficult to track down, but still within walking distance."

"Right."

"How do you know the towels aren't still at the hotel?"

Fenway stopped. "Because we had CSI go through the hotel trash already. And if housekeeping had found the bloody towels in one of the hotel rooms, we'd have heard about it."

"But," Sarah said, "what if the towels are hidden someplace besides the trash?"

"Ah," Fenway said. "The coaches, the owner, the general manager, the staff—they all have cars."

"And suitcases."

"But we can't search their cars or hotel rooms without a warrant." Fenway rubbed her chin. "Someone could have taken the plastic laundry bag from the room, stuffed the towels inside, and hid the bag at the bottom of their suitcase until they could get rid of it."

"So look at the players."

"Not just the players; staff, too—of both the team and the hotel."

Sarah furrowed her brow. "Do you think someone on the hotel staff is in on it?"

"I think I haven't considered the possibility until now. Maybe one of the coach's victims works at the hotel."

"Or a relative." Sarah winced. "I'm getting some more work tonight, aren't I?"

"Never a dull moment in this job." Fenway scratched her chin in thought. "When you get back to the office, can you cross-reference all the hotel employees with Levinson?"

"How far back?"

"I guess his whole career. Grudges like this can last a long time."

And if it's a staff member, it would explain how the killer had been able to avoid the cameras. Fenway sucked in a breath through her teeth.

"You know," Sarah said carefully, "if the Neons' ownership discovered Paul Levinson sexually assaulted one or two players on the team, it's more than likely he was doing it with a lot more players than that."

Fenway felt her stomach contract into a tight ball. "Honestly, Sarah—" Then she stopped.

"What is it?"

"Nothing." She tried to clear her mind. Levinson had been above the law for so long. The system had failed Maggie—and who knows how many others? All the preconceived notions she had of justice, of being one of the "good guys," of serving and protecting the community were clouding with doubt.

———

As Fenway entered the pristine, elegant lobby, she noticed the quiet. The police had left. One would never guess that a celebrity coach—or close to a celebrity, anyway—had been wheeled out of the hotel in a body bag.

Sarah was right: by focusing on the people who'd been on the ninth floor, and assuming they'd gone on foot somewhere to get rid of the towels, Fenway had been thinking too narrowly. The towels could be blocks or even miles away.

Twenty minutes had passed since Dez had gone to look at the parking video—plenty of time to note any suspicious cars going in or out when reviewing the security footage. That meant Dez had probably gone back to the station to interrogate Maggie. Fenway took her phone out and tapped the text message app.

Following a couple of leads

Still at the hotel

If you haven't already, start without me

She sent the text to Dez, then walked past the front desk and into the security office.

Ezekiel looked up. "Oh, Miss Stevenson, you're back. Anything else I can pull up for you?"

"Dez—Sergeant Roubideaux was just here, right?"

"Correct. We reviewed the camera footage from the parking garage. Not much foot traffic or cars coming *out* of the hotel, but quite a few cars—and people—going *in*. Mostly between six and seven in the morning. Ms. Christchurch had called the press conference by then."

"When did you get in today?"

"My shift started at six." He gave a sly chuckle. "I had to make sure none of those media types got out of hand."

Fenway grinned. "Yeah, I can see you keeping them in line." She scratched her temple. "I understand the cameras in the parking garage don't have great coverage."

"No, they don't, that's true."

"Who else knows that the cameras have blind spots in the garage?"

"Besides me?" Ezekiel thought for a moment. "Everyone who monitors the cameras. There's a staff of six of us who rotate our shifts."

"I'll need the names of those staff."

Ezekiel frowned. "Now, listen here, Miss Stevenson, the security staff is above reproach. We're vetted before we're hired. I don't like you insinuating—"

Fenway put up her hands, her mind racing. "I'm not accusing the security staff of anything."

"It sure sounds like you are."

"Let's say we arrest the killer, all right? Now the defense is going to look for alternate theories of the case, anyone else they can point to so the jury finds reasonable doubt. How's it going to look if I haven't done due diligence on your staff? You think the killer will stay locked up if we get surprised in the middle of the trial?"

Ezekiel narrowed his eyes, but after a moment, he nodded. "My apologies. That makes sense." He got to his feet and reached for a clipboard above the monitors. "Our schedule is posted here. You can make a copy of it."

"I appreciate that." Fenway took out her phone and took a picture of the schedule. "Any other staff besides the security team know about the blind spots?"

"We had a security briefing earlier this week with the soccer team's staff. We outlined our liability, the extent of what security services we could provide, the works. Coach Levinson wanted to check on players who broke curfew, and we pointed out the limitations of our surveillance."

"Were you here?"

"I *gave* most of the briefing." Ezekiel chuckled. "Coach Levinson got mad because they could only check on when the players came into the hotel, not when they went to their rooms. You ask me, if you run too tight of a ship, your crew can mutiny."

"Has anyone on the staff met Coach Levinson before?"

Ezekiel guffawed. "I'd have remembered someone *that* arrogant. No, I'd never met him before, and I don't know of any staff who did." He sat back down and rubbed his chin. "But we're in the hospitality industry. Putting up with difficult people is part of the job."

"Oh—I need to check on a car. A white Toyota Corolla."

"I knew that would give me a headache." Ezekiel sighed. "It's a car the players can check out."

"Check out—like a library book?"

"That's right. They give us a copy of the sign-out sheet, but the coaches are the ones with the keys." Ezekiel put his hands up in mock surrender. "I don't want the responsibility of keeping track of the car if you're not giving me the authority to hand the key out, you know what I mean?"

"Can I see the sign-out sheet?"

"I think one of the coaches has it—or it's around somewhere. You need it right now?"

"I can come back later. All right, Ezekiel, thanks for your help." Fenway turned toward the door, then stopped. "Hang on—just one more thing. I figured out that the stairwell doors don't have to be completely latched for the sensors to register the doors as being closed. Anyone ever try to trick those stairwell doors into thinking they're locked?"

Ezekiel scrunched his nose in thought. "People have tried. Duct tape over the latches, that kind of thing. But those latches are strong enough to stretch the tape after a few minutes—so the latches engage anyway." He grinned. "Mostly high school kids staying with their parents and sneaking out. We've had a couple of incidents in the last year, but nothing to be concerned about."

———

As Fenway got into her Honda, the sun disappeared behind a sheet of gray again. It was time for her to go to Maggie's interrogation.

She put the car in reverse but kept her foot on the brake.

How much value would she provide sitting in the observation room of the sheriff's office while Dez questioned Maggie? Much of the evidence suggested that Maggie had committed the murder—or at least should be a strong suspect. But Fenway didn't believe it.

Maggie had been drunk. She was under Levinson's thumb. Fenway believed Maggie had been passed out during the murder. As far as Fenway was concerned, Sandra Christchurch, Annabel Shedd, and even Ezekiel Washington had just as much means and opportunity—just as much knowledge, too—to commit the murder and get out through the stairwell.

So why go to the sheriff's office at all?

A knock on her window. Fenway jumped in her seat.

Deputy Donald Huke. Fenway rolled down her window.

"Deputy Huke, nice to see you."

"Likewise, Coroner."

"You here to see Melissa?"

Huke frowned. "I was part of the team that secured the evidence in the hotel room. Sheriff Donnelly assigned me to your case today."

"Oh, of course. What can I do for you?"

"I wondered if you could give me a lift back to the station."

"Actually..." Fenway found herself talking before her brain could stop her. "Maybe you can help me with something first."

"Sure—the sheriff said to give you whatever assistance you need."

"Great." Fenway tapped her chin. "A lot of people had reason to hurt Coach Levinson."

Huke nodded. "He was in a position of power. I'm sure he made some enemies."

"You heard that he was fired this morning?"

"I heard about the press conference, yes."

"It's possible that Christchurch only knows about a small fraction of Levinson's victims."

Huke pressed his lips together in a line. "That aligns with the statistical analyses of sexual harassment and assault I've seen in professional environments, yes."

"I've asked Sarah to see if any of the hotel staff have connections with Levinson. I was debating whether to stay and interview more of the staff."

Huke's face pinched. "Statistically speaking, Coroner, wouldn't talking to the players be a more fruitful use of your time and resources?"

"I suppose it would."

"The training camp bus left for Nidever University about a half hour ago," Huke said, "but you can go to their camp and interview them there, can't you?"

"Well, I—" Fenway pursed her lips; even after her conversation with Sarah, was she still too hung up on the physical evidence? "Yes. Of course I can. They might not like it, but since when did a suspect ever like getting questioned?"

"All right. If you're not going back, I'll just walk to the sheriff's office."

Dez might be interrogating the primary person of interest, but Huke was right: the players needed to be questioned. Coach Sunday, too. And there was only one of her. "You ever sat in on an interrogation, Donald?"

Huke tilted his head.

"Deputy Huke, I mean."

"I've taken classes in suspect questioning, and I've interviewed witnesses—but I've never been asked to sit in on an official interrogation. Would you like me to accompany you to Nidever University?"

Fenway debated internally. She'd rubbed Huke the wrong way since the day they met. But with more than twenty players to interview, he would prove useful.

"We could interview twice as many players. Plus, I seem to be a little scattered because of—" Fenway paused. *Because I see my Russian Lit professor all over this case.* "Because of all the different suspects and motives."

"Certainly. Anything I can do to assist."

"Excellent." Fenway unlocked her doors. "Get in."

Huke hurried to the passenger side and got in.

"Ready?"

"Not quite." Huke reached down the side of the passenger seat and fastidiously adjusted the position of the back, then carefully put on his safety belt. "All right. Ready."

She looked at the clock: it was almost one P.M., but she wasn't hungry at all. Ugh—this case *was* getting to her.

CHAPTER TEN

FENWAY AND DEPUTY HUKE STOOD AT THE SIDE OF THE SMOOTH, glassy lawn that stretched over the soccer field at Nidever University.

"This might be the most beautiful soccer field I've ever seen," Fenway said softly.

"Fescues Delta Tall blend," Huke said.

Fenway turned and blinked. "What?"

"The grass type. It's a hybrid tall fescue blend, probably with less than twenty percent Kentucky bluegrass."

"You can tell that from here?"

"The field gets a lot of wear and tear, but it doesn't have the dark shininess of a full—" Huke caught himself, then cleared his throat. "I worked at a garden center in high school. Got pretty good at recognizing plants."

Fenway turned back to the lush, verdant lawn. "It's a far cry from the muddy soccer fields we had at Western Washington." Certainly better than the weedy dirt patches she'd played soccer on as a preteen in Seattle.

Huke pointed across the field to two dozen women in black-and-gold uniforms. "I take it those are the players?"

"Right."

"What are half of them doing with those gold tank tops over their shirts?"

"Those are pinnies, so I bet they're prepping for a scrimmage."

The uniforms had no numbers on the back, but a stylized logotype was emblazoned on the front of every uniform.

"What does it say on the front of their shirts?"

"*Desert Treasure*. It's their sponsor."

"And those are the assistant coaches, right?" Huke motioned to the sideline. Rocky Portello wore a black baseball cap, a bright yellow T-shirt, and gray sweatpants. Lorraine Sunday was dressed in a black-and-gold tracksuit, her braids piled on top of her head.

The coaches still had their backs to them as Fenway and Huke walked onto the field. The pitch was damp from the sodden March morning under overcast skies. Fenway's black flats squished on the grass. Not ideal field conditions for the first practice of the new season, but Fenway admired Christchurch's decision to get her team away to a quiet town for training camp.

"Do you have a moment, Coach Portello?" Fenway intended for her voice to sound strong and commanding, but the wind and the chilly air took the power out of her words.

"'Rocky,' Coroner. As you can see, I'm busy now."

Fenway took a small step forward. "This is my colleague, Deputy Donald Huke."

"You and I spoke already."

"We may have allowed the team to leave the hotel, but I have additional questions."

Coach Portello looked out of the side of his eye at Fenway. "I spent the last forty-five minutes trying to get the ladies to concentrate on practice and not think about Coach Flash." Portello put his hands on his hips. "I'd prefer to do this later."

Fenway's feet sank slightly into the wet turf. "I understand where you're coming from, Coach. Unfortunately, I have a murder investigation to conduct. My superiors wouldn't like it if I prioritized a team soccer practice over solving a murder."

Portello turned his head until he was staring Fenway directly in the face. He hadn't seemed so when he was sitting in his hotel room, but Portello was a tall man, about six feet, and while Fenway's five-foot-ten-inch frame could be imposing, she still found herself looking up at the assistant coach.

"And *my* bosses," Portello said, "expect us to win the championship this year, whether or not our head coach has met an untimely demise. I understand you have a job to do, but so do I." Portello dropped his hands to his side and handed his whistle to the coach next to him. "And while I get that my goals aren't important to you, I hope you respect them." He turned and began to walk away.

Huke stepped in front of Portello, blocking his path. "The county coroner is being polite, Mr. Portello. I understand that you found the body this morning. Often, witnesses such as yourself are brought to the sheriff's office—treated as hostile, if need be, to ascertain the identity of the killer for the safety of the community." He held up his badge. "We'll be much more accommodating if you can find the flexibility to allow us to continue our investigation in a timely manner."

Portello drew himself up to full height but still had to lift his chin to make eye contact with Huke. "We don't have to come back to Estancia next year, you know. Gives your tourism industry a nice shot in the arm in March."

"Our tourism board probably doesn't think high-profile murders are good for business." Huke held up an index finger in front of Portello's face. "I have a proposal for you, Coach Portello. The coroner requires your players to answer a few questions each. You can make them available one by one so that your practice can continue with minimal interruption, or"—Huke patted the radio on his belt—"I can call the other deputies to come in and stop practice. They'll take you all down to the sheriff's office for questioning."

"No way, no how. You can't do that."

"All players and coaches were potential witnesses to a crime," Fenway said. "We only have one interview room, and we're interrogating Maggie Erskine right now. Everyone would have to wait." She cleared her throat. "I expect I can get all of you interviewed and processed in eighteen to twenty-four hours. I'm sure your players would love to spend the night in the police waiting room."

Portello folded his arms and looked down at the ground. "Fine. You can use the coaches' office in the athletics building. But I can't have any of my players off the pitch for more than fifteen minutes."

Fenway motioned to Lorraine Sunday, standing twenty feet away on the sideline. "Coach Sunday was on the ninth floor last night, and I have yet to speak with her."

Portello nodded. "Lorraine, you're up. Go show the coroner where the coaches' office is. You get to be the first one she interviews." Portello looked over at Fenway. "I'll get the players started on a couple of drills, then I can go next so I can get this out of the way."

"All right, Rocky," Sunday said.

Huke leaned toward Fenway. "Would you like me to join you or stay here and watch the field to make sure no one leaves?"

"Come with us," Fenway said.

"No more than fifteen minutes," Portello said. "I mean it."

Fenway and Huke followed Lorraine Sunday off the field, then Sunday turned to follow a concrete walkway into a set of buildings about two hundred yards farther. Huke caught Fenway's eye and slowed down until Lorraine was a few yards ahead.

"You mentioned we could question twice as many people with me here," Huke whispered. "Shouldn't you question Coach Sunday by yourself?"

"Listen to the questions I ask Coach Sunday, the type of information I'm looking to get, then I'll turn you loose on the players."

Huke nodded, then hesitated.

"Something else, Deputy?"

"I don't understand Coach Portello's reaction," Huke whispered. "He's acting like the first day of practice is more important than solving the murder of someone he considered a mentor. It doesn't make any sense."

"People process grief in different ways," Fenway whispered back. "Maybe I'll push him a little more after Coach Sunday's interview."

Lorraine Sunday was stoic as she walked. She stood a few inches shorter than Fenway, and her large brown eyes darted around the quad. Though Sunday wore no makeup, Fenway was shocked at how the assistant coach looked even younger in person than she had on the elevator camera.

"How long have you been with the team?" Fenway asked. She glanced over her shoulder; Huke walked about ten feet behind them.

Sunday never broke her stride. "This is my second year."

"You're the goalkeepers' coach, right?"

"I coach more than the goalies, but yes. Perhaps that's why Coach Portello had me interview with you first. Maggie didn't show up today. I can work with the backups, but Maggie not being here means a lighter load for me."

Fenway debated if she should tell Coach Sunday that Maggie was at the sheriff's office, then decided to keep her mouth shut. The assistant coach might already know Maggie had been brought in for questioning—though she was far away, maybe she heard Fenway say as much to Coach Portello—but if she didn't, she might be more forthcoming.

"Maggie has a lot of raw talent," Sunday continued, "and some good instincts. But for us to have any chance at the Pickering Trophy this year, she's got a lot of growing up to do."

"I see."

They came to a door in the side of an administration building and Lorraine opened it. Inside, the automatic lights switched on, buzzing. Fluorescent tubes sputtered on across the drop ceiling. In the cold, artificial light, the hallway looked sterile, like an operating theater.

Lorraine Sunday entered first, Fenway following on her heels, and Huke came in and closed the door behind them. Sunday stopped at the third office door on their left, a birch door with *Athletic Department Suite C* stenciled on its frosted glass window. Taking a silver key out of the pocket of her tracksuit, she turned the key in the lock.

The door swung in silently. In the middle of the room stood a worktable with a laptop and a stool with a back. The walls were a light tan, covered with pennants and posters of Coach Levinson's glory days at his previous clubs. Three desks: one on the left, one in the center behind the worktable, and one on the right. Directly behind the center desk hung a five-foot-wide banner with metal finial-tipped dowels at the top and bottom, reading *Las Vegas Neons—AFF Western Conference Champions.*

Huke, bowing his head, stepped to the side and leaned against the wall next to the door.

"Coach Levinson brought the banner all the way from Vegas?" Fenway asked. "I thought Ms. Christchurch wouldn't want it taken from the Neons' headquarters."

Coach Sunday shrugged as she walked to the desk on the right. "The official banner is still back at home. Coach Flash had this one made to hang up behind his desk. The idea was to walk in and see where we were last year and how much work still needs to be done."

"Were you close with Coach Levinson?"

Lorraine tilted her head and motioned to a chair in front of a desk with a laptop and a UCLA Bruins bobblehead.

Fenway sat.

"Would you like to sit, too?" Sunday said to Huke.

Huke held up a hand, palm out. "I'm fine standing."

Sunday focused her attention on Fenway. "How well do you know the history of women's soccer?"

"Maybe a little better than most, but that's probably not saying much. I know enough where I recognize Annabel Shedd."

"But not enough where you recognize me." Sunday sat behind the desk, steepling her fingers.

"You're Lorraine Sunday," Fenway said quickly. "You were the goalie for the World Cup team a while ago—ten, maybe twelve years ago?"

Lorraine cocked her head, and a crooked smile crossed her face. "Two games in goal. I was the backup."

"You shut out the Czech Republic." Fenway took a notebook and a pen out of her purse, then flipped to a blank page. "Why did you choose to join the Neons?"

"I spent a few years working with a few of the European clubs, but I wanted to build my AFF résumé. And to be honest, I got a little tired of the rain in northern England."

"Northern England?"

"I was at Liverpool WFC a couple of years ago." Lorraine interlaced her hands behind her head and stared at the ceiling. "And the Neons were offering me more money than the Anfielders. Christchurch seems to know what she's doing. But I'll tell you, getting dropped in the middle of the desert is a shock when you're used to gloomy Liverpool winters."

"I can imagine," Fenway said. "So you knew Coach Levinson before?"

"No, I'd never met him—I think I got the job offer based on my reputation."

"Risky move, then."

"Coach Flash has—uh, *had* such a knack for winning championships, and we seemed to be positioned to make a real run for it. Almost got it last year, too."

"But now you've got a rookie keeper."

"She was a rookie last year. Gabby showed her the ropes—now it's time for her to step up." Sunday put her arms down, resting on the top of the desk, then stared for a moment at the bobblehead.

"Did you know Levinson was going to get fired?"

"Sandra Christchurch sent the team a notification early this morning. About half the players slept through the announcement, but I was there. Everyone went back upstairs and made sure the rest of the team knew he'd been let go."

Fenway tilted her head. "How did you find out he died?"

"I saw the paramedics on the floor this morning. Then the police tape. Doesn't take a genius to put two and two together."

"Did you know about the allegations before today?"

She pursed her lips. "I've met men like Coach Flash before. Let's just say—I wasn't surprised he got fired."

"When did you find out about the allegations?"

Huke cleared his throat, and Fenway shot him a look. He pressed his lips together and bobbed his head, motioning for Fenway to come closer.

"Excuse me for a moment." Fenway got up and walked to Huke, about ten feet away from the desk. "What?"

Huke leaned in toward Fenway and whispered. "I apologize if I'm overstepping, but you're not asking questions relevant to the case."

"I'm not—what?"

"Shouldn't you be asking where she was during the murder, what she heard or saw?"

"I'm—I'm establishing whether she'd have any reason to want Levinson dead."

Huke took a small step back. "Okay. Like I said, I apologize if I'm overstepping."

Fenway walked back to the desk, Sunday looking at her expectantly. "Sorry about that—just some—some procedural minutiae." But she swallowed dryly. "I'm asking about the allegations because I need to get an idea of why Coach Levinson might have been killed."

Lorraine sat up straight. "Killed? What do you mean?"

Fenway tightened the muscles in her neck. "I thought you knew this was a murder investigation."

"Murder." Lorraine murmured it, letting her mouth slowly form the word. "No, I thought—I mean, especially after he was let go, and with the accusations—I thought for sure he'd—" Lorraine took a breath and cast her eyes to the floor. "Well, I guess you know what I thought."

Fenway leaned forward slightly in her chair, hoping it applied the right amount of pressure without scaring Coach Sunday off. "Can you tell me where you were last night?"

Sunday leaned back and looked at the ceiling. "I ate dinner at the hotel restaurant."

"By yourself?"

"Yes. Then we had a coaches' meeting with the owner."

"Where?"

"Her hotel suite. Flash, me, and Rocky."

"Did you see her with a diamond tennis bracelet?"

Sunday blinked. "A bracelet? Uh—I don't think I noticed."

Fenway thrust her jaw forward. "You compliment her on the bracelet a lot?"

"I—I told her it was beautiful when she was showing it off." Sunday frowned. "That must have been sometime last year, maybe at the end-of-season coaches' dinner. But I wouldn't say a lot."

"Have you seen the bracelet in the last twenty-four hours?"

Sunday shifted in her seat. "No—why?"

"During the meeting, did anyone leave to go into another part of the suite?"

Sunday shrugged. "We all got some water from the fridge. I think Rocky had to use the bathroom."

"Was he gone for a long time?"

"It didn't seem like it took too long."

"What did you do after the meeting?"

"Karaoke," Sunday said.

"I'm sorry?"

"Oh—not with the owner and the coaches. I went by myself. There's a bar a couple of blocks down on Fourth. I do a decent Whitney Houston."

"Did you sing?"

"Just a couple songs. Then I came back to the hotel—"

"What time was that?"

"About half past eleven, I think. I read some scouting reports and went to sleep around midnight."

Fenway ran her tongue along her teeth. "Anything awaken you during the night?"

"No."

"You stayed in your room between, say, midnight and six A.M.?"

The goalkeeping coach leaned forward slightly. "Slept straight through until my alarm woke me up at five."

"Nothing at all? No half-awake noises? No footsteps in the hall?"

"I didn't hear anything."

Fenway scribbled in the notebook, then stole a glance at Deputy Huke. His face was impassive.

"Okay—your alarm went off at five. Did you get up then?"

"Yes. Threw my workout clothes on, grabbed a bottle of water, and I was out the door. I'd guess ten minutes, tops. Then I went to the gym."

"Anyone see you?"

"Sure. Darcy Nishimura was on one of the ellipticals, and Aissa Oumar was using the free weights. I got on a stationary bike and did about twenty minutes of cardio. Aissa and I went down to the hotel restaurant to grab a quick breakfast."

Fenway scribbled in her notebook.

"That's when we saw the notification from Sandra Christchurch. We were already down there, so we went to the small conference room—there were only about twelve of us—and that's when Sandra told us Coach Flash had been let go."

"Did she tell you why?"

"Yes. Didn't exactly sugarcoat it, but she also avoided a lot of details. A lot of 'you'll hear some disturbing details in the next few days, which I can't legally discuss.' Stuff like that. I went back to my room to change, and then about, I don't know, eight o'clock or so, I got a knock on my door. One of the sheriff's deputies, telling me Coach Flash was found dead in his room. She talked to me for a few minutes, asked me where I was going. I said straight to Nidever to set up for the afternoon practice—but given the situation, I figured it'd be cancelled."

Fenway furrowed her brow. "But—practice wasn't cancelled."

"Rocky called. According to the AFF rulebook, we must have our first practice on the league's first day of training camp. He'd pulled up the rulebook online, and there aren't any stipulations for cancellation except for dangerous weather or threats to staff or players."

"Threats? One of your staff was murdered. That doesn't count?"

"First off, as I said, I thought he died by suicide. Secondly, the rule book doesn't mention death of a player or coach or other staff member as a reason not to hold practice on the first day of training camp. We sure weren't taking responsibility for the team getting fined." Lorraine sighed. "Rocky and I met in the lobby, and he drove us to Nidever."

"Do you think you could send me the relevant section of the rulebook?"

"Rocky's the one who told me. He'd be able to find it." Lorraine leaned forward. "As it turns out, it was probably the right call. Some of these players, they didn't even know the coach. We signed them in the off-season or traded for them. The players who did know him— they said they wanted the distraction. We told them if anyone didn't feel like practicing, they could stay at the hotel."

"Did anyone take you up on it?"

"Only Maggie, from the looks of it."

So Sunday hadn't heard Fenway say that Maggie was being inter-rogated. "We talked about why Coach Levinson was fired," Fenway said. "Do you know anyone who was particularly, uh, affected by his behavior? Anyone who'd have reason to want him dead?"

Coach Sunday paused, then took a deep breath and exhaled slowly. "I don't know how much more I should say."

CHAPTER ELEVEN

FENWAY SAT UNMOVING. SHE DIDN'T LOOK AT COACH SUNDAY, instead staring at a spot in the middle of the desk. Out of the corner of her eye, she saw Huke; he stood stock-still.

Finally, Coach Sunday spoke.

"These are all rumors."

Fenway raised her head slightly and met Sunday's gaze, then gave a slight nod of her head. "Obviously not *all* rumors if Coach Levinson was fired this morning."

Sunday frowned and leaned forward. "Let's put it this way: I don't have any hard evidence." She drummed her fingers on the desk, then took a sharp breath in.

Fenway twirled her pen in her hand. She was sure they had been talking for more than fifteen minutes, and she hoped Coach Portello wouldn't notice the time. Not when Sunday was just about to open up.

"The staff," Sunday said slowly. "Not only me and Rocky, but the administrative staff, the scouts, and probably some of the players—we're not dumb."

Fenway was quiet.

"Coach Flash," Sunday continued, "would often make the players go through grueling practices."

Fenway flipped in her notebook. "The Seven Summits. Maggie told me about running up the bleacher steps while balancing two buckets of rocks on either end of a six-foot pole."

"That's one reason I'm glad we don't practice in a place with bleachers this spring." Sunday gave Fenway a tight smile. "The Seven Vomits, as the players call them. But we started noticing that if Coach Flash and Maggie arrived at practice at the same time—no Seven Summits. And Coach Flash would sometimes cancel an afternoon goalkeeping session to run drills with Maggie, then no Seven Summits at the next practice either—at least, not after I started noticing."

"Did anyone discuss it?"

"Not with me, but I heard players discuss it."

"What did they say?"

"Some of them thought they should speak up, but they all thought they'd get cut if they did."

"Why would they think that?"

Sunday scoffed. "It's not just the Las Vegas Neons. If any of us want a job playing or coaching soccer—in the AFF, the European leagues, wherever—we can't talk about stuff like this. Besides, a couple of players thought Maggie was trying to get ahead."

"Like—she was using Levinson?"

"Gabby even said that's why she was traded."

"But you don't believe that," Fenway said gently, holding Sunday's gaze.

"Maggie started slow last year," Sunday said, her voice far away. "She didn't work hard at first. Coach Flash kept pulling her aside into one-on-one meetings, talking her up, saying she could be a star, then tearing her down—in front of the team, too—whenever she messed up."

Fenway's stomach tightened, remembering her professor.

"You know, there's only so much one person can take," Sunday said. "I knew he'd been her coach at Shellmont, too."

"How long have you known what was going on?"

Sunday folded her hands together on the desk.

"From my perspective, Ms. Sunday, it seems like the team normalized the head coach blackmailing players for sex with threats of torturing their teammates at practice."

Sunday's head snapped up. "I might have suspected something between Coach Flash and Maggie. But not that."

"Do the Neons have an HR department?"

"Not so you'd notice." Sunday lowered her voice. "Maybe Maggie finally did something about it."

Fenway turned the pen over in her hand and stared at it. The walls of the office moved in ever so slightly, and she tasted bile in her mouth.

Huke cleared his throat. "Ms. Sunday, when you say that Maggie might have done something about it..."

Fenway took a deep breath, and the walls receded.

Sunday bowed her head for a moment, then looked up. "Stood up for herself." Coach Sunday's eyes focused on the far wall. "She was playing scared for a while last year. But I worked with her. A lot. I built her back up, little by little, piece by piece, only to have Coach Flash flush it all down the toilet with one comment or tirade. Something—maybe someone—could have opened her eyes."

Fenway was quiet for a moment, then set down her pen. "You said you didn't know Levinson was getting fired until this morning's 6:30 meeting. What's going to happen now?"

"Now? *I'll* probably be fired."

"Fired? Not promoted?"

Sunday chuckled. "When a new head coach comes in, it's likely they'll clean house."

"You don't think they'll promote from within? Not you? Not Coach Portello?"

"If Christchurch wants to keep the ship steady—and she might—then she'll promote Rocky. He's the one who's worked closest with Coach Levinson, and I'd bet money that he'll let me go and bring in his buddy Jim Beaumont from Big Easy FC. They coached together when he was on Coach Flash's staff at Shellmont."

"And if she wants to shake things up?"

"She'll hire a head coach looking for a job—Addison Prowse or Kate Hayes. And they'll bring their own people. Either way, it means I'll be out of a job. And I'll have the stink on me."

"Stink? What do you mean?"

"Reporters asking if I looked the other way. If I told other staff or players to ignore what was happening. Did I tell a player Coach Flash 'didn't really mean it'?" Sunday shook her head. "No team will want me."

Deputy Huke stepped forward, and Fenway twitched—she had forgotten he was there. "This is a nice story, Ms. Sunday," Huke said. "And perhaps we can take you at your word that you wouldn't have gained professionally from Coach Levinson's death. But following your own train of thought, you knew your career was over as soon as Christchurch made the decision to fire Levinson. Is it possible you knew he'd be fired before this morning's notification? Is it possible you blamed him for putting your job and your career in jeopardy?"

"I don't—"

"Is it possible," Huke continued, "that you meant to go *talk* to him last night? I know people like Coach Levinson—I bet he doesn't apologize for anything. Blaming everyone but himself—maybe he started blaming you."

A scenario jumped into Fenway's head: Sunday knocking on

Levinson's door and finding Maggie in the room with him. Maybe in his bed, maybe in a state of undress—maybe both. And Levinson wouldn't have cared. He was still coercing Maggie into sex—even though he was about to be fired, whether he knew it or not.

So Lorraine Sunday might have lost her temper, grabbing the driver from his golf bag—

Sunday pursed her lips. "I did *not* visit Coach Flash's room last night."

Huke opened his mouth. "Is it possible—"

"That's enough, Deputy." Fenway shot a disapproving look at Huke.

He nodded and stepped back. Sunday shook her head, a smile touching the corners of her mouth.

Fenway tilted her head and frowned. "Why the grin, Coach Sunday? The deputy has a point, you know. The prosecution will ask me if you could have been angry enough at Levinson to kill him. Convince me you weren't."

Sunday stood up. "Convince you I wasn't angry enough to kill him? How about you come to me when you have anything resembling proof?"

Fenway reached up to run a hand through her short hair, dense and prickly.

"Am I free to go?" Sunday pulled up the sleeve of her track jacket and checked her watch. "It's been twenty minutes. Rocky won't be pleased."

Fenway pushed back her chair and started to rise.

"I've got another question," Huke said.

Fenway glared at Huke, but he took no notice.

"You know something you're not telling the coroner."

Sunday crossed her arms. "I've said all I'm going to say."

"When the coroner asked who might want to harm Coach Levinson," Huke pressed, "you mentioned Maggie Erskine. But she's just one person. You didn't tell us the rest of the list. Are you protecting someone?"

"I'm not—" Sunday leaned on the desk and looked down. "It's really not my place to say anything."

"But it *is*," Huke insisted. "This is a murder investigation."

Lorraine turned around and began to pace up and down the side of the room.

"You said you didn't have any evidence of Coach Levinson sexually assaulting anyone," Huke said, "but that's a lie, isn't it?"

What was Huke doing? Was he *trying* to piss off the witness?

Sunday stammered, "Not—not exactly."

Fenway stared at Lorraine Sunday, unblinking.

Sunday crossed her arms, took a few paces back and forth behind the desk, then grunted. "Ten years ago, Levinson did the same thing to Annabel."

"The same thing he was doing to Maggie?" Fenway asked. "Sexual coercion?"

Sunday averted her eyes. "It's not my place to tell you this. If Annabel wants you to know, she can tell you herself."

Fenway rubbed her chin. "Everyone thinks Maggie blew the whistle on Coach Levinson. And it was Annabel?"

Lorraine grimaced and sat back down. "It's complicated," Lorraine said. "Annabel brought her complaint to the AFF Board of Governors."

"But that was a decade ago," Fenway said.

"Finally, someone who remembers the news stories." Sunday gave a small nod. "Several players complained about certain coaches, but the media hardly mentioned it. And even with sworn testimony at the AFF hearings, those coaches still kept their jobs." Sunday rubbed her forehead. "But Annabel lodged another complaint last year."

"And this time the results were different?"

"The Board of Governors has a couple new members. And this

time, Annabel had documentation. She had photographs. She even had video from CCTV of Levinson behaving—uh, badly with her. She had recorded voicemails. Suddenly, it wasn't a 'he said she said' scenario."

"How did you find out about Annabel's new complaint?" Huke asked.

"Annabel came to me for advice." Lorraine gave Fenway a tight smile. "We were on the US national team together, remember? We were both backups. Her, the new star striker; me, the long-in-the-tooth goalie. We got to know each other. We had each other's backs."

"And you convinced Annabel to go to the Board?"

"I didn't just talk to her—I saw some of the footage. She showed me photos. Coach Flash was a bad guy, Coroner. His sexual misconduct—no, his *assault*—went on for years: at Shellmont, on two different AFF teams before that, and who knows where else. It went back to when Levinson was an assistant coach in the league. He did the same thing with Annabel years ago that he's doing right now to Maggie."

Of course. That's why Annabel was so adamant about keeping Maggie away from Levinson—because of the hell she had gone through.

Maybe it wasn't Maggie who'd had enough. Perhaps Annabel could handle it when it was her, but not when she knew other victims.

Annabel left the elevator after midnight. Was she trying to keep Maggie away from Levinson? And—if Annabel saw Maggie was already passed out in Levinson's bed, did *she* snap—much like Huke had accused Lorraine Sunday of doing?

Fenway leaned back and thought for a moment.

Just then, the door opened, and Annabel rushed in. Fenway turned quickly away.

Sunday looked up. "Practice isn't over already?"

Annabel stopped short. "Oh—Coach Sunday, sorry. We're on a water break. I just need somewhere to stash my bag until the locker room floor is dry. I didn't think anyone would be in here."

"No problem, Bel. Put it in the closet next to Coach Rocky's desk."

"Here?"

"Sure."

Fenway peeked at the bag out of the corner of her eye: a square duffel with gray and aquamarine stripes with *Desert Treasure* on the side. Annabel dropped a matching sweatshirt on top of it.

"Thanks. Sorry to bother you."

She left, and Fenway listened for the click of the door latch and Annabel's receding footsteps before she opened her mouth again. "Speak of the devil."

"Hmph. I hope she didn't hear any of that."

Fenway cleared her throat. "Why hasn't Annabel gone public with this? She's a superstar in the sport, only a year or two from retirement."

"Ten years ago, after the accusations about Coach Flash, the Board reminded her of the gag order in the AFF player contracts." Lorraine stood and began pacing again. "All the players sign an agreement saying any conflicts will be kept within the confines of the AFF and its arbitrators."

"Wait," Fenway said. "She was sexually assaulted by a coach. She couldn't go to the police?"

Sunday shook her head. "Or to the press. The penalties were strict. I believe the fines alone would have been enough to bankrupt her."

"That's—illegal," Fenway said. "And it's certainly unenforceable."

"Most players don't know that," Coach Sunday said. "At any rate, she never would have played professionally again."

"So why did she submit another complaint last year?" As soon as the words were out of Fenway's mouth, she knew. "Oh, right. She doesn't have to worry about money anymore—she married one of the richest women in the world."

"Who is also the CEO of one of AFF's biggest sponsors." Lorraine nodded. "Money talks. And look, I don't know about the legality of what she signed. I just know that Annabel got word from the Board of Governors right before training camp."

"About the investigation?"

"They told Annabel they had investigated Levinson and her complaint was 'without merit.'"

"What? No merit? That must have surprised her."

Oh—maybe not. Fenway hadn't accused her professor of anything because she knew the university would defend him and accuse her. New board members or not, Annabel was still fighting an uphill battle.

Fenway took a deep breath. "It probably pissed off Mathilda Montague."

"I think that's why the board didn't give Annabel the bad news until Desert Treasure signed a five-year sponsorship extension," Sunday said. "Say what you will about their ethics, but the AFF is full of savvy businesspeople."

Fenway nodded, then furrowed her brow. "Hang on—how can the complaint be without merit, but this morning he was fired for cause?"

"Annabel had video and photos of Coach Flash and Maggie, too. Stuff from her years at Shellmont University. Some of the footage was from Maggie's freshman year, when she was seventeen."

The pieces clicked into place in Fenway's head. "The team traveled. Levinson took a minor across state lines to have sexual relations with her. The textbook definition of sex trafficking."

Sunday nodded. "That's the phrase Annabel said she used—*human trafficking.* You better believe that scared the pants off the AFF Board. Threatening Annabel was no longer an option."

Fenway tilted her head. "How did she get those recordings?"

Sunday chuckled. "I don't know, but I'd bet Annabel's wife paid some private investigators a lot of money. Annabel packaged it all up a few days ago—after she got the 'without merit' response—and sent it to the US Soccer Federation." The corners of her mouth went up in a smile.

"I'm surprised it wasn't *her* we had to scrape off the floor," Fenway muttered. "So you and Rocky know all this."

"I've known for a week or two. I don't know if Rocky found out. I'm not surprised it went to the owner of the club, and that's why I'm not surprised Coach Flash was fired."

"And even after the formal complaints," Fenway said, "he kept doing it. He kept going with Maggie." *Even last night*, Fenway almost said. "Do you have the reports Annabel submitted?"

Sunday clamped her mouth shut and shook her head.

"We may need that information," Huke said.

Fenway shot another look at the deputy.

"Annabel released the information herself," Sunday said. "You already know about Maggie. I'm not identifying any of his other victims unless I get subpoenaed. And if you want to get the report from the AFF, you'll have quite a legal fight on your hands. The league won't simply hand those over because you ask nicely."

Ah, but maybe she could ask Annabel nicely. If Fenway pulled the right thread, the whole scheme of Levinson's might unravel. And it might reveal the killer.

Lorraine stood and walked toward the door. "Suddenly, those wet winters in Liverpool don't seem so bad."

CHAPTER TWELVE

Fenway's insides roiled.

As Lorraine Sunday walked back to the field, Fenway and Deputy Huke followed, but Fenway slowed her pace until Sunday was out of earshot.

"I thought you were just going to observe," Fenway said.

"You were digging for evidence of the victim's crimes," Huke said evenly.

"I was—" Fenway pressed her lips together and took a deep breath in through her nose. "I needed to establish motive."

"You hadn't yet established the suspect's whereabouts during the time of the murder."

"Donald—Deputy Huke—I am your superior—"

"With all due respect, Coroner, the sheriff may have asked me to assist you, but you are not in my chain of command. I followed protocol on questioning witnesses."

Fenway lifted her hand up—she almost held an index finger in Huke's face—then dropped it to her side.

Huke didn't say anything.

"And what were you doing calling out our witness like that for lying like that? She's the first one I've talked to who doesn't seem to be actively—"

"Just because she's willing to talk doesn't mean she's truthful." Huke furrowed his brow. "I thought you'd be happy. You got the answers you needed."

"What you did was risky."

"To whom?" Huke asked, cocking his head. "Ms. Sunday was ready to end the interview."

"What would have happened if your plan had backfired?"

"Then you blame me for being new and overly ambitious, apologize, kick me out of the room, then tell her some amusing anecdote about when *you* started the job. Then she might tell you a story from her soccer playing days, then you ask her, more subtly, if she has anything else to add."

Fenway stopped in her tracks. "You really thought that all through?"

"It's one of the standard interrogation methods. I create a situation of conflict through direct confrontation, and you resolve the conflict through engagement and empathy. To be perfectly honest, I didn't think the direct confrontation would work by itself."

It sounded like a fancy way to describe *good cop bad cop*, which she'd thought was only something that happened on TV. "You take a class for this?"

"Intermediate Interrogation Techniques. It's offered through our extended learning program. I took it a couple of months ago. Goes toward my professional certification." He took a few more steps. "Deputy Salvador isn't the only one who wants to get promoted to detective, you know."

Fenway nodded and began walking again, down the concrete path toward the field.

"What next?" Huke asked.

"Annabel," she said. "She's running drills on the other side of the field. Can you ask her to join us?"

The path ended at the edge of the grass, then Fenway's shoes squished on the lawn as she continued toward the players. She walked past Coach Portello, still standing at the sideline.

He cleared his throat. "I understand you're just doing your job, Coroner."

"A man has been murdered," Fenway said evenly.

Portello nodded. "We've *all* been through a trauma."

"Some of the players, more than one," Fenway said before she could stop herself.

Portello bristled. "Is that supposed to be some crack at me?"

Interesting—she'd hit a sore subject. Sunday's words—that Levinson had victimized more players than Annabel and Maggie—ran through her head. She started to speak, then stopped. She didn't want to take the bait.

"I asked you a question, Coroner," Portello said. "What did you mean with that last statement?"

Fenway chose her words carefully. "You told me this morning that Coach Levinson might have cheated with a player. Now that he's been accused—"

"It's awful, all right?" Portello snapped. "What do you want me to say?"

"You were close to Coach Levinson—"

"I had no idea what he was doing."

"That's not what I was going to say," she said sharply. From twenty yards away, Huke turned his head. She lowered her voice. "The owner is alleging Coach Levinson is guilty of sexual coercion, sexual assault, and statutory rape—"

"We don't have—"

"And from what I know," Fenway said over him, "the Neons didn't stop it. The league didn't stop it."

Portello gritted his teeth before he spoke. "I don't know any details."

Fenway scoffed. "You told me this morning he'd been cheating on his wife! How did you know that if you had 'no idea what he was doing'?"

"I'd heard rumors. Nothing definite."

Fenway took a step next to Portello on the sideline, following his gaze to the players. "You were Levinson's right-hand man for a long time. At Shellmont University. Even before that. You knew what he was doing."

"I don't—" Portello barked, turning suddenly away from the field, his eyes losing focus.

Fenway took a small step toward him but waited.

After a moment that seemed like an hour, Portello closed his eyes and took a deep breath. "I didn't know what was going on." He clenched and unclenched his fists.

"If you knew he was taking advantage of his players," Fenway said evenly, "and you knew he wouldn't stop, you'd know it was only a matter of time before his actions would screw up your job prospects."

Finally, Portello glanced at Fenway's face. "You think *I* did it? That makes no sense. He wasn't hurting me. He wasn't withholding playing time from me." Then he looked at the ground and chuckled. "When I think about who could have done it, I automatically think it was one of them."

"One of who?"

"One of the players who was sleeping with him—like Maggie. Maybe he didn't give her enough attention last year. Maybe he refused to leave his wife. Who knows?"

Fenway shook her head. "You can do better than that, Rocky. Paul Levinson wasn't having an affair with his players; he was sexually coercing them."

Portello scowled. "Consenting adults. The players could have left at any time."

"Not if they wanted to keep playing for the league," Fenway said, trying to tamp down her rising blood pressure. "Levinson put them in a position where they couldn't say no." She looked at Portello out of the corner of her eye. "And at Shellmont—when *you* were there—he sexually coerced a minor, too."

Portello sniffed, then raised his eyes and looked across the field at the players.

Not a big reaction from the assistant coach. He knew. Maybe he'd seen Annabel's report.

Fenway followed Portello's gaze; Huke and Annabel Shedd were walking toward the sideline. "Come on, Rocky. I might be the same age as some of your players, but I'm not stupid. You knew. Or you suspected."

Portello looked down at the ground, kicking the grass for a moment, then he raised his head and looked Fenway in the eye. "There was some rumbling, I guess."

"When?"

"Last year. I could see the interplay between Maggie and Coach Flash. He took her under his wing—but then, everyone knew she'd be starting in goal for us this year."

"Interplay—what do you mean by that?"

Portello sighed. "At first, I thought Maggie had a crush on him. But he was married. I figured the whole thing was kind of innocent." He shook his head. "I didn't know she had it in her."

"Had *what* in her?"

"You know. The ability to kill another human being."

Fenway looked up. Huke and Shedd were only about fifteen yards away. She raised her hand slightly toward them, palm out, and Huke stopped and said something to Annabel, who also stopped walking.

"You honestly believe Maggie killed him?" she asked, lowering her voice.

"Who else would it be? I saw them interacting. I didn't think much of it at the time, but now with the charges, his firing—hell, his *murder*—everything looks different."

Fenway tilted her head. "You and he were on the same floor. The ninth."

"Uh, yeah."

"The two of you always on the same floor when you travel?"

"Sure. Makes it easier for strategy sessions, especially if there's an injury we didn't foresee, whether it was one of our starters or one of theirs."

Fenway took another small step forward. "All the times last year when the Las Vegas Neons were on the road, in new cities, strange hotels—you mean to tell me the coach stayed on the same floor as you, but you never saw Maggie go into his hotel room?"

Coach Portello crossed his arms. "Maybe I *did* see them hanging out a lot more than might have been appropriate, you know, for a normal coach and player. But Maggie wasn't a normal player. She's our future. I didn't think anything of him putting her on a pedestal—because without her, we have no chance at the trophy."

"Coach Levinson isn't the first coach in the league who's been accused of sexual misconduct with his players," Fenway said quietly. "In every other circumstance, the people in power knew complaints were made, sometimes years ago, and they did everything they could to cover it up." Fenway glared at Portello, but he didn't return her gaze. "Maybe you've convinced yourself you didn't know anything, but you knew what he did."

"I never—" Portello caught himself, cleared his throat, then ran his hand over his face. "Didn't you say you needed to interview some of the players?"

Fenway motioned to Annabel standing next to Deputy Huke. "I certainly did."

He grimaced. "Our offense runs around her. You can't take someone else?"

"She and Maggie went out to dinner last night," Fenway said. "Don't you think it would be irresponsible of me not to follow up?"

Portello sighed. "Fine." He motioned to Annabel.

Deputy Huke walked over to them, Annabel following close behind.

"Fifteen minutes," Portello said.

"This is a murder investigation, sir," Huke said. "It will take as long as Coroner Stevenson needs."

Fenway glanced at Huke's face. "It's all right, Deputy. I can follow up later if I need to."

Huke pressed his lips together. "Coroner, can I talk to you for a moment?"

"Uh—I suppose."

Huke motioned with his head toward the quad, and the two of them walked about fifty feet away.

"What's this about?"

Deputy Huke looked at the ground for a moment. "I didn't hear everything you and Coach Portello discussed," Deputy Huke said in a low, firm voice, "but I didn't hear many questions regarding the murder."

"As I mentioned," Fenway said, feeling her jaw tighten, "I'm establishing motive."

Huke squared his shoulders and turned to Fenway, a skeptical look in his eye. "In my year on the job, I've been called to the scene of bar fights and some domestic altercations." He took a deep breath, placing his feet slightly farther apart. "In every one of those cases, the assailant has attempted to convince me that the victim *deserved* to be hit. It's easy for me to shut that down because the law is clear." Huke swallowed hard and drew himself to his full height. "I understand this is a sensitive situation, Coroner, but I suggest—"

Fenway cut Huke off. "I need to know who covered up for Paul Levinson." She caught her voice rising in volume. Then, softer: "Anyone who set up these clandestine meetings between our murder victim and his players had a good reason to want him dead. Levinson could have dragged other people down with him. Now he can't." She jerked her head toward Coach Portello. "And he might say that he was worried about his job, but he sure thinks he's going to get promoted to head coach."

"Then you should be asking details about how he found the body, or if he knew where to find the murder weapon. I get it—Levinson was a bad guy. But putting the victim on trial—"

"Deputy Huke," Fenway snapped, though her voice faltered. She steeled herself; she wasn't going to let memories of the Russian Lit professor make her sound weak. "Don't tell me how to run my investigation."

Huke blinked, then stood up straight. "Yes, ma'am. Sorry, ma'am."

Fenway felt a sharp sting in her hands and realized she'd balled up her fists so tightly that her nails were digging into the flesh of her palms. She opened her mouth to speak, but her voice caught in her throat.

Her phone rang in her purse. "Hold on," she told Huke.

It was McVie.

"I have to take this," she said, and her voice was rougher than she expected.

"Yes, ma'am."

Fenway turned her back on Huke and strode away.

Suddenly, her vision swam. What was she doing? She was in the middle of a set of suspect interviews—and she'd just left two of the biggest suspects standing on the sideline while she caught flak from a deputy, then took a call from her boyfriend.

She blinked and tapped *Answer.* "Hey, Craig—sorry, I can't talk."

"Just wanted to say dinner is up the air tonight. Megan wants to talk with me. She might not be coming over tomorrow."

Fenway sighed. "I was really looking forward to this—and it's the first night in a while where you don't have to work when I come over. You've been so busy with this case—"

"I know," McVie said. "But if Megan doesn't come over tomorrow, you and I can spend all weekend together."

Fenway gritted her teeth.

"Is—is everything okay?"

Fenway took a deep breath in, held it to the count of ten, then exhaled.

"Fenway?"

"It's the case," she finally said. "Too many ways things can go."

"Oh," McVie said. "You know, if you need to bounce ideas off—"

"I've got a couple of suspects standing about fifty feets away," Fenway said. "I'll call you later."

"Not if Megan—"

"Right, right," Fenway said. "Not if Megan and you are having your discussion. Maybe this weekend. Got it." She clicked *End Call* before McVie could respond.

She turned on her heel in the wet grass and strode back onto the pitch. "All right, Annabel. Let's get moving."

CHAPTER THIRTEEN

Annabel tilted her head. "You?"

"Me," Fenway replied.

Annabel hesitated. "*You're* the coroner?"

Fenway nodded. "Come on." She started walking toward the concrete walkway.

After a moment, Annabel began to follow, running to catch up with her. The overcast sky darkened. The breeze turned stronger, with a hint of menace. Fenway smelled the sharp, fresh aroma of ozone.

Annabel stopped. "You were at Maxime's last night."

"Yes."

"You talked to me in the ladies' room."

"Yes."

"I thought you were a fan."

"I *am* a fan. Your fans can have real jobs, you know."

"Right. Sorry."

Fenway felt a pang of guilt—Shedd knew something wasn't right.

"What did you say your name was?" Shedd asked.

"Sorry, I don't think I ever mentioned it." Fenway held out her hand. "Fenway Stevenson."

Annabel took her hand and shook it. "Fenway?"

"My dad is a big Red Sox fan."

Annabel looked into Fenway's face. The corners of her mouth turned down slightly.

Fenway returned Annabel's stare, though she tried a friendly—if neutral—look. Out of the corner of her eye, she saw Deputy Huke frown, then cross his arms.

Could Huke help with Annabel? Despite Fenway's dislike of his interruption, he *had* been valuable to keep Lorraine Sunday talking.

No. She didn't want him tagging along this time.

She caught Huke's eye and motioned with her head toward the other players. Huke nodded, took out his notebook, and strode onto the field.

Fenway turned back to Annabel and cleared her throat. "Coach Portello is letting me use the office to conduct my interviews," Fenway said. "We can go in there where it's quiet."

Annabel frowned. "I'm warmed up, and I don't want to sit for ten minutes." She turned back to the field. "Let's walk around the edge of the field so I can keep my blood flowing. I want to stay loose."

Fenway shook her head. "I don't want the other players hearing us."

Annabel pointed to an adjacent field. "How about that one? It's a hundred yards away from anyone else."

"It looks like it's about to rain."

"You afraid of a little water?"

"I suppose not." Fenway stole another glance at Huke, who had pulled one of the players to the side. She gave him a slight nod and turned back to Annabel.

They crossed the first field, Annabel picking up the pace, but Fenway kept up with her. Her feet were getting cold, but the change of scenery might do her good. Besides, Fenway was always sharper when she moved—pacing around the room, running the trail to the butterfly waystation, or taking a walk to clear her head.

When they got halfway across the second field, Annabel turned her head to look at Fenway. "Okay, Coroner, no one can hear us now."

"Let's get this out of the way first—have you seen a diamond tennis bracelet, either last night or today?"

Annabel frowned. "The only person I know with a diamond tennis bracelet is Sandra Christchurch—" She turned to look at Fenway. "It wasn't stolen, was it?"

"It's been reported missing. All right, back to Coach Levinson." Fenway wanted to ask about the report, but Huke's words rang in her ears. "Tell me where you were last night, all the way up through eight o'clock this morning."

"You already know I was at Maxime's for dinner." Annabel began a mock run, lifting her knees high.

"But you didn't leave with your dinner companion," Fenway said.

"That was Maggie Erskine, by the way."

Fenway felt like she should be mimicking Annabel's workout, but in her pantsuit, it would look silly. "This is Maggie's first year as the number one keeper, isn't it?"

Annabel nodded.

"I saw the two of you at dinner. It looked like you were fighting."

Annabel paused, stopping her mock run, and walked a few steps, thinking. "She's a big fan of Coach Flash. Played under him at Shellmont. I don't—" Then she lapsed into silence, stared at the ground, and slowed her walk.

"What is it?"

"He doesn't—didn't—always have her best interests at heart," Annabel said carefully. "Maggie didn't want to hear anything negative about Coach Flash, so she left. She told me she was getting an Uber. I assume she went back to the hotel, although I don't know for sure."

Despite the cold weather, Fenway felt herself break into a sweat under her blazer. "How did the two of you get to the restaurant?"

"I drove. The team has a car. Usually for errands, but sometimes the coaches let the players check the car out."

"What kind of car is it?"

"It's a white Toyota. A Corolla, I think."

Fenway nodded—the car in the parking garage. Sarah had been right.

"Coach Sunday has one of the keys," Annabel continued. "I checked out the car from her."

Fenway nodded. Interesting—Sunday hadn't mentioned it in her interview.

"So you left the restaurant, and Maggie was already gone?" As soon as the words were out of her mouth, Fenway inwardly grimaced —she was leading Annabel with what Fenway already knew. Better to let Annabel tell her own story, especially since she was a suspect.

Annabel nodded. "I drove back to the hotel. I thought maybe I could catch Maggie at the bar. She'd had a lot to drink, but I didn't think that would stop her from having more."

"What time did you get back to the hotel?"

"Uh—I don't know. I didn't look at the time. I didn't see Maggie in the bar."

"Did you see anyone else?"

"A few of the other players. Coach Flash was there, too."

"Did you stay and talk to them? Maybe have a drink? Wait for Maggie?"

"I went straight up to my room. First practice was today, after all. I wanted to get some sleep."

"Did you stay up?"

Annabel was quiet.

"You may not know this, Annabel, but there are cameras in the hotel."

"All right," Annabel said. "I texted Maggie to make sure she'd gotten back to the hotel safely. But she didn't respond. So I went to her room."

"She's on the same floor as you?"

"Right."

"Don't most of the players have roommates?"

Annabel tilted her head. "How do you know that?"

"I wasn't lying—I follow the game a little. I know the AFF is on a budget. Most players room together."

"I pay for my own hotel room," Annabel said.

"Who is Maggie's roommate?"

Annabel was quiet for a moment. Finally: "She doesn't have one."

Fenway tilted her head. "Why not?"

"I'm afraid I can't tell you any more."

"Suddenly you're not cooperating?"

"There's—there's an agreement preventing me from discussing the matter."

Fenway thought a moment and fell behind Annabel's rapid walking clip. The gag order in all the AFF player contracts. "I see."

Annabel wiped her forehead with the back of her hand and sneaked a look at Fenway's face. "You do?"

"Yes." Fenway broke into a slight jog to keep up with Annabel. "Did Maggie answer her door?"

"No."

"What time was this?"

"Around midnight."

"What did you do afterward?" Fenway asked.

"I—uh—well, I went to look for her." Annabel grunted. "I guess the cameras recorded me on the ninth floor."

"Yes."

"Can you blame me?" Annabel said. "I was angry. I didn't want—" She paused. "Sorry. I can't talk about why I was on the ninth floor."

Fenway wiped a bead of sweat from her forehead—then she remembered following Annabel in Maxime's.

"Let's go back to the restaurant."

Annabel glanced at Fenway. "Okay."

"I went into the restroom, and you were talking to someone on the phone."

Annabel didn't say anything.

"Can you tell me who you were talking to?"

"Uh—I'm not sure I remember."

"I'll tell you what I remember," Fenway said. "'I swear, if you don't do something about Maggie and that monster, I will.'"

Annabel grimaced. "Oh. Yeah. I guess that does sound bad."

"Were you referring to Coach Levinson?"

"I'm prohibited from talking about it."

"What?"

"I mentioned a signed agreement. I believe if I answer that question, it might put me in violation of that document. I'll have to consult with my lawyer before I answer your question."

"We can get a subpoena."

"Good. That's one of the ways I can talk to you about it without being in violation."

"Can you at least tell me who you were talking to?"

"Again, I'm prohibited from telling you."

Fenway sighed. "All right, then. When you got out of the elevator on the ninth floor late Thursday night, who did you go see?"

They reached the edge of the second field, right at a chalk boundary, and Annabel stopped walking so abruptly that Fenway got several feet ahead of her before turning around.

"What is it?"

"This is all regarding the same issue I can't discuss."

"You can't even tell me who you went to see?"

"I don't think I can, no."

Fenway was taken aback. She could get a subpoena, but it could take days—or even weeks. She decided to change to another subject. "I take it by now you've heard Coach Levinson was fired."

"Sandra Christchurch sent an email to the team before the press conference," Annabel said.

"To the best of your knowledge, did any of your conversation last night affect Coach Levinson's employment status with the team?"

Annabel considered for a moment, then said in an even tone, "I apologize, Coroner. I can't answer."

"Because of the agreement." Fenway exhaled, trying to disguise her annoyance. "I'm conducting a murder inquiry—and I know about the complaints you made to the AFF Board of Governors."

Annabel shrugged. "That was all over the news ten years ago."

"I mean the one you made last year. And I know you were just told the case had no merit."

Annabel looked stricken.

"You can't conceal information from the police. The gag order is unenforceable."

"I'd like nothing better than to talk about this with you, Coroner. I'd even help you get the subpoena if I could. But I can't."

"You can't?"

"We don't have a collective bargaining agreement, so we have no power. I won't talk without a subpoena."

Fenway looked back at the soccer field; she and Annabel had walked far away, with no one within earshot. "I'm going out on a limb here," Fenway said. "I'm willing to stipulate that you talked to—whoever you talked to on the ninth floor about..." Fenway's mind raced. "About the music they play at practices."

Annabel furrowed her brow. "What?"

"Surely your contract doesn't cover the team's music playlist, does it?"

"No, of course not."

"Hypothetically, let's suppose you'd wanted to discuss the music they play at practices."

"You mean—last night when I went to the ninth floor?" Annabel's brow furrowed.

"Absolutely correct. You're concerned about the team's motivation. You're afraid the current music selection is—is detrimental to the success of the team, especially since the coach always wants to use Maggie Erskine's playlist, even though he yells at her for having horrible taste in music. *That's* why you went to the ninth floor after midnight. You can talk about music playlists without violating your agreement, right?"

"Because Coach Flash is always playing Maggie's—" Annabel's forehead relaxed. "Oh. I get it now." A slight smile played on Annabel's face, and she stepped over the chalk boundary and resumed walking.

"When you went to the ninth floor, whose door did you knock on to discuss the music playlist?"

"I went to Coach Flash's room first. I knocked on the door."

"Was there an answer?"

"No. But..."

Fenway could see the gears turning in Annabel's head.

"Maggie has—she has, uh, a favorite band. And I could hear the band's music through the door."

"And you were concerned Coach Levinson was—was having undue influence over the kind of music Maggie wanted at practices."

Annabel squinted. "Are we still talking about the same thing?"

"So after you heard Maggie's music," Fenway said, "what did you do?"

"Oh." Again, the wheels turned in Annabel's head. "I—uh—I went to see Sandra Christchurch."

Fenway stopped in her tracks. "You went to see the owner of the Las Vegas Neons?"

"I did," Annabel said. "I'd called her earlier, too."

"From the restaurant?"

"Correct," Annabel said. "I—uh, was complaining about the music playlist Coach Levinson and Maggie were making together. The, uh, monsters of rock."

"So you went to see Christchurch at half past midnight?" Fenway asked. Sandra Christchurch had lied to her—

Then she replayed the conversation in the hotel restaurant in her mind. Sandra Christchurch had simply stopped offering information at one point. *I might have gone to bed at eleven, or it might have been three.*

She never mentioned Annabel banging on her door at about a quarter past midnight. A lie of omission, certainly. But not an out-and-out falsehood.

In fact, they'd gotten sidetracked on whether Coach Levinson knew he was getting fired—and then Fenway had asked what time Christchurch had gone to bed. Rookie mistake—Fenway hadn't paid close enough attention.

With effort, Fenway brought her attention back to Annabel.

"Sandra certainly wasn't expecting me to show up." Annabel chuckled lightly. "It took me a few minutes of knocking on her door pretty loudly before she answered."

"I see. And what was her reaction to her star player showing up in the middle of the night?" Fenway quickly added, "To talk about the music playlists."

"She was upset I had awakened her, of course. But I told her it was too important. Maggie was in Coach Flash's room"—she glanced at Fenway—"listening to his music. I told her it couldn't wait. I pretty much barged in."

"What did you do once you were inside?"

"I told her I knew she had seen the reports about Coach Levinson and the way he, um, forces his musical tastes on players. I accused her of protecting the team and the league over her players. I told her about what Levinson did. Not just with me. Not just with Maggie. I was graphic. I showed her videos I had on my phone. I showed her medical bills."

Fenway nodded. The floodgates had opened.

Annabel laughed. "I halfway expected her to call security, to be honest. I pretty much dragged her down the hall."

"She left her room?" Sandra Christchurch hadn't mentioned that.

"We stood in front of Coach Flash's door for about thirty seconds. And we listened to Maggie—uh, her playlist, I mean, come from the door."

"What did Ms. Christchurch do?"

"She didn't do anything. To be honest, I couldn't read her. If I owned a team and I heard the head coach fucking"—Annabel caught herself—"listening to music playlists with our starting goalkeeper— who's less than half his age, mind you—I'd be pissed." Annabel picked up the pace, and Fenway felt a bead of sweat trickle down her temple. "We went back to Sandra's room, and I went *off*. I was pissed off. I yelled at her. I think I even told her that her dead husband would be disappointed in her."

"How did she take that?"

"She was quiet. I think the crack about her husband was over the line. But I didn't let up. I played my last card. I told her I'd resign from the team, and I'd go to the press. I said I didn't care if I got sued by the team or the league. I told her I'm not keeping my mouth shut anymore."

Annabel's pace was even quicker now; Fenway had to almost run to keep up.

"The winning goal in the World Cup last year?" Annabel continued. "It bought me my freedom. I know I only have one or two years left. My face is on cereal boxes right now. Nobody wanted to listen to me ten years ago—well, you better believe they're gonna listen to me now." Annabel's voice was calm and assured, even though anger coursed through it.

Fenway could feel her pulse pounding and it wasn't completely because of the fast pace of their walk. "You hit her in the wallet."

Annabel breathed in deeply as the first sprinkles of rain started. "She told me she would take care of it, and she'd already started the conversations with her lawyers—she'd been on the phone with them earlier, she said."

"And that was enough for you?"

"Sandra showed me the press release her PR team had put together. It said the Neons and Coach Flash agreed to part ways at the end of the season."

"So bringing Maggie and Coach Levinson to her attention—that got her to move the timeline up?"

"I don't know for a fact. You know what they say—correlation doesn't prove causation. But she said she'd take care of it."

"Then what?"

"I went back to my room."

"Uh—no, you didn't."

"I most certainly did. Are you calling me a liar?"

"The camera doesn't show you getting back into the elevator."

"Oh—well, lots of adrenaline. I decided to take the stairs. But I didn't realize the doors from the stairwell lock from the outside. I couldn't get back to my floor—I had to go down to the ground floor, come back around, then take the elevator back to my room."

That story matched the video evidence, but Fenway wasn't fully convinced. "Did you, at any point, enter Coach Levinson's room?"

"No."

"Did you get visual confirmation of Maggie being in Coach Levinson's room?"

"Uh—no."

Fenway thought for a moment. "At any point, did you take anything from Coach Levinson's room?"

"I told you, I didn't go to his room."

"But someone could have opened the door and handed something to you."

"Handed something to me? Like what?"

"A trash bag, perhaps."

"No. Nothing."

"Were you happy when you saw the press release this morning?"

Annabel's nostrils flared. "You think I like reliving what that asshole did to me? Every time I talk to somebody about it, I have nightmares for a week." She shook her head. "No, I was not happy about reliving it. But I'm doing this so the next generation of AFF soccer players *doesn't* have nightmares."

The drizzle turned into rain, though it was still light. Fenway was glad she didn't have her longer curls—they would have exploded into frizz.

"It's the same everywhere," Annabel murmured.

"What?"

"Sorry, I was thinking out loud. Will it ever really change? People in positions of power—doesn't matter if they're coaches or religious leaders or whatever. Even if they get fired, they always go to the next town or the next team or the next school. If Levinson hadn't died, I bet next season he'd be coaching a women's team in Europe or at some big-name university, and he'd never stop."

Fenway was quiet for a moment. Only the sounds of their feet squishing on the grass could be heard over the breeze rushing in their ears and the gentle drops of rain on the ground.

"I didn't kill him," Annabel said.

Fenway shrugged. "You're very angry with Coach Levinson."

"Of course I am," Annabel said. "He needed to pay for what he did. I'm definitely not upset he's dead. As much courage as it's taken me to come forward, though, I don't think I'd have the guts to murder someone."

———

Fenway and Huke spent the next two hours interviewing the other players, and everyone else wanted to go to the coaches' office to get out of the rain.

Everyone asked where Maggie was—several of the players said they were expecting to win the Pickering Trophy with her in goal this year—but no one had seen anything. No one had heard anything. None of the players went anywhere near the ninth floor between the hours of midnight and six o'clock.

As Fenway and Huke walked to her Accord, she called Sarah.

"Hey, Fenway."

"Can you do some research? It might take some time tomorrow, too."

"Overtime on a weekend when all my friends are out of town? Sure."

"The stairwell's been bothering me. The doors should lock so no one can exit on any floor except the ground floor."

"Right—lots of hotels are like that."

"I need to find how to prevent the door from latching, but where a sensor mounted on the top of the door would still register it being closed."

"A strong adhesive tape over the latch might do it. Duct tape, electrician's tape, maybe."

"I asked security about that—the latch is strong enough to stretch tape like that. And besides, I didn't see any adhesive."

"Huh." Sarah exhaled. "I'll work on it."

"Thanks."

Fenway ended the call.

Huke piped up. "There are hinge-mounted door stops now. They're pretty exact. I can send you a link."

"How do you know about it?"

He shrugged. "I've done some work around Melissa's apartment. Saw 'em at the hardware store."

Fenway unlocked the doors and sat down heavily in her seat. Starting the engine as Huke got in, she pulled her phone out of her purse and texted Dez.

Are you still interviewing Maggie?

She waited a moment but got no response. The interrogation might still be going on.

Fenway and Huke drove back downtown in uncomfortable silence. The fifteen-minute drive felt like hours. She pulled into the parking garage next to City Hall, and Huke opened the door before she killed the engine.

"Thanks for helping out," Fenway offered. Not an apology, but something civil.

"Any time, Coroner."

Her phone rang—it was McVie. She tapped the answer button on her steering wheel.

"Hey, Craig."

"Hi, Fenway. Sorry about earlier."

Huke looked at her expectantly. She motioned for him to go, and he left the car, shutting the door behind him.

"No, don't worry about it," Fenway said.

"Will you be working late?"

"Probably. Are you having that talk with Megan tonight?"

"That's the plan." Then silence for a few moments before McVie spoke again. "Are we okay?"

"I think so." Fenway drummed her fingers on the steering wheel.

"Were you able to talk to your client about what you found yesterday?"

"I didn't find anything yesterday."

"Exactly—you said Mathilda Montague would expect a smoking gun about Annabel and Maggie sleeping together, and we didn't get it. Instead, we found a reasonable explanation about why the two of them have spent so much time together."

McVie hesitated a moment. "Ah. I did tell her about dinner last night and that I was unable to uncover anything suspicious."

"How did she react?"

"She told me to keep digging."

"Oh—so you're still on the case?"

"It's good money."

"Is that a 'yes'?"

"She wants me at it for another week. Mathilda showed me Annabel's cell phone bills. A bunch of calls to Maggie's number. Not a 'teammate' number of calls, either."

"Oh, I see. Where there's smoke, there's fire."

"Do you have a better explanation for all those calls?" McVie asked. "Because I sure don't."

"I do, in fact."

"Oh." A ticking sound on the other end of the phone—McVie was probably tapping his pencil against the desk. "Is it anything you can tell me about?"

"Uh—I don't think so." Fenway rubbed her forehead, then it came to her. "I bet Piper could find some things out."

"About what? Is *someone* having an affair?"

"No, no, not an affair. Not exactly. Have you seen the news article about Levinson?"

The sound of McVie typing on his keyboard. "Okay, hold on, I'm reading the press release—oh no. Sexual misconduct." He exhaled loudly. "With either Annabel or Maggie?"

Fenway said nothing.

"Right, right, you can neither confirm nor deny allegations relating to an open murder investigation. I get it. Still, thanks for pointing me in the right direction."

"I'm sure I don't know what you're talking about." Fenway killed the engine. "I've gotta go, Craig. Maybe I'll call you tonight."

————

Fenway stuck her head in the coroner's office suite for a moment, but Sarah told her Dez was still in the sheriff's office, questioning Maggie.

"Deputy Huke told me about these over-the-hinge door stoppers that might fit the bill," Fenway said.

"Great minds think alike." Sarah clicked on a window on her computer, and a hardware site appeared.

Onscreen, Fenway saw a beige triangular wedge with a notch running the length of the acute angle.

"This is a hinge pin door stop." Sarah mimed reaching up and sliding something vertically down. "They slide into the hinges at the top and prevent the door from opening too wide and slamming into the wall behind." She pointed at the screen. "These wedge types slide over the hinge too, but they allow stopping in both directions." She dropped her hand to her lap. "Someone could set this to close the door *almost* all the way—enough to let the sensors touch without allowing the latch to close."

"And it would be easy to take on and off?"

"As long as they could reach the top hinge, less than five seconds."

Fenway rubbed her chin. "I wonder." She brought her hand down and rapped softly on the counter. "Can you send me the link to that door stopper?"

"Email or text?"

"Both. Thanks, Sarah."

She walked across the street. The sky was dark and the rain, though not heavy, cast a dull light over the city street. Fenway pulled her thin blazer around herself and hurried through the amphitheater in front of the city building and in through the front door of the sheriff's office. As she strode past the front desk, she saw the doors to both the interrogation room and the observation room were closed.

Fenway knocked lightly on the observation room door.

Dez's voice, quiet: "Come in."

Fenway opened the door and walked inside, closing it gently behind her. "Didn't expect you to still be interrogating Maggie."

Dez stared at Maggie through the one-way mirror.

Maggie sat alone at the aluminum table in the middle of the interrogation room. Slumped in her chair, head tilting to the side, she looked miserable. Her mouth turned down at the corners, and her eyes were puffy and swollen. Her brown hair was pulled back into a ponytail.

"Does she remember anything else from last night?" Fenway asked softly.

Dez turned her head back to Fenway. "She did remember something else."

"What was it? Anything about the murder?"

"No, no. She remembered getting into an Uber with you in front of Maxime's."

CHAPTER FOURTEEN

FENWAY NODDED. "THIS IS GOOD. IT MEANS HER MEMORY IS coming back. Maybe she'll remember more about last night."

Dez set her mouth in a line. "It's not great. She sees you, she might think we're setting her up."

Fenway tilted her head. "You say that as if you think she's innocent."

Dez frowned. "Fine—she sees you, then she'll think she can get her attorney to say this was all a setup. You share an Uber, you sit next to her at the bar, and the next morning, there's a dead body in the hotel suite where she wakes up and says she remembers nothing."

Fenway stared at the floor. The cheap laminate tiles were a low-quality out-of-date design intended to look like marble. "It's fine. I don't need to be part of the interrogation." She looked back up at Dez. "What *does* she remember?"

Dez flipped pages in her notebook. "After she was here a couple of hours, she suddenly remembered getting the Uber." Dez flipped a page. "She reported getting in the car with a light-skinned Black woman around thirty years of age with short hair."

"Hey, that's me," Fenway said playfully, then grew serious. "What about the restaurant? Does she remember what she and Annabel fought about?"

"I'm focusing on the hotel," Dez said, "not the restaurant. After Levinson coerced her into sex in the living room, she remembers walking into the bedroom, but that's it. Vaguely remembers sex in the bed later. Maybe she passed out and was unconscious even when the killer came in and beat Levinson to death. And when the killer cleaned up, too."

"You think she's innocent."

Dez hesitated. "I have a couple of scenarios in my head, and in both of them, Maggie is the one with the golf club in her hand, but it doesn't all fit." She shook her head. "Why stay in the hotel room? And where did the towels go?"

"We thought maybe Annabel took them."

Dez nodded. "Right. In one of my scenarios, Maggie hits him over the head—maybe she doesn't mean to kill him, but he's dead on the floor in front of her. She panics, calls the only person on the team she trusts. Annabel comes up with a plan, cleans up just enough to make it look like someone else could have done it. Then she took the towels and used the stairs to get rid of them."

"But that's not what Annabel says."

"You interviewed her already?"

"I sent you a message—Deputy Huke and I went to Nidever this afternoon."

Dez pulled out her phone, tapped on the screen, and nodded. "Right. Sorry, I was in the interrogation room with Maggie."

"Then let me catch you up," Fenway said. She gave Dez an overview of all the coach and player interviews, including the conversations with Coach Sunday and Annabel Shedd, then told her about Annabel's AFF complaint that Levinson had victimized her ten years before.

Dez rubbed her chin. "Even if what Annabel says is true, that gets us possible motive, but we're still light on evidence. Remember, we're missing two towels with no theory about where they went."

"Sarah thinks they could be in someone's suitcase, or maybe a hotel staff member with a bone to pick with Levinson threw them somewhere we haven't looked yet." Fenway snapped her fingers. "The Toyota Corolla that the team uses. Someone might have stashed the towels in the car. I know it's one of a zillion possibilities, but one we should explore."

"I hate it when hours of hard work give you more questions than answers." Dez pressed her lips together. "What else?"

Fenway thought for a moment. "His wife," she said. "He's cheating on her. Maybe she thinks it's just cheating and not sexual assault, but when she finds out—"

"The widow Levinson," Dez said, "still lives in New York. She didn't make the move out to Vegas with her husband. She was at dinner with three friends last night. Confirmed it with all three friends and a few members of the waitstaff at the restaurant."

"Professional hit?"

"We're looking into the wife's financials, but I spoke with her. She doesn't seem to care enough to have done it. Her family is wealthy. Seems to me the marriage may have run its course—they live separate lives."

"Okay," Fenway said. "Then that keeps the suspect list local."

"Have you seen the report Shedd filed?" Dez asked.

"Not yet. We'll need a subpoena if we want to see it. I think we can get it—it'll go toward establishing motive."

"Hold on," Dez said. "Sandra Christchurch didn't say anything in her interview with you about Annabel coming to her room. You believe Annabel over the owner of the Neons?"

"Christchurch gave me evasive answers when I asked about what time she went to bed," Fenway said. "I suspect she purposely didn't tell me that Annabel showed up at her room."

"Why would she do that?"

Fenway was silent.

Dez nodded. "So—my theory is that Annabel and Maggie worked together to cover up the murder of Coach Levinson. If Christchurch can't vouch for Annabel's whereabouts, then maybe my theory needs to stay on the table."

"That's the problem," Fenway said. "Too many people had means and opportunity."

"And now I get to ask about McVie's investigation." Dez crossed her arms. "You said McVie's client is Annabel's wife. She's the CEO of a big Vegas-based entertainment company, right?"

"Mathilda Montague—she thinks Annabel is cheating on her with Maggie."

"And you were following the two of them to Maxime's when they had dinner last night." Dez leaned on the table next to the one-way mirror. "How did you end up sharing an Uber with Maggie?"

"Uh—Annabel and Maggie fought. Annabel says she was trying to warn Maggie not to trust Coach Levinson, but Maggie got upset and stormed out. I ran out after her and made up a story about staying at the same hotel and needing a ride." Fenway closed her eyes and remembered the hallway at Maxime's in front of the women's restroom. "'I swear, if you don't do something about Maggie and that monster, I will.'"

"What was that?"

"Annabel said it into her cell phone." Fenway paused. "She says that Christchurch was on the phone with her. That's another reason why Annabel needs to stay in the suspect column."

Dez squeezed her eyes shut and pinched the bridge of her nose. "We might need to talk with McVie. Or with his client."

"How is McVie's investigation relevant? It's about whether Annabel and Maggie are having an affair, not if Maggie is one of Paul Levinson's sexual coercion victims."

Dez dropped her arms to her sides. "Let's take a what-if scenario. Let's say that Annabel tells her wife that she was raped—or sexually coerced, however she might have phrased it—ten years ago. Mathilda Montague wants to find out who it was so she can hurt the perpetrator, but Annabel won't tell her. So Montague hires McVie under false pretenses. Let's say she knows it's ten years ago, so she suspects it has something to do with the soccer team she was on back then."

"So—wait, you're saying Montague *never* thought her wife was having an affair?"

"It's a good cover story when she hires McVie. And further, let's say she knows McVie is good at what he does."

"Why set us up with the expectation that Annabel and Maggie are sleeping together? They're clearly not."

"Did McVie tell his client they weren't having an affair?"

"Yes."

"And what was Mathilda Montague's response?"

Fenway felt the heat rise to her cheeks. "She told him to keep digging."

"So where do you expect he'll dig? Maybe into her previous relationships?"

"Uh—yeah."

"Piper still works for McVie, right?"

"Yes."

"She'll find Shedd's AFF complaint in about twenty seconds."

Fenway nodded—especially since she'd led McVie right to it.

"What if Mathilda Montague knew about the sexual coercion? One of her other investigators could have found that AFF complaint. Now Mathilda Montague knows Paul Levinson, her current coach, sexually coerced her. Raped her. Now she has motive as well as means: access to private planes, fancy cars—she could have hired someone to kill Paul Levinson." Dez spread her hands out. "Now do you think McVie's case is still irrelevant?"

"Then why hire McVie? He hadn't found out about the AFF complaint before Levinson was killed."

"To throw us off the scent. You have a better explanation?"

"Jealous. Control freak. Wants a reason to divorce. Any number of things that make a lot more sense than hiring a P.I. in an elaborate ruse to kill her wife's soccer coach."

Dez scratched her eyebrow.

"Occam's Razor, Dez. That's the far more *likely* possibility."

"We can't rule it out. Montague probably has other investigators who might have uncovered Annabel's complaint already."

"We go where the evidence goes." Fenway set her jaw. "But let's cover our bases. When you're done with Maggie's interview, see if any of Mathilda Montague's planes landed at—or took off from—the Estancia airport in the last three days. I don't know if we can find any large payments from Mathilda Montague's personal accounts, but I'll see what we can do."

Dez looked at her out of the corner of her eye. "Piper might be able to find things we can't. Especially if Montague has paid McVie electronically. Account numbers, transaction numbers—"

"We wouldn't be able to use any of that in court. Fruit from the forbidden tree and all that."

"Ah, but you're focusing on the wrong tree. We find out there are suspicious payments being made, then we use legal means to get information about—or from—Montague's other private investigators. If those payments come to light through those efforts, we'll be able to use that evidence."

It wasn't the intent of the system, but Fenway had read enough case law to know Dez was right. "Then I'll call Craig and see what Piper can find. But first, I'll type up my notes and get them over to you." Fenway motioned with her head toward Maggie. "And what do we do with Maggie? Hold her overnight?"

Dez frowned. "No blood on her. No fingerprints on the murder weapon. The clock started when she arrived this morning. Forty-eight hours, then we have to let her go. And every rock we turn over seems to point at everyone *besides* her." Dez shook her head. "I'm inclined to release her."

Fenway took a deep breath and gathered herself. "I agree. She didn't understand he was manipulating her. Thursday night, she got into a fight with Annabel because she was still defending him. She may realize he coerced her into a sexual relationship *now*, but not Thursday night, and certainly not when she was drunk."

"Sometimes drunkenness can provide a unique clarity."

"The clarity usually comes after the drunkenness." Fenway shrugged. "She doesn't seem like a flight risk to me. She's worried about her career—and that's especially true now that Levinson is gone. I'd bet a hundred bucks she'll go back to the hotel and show up at practice tomorrow."

"If she's guilty, she's a flight risk."

"I'll sign off on the release if you're worried about it. I'm headed back to my office to get my notes in the system."

Dez nodded and Fenway left the observation room.

———

As Fenway walked across the street to her building, the rain fell harder.

She took her phone out of her purse and looked at the time. Her stomach rumbled. It was already three thirty, although the dark afternoon made it seem like the early evening. And she had missed lunch.

She walked back into the coroner's suite, saying hello to both Sarah and Migs, and went into her office and shut the door. She searched through her drawers until she found an old granola bar, then tore it open and ate greedily, barely tasting it on its way down.

She typed up her notes and sent them to Dez, then went through her email and took care of some paperwork.

Not enough evidence to charge either Maggie or Annabel with murder. Maybe Dez was onto something. Even if Mathilda Montague wasn't involved in Levinson's murder, digging into her financials and travel might uncover something important.

Fenway pulled her phone out and texted McVie.

Can you talk?

She hit send, and less than twenty seconds later, her phone rang.

"Hi, Craig."

"Hi, Fenway."

She sighed heavily. "Sorry about earlier. I was—" She blinked and saw a flash of her Russian Lit professor's carpet. "I was juggling a bunch of things at once."

"I get it."

Then it hit her. She'd never told McVie about what happened to her in that professor's office ten years before. Her father knew—he'd been accused of the professor's murder, after all—and Dez knew. But McVie didn't know.

That might not be entirely true. McVie could have pieced things together—he was good at that.

Was Fenway putting a barrier between them because she hadn't told him?

She drew in her breath sharply.

"You okay?"

"I might need your help on the murder case. Or Piper's help."

McVie was silent for a moment. "I thought you were going to keep my client out of this."

"We have a—uh, possible theory that we need to explore."

McVie was silent.

"Montague said to keep digging, right?"

"Yes."

"It's possible that Montague had an ulterior motive for that."

"What do you mean?"

Fenway clicked her tongue in thought. "I guess I can't tell you. But I need to know if any large payments have been made from Mathilda Montague's personal accounts to individuals. Or any of her shell corporations."

McVie paused. "That's the kind of thing we'd focus on if we suspected she'd paid a hit man."

Fenway licked her lips, choosing her words carefully. "I suppose it is."

McVie sighed. "I can put Piper on it, but without a warrant—"

"Thanks, Craig," Fenway said quickly.

"I have an obligation to protect my clients. To give them the information they need to make better decisions."

"Like Annabel's complaint?"

"Yes, you were right—Piper found the complaint Annabel lodged with the AFF Board of Governors really fast." He hesitated. "Does this have something to do with—"

"I can't say any more, Craig." She paused. "Did you talk with Megan yet? Is dinner off?"

"She's coming by the apartment in about an hour. Won't tell me what she wants to talk about."

"Oh—when you said she wanted to talk earlier, I thought you just meant a phone call. Do you think it's something serious?"

"I'm trying not to obsess about it," McVie said. "Anything else?"

"When do you think Piper can get the information about Montague?"

"Piper might have found the AFF complaint in record time, but she needs a few hours to review it." A beep. "Speak of the devil. That's her on the other line. Gotta go."

Fenway ended the call, then took care of a few outstanding items in her email. She signed some more paperwork Sarah had left on her desk.

Then she opened her web browser and typed in the address for the Las Vegas Neons website. The news feed in the left column featured headlines:

Neons fire head coach Levinson for cause
New faces at training camp
What Levinson's departure means for Neons' season

Nothing about Levinson dying. No good way to spin his death, Fenway guessed. She clicked her monitor off. She packed up her laptop, picked up her purse, and walked out of the office, saying goodbye to Sarah and Migs as she went.

The rain had turned heavier. Fenway wished she had an umbrella, but it was only about a hundred yards between the office building and the parking garage. She looked up and down the street. About two blocks down, in front of the sheriff's office, a cruiser was parked up on the sidewalk, its lights flashing. Odd.

If it hadn't been raining, she might have been able to see what had happened, but with the streetlights reflecting off the wet asphalt, she couldn't make much out.

Her clothes were only a little wet when she stepped under the protection of the parking garage's overhang. Walking up to her Accord, she took the key fob out of her pocket and pressed the unlock button. The car chirped its greeting—

And Fenway heard a small shriek.

"What the hell?"

A head popped up on the passenger side of the car between the Accord and the Jeep parked next to it.

"Maggie?" Fenway said incredulously.

"Help," Maggie whispered. "Someone's trying to kill me."

CHAPTER FIFTEEN

"Someone's trying to kill you?" Fenway repeated.

"Keep your voice down," Maggie hissed.

"What happened?"

"The detective questioned me for a long time. I didn't know they could keep me in there so long. I mean, they let me stew in the interview room for hours."

Fenway opened the driver's side door. "Get in," she said.

They both got in and closed the doors. The Accord smelled faintly of tacos.

"I answered all of their questions," Maggie continued. "I don't know what happened. I told them about the Uber, they disappeared, and they were gone. For a *long* time."

Fenway opened her mouth, then shut it quickly.

"The detective came back in and told me I was free to go for now, but not to leave town."

"That's probably a good idea."

"I mean, where am I supposed to go?" Maggie shrugged. "I have—I have a job. I was supposed to be at practice today. I was gonna go right back to practice—maybe I could get in a half hour, or forty-five minutes if traffic wasn't bad. I even called an Uber to get down there."

"So what happened?"

"I was standing on the sidewalk, waiting for my ride."

"Even in this rain?"

"Well, excuse me for feeling sorry for myself," Maggie said, rolling her eyes. "Yes, in the rain. Anyway, this white Corolla guns it and heads right for me."

"A white Corolla?"

"Yeah—it looked a lot like the one Annabel drove last night."

"Did you get a look at the driver?"

"No—I jumped out of the way. The car went up on the sidewalk, then it skidded around the corner and was gone. It must have missed me by only a couple of inches."

Fenway's eyes went wide. "Somebody just tried to run you over?"

"Yeah, and in front of the sheriff's office. How screwed up is that?"

"You're sure it was a white Corolla?"

"I'm pretty sure. It's getting dark, but it was a small white sedan. I saw the Toyota logo on it."

Fenway tried to remember what the Corolla in the parking garage had looked like, then snapped her fingers. "Nevada license plate?"

"I didn't see it."

Fenway turned on the engine. "All right. All right. Let's get you somewhere safe."

Maggie nodded, her green eyes wide. "Do you think they'll recognize me?"

"They?"

"Whoever's trying to kill me."

Fenway appraised Maggie: her black-and-gold tracksuit was eye-catching. If someone had wanted to hurt Maggie, the tracksuit was a dead giveaway.

Fenway popped the trunk, got out of the car, and rummaged through a box in the trunk. She pulled out a sweatshirt, light blue with *Western Washington* on the front. A pair of gray socks. A pair of sweatpants, the hideous ones she had bought in Los Angeles two months before—they were so ugly, they'd never even made it inside her apartment. Aha—her Boston Red Sox cap.

Fenway closed the trunk and got back in the car, handing the sweatshirt and cap to Maggie. "Might be sweaty from a workout, but at least it won't be glaringly obvious you're wearing your tracksuit."

"Thank you," Maggie mumbled, taking off the jacket of her track-suit and putting on the college sweatshirt. Then she pulled her brown hair into a ponytail through the back of the Red Sox cap and put it on. She ran her hands along the brim of the cap.

"Is there a hole in this cap?"

Fenway grimaced and nodded. "Oh—yeah, sorry."

"Is it a *bullet* hole?"

"The story sounds more interesting than it is."

Fenway backed out of the space, and soon they were pulling out of the parking garage and driving down Broadway.

"Where do you think I'll be safe?"

"I think the sheriff—" Then Fenway stopped. Maggie was targeted in front of the sheriff's office. Maybe it was a brazen attempt to harm Maggie.

Maggie pulled the cap low over her eyes as they drove past the sheriff's cruiser.

"How sure are you that the white Corolla was the same one Annabel drove?" Fenway asked.

"I'd, uh, already had a couple of drinks when Annabel and I went to dinner. It looked familiar, but I don't know for sure."

"Do you know who drives the Corolla most often?"

"Training camp only started today. I think Annabel was the first one to drive it."

"Annabel checked it out Thursday night?"

"Maybe. The sign-up sheet is in the security office. Or maybe Coach Sunday has it. Anyone can borrow the car."

"Players? Assistant coaches?"

"Sure, although I think the coaches have their own cars."

"What about the owner?"

"Why would Sandra Christchurch take a Corolla when she literally has a fleet of cars?"

"If she wants to run someone over. Or hire someone to do it."

Maggie looked out of the side of her eye at Fenway. "You think it was Ms. Christchurch?"

"I'm not ruling anything out."

"Maybe—maybe I'm overreacting. Maybe it was a prank."

"Maybe." But Fenway knew it wasn't a prank. Somebody was targeting Maggie.

And so close to the sheriff's office, too. Fenway was sure there were cameras outside the sheriff's office, and those recordings could confirm whether Maggie was telling the truth about the Corolla almost running her over. That shouldn't be hard to prove.

She tapped her phone. "Call Sarah."

The phone rang. and Fenway heard the sound of Sarah's phone picking up.

"Hi, Fenway. Forget something?"

"No—we just had an incident right in front of the sheriff's office."

A sharp intake of breath. "What happened?"

Fenway paused, the gears turning in her head. "I've been told a pedestrian was almost run over. Is there any way you can get camera footage of it?"

"I'll do my best. You said it happened now? Did you see it?"

"Maybe ten minutes ago." Fenway glanced over at Maggie, who

pointed up. "Scratch that—probably closer to twenty or thirty. If you find the footage, send it to me."

"Will do." A pause. "Are you okay, Fenway?"

"I'm fine."

"All right. Do you want to head back into the office so you can see the video for yourself?"

"I can't do that right now. Think you can send it to my phone?"

"Well—I can send it to our encrypted storage, then send you the link. I know it's a pain in the ass to look at it through your phone, but you might be able to do it."

"All right. Thanks, Sarah." She hung up.

Fenway glanced in the rearview mirror. The last of the gray light, filtering through the clouds, was disappearing. The rain made it even harder to see. A few pairs of lights reflected in her rearview mirror.

"Why would anybody want to run me over?" Maggie's voice was small.

"Maybe whoever killed Coach Levinson thinks you might know something."

"What are you talking about? You all think I did it."

"Not all of us."

Maggie looked at Fenway. "Not you?"

Fenway scratched her head, her fingers coming away damp from her wet hair. She didn't want to tell her, but she couldn't see any way around it. "No, I don't think you did it."

"Why not?" Maggie's forehead wrinkled in confusion.

"I guess I need to explain." Fenway paused, thinking of how best to phrase it. "My boyfriend is a private investigator. And his client thinks you're having an affair. I was—uh—helping him out with the case."

Maggie sank down in her seat. "Your boyfriend is a P.I.?"

"Uh—yeah, he is."

Maggie covered her face with her hands. "He works for Coach Flash's wife, doesn't he?"

"I don't—" Fenway had said too much already. "I don't believe you're having an affair with the person you've been accused of having an affair with." There. Was that convoluted enough?

"But I *was* sleeping with—oh. So not *his* wife." She rocked slightly in the seat. "I don't—I don't want—it's hard to explain. Coach Flash and I don't have that kind of relationship."

"You're not the first person he's done this to," Fenway said quietly.

"Annabel," Maggie whispered. "She was telling me the truth?"

"I think so. And from what I gather, it's more than the two of you."

"I—" Maggie's mouth dropped open, then she shook her head. "I don't think that's true. Coach Flash believes in me as a player. No one else does."

"A lot more people believe in you than you think," Fenway said. "I talked to everyone on the team today. They *all* believe you can take this team to the championship."

Maggie was quiet.

"You don't need Coach Flash to scream at you in front of everyone. It doesn't make you a better player. You had two clean sheets in a row last year when Gabriela Fortuna was injured, didn't you?"

Maggie said nothing.

Fenway looked at her out of the corner of her eye.

A tear slid down Maggie's cheek. "I just want to play soccer," she murmured.

Fenway looked in her rearview mirror again. The two sets of headlights were the same—they'd followed her from the parking garage. Fenway exited the freeway at Estancia Canyon, and both cars followed.

It might have been a coincidence.

Fenway had to make a decision—the turn for her apartment was coming up.

She tightened her grip on the steering wheel and drove past her turn.

The two cars followed.

She turned down a side street. The car directly behind her kept going straight. But the car behind that one turned with her.

It was a small sedan—a light color, but in the darkness, it was hard to tell whether it was white—or whether it was a Corolla.

Still, that was one coincidence too many.

She'd been for a run on these side streets many times.

At the stop sign, she turned left.

"Nice and easy," she muttered, watching the sedan behind her turn also.

"Where are we going?" Maggie said.

"I think we're being followed."

"What?"

"I said, I think we're—"

"I heard you! What do I need to do?" The terror crept into Maggie's voice.

"Pull your cap down low over your face—and sit down in the seat a little bit more."

"Will that help?"

"If they're following us, I think they already know it's you." Fenway pushed herself more upright in the seat. "Hang on. I'll try to lose them."

Fenway turned left again, a slow turn around the corner—then when the Accord was slightly out of view of the tailing car, she smashed her right foot all the way to the floor.

The Accord lurched forward, then kept going—fifty, then sixty miles per hour. She blew through the stop sign—no cross traffic, thank God—onto Estancia Canyon Road and barreled toward the freeway.

In her rearview mirror, she saw the white sedan also stop and speed out onto the street, narrowly missing an SUV.

"Yep," Fenway said. "We're definitely being followed."

"Can't you call somebody?"

"Good idea. Hold down the voice activation key on the center console."

Maggie did as instructed. Two fast beeps.

"Call Dez."

The phone began to ring. On the second ring, Dez picked up.

"You *did* talk to McVie, didn't—" said Dez.

"Someone tried to run over Maggie in front of the sheriff's office about a half hour ago."

"Somebody tried to—what?"

"I've got Maggie in the car, and we're being followed—maybe the same car that tried to run her over."

"What—"

"I think it's a white Toyota Corolla."

"Isn't it the same make and model—"

"As the car registered to the Neons? Yes."

"Where are you now?"

"Estancia Canyon Road, heading east. I'm about to get on the freeway. We'll be safer if we're around a lot of other people." Fenway swallowed hard. "I hope."

"No high-speed chases," Dez said.

Fenway's mind raced. "I'll take Ocean Highway south toward Santa Barbara, then go as fast as I can in the left lane. Hopefully I lose my tail. But if there's a white Corolla following me, I want a cruiser to pull them over."

The stoplight ahead of Fenway, just before the Ocean Highway on-ramp, turned yellow.

"Oh, shit," Fenway mumbled.

"What is it?"

"I'm not stopping." Fenway maneuvered into the empty left lane and punched the accelerator. "Hang on, Maggie."

"Fenway, don't—"

The light turned red.

CHAPTER SIXTEEN

A LOUD HONK SOUNDED TO HER LEFT AS FENWAY SPED ACROSS THE intersection. She slid across three lanes, tires squealing, and onto the southbound Ocean Highway on-ramp.

She accelerated onto the freeway as her phone buzzed. Another call was coming in, but she ignored it.

Fenway exhaled and glanced at Maggie. Even in this low light, Fenway saw Maggie's face, ghostly white. "You're okay, Maggie, right?"

"Right." Maggie's voice squeaked.

"The Corolla isn't behind us anymore."

"Bring Maggie back to the sheriff's office," Dez said. "We'll set up protective custody for her."

"Whoever it was tried to run her over in *front* of the sheriff's office," Fenway said. "I'm not bringing her back there. Get protective custody set up for her first."

"Fenway, you need to bring her—"

"I'm keeping our—our prime suspect alive, okay?"

"Have it your way." Dez sighed. "I won't be able to set up a safe house for the next few hours anyway—probably not till tomorrow morning. Fine. Where are you going?"

"Uh—I'll tell you, Dez, but keep this under your hat. If anyone asks, you don't know where she is."

"Fine, I'll play along. I don't know where she is. So where exactly do I not know about?"

Fenway drummed her fingers on the steering wheel. Her apartment was not an option.

Her father's mansion? He had the security—but it was isolated, and it was easy to discover Nathaniel Ferris was Fenway's father. So maybe her father's house wouldn't be a great idea.

It was unlikely anyone on the Las Vegas Neons knew she was dating McVie, though. Maybe Annabel had seen Fenway and McVie together in Maxime's, but she didn't know who McVie was. Perhaps after some digging, she could put two and two together, but the chances were low.

She hoped.

"I'm taking Maggie to Craig's."

"No, no, no," Dez said. "You take her to a hotel or something. A hotel far away from the Broadmere."

"No one on the team knows Craig and I are dating. Maggie will be safe at Craig's apartment."

"Are you kidding? Everyone in town knows. His apartment could be the next place they look."

"We're talking about a member of the team, or the staff, maybe."

"Or a professional hitman with a multi-millionaire backer. Who might even be McVie's client."

Fenway was quiet for a moment. "Yeah, you're right, Dez. A hotel room. We'll get something out of town." Fenway drummed her fingers on the steering wheel. "I'll figure something out. I'll pay cash so it can't get traced. Maybe a motel over in P.Q. Maybe Cactus Lake. I know they take cash. And no one would look for us up there."

Dez was quiet for a moment. "You be careful."

"I will."

Fenway ended the call and looked over at Maggie. "You okay?"

Maggie's hand was gripping the handle next to her head, above the passenger door, and her knuckles were white. "No. You don't think the police can protect me."

Fenway was silent.

"What? We're spending the night at a crappy hotel?"

"I can't think of anywhere else where we can pay in cash and not be—" Fenway stopped mid-thought and turned a few scenarios over in her mind.

She held down the phone button on the center console. Two beeps.

"Call Piper."

Piper picked up on the first ring. "Hey, Fenway! You looking for a dinner companion now that McVie is meeting his daughter?"

"Maybe another time. I need your help."

"I've already left the office."

"I hope it will only take you a few minutes. And I think you can do this from your phone." Fenway hesitated. "I wouldn't ask you this ordinarily, but this is an emergency."

"Ha," Piper said. "You absolutely *would* ask me ordinarily."

"Maybe. But this is still important. Remember when you sent me the credit card when I was in L.A. a couple months ago?"

"Ah, your fugitive days. Those were fun, weren't they?"

"I have someone else in the car with me, Piper."

Piper tittered. "Sorry."

"Did you cancel those cards?"

"Uh—no, I guess I didn't. Why? Did your dad get a bill he wasn't expecting? Did someone skim the numbers?"

"No—I need some, uh, some way to disguise a payment. Can't be under my name."

"Oh. Sure, you should be able to use it."

"Thanks."

"Do you want to tell me what this is about?"

She thought about telling Piper, then heard Dez's angry voice in her head. "I'd love to tell you, but it's an ongoing investigation. Can't give you the details."

"Oh. It must be serious. Is this about the dead soccer coach?"

From the passenger seat, a muffled sob from Maggie.

"Like I said, I can't discuss it."

"Okay, fine. And as much as I'm annoyed that you won't give me the details, you know you can call if you need something." She paused. "Stay safe."

Piper hung up.

Fenway glanced over at Maggie. "Turn your phone off."

"I can keep it on silent if it bothers you."

"No. All the way off. I don't want anyone to be able to track you."

———

Fenway drove the twenty minutes to Paso Querido, and in the small downtown, they pulled into the parking lot of a Harkness Inn & Suites with a *Vacancy* sign lit. "Not the Broadmere," Fenway said, "but it's better than the places that take cash."

"A lot better," Maggie said.

They got out of the car. Live rock music was pouring out of a bar across the street. The singer was loud and slightly off-key, but the music was pounding and sounded fun.

"I don't have anything with me," Maggie said. "I don't have a change of clothes. I don't have a toothbrush. I don't have anything."

"Maybe we can get some of the stuff from the hotel."

Fenway opened the trunk and dug in the pocket of the ugly sweat-pants. She'd remembered correctly—a driver's license and a credit card, both with the name *Molly Lundgren*. The driver's license had a picture of a bald Fenway. She ran her hand over her short hair—she still looked like the picture.

Maggie followed Fenway in the front door and pulled the Red Sox hat down over her eyes. She bit her thumbnail and walked in short, stuttering steps.

Fenway got them a two-bedroom suite, then pulled Maggie into the gift shop and charged a T-shirt, a toothbrush, and some toiletries to the room.

They took the elevator to the third floor and walked to the end of the corridor, where Fenway pulled the key card out and opened the door to their suite. Fenway turned on the lights.

A different color scheme than the Broadmere, and less elegant furniture, but still functional. Sofa, television, coffee table. The doors to both bedrooms were open, queen beds in both rooms.

"Which room do you want?" Maggie asked, clutching the plastic bag of toiletries, the T-shirt draped over her arm.

"Whichever. They look the same."

Maggie walked into the room on the left, dropped her bag and shirt on the bed, then walked out, pacing around the suite.

"You're safe here, Maggie."

"How long do you think I have to hide out?"

"As long as it takes to make sure no one's trying to kill you."

"Sorry—that was rude. I mean, I appreciate everything you've done for me. But I need the practice time. Bonding with the team, running drills, getting comfortable in goal. I had a pretty good workout regimen in the off-season. But I haven't even played a formal scrimmage for months." She plopped herself on the sofa, her brow furrowed.

"Keeping you safe is my number one priority." Fenway sat at the opposite end of the couch from Maggie, who immediately stood and walked into the bathroom, closing the door behind her.

Fenway gritted her teeth, pulled her phone out of her purse, and texted McVie.

Can you talk?

Her phone rang. It was McVie.

"Hi, Craig."

"Hey. Megan only stayed long enough to grab some of her things. I thought you and I could have an evening out. Or maybe an evening in."

"Things got complicated at work."

McVie was silent.

Fenway took a breath. "When I walked out of the office tonight, I saw a police action right in front of the sheriff's office. Swirling red-and-blue lights, a cruiser parked up on the sidewalk, the works."

McVie sucked in air through his teeth. "What happened?"

"After we interviewed Maggie, we let her go. While she was waiting for a ride, someone tried to run her over—right in front of the sheriff's office."

"Is she okay?"

"She jumped out of the way in time."

"You think the driver is the same person who killed Paul Levinson?"

Fenway shrugged. "Maybe. Probably."

"Why isn't Maggie in protective custody?" McVie's voice rose in pitch, if not volume.

"Dez said they'd probably need till the morning to set it up."

"Why the hell are *you* responsible for her?"

"She was hiding next to my car when I got to the parking garage. She's in the bathroom now."

"At your apartment? They could find out where you are—"

"At a hotel."

McVie paused. "I can't believe they let her go. I thought for sure they'd have enough to hold her."

Fenway pursed her lips. "How do you know that?"

"I still have one or two contacts in the sheriff's department."

"They probably *do* have enough to hold her. But Dez doesn't believe Maggie did it. And neither do I."

"Why not?"

"A lot of reasons. She was falling down drunk, for one thing—I don't think she could have lifted a golf club above her head without falling over. And she thought Levinson was crucial to her success. Plus—we're missing some physical evidence that would likely be in the room if she'd murdered him."

"I see," McVie said. Then, a touch of restraint in his voice: "Why did you put yourself in harm's way for someone involved in a murder investigation?"

"I couldn't leave her there when I knew somebody was trying to kill her. And when we drove out of the parking structure, the same kind of car that tried to run her over was following me."

McVie gasped. "What kind of car?"

"It was a white Corolla. But I lost them."

"But if they recognized your car, they could be driving all around Estancia, looking for your Accord."

"We drove out of town."

"Out of town? Where?"

"I—I'm not sure I should tell anyone."

"I know that tone in your voice. You got Piper involved."

"So what if I did?"

"It means things are serious." McVie cleared his throat. "I think I should come stay with you."

"I can take care of myself, Craig."

"Someone is trying to kill Maggie, Fenway. Don't be an idiot. You just learned how to shoot a gun last year. Did you at least *bring* a gun with you?"

"Well—no."

"Let's say the person who ran Maggie over followed you to your hotel. Or figures out you're there. Let's further assume they'll find out what room you're staying in."

"Not very likely. I covered my tracks."

"Even though you don't know how they could find you doesn't mean they can't."

"I think you're being paranoid."

"Let me ask you this: would Piper be able to find you?"

"Of course. She helped me figure out how to cover my tracks."

"But if she hadn't helped you—let's make it, hypothetically, someone as talented as Piper. Could that person find you?"

Fenway was quiet.

"I'm coming over," McVie said. "Where are you staying?"

————

A knock at the door—three quick raps, then two slow ones. Fenway opened the door with the latch on.

"Hey, beautiful," McVie said.

"Don't get any ideas about tonight." Fenway closed the door, unfastened the latch, then opened it again. "I only invited you over here because you make me feel better about keeping Maggie safe."

McVie came in and dropped Fenway's overnight bag on the sofa. "I'd feel better if you moved your Accord around to the back of the hotel."

"I already checked—the back lot is full."

"Then park on the street."

Fenway sighed. "I don't think the Accord will give me away. If the killer passes by this hotel, they'll already know where I am."

"Good point." McVie glanced around the room. "Where's Maggie?"

"Her bedroom. I think she's trying to get some rest."

"Was she okay with me coming over?"

"Not really, but I insisted. I don't think she wants to be judged by the P.I. who thinks she's having an affair."

"I don't—" McVie stopped and shook his head. "No, it doesn't matter. As long as she stays safe."

"I think we're in a pretty good spot. No one knows we're here."

"But the elevators aren't very secure. I came up here without a room key. It makes me a little nervous."

"No one will be looking for Molly Lundgren."

"Oh—you kept your fake ID."

"Only by dumb luck. It was in the pocket of those ugly sweatpants." Fenway elbowed McVie. "And you're always bugging me to clean my car, but I'm really glad I didn't."

"Oh, I'll never hear the end of that one." McVie paused. "Did you get a good look at the Corolla?"

"I saw it this morning in the parking garage. And didn't you see Annabel drive it last night?"

McVie nodded. "It was dark, though. Have you told Dez about the Corolla?"

"Yes. She knows the Corolla was in the parking garage this morning, and she knows I thought it was the same car following us."

McVie cocked his head. "Who else knows Maggie's here?"

"No one. You, me, and Maggie—that's it." Fenway paused. "I should probably call Dez and tell her, too."

McVie dropped his arms to his sides and began pacing around the room. "Okay. If you're sure no one followed you here, we can—" Then he stopped and raised his head.

Fenway turned to look: Maggie was standing in the open doorway to her bedroom.

"Hi, Maggie. Everything okay?"

Maggie shrugged.

Fenway motioned to her. "Maggie, this is Craig McVie."

"You were in the restaurant last night."

McVie nodded.

"I heard you were a private investigator, too."

"He used to be the county sheriff," Fenway offered.

"I heard your client thinks I slept with her husband."

McVie furrowed his brow. "Husband?" Then he caught himself. "Sorry. I shouldn't be talking about my clients. It's unprofessional."

He shot a look at Fenway.

Fenway walked to the sofa and unzipped her overnight bag. McVie's toiletry bag was on top. "I had to tell her something."

"You had to tell—"

"I was in the Uber with Maggie, Craig. She wanted to know why I wound up in the hotel having a drink with her last night. I figured the truth was as good as anything."

"I see," McVie said, crossing his arms.

"Look. I know it wasn't—"

"It's fine," McVie said. "The priority right now is keeping Maggie safe." He looked around the room. "We can push some of the furniture against the door, maybe wedge it against the wall so we're sure the door can't open."

Fenway smiled. "I thought you'd sleep out here so you could be sure no one could break in." She turned to Maggie. "This is kind of a new situation for me. Craig was sheriff for a long time. I'd feel better if he stayed."

Maggie stared at the floor, her eyes unfocused. "Yeah, fine."

McVie and Fenway pushed the sofa up against the door, then Maggie wedged the end table between the back of the sofa and a half-wall near the door. McVie pulled on the sofa from several angles, and it wouldn't move.

"I think this is good enough for tonight," McVie said. "We'll figure out what we're dealing with tomorrow."

"Tomorrow—it's Saturday. Will you have to work?" Fenway asked.

"Let's talk about it later."

Maggie looked from Fenway's face to McVie's, then put her hand over her mouth. "Your client will be pissed if she finds out you helped the woman who's supposed to be sleeping with her husband."

"You let me worry about my client." McVie tried to give Maggie a reassuring grin, but the smile didn't reach his eyes.

"She can still fire you," Fenway said under her breath.

"I'm not leaving, Fenway. Your safety—Maggie's safety—is more important."

They were quiet for a moment. Then Maggie leaned against the wall. "This doesn't seem real."

"I'm sorry," Fenway said.

Maggie swallowed hard. "I feel like I should call the team. Let them know where I am. So they don't worry."

Fenway pulled her laptop out of its case. "I can send the team an email. Say we have you in protective custody. That way, they don't think you're still the prime suspect." She opened the laptop on the coffee table and sat on the sofa.

Maggie walked over and plopped down resignedly on the couch next to her.

A Wi-Fi connection for the hotel appeared on the screen, and Fenway clicked *OK*. The Neons' website appeared.

And the news feed had changed.

Neons release goalkeeper Erskine

Fenway sucked in air through her teeth and looked at Maggie, who stared at the screen, eyes wide.

"They cut me?"

"Oh, Maggie, I'm so sorry."

"They can't cut me! I'm the starting goalie!" Maggie stood. "I didn't even *do* anything!"

"Maybe this is all a misunderstanding."

Maggie glared at Fenway. "The one person who believed in me, and as soon as he's not around, they drop me. I thought you told me my teammates believed in me."

"They do—they do, I know they do. They must have thought you were guilty of—"

"I'll tell you what I was guilty of." Maggie paced around the room, arms folded and head down. "I was having sex with the head coach, that's what I was guilty of."

"But you didn't—"

Maggie shook her head. "Coach Flash kept telling me I wanted it. Saying I wouldn't have come back to play for him so many times if I didn't want it." She scoffed. "Like I had a choice after they drafted me."

Fenway closed her laptop. "We can get this all straightened out tomorrow."

Maggie sat down on the sofa again and put her head in her hands. "What am I supposed to do? This isn't right."

"You can't do anything tonight." Fenway set her computer on the coffee table. "Maybe we can fix this. If the team—one of the coaches, or the general manager, or even the owner—thinks you were involved in Coach Levinson's death, it might be why they released you. Maybe we can get Sergeant Roubideaux to call and set them straight. She interrogated you all day, and we let you go. It's not what we do if we think someone's guilty."

Maggie's shoulders started to tremble. "Think of how it looks, though," she whispered. "He was dead in the hotel room, and I was passed out naked in his bed. The murder weapon and all my clothes were in the shower. I'm so stupid. Of course it looks like I killed him.

And they can't have me around."

A light bulb went off in Fenway's head. "All your clothes were in the shower."

"That's what your sergeant told me. I didn't put them there—at least, I don't think I did."

"Right," Fenway said. "The idea was you killed him with the golf club, washed off the murder weapon and all your bloody clothes in the shower, and then you were so tired—or maybe so drunk—you passed out in the bed."

A dark cloud passed over Maggie's face. "I was definitely drunk."

"But if you had done all that, would you have taken the time to dry off and clean up?"

"I don't know. Drunk me does some crazy shit."

"But you didn't get into bed soaking wet, did you?"

Maggie paused. "Uh, I guess not."

"Not even a little wet, right? Even if you had dried off and gotten rid of the towels, there would have been *some* evidence you'd been in the shower—if you sleep with wet hair, it gets messed up."

"I guess."

"So I don't think you were in the shower. I think you were passed out drunk and you slept right through everything." And what Fenway didn't say: if the killer threw Maggie's clothes in the shower, it looked like they were trying to pin the murder on her.

"So wait a minute," Maggie said. "Do you believe I didn't kill Coach Flash?"

"That's what I've been saying."

"This day has been so crazy," Maggie muttered. "I don't even know if I should pinch myself to try to wake up." She rubbed her eyes. "Maybe I need a good night's sleep." She walked toward the bedroom. "Maybe I'll wake up tomorrow and this will all be a big misunderstanding. Or a dream."

Maggie shut the bedroom door behind her.

Fenway took out her phone and called Dez.

Dez answered on the second ring. "Everything okay?"

"No." Fenway sat forward, lowering her voice. "The Neons just released Maggie."

Dez sighed. "I was afraid of that."

"Why? We didn't arrest her for Levinson's murder. We haven't even named her as a suspect."

"The hotel's housekeeping staff alerted the team this afternoon."

Fenway blinked. "Housekeeping? What do they have to do—"

"They found Sandra Christchurch's diamond tennis bracelet on the floor in Maggie's room."

PART 3

SATURDAY

CHAPTER SEVENTEEN

A HAND ON FENWAY'S SHOULDER. MCVIE'S DEEP VOICE BURROWED through her subconscious. "Fenway, wake up."

"Mmph."

"Maggie's gone."

Fenway sat bolt upright. Her eyes were gummy with sleep, and she blinked hard, willing her eyes to water. "What?"

"Maggie's not here. She left."

"What do you mean, she left? What time is it?"

"It's about six thirty. I went to the bathroom a few minutes ago, then I walked out into the living room and noticed the sofa and the end table weren't next to the door anymore. Then I went into Maggie's room, and she was gone."

"Where did she go?"

"Well, I don't know, Fenway. I just found out, and I came in and woke you up."

"Right, right, sorry." Fenway rubbed her temples, kicking off the sheets.

"She was upset last night, wasn't she?"

"Yesterday would have been hard for anyone." Fenway got out of bed and dug through the overnight bag, finding clean underwear and a bra, but no other clothes. "Especially when she found out the Neons released her. She was really upset." Fenway paused. "I didn't even tell her about the diamond tennis bracelet."

McVie nodded. "I was thinking about that. I know you haven't told me much about her movements yesterday, but from what I could piece together, there's no way she'd have stolen the bracelet. Did she even have an opportunity to go into her hotel room yesterday?"

Fenway nodded. "When Dez walked her out of the hotel, they stopped in her room so she could change."

"Isn't it just as likely that someone planted the diamond tennis bracelet in her room?"

"Someone like who?"

"Like the hotel staff, for one. They take it from Christchurch's room, they realize it's a big deal and they won't be able to pawn it, so they do the next best thing: hide it in the murder suspect's room."

Fenway shrugged. "It's a possibility."

McVie furrowed his brow. "You're not thinking about the tennis bracelet."

"No. I'm trying to keep Maggie safe."

"So let's figure out where she would have gone."

Fenway stood. "Did you bring my work clothes?"

"I even hung them in the closet," McVie said. "Left side, all the way over."

Fenway slide the closet door open. "Maggie may have gone back to the Broadmere to try to get her things." Fenway reached up to take the cream blouse from the rack. Woof. Deodorant first. Definitely deodorant first. She didn't have time to shower.

"Would she have contacted anyone on the team to try to get them to change their minds?"

"It's possible," Fenway said, hurrying into the bathroom, grabbing the deodorant from her case on her way to the toilet. "Dez let her go yesterday without pressing charges. But I thought she believed me when I told her we thought she was innocent."

McVie pulled on his jeans. "She may have in the moment, but sometimes when you replay the day over in your head, you start to think of things differently."

Fenway flushed, then stood and put on her deodorant. "You mean she believed me when she went to bed, but not when she was lying there, staring at the ceiling."

"Right. It's hard to accept you're no longer the prime suspect after the police interrogate you all day." Fenway stopped for a moment. "Or maybe she heard me talk about the tennis bracelet. I tried to keep my voice down."

"The walls are thin." McVie put on a T-shirt, tight on his muscular arms. "Maybe she went to talk to someone on the team to get their take on the situation—figure out what she needed to do."

"Good idea. She might risk contacting someone if she thought she could get back on the team." Fenway buttoned up her blouse, then walked out to the living room. "I guess we start with the Broadmere. It's the most obvious place she would go, right?" She grabbed her purse, opened it, and immediately cursed.

"What is it?" McVie hurried out of the bedroom.

"I left my purse out here like an idiot," Fenway said, rummaging through her bag. "My keys—I think she took my keys."

"How do you—"

"My purse is too light. With all the keys to the offices at work, I've got, I don't know, a zillion keys." Fenway dumped her purse upside down on the coffee table: makeup case, wallet, receipts, sunglasses, a folded piece of paper. But no keys.

McVie knelt down, and Fenway heard a jingle.

"They were on the floor?"

McVie stood, holding a keychain with over a dozen keys, and Fenway's face fell.

"My Honda key is missing."

McVie unfolded a piece of paper that had fallen out of her purse. He opened it, glanced at it, and then showed it to Fenway.

Sorry—I took your car to try to get my job back
Find me at the Broadmere and I'll give you back your key and money
    for gas

"Dammit, Maggie, you idiot." Fenway tossed the paper on the table.

"At least we know where she is."

Fenway scooped up the contents of her purse and dumped everything back in. "Can you drive?"

They rushed out of the hotel room.

From the passenger seat of McVie's Highlander, Fenway took out her phone and dialed. McVie started the engine and raced out of the parking lot.

Three rings. Then the phone picked up, and Dez sleepily exhaled on the other end. "Hello?"

"Maggie's missing."

"Maggie's—what? Fenway?"

Fenway held on as they turned a corner sharply to get onto the highway back to Estancia. "We stayed in a hotel in P.Q. last night, but when McVie got up a few minutes ago, Maggie was gone."

"Gone? Does she realize her life—"

"The Neons released Maggie yesterday—she saw the news online. Soccer is her life, Dez. She left a note—she went to talk to someone on the team to get her job back."

"Wait—you said McVie got up a few minutes ago? What's he doing there?"

"Maggie's life was in danger. Craig thought he could help."

Dez exhaled loudly. "He's not sheriff anymore. He can't get involved with a police investigation just because he's worried his girl-friend is in danger."

"I was trying to keep Maggie out of harm's way until you could set up a safe house. McVie was helping protect her."

"And how is that working out?" Dez snapped.

Fenway was quiet for a moment, then ran her tongue over her teeth and sat up straight in her seat. "Anyway, Maggie's note also says she'll meet me at the Broadmere Hotel to give me my keys. We're headed there now. If you have the safe house set up, we should take her there."

"The safe house will be my next call," Dez said. "Maggie went directly to the Broadmere?"

"I assume she did. It doesn't say if she stopped somewhere else. Oh, and I don't think she knows about the tennis bracelet."

"You mean she doesn't know the team fired her because of the theft?"

"I don't even think she knows the bracelet is missing." Fenway hesitated. "Unless you mentioned it in your interrogation."

"No." Dez paused. "She still had her phone on her?"

"I had her turn it off last night. I didn't want anyone tracking us. But I didn't take the phone away from her."

"Okay. We can check the rideshare companies, see who picked up anyone from the hotel in P.Q."

"Uh—well, she took my Honda."

A note of disbelief in Dez's voice. "She took—"

"Maggie left in the middle of the night. Or early in the morning."

Dez harrumphed. "Like she'd win anyone over waking them up at four in the morning."

"They're all early risers, Dez. Everyone I interviewed was up at five or five thirty."

"Another reason I'm not a professional athlete," Dez said. "Okay —she's in a stolen vehicle. That will make it easier to find her since we can associate her with a crime in progress. It'll make it easier to hold her, too, since there's something we can charge her with."

"I don't want her to get in trouble. I know she's twenty-two, but in a lot of ways, she's just a scared kid."

"We'll figure stuff out after she's in custody." A rustling noise on Dez's end. "What's your Honda's license plate number?"

———

McVie pulled into the driveway of the Broadmere, and Fenway opened the passenger door of the Highlander before McVie had even come to a complete stop. She jumped out and rushed into the hotel lobby, holding her badge up.

The receptionist looked up from his computer monitor. "Oh— officer, is everything okay?"

"Did you see this woman come in here during the last few hours?" Fenway held up her phone, a photo of Maggie from the Neons' website on the screen. "She's with the soccer team."

"Ah, yes."

Fenway let out a sigh of relief. "Oh, good. Did she go up to her room?"

"No, no—I mean, I've seen her, but she hasn't been in here this morning."

"Are you sure? She would have been driving a silver Honda Accord sedan."

"I've been working since midnight. I had a meal break at four, so you might ask Patti."

"Patti?"

"She covered the front desk while I was on break, but she finished her shift at six. You'd have to call her at home."

Fenway ran a hand over her face. "The security footage," Fenway said. "You've got a camera in the lobby, right?"

"Sure. You said a silver Honda? It might be on the parking garage camera."

"Think I can take a look?"

"I'll see if our security team is available."

While the receptionist picked up the phone and dialed, McVie rushed in. "Any luck?"

"Not so far." She motioned with her head to the front desk attendant. "He's checking with the security team."

"I had a quick look in the front parking lot and on the street." McVie ran a hand through his hair. "Your Honda isn't there."

"It might be in the parking garage."

"She said she'd meet you here, right? But that doesn't mean she's here yet. Maybe she was meeting someone at a coffee shop. Or an all-night place like Jack and Jill's." He paused. "I assume she left our hotel to talk to somebody about getting back on the team."

"Okay," Fenway said. "Let's think about who Maggie would talk to."

"If housekeeping found Sandra Christchurch's tennis bracelet in Maggie's room," McVie said, "I assume Christchurch herself made the decision to fire Maggie."

"Not necessarily. Either one of the assistant coaches could have done it."

McVie nodded. "Sure—'we can't have a thief on our team.' Takes a potentially unpopular decision off Christchurch's shoulders, too."

"So she probably talked to Sunday, or Portello, or Christchurch."

"Or a player she trusted. You know, to try to get a good strategy together."

"Like Annabel Shedd. She's the most powerful player on the team —Annabel runs to Christchurch, saying, 'I'm not playing for you unless Maggie is reinstated'?"

"Yeah," McVie mused, "that could be effective."

"Or..." Fenway stared at the floor for a moment.

"What is it?"

"I'm worried."

"About what?"

"Shedd had the key to the white Corolla on Thursday night."

"Are you suggesting that Annabel Shedd tried to run Maggie over?"

"I don't know. We need to figure out who had the key last." Or even if Annabel gave Sunday the key back.

Maybe Lorraine Sunday had the key to the Corolla.

The receptionist hung up and turned to Fenway. "The security office says they can cue up the footage in about ten minutes."

"Thank you," Fenway said. "Would you please ring Annabel Shedd's room?"

"This early on a Saturday?" the man said. "I'm sorry—it's against our hotel policy. No calls before eight o'clock on Saturday."

"Did you see my badge?" Fenway asked. "I know I said 'please,' but it wasn't a request. And I don't need a warrant for a phone call."

The man frowned, then gave Fenway a curt nod. "Shall I ask her to come to the lobby?"

"I can speak with her over the phone."

"Of course." The man gave Fenway a tight smile. He dialed, waited a few moments, then hung up. "No answer."

Fenway glanced at McVie, whose jaw tightened.

"How about the owner?" Fenway said.

"You think a rookie goalkeeper would call the owner of the Neons to convince her to keep her on the team? Besides, if Annabel isn't in her room—"

"She could be in the bathroom. Or going for a morning jog. Even though she's not here, it doesn't mean she's meeting with Maggie."

"Fine," McVie said. "Call the owner."

Fenway turned to the receptionist. "Sandra Christchurch, please."

The man typed into the screen, then frowned and looked up at Fenway. "Ms. Christchurch has a *do not disturb* request on her room."

"A what?"

"She called the front desk last night. They made a note of it—not to be disturbed until ten thirty."

"Call her anyway."

The man hesitated.

"Please call her anyway."

"Calling a guest when they have a *do not disturb* on their line is against corporate policy. I'll get written up."

"Even with the police right here?"

"I'm afraid I don't make the rules. If you had a warrant or subpoena—"

"Never mind." Fenway took the phone out of her purse. "I'll call her myself."

"It'll go straight to voicemail."

"I hope she didn't fly her private plane to Mexico," Fenway murmured.

"Like a dine-and-dash, but with the hotel?"

"She's rich, right?" Fenway whispered, taking a few steps away from the desk as McVie followed. "Why would she care about leaving a hotel without checking out, especially if she's the one who beat her coach over the head?"

McVie blinked. "You—you think *she* killed Coach Levinson?"

"I think she's a viable suspect. She doesn't have a good alibi. The coach would have opened his door for her. And she assembled the press conference so fast, it looked like she didn't know he was dead, even though he'd been dead for hours."

"Don't jump to conclusions. She might have wanted to sleep in. I know she's rich, but I assume she's been busy the last couple of days with everything going on with the team."

Fenway tapped her chin. "I wonder..."

"What?"

"A little bird told me that Sandra Christchurch might sell the Neons."

"A little—" Then McVie raised his eyebrows knowingly. "Ah. Your father."

"What do you think is worth more money, Craig? A team with a head coach who's a sexual predator and who might have lawsuits coming down the line, or a team with a dead head coach?"

"You think that will make any difference to the lawsuits?"

Fenway nodded. "If Levinson isn't around to affirm or deny those claims? Absolutely. I'd think it would be a much weaker case."

"You don't think there's enough evidence to hold Maggie Erskine," McVie said. "There's even less for Sandra Christchurch."

"You're right. But I think Christchurch lied to me about where she was the night Levinson was killed." Fenway stepped back to the front desk and spoke to the clerk. "I need you to call another two rooms."

"Of course."

"Lorraine Sunday and Rocky Portello."

"Oh," the clerk said, "I saw them leave a few minutes before you arrived."

"I thought you said you didn't see anyone."

"I said I didn't see anyone come *in*; you didn't ask me if I saw anyone leave. The coaches came down in the elevators and went out through there." He pointed at the hallway leading to the parking garage.

A light bulb went off in Fenway's head. Of course. Even though it was Saturday, it was the second day of training camp. The coaches would be setting up for the players' arrival. And for that matter, Annabel was probably getting breakfast or in the shower.

"They've got training camp this morning," Fenway said. "We'll have to head over to Nidever University."

"Didn't you want to see the security footage first?" McVie asked.

"Yes, I do."

"I don't think security is ready for you yet," the receptionist offered.

Fenway furrowed her brow but wanted to play it cool. "Let's go up and see if Maggie is in her room." She looked at the receptionist. "Does Maggie Erskine still have a room here?"

The man clicked a few keys on the computer and nodded. "Room 612. Do you want me to call first?"

"I don't think so." She began to turn away, then stopped. "Thank you for your assistance."

"My pleasure."

Fenway and McVie walked to the elevator and Fenway pushed the button. The elevator dinged, the doors opened, and they got in.

McVie pushed 6, and the doors closed. "Do you think Maggie's here?"

"No, I don't."

"Why go up then?"

"I've been wrong before." Fenway paused. "Plus, most of the players are on the sixth floor. We might be able to get some information. Maybe Maggie talked to one of them."

"It's a long shot."

"We'll also go up to the ninth and see if Sandra Christchurch is in."

"Oh—of course. That's probably why the clerk gave you a dirty look when we went to the elevators—he knew you'd do that."

The elevator dinged, and the doors opened onto the sixth floor.

Fenway and McVie stepped out into the hallway. Turning right, they followed the narrow hallway to Room 612.

"You want to do the honors?" Fenway asked.

"I'm only here for my good looks."

Fenway knocked. "Maggie? It's Coroner Stevenson."

Silence.

She glanced at McVie, who shrugged. She knocked again.

Across the hall, a door opened, and a tall Asian woman with short black hair stuck her head out. "Hey—you're looking for Maggie?"

"Yes," Fenway said. "Have you seen her?"

"You must not have seen the news last night. Maggie's not on the team anymore."

"I thought she might have come back to pack."

"Well, if she did, I haven't seen her," the woman said.

"You're—" Fenway squeezed her eyes shut, the name out of her reach. "Darlene?"

"Darcy—Darcy Nishimura. We spoke yesterday at Nidever."

"Right, right. Thanks for letting us know."

Darcy nodded. She shut the hotel room door, and Fenway and McVie were left alone in the hallway again.

Fenway turned and knocked again, louder this time. "Maggie?"

"If she hasn't answered by now," McVie said, "she's either not there or not answering."

Fenway took her phone out of her purse, tapped the screen a few times, and found the phone number for the Broadmere Hotel.

The receptionist picked up on the second ring. "Broadmere Hotel, front desk. How may I direct your call?"

"Good morning. It's the coroner."

"I'm sorry?"

"The law enforcement person who just went up the elevator to Maggie Erskine's room."

"Of course. Sixth floor, correct?"

"Yes. We knocked, but there's no response. Is it possible to get someone up here with a master key and let us into Maggie Erskine's room?"

McVie looked up and shook his head.

"Uh—" the receptionist said.

"Hold on." Fenway placed the call on hold and turned to McVie. "What?"

"Even if the hotel comes up with a key, you can't go in."

"Ordinarily, I know I need a warrant," Fenway said, "but these are exigent circumstances."

"Exigent circumstances are when you think the person in the room is dead—not if you don't know where they are."

"But Maggie is in danger."

"Says you," McVie said. "In fact, everything you've done since you left the office yesterday is predicated on your unsubstantiated statement that Maggie is in danger."

"But she is!"

"I believe you. I talked to Maggie. But look at it from the D.A.'s perspective."

"What does the D.A. have to do with this?"

"Let's suppose you burst in there and find a bloody golf club with Maggie's fingerprints all over it."

"But that's not—"

"Evidence that Maggie did it, whatever it is. Or evidence someone else did."

"So? When there's a missing person, if you have reasonable suspicion the missing person is in danger, you're allowed to enter private property."

McVie rubbed the back of his neck. "Think about what Maggie's defense lawyer might say."

Fenway thought for a moment, then grimaced. "That I made everything up. That I only said Maggie was missing so I could enter her hotel room without a warrant." She looked at McVie. "But you could back up my story."

"We're romantically involved. A good defense lawyer could get reasonable doubt in a jury's mind in an instant."

"Right. Maggie could say I asked her to—I don't know—hide in my Accord to keep herself safe, while instead I'm at the Broadmere planting evidence in her hotel room." Fenway sighed. "And I won't be able to use anything I find in court—and the rest of the investigation will be tainted, even if I'm not on the active investigation."

"And then you'll be back at square one."

Fenway took the call off hold. "You still there?"

"Yes, ma'am."

"I'm sorry—I won't need the room key after all." She apologized for the inconvenience and ended the call, then turned to McVie. "Ready to go?"

McVie stared at the carpeted floor in front of Maggie's hotel room, then pointed at the bottom of the door. "Do you see that?"

Fenway squinted. A corner of cream-colored paper sticking out a quarter inch.

"You should see what that is."

"We can't get the staff to let us into the room, but we can take that paper?"

"The plain view doctrine."

"I'm not sure—"

"Take a picture of it first."

Fenway opened the camera app on her phone and snapped a picture of the paper, then bent down, pulling a pair of blue nitrile gloves out of her purse.

"What is it?" McVie asked.

Fenway snapped on her gloves, then carefully pulled on the corner of the paper. It was thicker than regular paper—cardstock. And it was stuck on the bottom of the door—maybe by something sticky, or maybe the corner of the card got wedged between the door and the seal.

Little by little, more of the card became visible.

A painting was printed on the cream cardstock: flowers in a vase in warm colors. In calligraphy below: *Thinking of You.*

"A greeting card," McVie said, disappointment in his voice.

Fenway patiently wiggled the card back and forth, little by little, until the small greeting card was completely out.

She turned the card over.

Maggie—
I know how happy this makes you
Lorraine

Fenway furrowed her brow. "Lorraine? As in Lorraine Sunday?" She held it out for McVie to read.

"What do you think this refers to?"

Fenway shrugged. "Maybe it's a 'Congratulations, you're our starting goalie' card." She dug in her purse with her free hand for an evidence bag, then found one and put the card inside. "Or maybe..."

"What?"

"You had a good point about Maggie not having enough time to hide a tennis bracelet—much less steal it in the first place. Maybe Lorraine stole it and put it in Maggie's room. Christchurch did say the coaches were in her suite last night for a meeting—Lorraine could have taken it then."

"You're saying Lorraine had a key to Maggie's room, too?"

"I guess that doesn't make sense." Then Fenway shook her head. "Of course. Lorraine Sunday doesn't have a key, but she wants to give the tennis bracelet to Maggie." Fenway got down on her hands and knees, turning her head toward the door and laying it on the carpet. "There's just enough space under this door to *maybe* slip in a thin piece of jewelry like a tennis bracelet." She pushed herself to her feet. "The housekeeping staff found it on the floor. Suppose the bracelet went farther into the room, but the card got stuck?"

"Another potential scenario." McVie looked up and down the hall. "Okay, we look suspicious. We should go."

They walked to the elevator. Fenway's phone rang in her purse. She pulled it out and tapped the screen. "Hi, Sarah."

"Oh, good, you're okay."

"Why wouldn't I—" Fenway grimaced. "Right. I didn't come into the office."

"Usually you leave me a message."

"It's been a crazy morning."

"Then I'll make this quick—I've got the results for the Broadmere staff."

"The results..." Fenway blinked, trying to remember.

"Yesterday," Sarah said, her voice touched with exasperation, "you asked me to see if any of the hotel staff were connected to Paul Levinson."

"Right—was that only yesterday?" Fenway took a few steps down the hall of the sixth floor and lowered her voice so McVie couldn't hear her easily.

"It was," Sarah said. "I found a Broadmere employee whose daughter went to Shellmont University. She was a senior the first year Paul Levinson coached the women's soccer team."

"Was she on the team?"

"I'm still digging into that."

"You have a name?"

"The student was Zuri Washington."

Fenway's mouth fell open. "Ezekiel."

"Yes, that's the father. You've met him?"

"He's been my main contact at the security operations center at the hotel." And he knew the ins and outs of the place. He'd know how to disable the doors in the stairwell to get in and out. He'd know where to stash bloody towels where the CSI team couldn't find them.

Fenway thanked Sarah, ended the call, and walked back to McVie, who reached out and pushed the button for the elevator. It immediately dinged, and the elevator slid open.

"So," Fenway said, pressing 9, "before we conclude that Maggie didn't come back to the hotel, we should check the security footage."

McVie elbowed Fenway gently as the doors closed. "You're still using 'we.'"

Fenway nodded, then looked straight ahead. The brushed silvery surface of the elevator door reflected the colors of their faces and hair and clothes, but no definition to their features.

"Can you pull Maggie's phone records?" McVie asked. "Those might at least tell us who she spoke with."

The elevator stopped and Fenway got out, McVie a step behind her. "It'll take some time—and depending on the phone company, we might need to wait until Monday." Fenway stopped in front of Sandra Christchurch's hotel suite door and turned to McVie. "Hold on. Your client thinks her wife is having an affair."

McVie rocked onto the balls of his feet, then lowered himself back to his heels. "That's right."

"What would she do if she found out you were trying to protect Maggie?"

"It's not like I'm billing her for this time." He paused. "Not unless it becomes relevant to the affair."

"Why are you doing this? Mathilda Montague could fire you—or worse, she could go after your P.I. license."

"Don't worry about it," McVie said softly.

Fenway scratched her head. "You're sticking your neck out on this one, Craig."

McVie motioned toward the door. Fenway rapped just below the eyepiece, then took a step back.

They waited a moment, the hallway eerie in its silence.

McVie glanced at Fenway, who took a step forward and knocked again, more forcefully this time. "Ms. Christchurch? It's Coroner Stevenson. I have a few follow-up questions for you."

"You do?" McVie asked quietly.

"'Have you seen or spoken to Maggie Erskine?' will be the first thing out of my mouth."

But no one opened the door.

"Do you hear anything inside?" McVie asked after a moment.

"No. But it's hard to tell."

Fenway rubbed her chin. "Do you suppose that Maggie somehow managed to talk herself back onto the team? That maybe she's over at Nidever with the coaches?"

Suddenly, the door was pulled open so fast it hit the wall behind it.

"What?" the woman in the room croaked. Fenway blinked a few times—the woman was Sandra Christchurch, but her shoulders were slumped under a long floral robe, her white-blonde hair disheveled, and her gray eyes tired. "I told the front desk I wasn't to be disturbed."

"I don't work for the hotel." Fenway gave her a tight smile. "Have you seen or heard from Maggie Erskine today?"

"I assume the staff made arrangements for her to return to Las Vegas. Or perhaps home," Christchurch said.

"Is that a yes or no?"

Christchurch smiled darkly. "No, I haven't seen her, Miss Stevenson."

"The Las Vegas Neons have a white Toyota Corolla they use—"

"A what?"

"A white Toyota Corolla. Have you used the Corolla in the last two days? Last night, say, around five or six o'clock?"

Christchurch put her right hand on her hip, her left hand holding the door open. "Coroner, I don't drive anywhere I don't have to. Now —if there's nothing else, let me get back to bed. I've had two late evenings in a row, and I need to be alert for a meeting later this morning."

"My apologies," Fenway muttered, and Christchurch let go of the door, the automatic mechanism slamming it shut.

CHAPTER EIGHTEEN

FENWAY AND MCVIE STEPPED OUT OF THE ELEVATOR INTO THE lobby. The receptionist was talking on the phone, the receiver pressed to his ear. He made eye contact with Fenway, then pointed to his ear with his free hand. Then, in a stage whisper: "I believe security is ready to review the footage."

He listened for a few more seconds, then hung up. "Yes, they're ready for you now. I can take you to the security office if you like."

"I know the way," Fenway said. "Is Ezekiel Washington on shift?"

The receptionist gave a nod as Fenway and McVie crossed the lobby into the hallway. Then Fenway stopped.

"You need to wait for me, Craig."

McVie gave Fenway a mischievous smile and held up both hands with his thumbs touching and index fingers extended. "Whatever. I bring you down here early on a Saturday, and you abandon me in the lobby."

"What's with the hand gesture?"

"I just saw my teenage daughter, remember? I'm trying to be more hip." McVie grinned and dropped his hand to his side. "I'll wait for you in the car."

They separated, McVie leaving out the front door, Fenway following the hallway. At the security office door, she knocked.

The door opened, and Ezekiel's head appeared. "Why, Coroner Stevenson," the man said, opening the door farther. "Nice seeing you two days in a row."

"Hi, Ezekiel. I need to see the camera footage from early this morning. The front parking lot as well as the recordings of the parking garage."

"Come on in. Bobby told me you needed the recording cued up to midnight."

Fenway smiled and stepped inside the security office, closing the door behind her.

"Oh, before we get started on the new video," Ezekiel said, "I got Friday's copy of the team's sign-out sheet for the Toyota Corolla you were asking about." He pulled open a file cabinet drawer at his feet and pulled out a folder. "On Thursday night, Annabel Shedd checked out the car. She hasn't checked it back in yet."

"Right. I forgot to ask earlier—you said you don't keep the key here. Who usually has it?"

"Two keys—Coach Levinson has one, and Coach Sunday has the other."

Fenway tilted her head. "Who usually signs the car in? The player who took the car, or the coach?"

"I don't know the team's protocol."

"And what's to keep Coach Sunday—or Coach Levinson—from taking the car out and not signing it back in first?"

Ezekiel shrugged. "As far as I'm concerned? Nothing. Now, if it's against a team rule, it's on them to enforce it."

"Who else has access to the car keys?"

"I have no idea."

"There isn't a key that the team gave to the hotel? Maybe the valet key?"

"If there is, no one told me about it."

That sounded like a no—but it was carefully phrased. Fenway nodded, not calling him out on the non-answer just yet. Ezekiel turned to the bank of monitors.

"It's all ready to go. I'm starting at 23:45. Figured you'd want a little cushion."

They reviewed the footage. After an hour sitting through sped-up recordings of both the parking lot and the parking garage, it was clear Fenway's Accord had never entered.

Fenway stood to leave.

"Sorry you didn't find what you were looking for, Coroner."

"No worries. It was a long shot anyway." She opened the door, then turned back around. "Oh—one more thing, Ezekiel."

"Sure."

"I couldn't place your accent at first, but you're from South Carolina."

He raised his hand with an easy smile. "Guilty as charged."

"Are you familiar with Shellmont University?"

Ezekiel slapped the table lightly. "Sure, sure. My daughter graduated in mechanical engineering from Shellmont. Summa cum laude, too. Proudest day of my life." He beamed.

"Did you know that Paul Levinson was soccer coach when Zuri was there?"

His easy smile slowly slid off his face. "How did you know my daughter's name?"

Fenway shrugged. "It's an investigation. We cover all our bases."

Ezekiel frowned. "My daughter didn't play sports in college. I wouldn't be able to name any of the coaches there."

"You had no idea that Coach Levinson ran the women's soccer program while your daughter—"

His dark brown eyes bored a hole into Fenway. "Absolutely none."

Fenway opened her mouth to ask a follow-up question but saw the look on Ezekiel's face and decided to change tactics. "That's good. You'll forgive me—I had to ask. They want us covering all the bases, you know."

He nodded, his eyes wary. "I understand. You have a good rest of your day."

"Thanks. You too."

Fenway made her way through the hallway and back to McVie's Highlander in the parking lot. He was engrossed in his phone and jumped slightly when Fenway rapped on the window.

Fenway opened the door after McVie unlocked it. "No dice. The Accord never came back here."

"I have something—and it might be urgent."

Fenway sat and put her seat belt on. "What is it?"

"I was about to get into the car when the player we met on the sixth floor ran up to me."

"Darcy Nishimura."

"She was about to get on the team bus to go to practice, but she saw me in the parking lot. She and I had an interesting conversation. Darcy said Maggie sent her an email this morning, and she just got it. She was worried about Maggie's safety."

"Wait—an email from Maggie? How early?"

"About five thirty. I think she was ready to show it to me, but she asked if I was with the police."

"And you told her no?"

"Impersonating a police officer is a felony, Fenway, even for a former sheriff. I told her to forward it to you immediately. Fortunately, I had a few of your business cards in the center console. I think she was planning to send it to you before practice started."

Fenway took out her phone and clicked on her email.

"Nothing but spam."

"Check your junk folder."

Fenway clicked again. "Empty. All right, I guess we have even more reason to go over to Nidever now."

———

The ride to Nidever University seemed to take longer than usual. Fenway stared out the passenger window through the gray morning mist. The low clouds made it difficult to see too far, and McVie kept his lights on.

She looked over at him. She admired his jawline, the cut of his shirt, his eyes staring intently at the road ahead. Dark circles underneath, though. He looked tired.

When he'd been sheriff, sometimes the demands of the job made him tired, too, but he seemed to enjoy the work. Running his own business—Fenway wasn't so sure. It seemed to take a lot out of him. Maybe part of it was the feast-or-famine business model of a P.I. agency, with fickle clients and seasonal work.

"Do you enjoy your job, Craig?"

McVie twitched his lips to the side and glanced at Fenway, then focused his eyes back on the road. "I don't know. Sometimes I do. When I have an interesting case to work on, I get to use my investigative skills. Honestly, before you came along, I rarely got to use those at the sheriff's office. It was always domestic disputes or busting drug dealers."

"And now?"

"As a P.I.? Now it's cheating spouses or parents who think their kids are on drugs."

"All you did was move a little further back on the timeline, huh?"

"No—I get the people who don't have enough evidence to get the cops involved. Most of the time, my clients are wrong."

"Really? Even in the cheating spouse cases?"

"One client came in completely distraught. Her husband said he was working late, but she called him in his office and he wasn't there. So I followed him the next time he said he was working late. He left the office on time—I thought for sure I'd follow him to a hotel. But no. He went to the beach down at Vista del Rincón, got out of his car, and watched the sun set. And then he got back in his car and started sobbing."

"Sobbing?"

"Yep. About, I don't know, five or ten minutes later, he got ahold of himself, started the car, and drove home. He went to Vista del Rincón twice a week, later and later, of course, as the days got longer."

"So—what happened?"

"I told the wife. She didn't want to believe me. She said she *knew* he was cheating. The next time, I took a video of the whole thing. She accused me of doctoring it, but she paid me."

"Did you ever figure out why the husband was at the beach?"

"He'd gotten a big promotion at work a couple of months before he started 'working late.' I don't know for sure, but my theory is that he hated it and didn't want to tell his wife. Call it an educated guess."

"You'd think it would be a relief to find their spouse *isn't* cheating."

"A lot of people are so sure, they refuse to believe anything else. They *want* their spouse to be cheating on them or want their child to be addicted to meth. They're so convinced they're right they won't even look at the evidence in front of them." He shook his head. "There are exceptions, of course, but mostly this job keeps whittling away at my faith in humanity."

"Because people suck," said Fenway.

"Right," McVie said.

"You're not driving out to Vista del Rincón after work and crying, are you?"

McVie's mouth curved into a sad smile. "Not yet."

Fenway tilted her head. "Have you thought about doing something else?"

McVie shook his head. "First of all, I know Piper took a big chance coming into my employ. And I don't want to let her down. Second, I owe it to myself to spend at least a couple of years at this." He rubbed his forehead. "I've got enough money in the bank where I could go without a client for a couple of months." McVie looked at Fenway out of the corner of his eye. "And it doesn't hurt that business is up."

"Business is up? That's great!"

"I don't know if it's because I'm a good investigator. I'm pretty sure it's because I'm now the only private eye in Estancia."

Fenway bit her lip. "Was it a mistake for me to go out to dinner with you on Thursday night? Maybe your date shouldn't have been a law enforcement representative."

"Lots of deputies have side jobs." McVie sighed heavily. "Callahan works private security, and I don't think he's the only one." He turned his attention completely to the road in front of him. "When are you planning to give Dez an update?"

"Oh—now, I guess," Fenway said, taking her phone out of her purse. Dez picked up on the first ring.

"I know, I know," Dez said grumpily. "I got held up. I'm almost there."

"Don't bother—the Broadmere was a bust. We left a couple of minutes ago. The team is having their training camp again this morning, so we're on our way to Nidever University."

"McVie is *still* with you?"

"We're trying to find Maggie." Fenway paused. "How's the safe house coming?"

"Still working on it."

After Fenway hung up, McVie drummed his fingers on the wheel. "I don't suppose there's any chance of stopping for breakfast."

Fenway sucked in air through her teeth. "Why don't you drop me off at Nidever and then go eat? You can bring me back something."

"Oh, can I?" A smile touched the corners of his mouth as they passed the Nidever University campus sign.

"You know how irritable I get when I'm hungry." She punched him lightly on the arm. "Hopefully this won't take too long, and we can get Maggie into a safe house. I still want to spend time with you this weekend."

"In that case, maybe I'll use the time you're at Nidever to put my reports together. So we can go to a movie or a *real* dinner date." He pulled into the parking lot behind the soccer fields, then parked.

Fenway leaned over and kissed his cheek. "I'll text you when I'm done. Hopefully, Maggie is here and has my car."

"Or maybe someone knows where she is, anyway."

Fenway smiled, grabbed her purse, and exited the car. She took her badge out of her pocket and clipped it to the belt loop on her trousers.

The soccer pitch was about a hundred yards from the parking lot. Fenway felt her flats grow wet again as she trudged through the damp grass.

Much like the day before, the players ran drills on the field. They shuttled back and forth between two lines of orange cones while Coach Portello walked alongside, a gray windbreaker on, a Las Vegas Neons cap low on his head, a scowl on his mustachioed face.

Lorraine Sunday stood on the sideline in her black-and-gold Neons tracksuit, and as Fenway walked up behind her, she turned.

"Coroner Stevenson," she said. "I'm glad to see you."

"You are?"

Sunday nodded. "I received an email this morning—didn't read it until I was on my way to the field, and to be honest, I was a little conflicted on what to do. Now that you're here, I can show it to you."

"What a coincidence," Fenway said. "I've got something I want to show you, too."

Sunday pulled her phone out and tapped on the screen. "Coach Portello and I both got this email, as well as a few of the players Maggie was close to."

"Like Darcy Nishimura?"

"I believe so." Coach Sunday handed the phone to Fenway, who began to read.

To: Lorraine Sunday, Rocky Portello, Annabel Shedd, Darcy Nishimura, Kylee Hathaway, Elena Campos
From: Maggie Erskine
Sent: Saturday, March 23 5:41 AM
Subject: I'm sorry

To my teammates and coaches—

I apologize for letting you all down. I had everything in the palm of my hand, and I let it slip through my fingers because I made some bad decisions.

I can't undo what I did to Coach Flash. We had so much promise this season, and it's all thrown away because of me.

I can't go to jail and I can't disappoint my parents.

If the police are reading this, the towels I used to clean up the blood are in a trash can at Paseo Fuentes Park.

—M

"We're worried," Lorraine said. "It looks like a suicide note."

Fenway bit her lip and felt her heart race. "It ticks all the right boxes. Regret. Thinking she has no way out. Shame." She rubbed her forehead. Sent before six o'clock—over two hours ago. She glanced up at Coach Sunday, whose jaw was tight, a vein in her forehead prominent. "What is it?"

"I called 9-1-1. But I couldn't tell them where Maggie was. I assumed she was still being held by the police." Sunday shook her head. "I debated calling her mother, but I didn't want to talk to her without having more to say. I called Maggie's phone, and she didn't pick up."

"So you just came to practice?"

"Rocky was driving when I read the message. I told him about it. He said he hadn't checked his email yet."

Fenway cocked her head. "He didn't ask if she was all right? He didn't turn around and go back to the Broadmere?"

"No." Sunday hesitated. "To be honest, it felt like it wasn't real."

"What do you mean?"

"That's not exactly the right word for it—but, you know, have you ever gotten an email from a co-worker that wasn't accurate? It mischaracterized something you did, or misrepresented the facts so the co-worker could shift blame or something? Sometimes you can't even put your finger on it; it feels, I don't know—*off*."

Fenway nodded. "Yeah, I've worked with those kinds of people."

"That's how this email felt. I hate to say Maggie was dramatic, but she was young. You've already seen how Coach Levinson set her up to think forcing her into a sexual relationship was okay. The email sounded off. It sounded like she was reaching out for attention— maybe a misguided attempt to say that if we got her back on the team, she wouldn't kill herself. Or maybe setting herself up for an insanity defense for killing Coach Flash." Sunday crinkled her nose. "It's more likely to have the opposite effect, but you can't tell Maggie that."

"You shared your opinion with Coach Portello?"

"Yes. He said he thought Maggie's confession was true, but he agreed the rest of it sounded like she was trying to get attention. Then he reminded me Maggie wasn't on the team anymore. Our priority was the well-being of our current players."

"He wanted to wash his hands of the whole thing?"

"Everyone deals with stuff like this differently," Sunday said. "Maybe Rocky's in denial. He's acting like Coach Levinson is out sick."

"Can you forward me that email?" Fenway said, pulling out her phone. She gave Coach Sunday her email address, and Sunday sent the email off. Fenway's phone dinged with the receipt notification.

"One more thing, Coach Sunday."

Sunday turned to Fenway, unblinking.

Fenway took the greeting card in the evidence bag out of her purse. "What can you tell me about this card?" She handed it to Sunday.

Sunday frowned. "I've never seen it before."

"Turn it over."

Sunday blinked, then looked closer. "Am—Are you suggesting I gave Maggie something with this card?"

"Did you?"

"This isn't my card."

"That's your name."

"But it's not my handwriting."

Fenway looked up from the card to stare Sunday in the face. "It's not?"

"No. I don't know who wrote this, but it wasn't me."

Fenway ran a hand over her hair. "Excuse me for a moment."

"I've never seen this before, Coroner." Sunday frowned, a waver in her voice. "Someone's trying to impersonate me."

Fenway nodded and turned away.

Walking away from the field, trying to get out of earshot, Fenway tapped on her phone and forwarded the email to Dez, with Sarah on the cc: line. Then she called her.

"Fenway—I thought I might be hearing your voice."

"Really?"

"As soon as I got off the phone with you, I got a call from dispatch. Maggie sent an email to some of her teammates and coaches."

"Right—I forwarded it to you."

"I was close to the Broadmere anyway, so we did a check of Maggie's room. No answer at the door, so we got a master key and went inside."

Fenway paused—why could Dez go in and not her? But of course —because the email looked like a suicide note. Exigent circumstances that Fenway hadn't had earlier.

"No sign of Maggie," Dez continued. "We found her laptop, though. Took it into evidence, and we called Patrick in so he might be able to bypass the login and see if it was the machine that sent the email."

"Maggie confessed to killing Coach Levinson in the email," Fenway said, "but something isn't right. One of her coaches said Maggie was trolling for attention, but I don't think Maggie ever went back to the Broadmere. She's not on camera."

"But haven't you established that whoever killed Paul Levinson was able to use the stairwell and evade the cameras?"

Fenway clicked her tongue. "Yeah, yeah. Still, I think the email is suspicious."

"You think someone else wrote it and is trying to frame Maggie?"

"Maybe more than Maggie," Fenway said. She told Dez about the card she'd found wedged under the door. "If Lorraine's card is fake, maybe the email is too. Someone could be trying to put the blame on Maggie. So they might kill her and try to make it look like a suicide."

"We've already got an APB out on Maggie," Dez said. "And an APB out on your car, too. I've pulled a couple of deputies to sweep the highway between P.Q. and Estancia, but she could literally be anywhere. If she sent the email from her phone and not the PC in the hotel, she could be halfway to Mexico by now, or halfway to Vegas— or she could really have intended self-harm. How many bridges or canyons or cliffs are there within a hundred-mile radius of Paso Querido?"

Fenway was silent.

"You're at the university?"

"Yeah."

"Ask all the players when they saw Maggie last. What her state of mind was, that kind of thing."

"I'll ask them if there are any local places Maggie talked about. Maybe she wanted to see the ocean one last time." Fenway's voice caught, and she cleared her throat. "Or the waterfalls up by Querido Pass."

"Uh—look, Fenway, I know you were trying to do the right thing by keeping her safe. Taking her to P.Q. was the right thing to do. I probably would have asked for backup from someone I trusted—like McVie—if I had been in your situation. This situation with Maggie? You went above and beyond. If it turns out she *did* kill herself, and even if it turns out she murdered Paul Levinson, it's on her. Not on you."

"Thanks, Dez."

"I gotta go. Patrick's calling."

Fenway ended the call and walked to the sideline of the soccer field.

She stood next to Sunday. "When was the last time you saw Maggie?"

"Thursday evening, before she and Annabel went to dinner. Girl was already a couple of drinks in."

"Did Maggie mention anything she wanted to see around Estancia?"

"We're here for training camp, not for sightseeing."

"That doesn't mean Maggie didn't *want* to see the Querido waterfalls or go down to Vista del Rincón. I'm trying to find where she might be. Did she mention anything? Any particular beach? Whale watching? Going all the way to Yosemite, maybe?"

Sunday shook her head. "She was focused on soccer. When she wasn't playing or practicing, she was going over strategy with Coach Flash—or, you know, she *said* she was."

"Right."

"For what it's worth, I don't believe Maggie killed herself. Either she's hiding out somewhere, hoping this will all blow over, or she ran."

"Even if she never plays soccer again?"

Coach Sunday sighed. "I don't know. You're the expert."

"The last time I spoke with Maggie," Fenway said carefully, "she was heartbroken about getting kicked off the team. That was last night—and this morning, I was under the impression she hoped to fight her way back."

"Fight her way back?"

"Maybe by talking to the owner." Fenway glanced quickly at Sunday. "Or someone she trusted. Like a coach."

"She didn't reach out to me." Coach Sunday clicked her tongue. "I wish she had."

Fenway hesitated, then barged ahead. "Any thoughts as to who could have written that card?"

Coach Sunday shook her head. "It makes me angry. If she saw that card and thought I was being inappropriate, maybe that kept her from calling me. Maybe she got desperate and *did* write that stupid email."

Fenway nodded, searching Sunday's face for signs of lying—but it was hard to tell. "Are you familiar with a white Toyota Corolla? It seems to belong to the team."

Sunday nodded. "We use it as sort of an errand car. Most of the players didn't bring a car here, so we allow some of the players to check the Corolla out. Go grab groceries, go to dinner. There's often a mad dash on the nights off. There's a sign-out sheet."

"Do the coaches ever borrow the Corolla?"

"Not since I've been part of the coaching staff," Sunday said. "We either drove our own cars here from Vegas, or the team gives each coach a long-term rental."

"But you hold the keys."

"Oh—right, Coach Levinson has one of the Corolla keys, and I have the other."

"I think I saw Paul Levinson's red Italian sports car in the parking garage," Fenway said. "Is it his personal car, or was it a rental from one of those exotic car places?"

"It's his own ridiculous car. Didn't you see the license plate?"

Fenway blinked, then remembered. "Oh, right—*FLASHEEE*, with three E's at the end. I think our forensics team is examining his car. But I'm concerned about the Corolla. Do you know where it is now?"

"I expect it's back in the parking garage," Sunday said. "Where it should be."

"Do you know if anybody took it out yesterday?"

"I know Annabel Shedd borrowed the car on Thursday night. I don't know if anybody else took it out after she brought it back."

"What's the checkout process?" Fenway asked. "You said you had a sign-out sheet, right?"

Sunday nodded.

"First come, first serve?"

"The players can reserve the car if they want."

"Did Annabel reserve the Corolla for Thursday night?"

"No, no one had reserved it, so I signed it out to her and gave her the key."

"Honor system?"

"I admit it's not efficient." Coach Sunday tilted her head. "You have a lot of questions about Annabel taking out the Corolla."

Fenway gave Coach Sunday a small smile. "And I'm afraid I'm not done yet. Do you remember what time Annabel said she'd bring it back?"

"She told me she'd bring the car back at player curfew."

"When is that?"

"Ten o'clock on nights before practice."

"Even when you're not starting until after lunch?"

"Even then."

Fenway tapped her chin. "Did she bring the key back?"

"Not to me," Lorraine said. "But the players usually bring the key back the next morning if they've got the car out close to curfew."

"And she would have given the key back to you?" Fenway asked.

"Well—she didn't give it back to me. Annabel might have returned the key to the security office or given it to Coach Flash." Coach Sunday smiled. "Most of the players are fairly responsible, but some of the younger ones haven't been out on their own—especially the rookies. They might go out with the car and maybe have too much to drink at dinner. Or pop a tire in a dirt lot in front of a country western club. It's better if Coach Flash and I both have a key so the two of us can do damage control if it's necessary."

"Not Coach Portello?"

"He doesn't want to deal with the sign-out process. It's just as well —we only have two keys anyway."

"I see," Fenway said. "And you don't have the Corolla key now."

Sunday shook her head. "With everything that happened yesterday morning, I didn't think to ask Annabel for the key back. I expect security would contact me if they got it, but this early in training camp, we haven't established a routine yet."

"I see." Fenway tapped her chin. "I'd like to talk to the players—find out when they last saw Maggie and see if they have any suggestions for where she may have gone."

Coach Sunday wrinkled her nose. "You don't think she went to turn herself in, do you? I know the email says she can't go to jail, but—"

"She hasn't yet. Not as far as I know."

Sunday snapped her fingers. "Her parents."

"What—Maggie might have gone to see her parents? They're in Arizona—"

"No, no, that's not it. Her father passed away two years ago." Sunday pulled her phone out, tapped a few times on the screen, and held it out for Fenway to see. "Look. 'I can't disappoint my parents.' Parents—plural. But she only has one."

"Maybe her mother remarried?"

"No."

Fenway frowned. "Maybe it was a typo. Or an autocorrect error."

Coach Sunday took her phone back. "But wouldn't Maggie have written, 'I can't disappoint my mom'?"

Fenway didn't speak for a moment. Sunday might have a point—the email might be a hoax.

And that meant Maggie was in danger.

"You're right," Fenway said. "Thanks for your time." She turned to the field; Annabel was running a passing drill with three other players. Fenway walked onto the pitch, making a beeline for Shedd.

"Hey!" Coach Portello's voice boomed across the field. "What do you think you're doing?"

Fenway kept walking, but Portello ran up to her. "I'm talking to *you*."

"I'm about to interview a witness."

"No, no. You talked to all the players already. I was accommodating yesterday—you took all my players away from practice. You're
not doing it two days in a row."

"Yesterday's interviews were about Coach Levinson's murder
investigation," Fenway said. "Now we have a missing persons case."

"This is outrageous."

"You think it's outrageous that your head coach was murdered
and now your starting goalie is missing? I agree."

Coach Portello took a deep breath, still walking beside Fenway. "I
understand you have a job to do, but Maggie isn't with the team
anymore. You had her in custody all day yesterday, and I was led to
believe she was the prime suspect." He pursed his lips. "Do you know
I received an email confession from her this morning?"

"I've seen the email, yes."

"So why are you interrupting our training again? I have the monu-
mental task of getting our players ready for our opening match, and
without a head coach or goalie, I just leveled up in difficulty."

"One of your players may have been involved in Maggie's disappearance."

"This is ridiculous," Portello said. "It's borderline harassment."

"I only need ten minutes, Coach."

Portello scowled and looked at the ground.

"I find it strange that Maggie was a member of this team for a
year, yet you don't seem to care if she's missing."

"She was a major talent, yes. I didn't want her to leave. But it's
water under the bridge."

"So that's it? She's no longer a player on your team, so you don't
care that she may be in danger?"

"I still have a job to do, if you haven't noticed," Portello said.
"Besides, she was having an inappropriate relationship with Coach
Flash, whether or not she was the one who beat him to death."

Fenway bit the inside of her cheek. Portello sounded like he was blaming Maggie for her own sexual coercion. "If you prefer," she said, taking a few steps closer to the assistant coach, "I can start with you." She stared into his eyes—dark circles were underneath, and his skin was paler than the day before. Perhaps the head coach's murder was taking a grimmer toll on Rocky Portello than he was letting on.

"Me?"

"Maggie was planning to talk to someone this morning about getting back on the team. Maybe it was you."

Portello shook his head vehemently. "I don't know anything about that. If she was planning to see me, she either changed her mind, or we missed each other."

"Missed each other?"

"Well—I called her to see what her status was for practice today. Then I found out she'd been let go. So if she called me back, I didn't get it."

"Where were you this morning, Rocky?"

"Me? You think I had something to do with her disappearance?"

"Can you answer the question, please?"

"Okay. Lorraine and I met for a quick breakfast at half past six. We grabbed bagels and coffee, then we left the hotel. We were here a few minutes after seven."

"Before that?"

"I showered and dressed."

"You were in your hotel room all night?"

"What?"

"All night—from the time you went to bed until you left to meet Coach Sunday for breakfast?"

"Oh—uh, yes. All night."

"You didn't leave your room to get ice or a snack from the vending machine?"

He hesitated. "No."

"You're sure?"

"I had trouble sleeping. I thought about getting up, but I didn't."

Fenway nodded. "And whose decision was it to release Maggie?"

"Like I said, she was a distraction. She was Coach Flash's project anyway—she's got talent but no discipline."

"So it was your decision?"

He set his jaw. "Sandra Christchurch made the call. Once housekeeping discovered her bracelet in Maggie's room, that was it."

"She thought Maggie had taken the bracelet?"

He sighed. "I tried to tell Sandra she hadn't been in her room all day. But you already know Maggie was the prime suspect in the coach's murder, and she was banging him. This was the last straw."

Fenway blinked. *She was banging him.*

Did Portello not see Levinson as the bad guy in this situation? Did he think Maggie was the instigator, using sex to get the starting goalie position, rather than the victim of a predator?

Fenway stopped about fifty feet from where Annabel was running the drill. "Do you know anything about where the team's white Toyota Corolla was at any time on Friday?" Fenway asked.

"That's the car for players to use if they need to." Portello frowned. "Given what happened yesterday, the players' use of the team car is a policy I'd like to rescind."

"Yes, but where was the Corolla yesterday?"

"How should I know? I don't have a key for it. Coach Flash and Coach Sunday do. As far as I know, it's wherever Annabel left it."

"Ah. An excellent transition to my questions for Annabel." Fenway turned away from Portello. "Annabel," she called across the field, "can I speak to you for a moment?"

"Hey, hey," Portello said, "I talked to you so you *wouldn't* speak with my players. They have to get their heads in the game."

Fenway unclipped her badge from her trousers and held it up. "If you'd known where the Corolla was, Coach, I might have the answers

I need. But as you said, the car is wherever Annabel left it. And I need to know where that is."

"You're a real piece of work, Coroner."

"I'll take that as a compliment."

Annabel jogged over. "Yes?"

Portello stared daggers at Fenway but turned on his heel and walked away.

"Let's talk for a minute," Fenway said, stepping sideways off the pitch, away from Portello. "I've got a few more questions."

"Is it about the weird email Maggie sent?"

"I do have some questions about the email—but first, did you know a white Toyota Corolla tried to run her over yesterday?"

Annabel's head snapped up. "What? No!"

"The team has a white Toyota Corolla," Fenway said quietly. "You were the last person to check out the Corolla Thursday night."

"You know where I was. I was having dinner with Maggie. You're also fully aware Maggie didn't come back to the hotel with me." Annabel kicked at the turf with her cleat. "I left the restaurant, I came back to the Broadmere, and I went to bed."

"Where is the key to the Corolla now?" Fenway asked.

"I gave it—" Annabel stopped, furrowed her brow in thought, and stared at the ground for a moment. "I guess I forgot to give it back. I would have returned it to Coach Sunday yesterday morning, but after we heard about Coach Levinson, it completely slipped my mind."

"So you had a key to the Corolla all day yesterday?"

Annabel frowned and crossed her arms. "I didn't take the car anywhere on Friday," she said. "And if anybody says they saw me with it, they're lying."

"Where is the key now?" Fenway asked.

"I took it out of my purse when I came back from that fancy restaurant." Annabel dropped her arms to her sides. "What did I do with it?" Her brow creased, then she brightened. "Oh, right, I knew I'd be seeing Coach Sunday on Friday morning, so I put it in my gym bag. But then when I heard Coach Flash was dead—I guess I forgot about it." She looked at Fenway, then her eyebrows knitted. "Are you telling me you think *I* tried to run her over?"

"I'm covering all avenues of inquiry."

"I was trying to *protect* her. Why would I try to hurt her?" Annabel clenched her fists.

Fenway shrugged. "It doesn't matter what makes sense to me. It only matters what made sense to the killer at the time. And someone tried to run Maggie over with the car you last had in your possession."

"I swear I didn't try to run Maggie over. I didn't even touch the car after I got back to the hotel on Thursday night." Annabel's chin quivered. "Did you ever think that there might be a bunch of other keys to the Corolla? The other coaches?"

Fenway shook her head. "Only Coach Levinson and Coach Sunday. And you have Coach Sunday's key."

"I don't know what to tell you. I didn't touch the Toyota on Friday."

Fenway rubbed her chin. She had yet to do an inventory of Coach Levinson's possessions. Could his key be accounted for? For that matter, could Coach Sunday's? Fenway had never seen the key. "If you still have the Corolla key, I need it."

Annabel fixed Fenway with a steely gaze. "Come on," she said thickly.

Annabel took off at a fast walk across the pitch, onto the concrete walkway, and across the quad. Fenway could barely keep up with her. Annabel said nothing, her shoulders tight. She didn't look back at Fenway.

Annabel kept up the rapid pace, turning behind the athletic building offices. As Fenway went around the corner, a locker room came into view, a large *W* painted on the wall on the side of the building.

The soccer star pushed the door to the locker room hard, and its hinges squealed in protest. Annabel's cleats clomped on the tile floor of the locker room with every step, the heavy footfalls echoing throughout the room, bouncing off the metal lockers and the hard surfaces of the sinks, the benches, and the floor. Annabel stopped at a locker about halfway down the first row, twisted the lock back and forth quickly, and opened the metal door. She thrust her hand inside. Grabbing her gym bag with the *Desert Treasures* logo, she rummaged around for a moment.

"What's the matter?"

"I thought for sure—" Annabel let out an exasperated sigh. "I thought the key was under my sweatshirt."

"No key?"

"No sweatshirt. Hold on." She dug in her gym bag further, then pulled out a key fob with the Toyota logo on it. She held it out wordlessly to Fenway, putting her bag back in the locker with her other hand, then slammed the locker shut.

Fenway took the key. "Thank you."

Annabel glared at Fenway and stomped out of the locker room.

The door slammed behind her, and the locker room was eerily quiet.

CHAPTER NINETEEN

There was a bench between the rows of lockers, and Fenway sat down heavily on it. She rested her elbows on her knees, then dropped her head into her hands, staring at the floor between her feet.

After a moment, she dug in her purse and pulled out an evidence bag, then dropped the key inside.

Maggie was in trouble; Fenway was sure of it. She suspected whoever had run Maggie off the road had written the fake suicide note and would try to finish the job.

On one hand, Annabel was the perfect suspect on paper. She was the last person Fenway could definitively put into the white Corolla. She admitted she was in Sandra Christchurch's room—so she could have stolen the tennis bracelet. And she had perhaps the strongest motive of anyone to kill Paul Levinson.

On the other hand, Annabel always tried to protect Maggie. Why would she hurt her?

As soon as the question flitted across Fenway's mind, the answer did too: self-preservation. If Annabel had killed Paul Levinson, she could have also killed the only witness to the crime. It wasn't a very satisfying motive, but it was enough.

She took out her phone and texted McVie.

I'm done for now

Fenway stood up and plodded out of the locker room. Like yesterday, the forecast didn't call for rain, but the dark clouds above seemed to have other ideas. Her phone dinged: it was a text from McVie.

i'm in the parking lot where i dropped u off
hope a bkfst sandwich is ok

She shuffled her feet on the concrete walkway and wound her way through the campus back to the parking lot. McVie was waiting for her in his Highlander, and he held up a circular, foil-wrapped package. Her stomach growled.

Fenway opened the door and took the proffered sandwich.

"Spinach and pepper jack. Any new information?"

Fenway opened the foil. "What looks like a suicide note, signed by Maggie."

The color drained from McVie's face. "A suicide note?"

Fenway took a bite. "I contacted Dez," she said through a mouthful of egg and English muffin. "There's an APB out on her and my Accord."

"So she's not dead in her hotel room?"

"No. No sign of her in there—just her laptop." Fenway took another bite—she hadn't realized how hungry she was. "But there are some major discrepancies." She pulled her phone out of her purse, tapped on the screen, and showed McVie the email.

"Uh—should I be seeing this?"

"You're looking for her too, right? We're still trying to make sure she's safe."

McVie hesitated, then started to read. "Wait—she confesses to the coach's murder in the email?"

"Scroll down."

"Okay."

Fenway pointed with her pinkie—her only finger not covered in melted cheese. "Look here. Maggie refers to her parents, but her father passed away a couple of years ago. Her coach thinks she would have just referred to her mother, so she doesn't think this note was written by Maggie."

"Did you call Dez?"

"Yes."

"Good. If there's a garbage bag with two bloody hotel towels in it, the police need to get to it sooner rather than later." McVie turned the engine on, and warm air blew onto Fenway's feet. "We don't know when the trash gets picked up from Paseo Fuentes Park, and we'll be lucky if the towels are still there. It's a pretty big park, but if we get a few deputies there—"

"I'll call Dez back." Fenway looked at McVie out of the corner of her eye. "And you have to stop saying 'we.'"

McVie shook his head. "I miss it," he murmured. "I was sheriff for so long, things like this seem second nature to me."

Fenway gave him a sympathetic nod, then tapped her screen to phone Dez. The call went to voicemail. She cleared her throat as the phone beeped in her ear. "Hey, Dez, it's Fenway. We talked about the email from Maggie earlier, but we didn't discuss the mention of those two bloody hotel towels I was looking for earlier. The email said the towels were thrown away at Paseo Fuentes Park. You might already be on it, but make sure you get some uniforms to canvass the trash cans there."

She ended the call, leaned back in her seat, and closed her eyes.

"There's something else," Fenway said. "Annabel had the white Corolla on Thursday night. She still had the key until—" She pulled the evidence bag out of her purse and held it up for McVie to see.

"Did you *steal* that?"

Fenway laughed. "You think I *stole* this? What kind of investigator do you think I am?"

McVie's ears reddened. "A resourceful one?"

"Nice save." Fenway rolled her eyes. "No, she dug it out of her gym bag and gave it to me. And now I need to go to the sheriff's office and log this into evidence."

———

McVie drove to the city center and dropped Fenway off in front of the sheriff's office. She walked in the front door and went down the hall to the evidence room. Deputy Huke sat behind the screen, tapping on the keyboard.

"Good morning, Deputy."

"Coroner Stevenson." His tone, even and measured, couldn't disguise his annoyance—probably at the way Fenway had behaved herself at Nidever University the day before.

"I appreciate the help yesterday."

Huke nodded. "Happy to do it."

Fenway hesitated, then leaned forward and lowered her voice. "You made some good points. And I appreciate what you did to get more information out of Lorraine Sunday."

"You're welcome." Huke's voice softened slightly but not completely. "Do you have evidence to log?"

"I do. A Toyota key, which I believe is to the white Corolla that tried to run over our murder suspect last night in front of this very building."

Huke reached over and pulled out a form, then set it in front of Fenway. "I heard. Have you found the Corolla?"

"Not yet." Fenway began to fill out the form. "Maybe we can drive around the city, pushing the button on the key fob and listening for the honk."

"I don't think that's an efficient—"

"Joking, Deputy Huke."

"Right." He cleared his throat. "How about your Honda?"

"You heard about my Accord too, huh?"

"Hard not to—there's an APB out for it. And Maggie Erskine, too."

"Right, right. Hey—speaking of the Corolla, I heard the murder victim had the other key. Could I see the contents of the victim's pockets, please?"

"Coach Levinson? Sorry, we haven't received his belongings from San Miguelito yet."

"Well, Deputy," Fenway said, tilting her head, "maybe you should call Melissa and set your girl straight!"

Huke looked up from his computer, his brow furrowed. "I hope you're joking again, Coroner."

"I—I am." She cleared her throat. "Sorry. I know you take your job seriously."

"Melissa has a wild side, which frequently pulls me out of my comfort zone," Huke said. "But she respects my boundaries." He took the form from Fenway and gave her a look.

Ouch.

Fenway's phone rang—it was Deputy Salvador. She tapped *Answer*.

"Celeste—hi. How can I help you?"

"I found your car," Salvador replied.

"Oh—where is it?" Fenway could hear birds and rustling wind in the background.

"Parked on the side of Route 326. I radioed it in. You're lucky it's still here. It was unlocked when I found it."

"My Accord went missing this morning. Maggie borrowed it without asking."

"The suspect we have the APB out on? Wasn't she the woman found in Coach Paul Levinson's hotel room yesterday morning? What was she doing with you?"

"Someone tried to run her over last night. I was trying to keep her alive until we could arrange a safe house." Fenway pinched the bridge of her nose. "Any sign of Maggie?"

"I found the car a couple of minutes ago. I'll begin searching for her."

"I think Maggie is still in danger. Do you see footprints in the dirt? Any signs of a fight or a scuffle?"

"She's at risk for suicide, isn't she?"

Fenway rubbed her forehead. "If the email is to be believed."

"There's a big drop-off next to the shoulder," Salvador said delicately. "There's a ravine that runs parallel to the beach and the road, and if someone were to jump off the side, it's at least a hundred feet down." The wind picked up on Celeste's side. "But the underbrush is thick here. And the trees are growing all the way up the side of this cliff. If somebody's down there, I can't see them."

"We need to get search and rescue out there," Fenway said, her voice rising. "I think somebody faked a suicide email in Maggie's name, and I believe they intended to kill her."

Salvador clicked her tongue. "I'll radio that in, too. It usually takes a couple of hours to organize, but I'll give you updates on when a rescue team will get here."

"I'll join you now," Fenway said. "Where are you on route 326?"

"About three hundred yards north of Bixby Road," Salvador said.

"Near the turnoff for Cypress Point Beach," Fenway said. "There's a set of stairs descending to the beach, over the ravine, right?"

"I'm not real familiar with this area."

"I've been there a couple of times. The first set of steps goes down to a footbridge over the ravine, then the second set of steps takes you the rest of the way. Once you get to the beach and start walking south, you'll come to a point where you can look up and see the sign for Bixby Road. I bet you'd be able to see my car on the side of 326."

"And there's a trailhead there?"

"Right. It doesn't go all the way up to the highway, but it goes to the edge of the ravine, Someone could probably scramble down into the ravine safely if they chose the right spot."

"So if Maggie jumped—or fell—"

"Or was pushed," Fenway said.

"—then we'll at least be able to establish a visual." A car passed by on Celeste's end. "I better call search and rescue. They'll know what to do."

"I'm on my way," Fenway said.

Fenway ended the call and turned away from Deputy Huke.

"Excuse me—"

Fenway turned. "Sorry—emergency."

"You didn't sign the form."

"Sorry, sorry." Fenway hurried over to the form, signed her name at the bottom, and ran down the hallway. She called Dez.

"Hey, Fenway. Got your message. I'm in the office—I sent Deputy Callahan over to Paseo Fuentes Park. And I heard over dispatch they found your Honda. Parked on the side of 326."

"No sign of Maggie, though," Fenway said. "And my Accord is parked right at the edge of a cliff overlooking the ocean."

Dez was quiet.

"I think whoever tried to kill her yesterday went to finish the job this morning." Fenway grimaced as she pushed open the door to the street. "I need a ride down there. I hope I'm not too late."

————

"Stop tapping on the armrest."

Fenway snatched her hand back and put it in her lap. "Sorry, Dez, but I'm nervous."

Dez nodded and stared straight ahead.

They turned off Ocean Highway onto the 326 off-ramp. "Remember when you first got to Estancia? Your first day on the job? You tried to call one of the suspects in the murder and tell him you were gathering evidence at the crime scene."

"I remember." Fenway felt the color rise to her cheeks. "I know it was a rookie mistake, and I appreciate you taking me under your wing."

"You've had a lot of success since then," Dez said. "You've had so much success, sometimes I forget you haven't even been in this job a year yet. And I don't recall you making any big mistakes like that in a while."

Fenway was quiet.

"Sometimes you do what you think is the right thing, and people still get hurt."

"I get it, Dez." She saw the sign for Bixby Road on the right.

"But we all make judgment calls. Sometimes they work out. And sometimes the person we're trying to protect makes a bad decision, and it costs them their life." Dez sighed and slowed the car. "Okay, here we go."

The silver Accord was parked on the shoulder closest to the ocean. A police cruiser was parked behind it.

"Should we go down to the beach first?" Fenway asked.

"I think we should see what we're dealing with from the highway." Dez turned the steering wheel hard to make a U-turn in the center of the road. "There's no telling where Maggie could be."

Fenway turned around in her seat, looking behind them, then

slowly turned back to the front of the car, taking in all of the scenery along the side of the road. "I suppose if somebody wanted to do her in, they might do it farther away from the road."

Dez pulled her Impala behind Deputy Salvador's cruiser and killed the engine.

Fenway opened her door. The wind whipped off the ocean, and Fenway's breath caught. On a winter day at Western Washington University in Bellingham, Fenway would have barely noticed a cold wind gusting across campus. Now, with the chilly ocean wind, a shiver went down her spine, and her body broke out in goosebumps.

She followed Dez to the cruiser, then looked down into the ravine. The ravine here ran parallel to the beach, and staring into the hundred-foot drop made Fenway slightly dizzy. Fifteen or twenty feet past the other side of the ravine was a hiking trail on a ridge, at a much gentler incline.

Even in the late morning, there wasn't enough light to see into the shadowy ravine. The dark clouds above obscured the sun, and the heavy underbrush and thick trees obscured everything more than five feet down the hill. Fenway raised her head.

She knew this trail; it led downhill in switchbacks to Cypress Point Beach. Fenway raised her head and squinted; she could barely make out the shape of Deputy Celeste Salvador walking on the beach, along the coastline toward the trailhead. Fenway turned slightly to look at the trailhead. She knew it wound from the beach up into tall scrub brush and short ironwoods, but because it was winter, the paths were overgrown.

"How do you want to do this?" Dez asked.

Fenway rubbed her forward—with incomplete information, there was no obvious way forward. She checked the clock on her phone: it was almost eleven. Maggie had been gone for at least five hours, probably more.

Fenway closed her eyes. "We need to think like the—" She didn't want to say *killer* because she didn't want to believe Maggie was dead.

Dez broke in. "Could've pushed her off the edge."

"True." Fenway opened her eyes. "But there's a lot of brush, trees —lots of stuff to break her fall. Maybe whoever it was didn't want to take the chance of her surviving." She felt a different kind of dizziness as she scanned the brush and trees for any broken branches. "And I don't see any signs that a body fell down here. But her body could still be in the ravine. So we better check."

"Why would Maggie meet someone all the way out here?"

"Maggie's an athlete," Fenway said. "Walk and talk. Maybe even a workout on the beach, saying they'd watch the sun rise."

Dez scratched her chin. "Celeste is already scanning the beach for signs of a struggle."

"So while she's doing that, let's come up to the ravine from the other side." Fenway pointed to the beach, raising her voice over the whipping of the wind. "I've been here a couple of times before. We can go down to the beach and take one of the trails to get to the lower ridge of the ravine."

"We should get a K9 unit down here," Dez said.

"How long will that take?"

"Won't know until I ask."

"If Maggie is still alive, she might be lying in this ravine. If she went in early this morning, she may be suffering from hypothermia or bleeding out." Fenway crossed her arms. "We need to get down there now."

"I'm not saying we don't," Dez replied. "But I don't think you and I will find Maggie in the next half hour. It'll take that long to go down to the beach and hike up the trail to get to the lower ridge of the ravine. Let me call this in, then I'll be down to help you as soon as I can."

Fenway nodded, blinked hard, then turned north and hurried

down the side of the road where the cliff edge softened into a steep trail. Twenty yards later, the trail turned into a set of wooden steps, leading down to a footbridge over the ravine, then more wooden steps with ice plant growing on the hill on either side. She wished she'd worn her running shoes instead of her flats.

Fenway felt her heart beat faster, and it wasn't only from the physical exertion. If she had done a better job keeping Maggie safe, or done a better job at convincing her the threat was real, she wouldn't be in this situation now.

The scenario flashed in her head: a dark, secluded beach an hour before sunrise, a young woman who was desperate to stay a member of the team, and a falsified suicide note.

"Please," Fenway whispered under her breath, "be alive, Maggie. You've got to still be alive."

Her murmured words spun away from her in the cold March wind.

A few minutes later, Fenway reached the bottom of the wooden steps, and her feet sank into the loose sand of the beach. Fenway swore loudly, and kicked her shoes off, then bent over and picked them up.

A large rock formation jutted into the sea on Fenway's right. She looked south and set out toward the trailhead.

After walking on the beach for several hundred yards, Fenway saw the ice plant fade into taller scrub. She must be close to the trailhead now.

She stared up at the cliff as a ray of sun poked through the gray sky. The light glinted off the cars: her silver Accord, Deputy Salvador's cruiser, and Dez's Impala, all parked on the side of Highway 326.

The fact Fenway's Honda was still there gave Fenway a sinking feeling. She tried to think of scenarios where Maggie was okay. But each scenario seemed increasingly unlikely.

Fenway blinked; Deputy Celeste Salvador waved at her about a hundred yards farther on. As she came closer, she saw Salvador standing next to the trailhead. She followed the path with her eyes as best she could: it led up to the lower ridge of the ravine in long, meandering switchbacks. After twenty feet of ascent, though, she lost the visual clues.

"Find anything?" she called to Salvador.

"Nothing yet."

Fenway shook her bare feet as she came close to the trail, then dropped her shoes, stood on one leg, and rubbed the sand off her feet before sliding her flats back on.

"No sign of a struggle anywhere on the beach," Salvador said. "But I've got more to walk." She motioned with her head toward the trail. "Want me to go with you?"

Fenway shook her head. "Dez is coming in a minute. Keep going along the beach. If you find anything, radio us."

Salvador nodded.

Fenway rubbed her hands together for warmth, then shoved them in her pockets and began walking up the path toward the lower ridge of the ravine.

The wet winter had been a boon for the plant life, and in a few places, Fenway had to backtrack to get back on the trail. The gray light filtering from the sky barely illuminated her way.

A flash of light in the sky.

Thunderstorms in Estancia weren't common, but they came every so often. She counted—one, two, three, four—then a distant clap. Still far away.

A drop of rain landed on Fenway's nose, and she cursed softly. Because of the heavy rain the day before, there was a chance they would find footprints on one of these trails—assuming the killer had taken Maggie out this way.

But if it started to rain again—especially before the CSI team could get on scene—the killer's identity might get washed away.

"Fenway!"

Fenway turned toward the beach and looked down. Dez was waving at her.

Fenway pointed down the beach, farther away from the staircase. "Find the next path up toward the ravine," she shouted.

Dez held an upturned thumb aloft and hurried down the beach.

The path merged with another and evened out, and Fenway was relieved to be on more solid footing. This might have been the path the killer and Maggie had taken.

And now the trail followed the edge of the ravine—a sheer drop about fifteen feet on this side, but a hundred feet up to the highway. Fenway stared up the cliff, but trees obscured her view.

She dropped her gaze to keep her eyes on the sides of the trail, looking for broken foliage that might reveal where Maggie had fallen.

The path was uneven, her footing unsure. It was frustrating how slowly she had to walk. But the rain was still holding off—only a drop or two every few minutes.

Then she saw it.

The crawling vines and the branches intruding onto the trail were broken at her feet. Fenway stopped in her tracks. She glanced up the trail; the disturbed foliage and broken branches continued up the path.

"Hey!" Fenway yelled. "Hey, I found something here!"

Fenway's gut told her Maggie was near. Had someone led Maggie up the trail, or had Maggie's body been pushed over the cliff from the highway and struck the path here? The trail sloped down on both sides, away from the edge of the ravine: the left side to the switchback trail leading to the beach, and the right side off into the trees.

Fenway closed her eyes and took a deep breath, which she held for a moment. Opening her eyes, she got on her hands and knees and peered down the side of the path into the ravine.

It wasn't as steep as she'd expected. Green and brown everywhere: branches, rocks, bushes, and brambles. She scanned one side in a grid pattern, as she'd been taught to do in her forensics classes, though it was easier with a field or a carpeted room than it was with a ravine.

Another raindrop landed on Fenway's head.

Wait—

A stylized B, outlined in red on a navy blue background.

Fenway squinted. It looked like her Boston Red Sox cap.

The underbrush and the foliage were thick, blocking Fenway's view on either side of the hat. But as she looked from a different angle, a light-blue sweatshirt came into view.

Western Washington.

The sweatshirt Fenway had lent Maggie the day before.

Fenway tried to yell, but her voice came out in a strangled whisper. She stood and cleared her throat.

"I found her!"

Fenway scrambled down the side of the hill into the ravine. The toeholds were tenuous, and the brambles bit at her ankles and hands. But she got onto solid ground, then scrambled over to the light-blue sweatshirt.

The outline of a body. Brown hair in a fan around a freckled face.

Maggie's sightless green eyes staring back at her.

CHAPTER TWENTY

FENWAY'S VISION BLURRED AS SHE SLOWLY CLIMBED OUT OF THE ravine. Grabbing onto a tree root sticking out of the side of the hill, Fenway pulled herself up over a bush and onto the trail. She got to her feet and stood for a moment, her hands on her knees, wiping her eyes and trying to catch her breath.

She looked up—the trees were standing solidly. Maggie had likely gone into the ravine from this part of the trail, not from the road above.

Fenway scanned the edge of the trail where a lip of bushes and dirt separated it from the ravine.

Aha. Broken brambles and the tamped-down underbrush gave her a good idea of where Maggie had last been standing, probably next to her killer. She pulled her phone out and tapped the camera app.

The single drops of rain falling every few seconds had turned into a light drizzle. The sky was growing darker with the approaching rain clouds. Fenway stayed to the side of the trail, searching the ground for any telltale signs of the killer.

There.

A good ten feet back from where Maggie had gone into the ravine: half a shoe print in the mud on the trail. It looked to be from the toe and the ball of the foot. Fenway snapped a picture—she was sure the coming rain would wash the print away before CSI could get here.

She stared at her screen, then enlarged the photo.

Wavy lines coursed horizontally on the sole from side to side, spaced further apart on the outside and closer together near the instep. A circle with two ridges around the outside was located at the ball of the foot, interrupting the waves. The print showed a sole deeply grooved toward the edge of the instep but lighter near the middle of the foot. This wasn't a new pair of shoes.

Faintly, she heard sirens growing closer. Now that Fenway had found the body, Dez had probably called an ambulance. She walked down the trail another twenty feet before she heard a voice behind her.

"Fenway!"

She turned around. Dez had drawn herself to her full height on a switchback below her, about fifty yards away. Dez cupped her hands around her mouth. "Where's Maggie?"

Fenway pointed down the ravine to where Maggie's body lay.

Dez motioned her closer with her arm. "Is she alive?"

Fenway pursed her lips and shook her head.

"Cause of death? Time?"

"I—I haven't examined the body."

"Well, get down there—you're the coroner." Dez hurried up the trail toward Fenway. "Find something for us to go on."

Fenway stared down into the ravine and took a deep breath. She hurried over to where the broken branches ended and began to climb down into the ravine again. She heard rustling and looked above her; Dez was following her down.

Fenway climbed over the underbrush and around a cypress tree to get to Maggie's fallen body. She pulled her phone out again and took pictures from several angles, making sure to be clear what Maggie's final resting position was—her arms, her legs. Fenway scooted around on the side of the hill to her feet, then bent down and looked at the soles of Maggie's shoes. Her white athletic shoes had a sunburst pattern on the bottom. Not a match for the footprint in the muddy trail above her.

Gently, Fenway reached out her hand and lifted Maggie's leg, then scurried around her side and lifted her arm. It was beginning to stiffen; Maggie had been dead for several hours. Fenway glanced at her phone screen.

"Based on rigor mortis," Fenway said, "I would put time of death sometime this morning. Probably between 5:00 and 8:00 A.M."

"Quite a window."

Fenway shrugged. "I don't have my kit with me. When CSI gets here, they can do liver temp and some other readings that might narrow it down more." She crab-walked cautiously toward Maggie's head, which had turned awkwardly to the side, and looked as carefully as she could at the back of the skull without touching it. The greenery of the underbrush was stained brownish red with blood.

Could she move the body to see the wound without Maggie sliding down further into the ravine?

Gingerly, she held Maggie's neck with her left hand, then placed her right hand on the crown of the head and lifted slightly. Matted hair obscured much of Maggie's scalp, but it was clear an object had hit the back of her head with sufficient force to crack her skull.

In the field, with only her gloved hands and the muddy ravine to deal with, Fenway couldn't be sure if the weapon had been a golf club like the one used to kill coach Levinson, a rock, or perhaps a thick walking stick. She supposed it was possible Maggie had hit her head on a rock on the way down, but given there was little damage to the rest of her body, Fenway suspected foul play.

"Anything?" Dez called.

"The back of her skull is smashed in. I can't get much more detailed out here."

"Does she have anything on her?" Dez asked. "A purse nearby, or a phone?"

Fenway checked the pockets of Maggie's track pants. There was a jiggling lump of metal in her left jacket pocket. Fenway reached inside, and her finger went into a metal loop.

"Find something?" Dez asked.

"My car key," Fenway responded. "No phone."

"Maybe her stuff is in the car," Dez called.

Fenway nodded, then turned back to the body. If Maggie had thought she was meeting someone to talk about getting back on the team, maybe an early morning run or hike was part of the killer's suggestion. Maggie might have left her belongings in the car while she went to talk or work out with her teammate or her coach.

The drizzle came down a little harder as Fenway and Dez swept as much of the ravine area as they could around the body, and others began to show up. Fenway lost track of time. First, two paramedics came on scene, then Melissa de la Garza from San Miguelito CSI.

Fenway was far away from Melissa, and by the time she climbed out of the ravine to the trail, her leg muscles were burning from going up and down the hill.

She looked out over the ocean, getting wetter by the minute. Then she carefully made her way down the trail the way she had come, and ten minutes later, she was back on the beach, the wet sand squishing in her shoes.

———

"You're not doing anybody any good sitting here moping," Dez said.

Fenway startled as the steady patter of the rain hitting the top of her head ceased, replaced by the sound of raindrops hitting plastic. She opened her eyes. Dez held an umbrella over her with one hand and with the other, handed her a large paper cup with a plastic lid. Fenway reached up and took it; it was hot, and it felt good in her frigid hand.

"I'm not moping," Fenway said. "Where'd you get coffee?"

Dez motioned with her head to the road above them. "Your boyfriend." She tilted her head. "You sure *look* like you're moping."

"I need to figure out what was going through the killer's head. I need to figure out who Maggie would have trusted enough to meet on the side of a highway at six in the morning."

Dez put her hands on her hips.

"I told her that keeping her safe was my number one priority, and here she is, dead in a ravine overlooking Cypress Point Beach."

"Because she didn't stay in the hotel room with you."

"Yeah, well, the least I can do is catch Maggie's killer."

Dez turned back to look at the ocean. "From the first day you were here, I've been trying to get you not only to play to your strengths, but also to rely on other people on your team. They have strengths, too—ones you don't."

Fenway pressed her lips together. "Maybe if I'd been paying closer attention, Maggie wouldn't be dead." She felt teardrops, hot and wet on each cheek.

Great. She was crying in front of Dez.

She hoped the raindrops on her face were hiding her tears, but she turned her face anyway. Fenway adjusted her seat on the bottom stair, dug her heels into the sand, then crossed her arms on her knees and buried her face in the sleeves of her wet jacket.

"You'll have enough time to feel sorry for yourself later," Dez said softly. "If you're going to find Maggie's killer, you need to think. Analyze. Observe."

A huge wave crashed on the shore, the roar a crescendo. "Whoever the killer is," Fenway said, catching her breath, "Maggie would have known them and trusted them. And they must have been an influential person to get her potentially back on the team."

"Maggie's killer or Levinson's?"

In the distance, three lights on the water, spaced far apart, began to flash. "They're the same person. I'm sure of it." Fenway sighed. "I used to love this beach."

"Stay in this job long enough, and it'll ruin everything," Dez said.

Fenway was silent. She stood, then paced slowly back and forth, feeling her shoes sink into the wet sand. "I don't really know what to think right now, Dez. I know we need justice for Maggie." Fenway bowed her head, her chin almost touching between her collarbones. "I thought if I could get her to the hotel in Paso Querido, she'd be safe. I thought she *was* safe."

Fenway heard Dez's shoes squish on the sand, then felt a hand on her shoulder.

"I know you did."

Fenway looked back to the water. The three lights were glowing out of sync, giving a hazy, dreamlike quality to the fading light of the late afternoon.

Dez shifted her weight from foot to foot. "By the way, they're taking your car for evidence."

"I figured." Fenway turned around, squinting at Highway 326 above them. "Is McVie still here?"

Dez nodded. "He said he'd forward us some emails about his investigation—he thought we might be able to find something to point us in the right direction. But I don't know how much help they'll be in finding Levinson's killer."

Fenway ran her fingers through her short, wet hair, a stream of water cascading onto her shoulders and down her back. She shuddered. "If we find Maggie's killer, we'll find Levinson's killer."

After crossing the sand and climbing the wood-and-stone staircase, Fenway reached Highway 326 and looked down the road. McVie's Highlander was parked about a hundred yards in front of Fenway's Accord. The Honda was now surrounded by police tape and three police cruisers. Fenway walked around her car, trying not to make eye contact with the officers inside, who were searching the glove compartment and the area beneath the seats. She wondered vaguely if the car still smelled like lengua tacos.

Fenway stared ahead through the thickening rain and saw McVie's silhouette in the driver side of the Highlander. She walked to the passenger side window and rapped lightly on the glass.

The door locks clicked open, and Fenway opened the door. A fluffy beach towel was draped over the seat and another on the seat back.

"Hey," McVie said.

"Hey yourself," Fenway said, an exhausted smile touching the corners of her mouth. "What's all this?"

"After Dez told me you found Maggie's body, I figured you'd be out here awhile." He looked up at the rain an awkward angle. "And the skies hadn't opened up when I dropped you off at the sheriff's office earlier. So I went home and picked up a few things."

"A few things?"

"I made a run to Java Jim's, for one," McVie said, smiling. "I figured you all could use some hot drinks. Got some for the other officers too."

"And towels so I wouldn't mess up your car." She sat down heavily in the passenger seat the towel at her back falling and landing on top of her shoulders. She reached behind her and began to towel off her wet hair.

"Towels so you can dry off. I even put the seat heaters on, so they're nice and warm." He pointed with his thumb into the rear seat. "I've got some sweats for you in the back if you want to change."

"You think of everything, don't you?" Fenway's shoes squished. For a moment, she wasn't sure whether leaving her shoes on or taking them off would cause more of a mess. She leaned back in the seat—against the warm, fluffy towels—and tried not to think about it.

"Are you okay?"

Fenway closed her eyes and concentrated on her breathing. She noticed her breaths coming short and fast and took a deep breath in through her nose, releasing it out through her mouth. One more: in, out. "I—" She put her hands over her face and felt hot tears on her palms where they were touching her cheeks. "I failed her."

Then McVie's arms were around her, pulling her into an awkward embrace. "I'm sorry." McVie ran his fingers gently over the back of Fenway's head, the way he used to run his fingers through her hair when it was longer. "You'll figure this out."

After a few moments, Fenway pulled out of McVie's hug and wiped her face with the towel. McVie wordlessly started the engine and pulled the Highlander out onto 326. They followed the winding road back to Ocean Highway and entered the freeway going south toward downtown.

McVie cleared his throat. "Do you need to pick anything up from home?"

Fenway looked at McVie out of the corner of her eye. "I think I need to go back to the coroner's office."

McVie shook his head. "It's past five o'clock, Fenway. I don't think you've eaten since that breakfast sandwich. And you've been running after Maggie since early this morning."

"But the first forty-eight hours—"

"You won't do anybody any good with how worn out you are right now." McVie changed lanes and passed the Broadway exit.

"Where are we going?"

"If you don't need to pick up anything at your apartment, I'm taking you to my place."

"What about Megan?"

"I talked to Amy after I got to the beach—she told me Megan spent the day with her friends. I think she skipped her tutoring session today, too." McVie ran a hand over his face. "I get that she's seventeen and doesn't really want to be a part of our messed-up family anymore—anyway, it's not important. The point is, she's not coming."

"Oh." Fenway touched her finger to the cold passenger window, tracing the path of a raindrop inching from the front to the back of the window with the wind. "So you basically waited all day for me."

"I ran a few errands," McVie said, waving his hand dismissively. "I had a report to write. I got my laptop from my office, and I paid some bills."

Fenway kept staring out the passenger window as they exited at San Vicente Boulevard. "You don't think your client has anything to do with the death of Paul Levinson, do you?"

McVie rubbed his chin. "I don't think so. Why?"

"Montague's wife was the last person seen with the white Toyota Corolla."

McVie frowned. "Montague hasn't communicated with me at all since Coach Levinson's body was discovered Friday morning."

"She must have seen the news articles by now. It's her wife's team, after all. Don't you think it's a little odd that she hasn't said anything?"

"Maybe. But she's the CEO of a big organization." McVie tapped the steering wheel. "Honestly, I expected to be chewed out two or three times by now. Every time my cell phone rings, I think it's Mathilda Montague calling me to ask how I let something like this happen."

"Something like what?"

"Mathilda wanted to keep her spying on Annabel hush-hush. Now with the deaths of both Annabel's coach *and* the woman Mathilda suspected—"

"She can't blame *you* for that, surely. Like you had anything to do with—"

McVie smiled sadly. "It's sweet that you think my clients are rational."

"But she hasn't said anything to you yet? Not since Coach Levinson was killed?"

"Her assistant has called a few times to ask for status updates, and I've gotten electronic payments for the work I've done so far."

"So that's good, right?"

He shrugged. "Maybe I'm reading too much into Montague's radio silence."

They pulled into McVie's apartment complex. He guided the Highlander into his parking space.

Fenway exhaled slowly.

"So," McVie said, "who's left as a suspect now?"

Fenway bit her lip. "Annabel had the car last. She had motive for wanting Levinson dead—he'd raped her ten years before and gotten away with it."

"But why kill Maggie?"

Fenway shook her head. "My only hypothesis is that Maggie witnessed the murder and had to be eliminated."

"Then why wasn't Maggie killed along with Coach Levinson?"

Fenway crinkled her nose. "I didn't say it was a *good* hypothesis."

"Maybe you haven't uncovered the real motive yet." McVie drummed his fingers on the armrest. "You know, just because we didn't see evidence of an affair between Annabel and Maggie doesn't mean there was nothing between them. They could have been very good at hiding it."

Fenway shook her head. "Okay, for the sake of argument, let's assume that Annabel and Maggie *were* having an affair. Let's even assume that Annabel wanted to leave Mathilda Montague and be with Maggie."

"That would give her a really good motive for killing Levinson."

Fenway crossed her arms. "But not for trying to run Maggie over."

McVie shrugged. "Here's a hypothetical scenario. Annabel wanted to leave Mathilda, but Maggie rejected her because she was too scared to come out from under Levinson's thumb. Maybe that's what they were arguing about in the restaurant. Then Annabel kills Levinson, thinking Maggie will finally be with her. But Maggie rejects her again."

"So Annabel tries to run her over?"

McVie paused, thinking. "If Annabel was the one with the Corolla key, why wouldn't you think Annabel was the Corolla driver who tried to kill Maggie?"

Fenway traced the edge of the window with her finger. "Granted, Annabel was the last person who checked the Corolla out. And she had the key."

"Were there other keys?"

Fenway nodded. "A second key—Coach Levinson had it."

"Did he have it with him the night he died?"

"I don't know. In fact, I don't know where it is."

"If it's missing, whoever killed Levinson could have used *his* key to steal the Corolla."

Fenway dropped her hands to her lap. "Yeah, yeah, Craig. I see what you're saying. It's not likely, but it's possible."

"And Annabel would have been one of the few people Maggie would have trusted to try to get her back on the Neons."

"I guess we need to establish where Annabel was this morning." Fenway took her phone out of her purse. "I'll call Dez. Can you drop me off?"

———

An hour later, Fenway and Dez stood at the entrance to Annabel's hotel room. Two officers were behind them.

"You don't think we can take Annabel in for questioning by ourselves?" Fenway whispered.

Dez put her hands on her hips. "You've spun a hypothetical tale of Annabel bashing Coach Levinson's head in with a golf club, then trying to run over Maggie with the white Corolla, stalking you in the same car, then hitting Maggie over the head and throwing her body into a ravine. Did I miss anything?"

"I guess not."

"Great. So I'm not taking any chances."

Fenway reached out and knocked on the hotel room door.

Annabel opened the door a moment later. Her hair glistened, wet from the shower, and she wore pajama bottoms and a ratty white T-shirt a couple of sizes too big for her. "Coroner—hi. What can I do for you?"

"We have some additional questions for you," Fenway said. "Can you come with us?"

"Is this about Maggie? Did you find her?"

"Have you seen the news this evening?" Dez asked gently.

"No—wait, what happened?"

"Like I said," Dez said, this time more firmly, "we need you to come with us."

"Oh—yes, absolutely. Let me throw some clothes on, and I'll be with you in a few minutes."

Dez stepped past Fenway until she was inside the threshold. "Just grab your shoes, Ms. Shedd. With any luck, we'll have you back here within the hour, and you can continue with your evening."

"I'll be fast. Two minutes, tops." Annabel looked from Fenway to Dez, then frowned. "Shit, you're not kidding."

"I thought for sure you would prioritize helping us figure out what happened to Maggie," Dez said.

"Of course—I'll do whatever I have to do to make sure Maggie is safe."

"While we have you here, Ms. Shedd, would you mind if we took a look around your hotel room?"

"I can't change out of my pajamas, yet you want to take a look—" Annabel cocked her head to the side, realization dawning on her face. "Coroner Stevenson already knows about the key to the white Corolla." She blocked Fenway and Dez from stepping too far into the hotel room, setting her body between the edge of the door and the wall. "You know, I don't think I *will* come down to the station with you. I'll give my lawyer a call first."

"You can call your lawyer from the car and ask them to meet us there." Dez smiled a half-smile that Fenway thought looked smarmy, not easygoing. "It'll be much faster anyway."

The cords in Annabel's neck tightened. "Am I under arrest?"

A slight hesitation in Dez's voice. "No, we just need to ask you some questions."

"The coroner has already asked me quite a few questions over the last couple of days." Annabel's shoulders tightened. "Let me ask *you* a question first: do you know where Maggie is?"

Fenway glanced briefly at Dez, then quickly turned her attention back to Annabel. But it was enough of a tell.

Annabel's face crumpled, the creases of her umber complexion deepening, and her breath hitched. But then her face turned inscrutable. "If anything has happened to Maggie, and if you're asking me to come down to the station, I *definitely* won't be there until my lawyer joins us." Annabel took another step forward. "Now, unless you're arresting me, please get out of my room. I have quite a bit of work to do tonight." She walked toward them, herding them out the door. Dez grunted, but turned and stepped over the threshold into the hallway, Fenway following.

"What size shoe do you wear?" Fenway asked.

"What?"

"Your shoe size," Fenway repeated. "What is it?"

"I don't see how that's any of your business."

"Humor me."

Annabel looked down at her long feet, encased in white cotton athletic socks. "Take a guess, Coroner."

The door shut gently but firmly.

Dez shook her head. "She scored the winning goal in the World Cup. You think her shoe size *won't* be on a fan site somewhere?" She took her phone out and began tapping on the screen as they walked down the hall.

Fenway pushed the button for the elevator.

Dez held up her phone for Fenway to see, then turned it back to read it. "Here it is. 'The 5-foot-11 Annabel Shedd thrives on the stress of high expectations. In high school, she was self-conscious about her large feet, but she now views her size 11s as one of her greatest advantages. It's hard to argue, as those size 11s have kicked in 34 goals in international play.' Why did you want to know?"

"I took pictures of a shoe print at the scene where we found Maggie's body."

"Did you show the print to CSI when you were out on the trail?"

The elevator dinged, and the doors opened. "The rain washed it away before CSI could get an imprint," Fenway said, stepping in and pushing the button for the ground floor. "I'll send the photo to Melissa—I should have sent it as soon as I took it."

"Did you put anything in the photo to measure it against?" Dez asked. "Otherwise, they'll have a lot of trouble determining the size."

Fenway swore at herself in her head as the elevator doors closed behind them. She should have put something—a pencil, her hand, *anything*—next to the shoe print when she photographed it.

The elevator began to descend. "It'll be better than nothing," Fenway said. "You can see the sole pretty clearly—and the wear pattern. If it's smaller than an eleven, we can rule Annabel out as a suspect."

Dez turned to face Fenway, narrowing her eyes. "You saw the shoe print. You've been doing this for a while. What do you think?"

"It could be the same size Annabel wears."

A ding, and the doors opened. Dez walked out of the elevator. "It's late, and I've had a hell of a day." She glanced at Fenway over her shoulder. "I know you have, too. Send the photo to Melissa and get some sleep. We can get a fresh start tomorrow."

PART 4

SUNDAY

CHAPTER TWENTY-ONE

FENWAY STARED AT THE EMAIL SHE HAD OPENED ON HER PHONE, her eyes unfocused. She was missing something. She leaned back in the rear seat of the rideshare. She'd gotten the message at six A.M. that Dr. Yasuda was performing the autopsy on Maggie—at eight. Fenway had rushed through her shower and hurried downstairs before she remembered her car was being held as evidence in Maggie's death.

Fortunately, the Uber had arrived in five minutes, but the trip was costing her over a hundred fifty dollars.

Her phone rang in her hand. McVie.

She hesitated, then clicked *Answer*.

"Hey, Craig. It's a little early for you to be calling."

"I thought you were coming over last night. Everything okay?"

"Yeah, yeah." Fenway closed her eyes. "I meant to come over after I went to the hotel with Dez last night. But afterward, Dez dropped me off at my apartment, and, I don't know. I didn't feel like going anywhere."

A pause on the other end. Then McVie cleared his throat, his voice brittle with forced enthusiasm. "I understand. You went through a lot yesterday, and I had a lot of work to catch up on last night anyway."

She gritted her teeth. "It doesn't have anything to do with you, Craig."

"I said I understood."

Fenway tilted her head forward and looked out the window. They were at the fork in the highway, and the driver turned towards San Miguelito. "I guess maybe I should have called."

McVie cleared his throat. "Do you want to go to breakfast? Jack and Jill's?"

"I'm on my way to Maggie's autopsy."

"Oh—that was fast. Usually it takes a day or two to schedule."

"Dr. Yasuda scheduled it herself. It's a high-profile death."

"Hang on—the autopsy in San Miguelito? You don't have your car. Do you want me to drive you?"

Fenway bit her lip. "I thought you had a lot of work to do."

"I do."

"So, you don't really have time to drive me to San Miguelito."

"No," McVie said, a sharp edge in his voice. "But if you're in a jam—"

"I'm in an Uber," Fenway said.

"An Uber? It'll cost a fortune."

"One fifty. I'll expense it."

Another moment of uncomfortable silence followed.

"Did I do something to upset you?" McVie asked.

"No," Fenway said quickly, then turned and stared out the window. She had made this drive in her Accord at least a dozen times, but she'd never gotten to really pay attention to the scenery. If Maggie hadn't stolen her car, she'd be making this drive and ignoring the landscape.

Of course, if Maggie hadn't taken the Accord, she might still be alive. The ironwood trees and sagebrush on the side of the road whooshed by and started to blur in Fenway's vision.

"Fenway? Are you still there?"

"The woman I was supposed to keep safe was killed yesterday," Fenway whispered. "I'm processing it. Everything that happened yesterday, and you think I'm in a bad mood because of you?"

"No, of course not," McVie said quickly. "I wasn't thinking."

"I have to go." Though it would be at least another twenty minutes in the car. Fenway exhaled, long and slow. She thought back: Akeel, only a couple of months. A high school boyfriend had lasted six weeks. Another boyfriend in college had lasted six months, but it was long distance, and they didn't talk to each other more than once a week for the last two months. She and Craig had been together for a while, but with all the false starts and stops, she wasn't sure exactly how long it had been. This was the longest romantic entanglement she'd ever had. "I need to get in the right headspace for the autopsy, Craig."

"Okay," McVie said softly. "Maybe you can give me a call if you need a ride home."

"Sure."

"I, uh, I hope the autopsy gives you some answers."

Fenway opened her mouth, but nothing came out.

"I guess I'll talk to you later."

Silence. Fenway lifted the phone off her face. McVie had hung up.

———

The brown plastic chairs in the medical examiner's office waiting room cut off the circulation to Fenway's legs, and she had to shift her weight every few minutes. She took her phone out of her purse and glanced at the time: 8:23. It wasn't like Dr. Yasuda to keep people waiting.

Fenway stood up and shook each leg to get the blood flowing. She noticed with irritation that her bone-colored flats and her gray pantsuit clashed. She frowned—after spending yesterday in the sand and on a muddy trail, maybe she should have worn her hiking boots. Who knew what the day would hold?

The door on the left side of the lobby opened, and a familiar face popped out, a mass of black curls surrounding a serious expression.

"Melissa?"

"Good, I'm glad you're here." Melissa opened the door wider. "Dr. Yasuda is stuck consulting on another case right now. But I have some things to go over with you. Can you follow me back to the lab?"

Fenway followed Melissa down a corridor, making a hard right turn. Fifty feet later, they were at the laboratory door, and Melissa pulled the key card down from her lanyard. A beep and a click and Melissa pulled the door open.

"I got the photo you sent me of the footprint," Melissa said. She walked to her workstation, Fenway following, and woke up her computer. A photo of the shoe print filled the screen.

"Did this get you anywhere?" Fenway asked.

Melissa clicked the mouse and zoomed out. "It's not clear from the photo how far away from the ground the phone was when you took the picture."

Fenway held her hand in front of her, about waist height, and mimed taking a picture of the floor. "That's where I took it."

"Even a couple of inches each way would alter the results." Melissa clicked onto a window showing a large set of numbers in a complex spreadsheet. She reached into a drawer and pulled out a measuring tape. "Keep your hand in front of you, right there, and hold that end."

Fenway held the end of the tape measure, and Melissa knelt in front of her and pulled it taut.

"Were you were holding the phone right there?"

"Uh—more or less."

"Put it *exactly* where you think you held it."

Fenway furrowed her brow. "The ground sloped a little to the right. So I don't know exactly how far from the ground I was."

"Put your hand as close as possible to where you were holding the phone."

Fenway hesitated, then lifted her hand about an inch.

"There? Are you sure?"

"It's my best guess."

Melissa squinted as she looked at the tape measure, then grunted and stood up. "Thirty-one and a half inches," She leaned over her desk, typing the number into the spreadsheet. Melissa hit the enter key with a flourish, then she put her index finger on the screen. "According to these calculations, the shoe size is somewhere between an eight and a ten."

Fenway winced. "What degree of certainty?"

"It depends on how certain you are about how high you were holding the phone when you took the picture. But within this range, I'd say eighty, eighty-five percent."

"I might have had my hand lower."

"Okay." Melissa typed again. "Let's say you had your hand an inch lower. Now we're looking at a seven and a half to nine and a half."

"We're going the wrong way." Fenway loudly exhaled through her mouth, teeth together, making a whooshing sound. "It's close, but not close enough. There goes our prime suspect."

"Prime suspect?"

"The woman who had access to the car—"

"Wait, wait." Melissa held her hand up. "That's a *men's* shoe size eight to ten."

"Oh, so I add—what? A size and a half for women, right?"

"Nine and a half to eleven and a half. But remember, there were a lot of variables with your photo."

Fenway rubbed her forehead with the fingertips of both hands. She could feel a headache coming on. "What type of variables are we talking about? Different shoe manufacturers size their products differently. Don't you get half or even a full size difference in certain brands?"

"True, but I was referring to variables in the soil." Melissa crossed her arms. "I don't think you appreciate how unusual it is to get a clear tread print in soil to begin with. The soil was moist but not muddy. And you got to it before the rain blurred much of the sole. You were lucky."

"I'll make sure to buy a lottery ticket."

Melissa gave Fenway a wry smile. "But the quality of the photo itself—and the fact it's a photo—will make further identification difficult."

"It was about to rain."

"No—sorry, you did the right thing, no question. But to run it against the national database, we usually need a higher resolution image, or ideally a plaster impression."

"Wait—database? There's a government database on shoe prints?"

"It's not governmental, it's commercially maintained—two guys up in Montana. They call it SoleBrothers." She clicked a window, and the SoleBrothers website popped up, a progress bar almost two-thirds complete. "Never underestimate the power of a bad pun when selling to state and local officials."

"So what are the odds of finding the shoe?"

Melissa shrugged. "Hard to say. When I was trained on the system, we used plaster impressions. Those have better accuracy than photos."

Fenway pointed to the screen. "How much longer will this take?"

"I didn't start running it until after I came in. So maybe another ten minutes."

The computer beeped, and the screen changed.

"Or maybe sooner," Melissa said.

The photo Fenway had taken of the shoe print took up the left-hand side of the screen, and a photo of another shoe sole appeared in the middle of the screen. Text flowed down the right-hand side.

"Today is your lucky day. Maybe you *should* buy a lottery ticket." Melissa clicked on the screen and the whole shoe appeared on the screen in profile. "This is a Bronson Eagle GTX4."

"Bronson?" Fenway asked. "I've never even heard of them."

"Small manufacturer in New England." Melissa tapped the screen with her index finger. "And this Eagle GTX4 had a limited run. It was only manufactured for about three months, and that was two years ago."

"Was something wrong with the engineering?"

"I don't know the details, but I seem to remember the design wasn't popular." Melissa smiled. "Before I started dating Donnie, I went out with this guy who was kind of a sneakerhead. I remember him making fun of this shoe. He wouldn't shut up about it."

"So we're looking for somebody from New England?"

"Not necessarily." Melissa pulled her chair out from her desk and sat down. "If it wasn't popular, it may have been sent to other regions on clearance. Shoes like that wind up at one of those designer-names-for-less places."

"Is this a men's or a women's shoe?"

"I think it was marketed as a men's shoe, but plenty of women wear men's sneakers. Especially if they have larger feet."

"Does this SoleBrothers site track where the shoes were sold?"

Melissa shook her head.

Fenway leaned on the desk and ran her hands through her hair. "We *might* be able to get a warrant to search everyone on the team for a pair of Bronson Eagle GTX4s with a muddy sole," Fenway said. "But if the killer's smart, they would have dumped the shoes by now."

"Why wouldn't you get a warrant?"

"I've pissed off enough people on the team," Fenway said. "The Las Vegas Neons will find a different place to hold training camp next year if I keep this up. Then the whole city will be mad at me."

———

Fenway had forgotten how fast Dr. Yasuda walked down a flight of stairs. After climbing in and out of the ravine the day before, Fenway's quadriceps and calf muscles were screaming by the time she got to the bottom of the stairs and pushed open the morgue door behind the medical examiner. Fenway put on a gown, gloves, a cap, a mask, and goggles, and joined Dr. Yasuda next to an aluminum table, a body lying under a sheet.

"I scheduled this as soon as I could," Dr. Yasuda said gently.

Fenway shifted her weight from foot to foot.

Dr. Yasuda folded the sheet down, revealing Maggie's head. The young goalkeeper had been wound tight in life, but now her eyes were closed, her body still, peaceful.

Dr. Yasuda folded the sheet at Maggie's chin. "Before we make any incisions," Dr. Yasuda said, "we should look at the head wound."

Fenway stared at Maggie's face and murmured her assent.

"Can you assist me with turning the body into a prone position?"

Maggie's body was lithe and wiry. She seemed surprisingly light as she and Yasuda maneuvered her onto her stomach.

Using scissors to cut the longer strands of hair, then shaving around the wound with clippers, Dr. Yasuda cleared a small area of Maggie's scalp.

"Blunt object, base of the skull," Fenway said. "Probably fatal."

"Yes, I would say so." Dr. Yasuda shined a light over the wound. It was about an inch and a half in diameter, one end rounded, one end flatter.

"This looks almost like the mark left by the head of a golf club," Fenway said.

Dr. Yasuda frowned and grunted. "Do you see how round this area is?" Yasuda pointed to the rounded edge. "Golf club heads are rounded, yes, but they aren't perfectly round—the heads almost always have their rounded sides in asymmetrical shapes. I believe this was a stick of some kind with a round end."

"What kind of stick has a round end?" A walking stick? A scepter prop from a movie with warlocks and elves? "Maybe a rock? Could she have jumped and hit her head on a rock?"

Dr. Yasuda shook her head. "Unlikely. The rocks in the area aren't smooth, and there would be more complex injuries around the wound. No—this was homicide."

Fenway crinkled her forehead. "If someone was trying to make it look like suicide, they did a bad job."

"I agree—but I believe that's what happened. There are other lacerations and wounds consistent with a fall from, say, fifteen or twenty feet. But the head wound would have been shallower from that height."

"The murder weapon," Fenway said. "Was it a wooden walking stick? Or a hiking pole made of metal?" Fenway tilted her head and squinted. "I suppose it's too thick to be a metal hiking pole. At least not the ones I've seen."

"From the angle of the blow," Yasuda said, "the assailant was right-handed."

"Same as Coach Levinson's killer," Fenway murmured.

"The tip of the weapon was spherical," Yasuda said.

They worked in near-silence, Yasuda collecting tissue from the wound itself to pick up any clues that might have been left behind by the weapon. They turned her over into a supine position.

Dr. Yasuda led the autopsy with Fenway assisting, but there were no further clues to be gleaned from Maggie's body. Nothing was in her mouth, and aside from the dirt and mud on her head, face, and hands, nothing was found suggesting where Maggie was prior to the hillside.

"She was sexually active," Yasuda said. "But I see no sign of sexual trauma."

"Was she pregnant?"

"I ran a blood test last night," Dr. Yasuda said. "She was not pregnant, and it doesn't appear she has ever been pregnant."

"So the body isn't telling us anything."

"It tells us where *not* to look. Her stomach was empty, so she likely did not stop for coffee or breakfast between the time she woke up and the time she arrived at the hiking trail near the beach."

Dr. Yasuda and Fenway worked together to stitch Maggie back up. "If the body has any clues besides the head wound, I don't see them." Yasuda clicked her tongue. "Of course, it will take a few days to get the tox screen back, but there appear to be no signs of drug abuse."

They finished, and Fenway removed her protective equipment and washed up. She was surprised to discover two hours had passed. She had performed a few autopsies on her own, but never on a murder victim. She was glad Dr. Yasuda had taken the lead.

"It was nice to work with you again, Miss Stevenson," Dr. Yasuda said. "It's a shame I only see you in unfortunate circumstances."

"Melissa said the same thing." Fenway shifted her weight uncomfortably. "Sometimes you ask me to give a message to Dez—"

Dr. Yasuda glanced up at Fenway and gave her a small smile. "That won't be necessary. I'll see her this afternoon."

A smile spread across Fenway's face. "Good for you."

They said their goodbyes, and Fenway walked out of the morgue, then took the steps up to the ground floor. She started to turn left to go down the hall to the lobby but stopped in her tracks. She made a right turn instead and knocked on the door of the lab.

A moment later, Melissa opened the door. "Oh, Fenway. Did you forget something?"

"You did the autopsy for Coach Levinson here, didn't you?"

"Dr. Yasuda did."

"You might still have his personal effects. I wondered if I could see them."

Melissa raised her eyebrows. "Ah. I believe we logged them yesterday. I know we have the package scheduled to go to the Dominguez County Sheriff's Office, but the courier hasn't made the run yet. You want to take them back?"

"I don't have a car," Fenway said. "I took an Uber here. But I need to check his belongings. It could be important to the case."

"Gotcha. Come with me." Melissa walked out of the lab, Fenway following, and turned down the hallway, away from the basement entrance. A series of flat metallic blue doors went by on the left. At the fourth blue door, Melissa stopped, took a large ring of keys from her purse, and opened the door.

"This is where the M.E. keeps all the evidence? No one would ever find it."

"That's the idea. Some people who lose loved ones get a little crazy and try to steal their things. Makes it easier if they can't find where we keep them."

Fenway stepped into the room behind Melissa. Floor-to-ceiling metal gates surrounded the five-foot square entry area on three sides.

"All right, let me get Coach Levinson's box." She nodded at a clipboard hanging by a chain on the gate. "Go ahead and sign this out."

Melissa returned a moment later with a white cardboard box. A string of numbers and letters was written on the side.

Fenway opened the lid. Very little was inside: his clothes, a keychain, and a fitness tracker. "No wallet?"

"He had the keys in the pocket of his sweats. His wallet was on the table in the hotel room, and the exercise tracker was on his left wrist." Melissa gestured to the box. "I catalogued that room myself. I can tell you he didn't have anything else on his person."

"No wedding ring?"

"In a pocket of his carry-on."

Fenway picked up the keychain and stared at it. A key fob with a logo for the fancy Italian sports car, a large metal key with a ProLoc logo that perhaps went to Levinson's house back in Las Vegas, and several smaller keys, perhaps to the Nidever University facility. Finally, a thin wire key ring was on the keychain, but without a key. It was laced through a small punch hole in a laminated card. The card, about an inch and a half wide by four inches long, was white, with dark blue pre-printed lines labeled *make, model,* and *license number.* None of the lines were filled in.

"Did anybody notice this keychain has a *second* keychain on it?" Fenway squinted. The wire of the smaller keychain was bent, as if somebody had pulled on it with a lot of force.

"That's your detectives' job. We logged it into evidence here, but it probably won't be reviewed until it gets back to Estancia."

"Did this keychain get printed?"

"Partials. Nothing usable, though most of the partials are consistent with the victim."

"Hmm." Fenway stared at the keys. "Why would there be a second keychain with no key on it?"

"I don't know. Maybe he took the key off and gave it to his wife before he left Las Vegas."

"I'm not sure." Fenway held up the keychain, letting the card dangle. "These cards are often used by rental places or dealerships."

"Maybe he bought a new car?"

Fenway shook her head. "The assistant coaches say he had a key to a white Toyota Corolla that belonged to the team. I think it was on here."

"The car that almost ran Maggie over the night before last?"

"Yes." Fenway gave Melissa a sideways glance. "How do you know about that?"

"The APB. Everyone at the sheriff's office knows the story behind it." Melissa pursed her lips. "I don't know, Fenway. If the car belonged to the team, he probably kept the key in his office. There are other explanations—not necessarily the Corolla key."

Fenway raised her eyes from the keychain to Melissa. "Did you log a Corolla key into evidence when you examined the hotel room?"

Melissa shook her head.

"Annabel had access to the Corolla," Fenway said, "and we've been treating her as a suspect. If Levinson had the Corolla key, she'd be our prime suspect. But now it's missing—and so I think whoever killed Coach Levinson stole the other key and used the Corolla not only to try to run over Maggie two days ago, but also to meet her at the beach where they killed her."

"If that's the case," Melissa said, her eyes lighting up, "then I should probably get you get back to the sheriff's office in Estancia as soon as possible—with the evidence box."

Fenway grinned. "That'll sure beat waiting for an Uber."

CHAPTER TWENTY-TWO

DEZ WAS THE ONLY ONE IN THE CORONER'S OFFICE WHEN FENWAY walked in and set the box on the counter. The sergeant stared at her computer screen with her jaw clenched.

Dez glanced up. "How did the autopsy go? Did you find anything that helps the investigation?"

"It wasn't a golf club that killed Maggie," Fenway said. "The rounded edge of the wound was too circular—it was a stick with something spherical on the end."

Dez furrowed her brow. "Like what?"

"I don't know. A walking stick?"

"I've never seen a walking stick with a ball on the end."

"Me neither." Fenway pointed toward the door of the office. "Can you review the evidence I brought back from San Miguelito?"

Dez stood and walked over to the counter. "What do you have there?"

"Coach Levinson's personal effects." Fenway pushed the box over to Dez.

"This has all been logged?"

"Yes. I want your opinion on the keychain."

Dez lifted out Levinson's keys with one hand and squinted. "What's this?" She pointed to the small key ring.

"It's one of those temporary cheap wire key rings you see at dealerships, right?"

"But there's no key on it."

Fenway nodded. "And the wire looks like it's been pulled."

"You're thinking there was a key on here that someone grabbed and yanked off."

"Right."

"Any fingerprints?"

"Nothing usable."

Dez turned over the tag in her hand. "Make, model, license plate. But it's blank." She looked up at Fenway. "You think this wire key ring held the key to the white Corolla."

Fenway pointed at Dez and touched her nose with her other hand. "Even though Annabel had the other key, both the assistant coaches said Levinson had the second key. And I think the killer took it."

"And tried to run over Maggie in front of the police station."

Fenway nodded.

Dez closed her eyes and put her hands on her temples. "There could be other explanations."

"That's what Melissa said, too. Key could be in his office instead." Fenway shook her head. "But I don't think so. The team's only been in Estancia a few days, and Annabel was the first person to borrow the Toyota. It makes sense that it hadn't come off his keychain yet."

"Maybe he didn't want the responsibility of the Corolla."

"If that were the case, he never would have put it on his keychain. He would have been looking for another coach to take care of the key. And he wouldn't have yanked it off the wire. He would have handed the whole key ring over to the other person."

"Maybe that's true—maybe he never put it on his keychain." Dez put the keychain back in the box. "Did you look in the coaches' office for the Corolla key?"

"Not yet." Fenway rubbed her chin. "We can get a warrant. I don't want to ask anyone if I can look in Coach Levinson's desk—they're all suspects."

Dez nodded. "I can get the paperwork started."

"If my gut is right and the killer *did* take Levinson's key, there's a good chance they don't know we're looking for it. We've focused all our attention on Annabel, and anyone who was on the field earlier today—or in the hotel—knows we think Annabel is the only one with a key."

"Don't you think they'll have tossed the key by now?"

Fenway leaned back against the conference table. "Maybe. But you'd be surprised at how many people don't want to throw away something with so much perceived value, like a car key. Besides, they might need to use it again. If we can find the Corolla key, we might find our killer."

Dez walked around the counter. "I've got something to show you, too."

"Yeah?"

"We got lucky with the canvass we did of Paseo Fuentes Park."

"Oh," Fenway said, her eyes growing wide. "That means—"

"They hadn't picked up the trash yet." Dez tilted her head. "But I'm not sure you'll like what we found."

———

The logo of the Broadmere Hotel was printed in a deep navy blue on the white plastic laundry bag, so shiny it was almost silver.

Dez held the bag up. "I thought you'd want to see this."

"A laundry bag from the Broadmere."

Dez took out a white hotel towel, more than three-quarters of it pink, and still wet, consistent with the towel being used to clean up the blood, then washed in the shower. Dez removed the second towel from the bag, and it was even bloodier than the first. Fenway was glad there was a plastic sheet covering the table.

"So I was right—the two missing towels were thrown away. I wasn't looking far away enough." Fenway glanced up at Dez. "Samples sent to the lab?"

"Already done. I'd wager that's Paul Levinson's blood."

"Good."

"But that's not all." Dez reached her gloved hand into the bag and pulled out a gray-and-aquamarine striped sweatshirt. The sweatshirt was spotted with blood as well. Dez grabbed the shoulders of the sweatshirt and unfolded it. *Desert Treasure* in embossed gold letters snaked across the chest of the sweatshirt. Fenway blinked. "That's the name of Mathilda Montague's casino empire—or, you know, legitimate business interest."

"We've talked with several players on the team," Dez said. "Annabel is the only player who owns a sweatshirt like this."

"Are you sure? I thought Desert Treasure was the sponsor of the team."

"Yes, but this is a different sweatshirt than the corporate gear the team members of the Neons have. Lorraine Sunday even sent me the electronic order form for the team gear, Fenway, and the Desert Treasure gear is a different design. This is exclusive—it was a limited edition—and it's Annabel's sweatshirt, no question about it. She even has a matching gym bag."

Fenway frowned. Annabel's sweatshirt. She closed her eyes and thought back. The interview while walking around the field. Annabel stomping angrily through the locker room to get the Corolla key—

"The Corolla key," Fenway said.

Dez cocked her head. "What does that have to do with the sweatshirt?"

"When Annabel gave me the Corolla key, she dug through her gym bag and said it was under her sweatshirt. But her sweatshirt was missing."

Dez wrinkled her nose. "She offered that information to you?"

"Yes." Fenway took the sweatshirt and laid it flat, looking at the bloodstains. "The question is, was it missing because she'd forgotten she'd cleaned up the murder scene and thrown it away? Or was it missing because someone had taken it and was trying to frame her?" Fenway pointed at the stains. "The sweatshirt isn't as bloody as the towels."

Dez leaned over the table, studying the sweatshirt. "Here's one possible scenario. Annabel wore a sweatshirt when she killed Levinson, getting some spatter on it, and perhaps more when she tried to clean up with the towels. Maybe she carried the bloody towels and the blood transferred to the sweatshirt."

Fenway pinched the bridge of her nose and thought a moment. "That also fits with our old theory that Maggie killed him and Annabel cleaned up after her."

"True."

"But why point out to me that the sweatshirt is missing?"

Dez put the towels and sweatshirt back into the bag. "Let's say Annabel comes to the realization that she tossed a bloody sweatshirt that could be traced back to her. So she lets slip in front of the coroner that the sweatshirt is missing. Now you're thinking she was framed—her plan worked." Dez folded the sweatshirt. "Consider the source of your information."

Fenway pulled off her blue nitrile gloves and threw them in the hazardous waste bin. "The blood on Annabel's sweatshirt *does* make it look like we need to bump her to the top of our suspect list. But let's keep an eye out for things that don't fit. You're right—I *am* thinking that someone's trying to frame her."

"The evidence points to Annabel." Dez cracked her knuckles. "She was on the ninth floor the night Levinson was killed and didn't come back down the elevator. She had the key to the Corolla, no matter if there was a second key. Means, motive, and opportunity for both Coach Levinson and Maggie."

"Weak physical evidence and a weak motive to kill Maggie," Fenway said.

"Self-preservation can be very compelling," Dez said. "Even if she killed Levinson to protect Maggie, she might have killed Maggie to protect herself."

Fenway bit her lip and stared at the floor, thinking. "It's possible." She raised her head, looked at Dez, and tapped her chin.

"What?"

"I think we need to check the security footage from Thursday night again."

———

"I'm sorry," the hotel clerk said, "but Mr. Washington has asked for you to get a warrant for any further review of the security footage."

"He *what?*" Dez asked, drawing herself up to full height. "He's been cooperative up till now."

Fenway motioned with her head, and she and Dez took a few steps back from the desk. "Sarah did some digging," she said softly, "and Ezekiel's daughter went to college at Shellmont University when Levinson was the head coach. I mentioned it to him when I came here yesterday—and I guess it rubbed him the wrong way."

"So we need to add him to the list of suspects?"

"I'm not sure. His daughter wasn't on the soccer team."

Dez pursed her lips. "Did you confirm that, or did he just tell you?"

"I haven't confirmed it yet."

"So now," Dez said, her voice rising slightly, "he's prevented us from watching the security video."

"I'll go above his head." Stepping toward the desk, Fenway cleared her throat. "May I speak with the security supervisor? Or maybe the manager of the hotel?"

"It's Sunday. Neither are available."

"This is important. It's regarding the security footage."

The clerk blinked a few times. "I suppose I can try to make a phone call."

"Please." Fenway stepped back and lowered her voice. "I wish we could see that video. I'm almost positive Annabel *didn't* have the sweatshirt on when she got off the elevator on the ninth floor."

"I don't remember." Dez exhaled through her nose. "If she had it on when she exited the elevator but didn't have it on when she came back in through the front entrance, I'd arrest her tonight."

Fenway nodded. "And if we can search the coaches' office and find the key, it'll mean that no one had a Corolla key *but* Annabel."

"I apologize," the clerk said, hanging up, "but I'm afraid our manager isn't answering."

"Thanks for your assistance." Fenway motioned to Dez, and they walked through the front doors, stopping just outside the entrance.

"That's it?"

"We can go down the warrant road, but that'll take at least until tomorrow morning."

"We should go to the security office anyway," Dez said. "Ezekiel could be deleting footage right now."

Fenway ran a hand over her hair. "No reason to go there now—he could have deleted footage at any point during the investigation. A judge would never sign off on an injunction without more to go on."

Dez's mouth curved down. "I'm looking at Mr. Washington as a suspect now. Ezekiel had means and opportunity for Levinson's murder—and if we find out that Levinson did something to his daughter at college, he has motive, too."

"He's one of the few people who knows exactly how the doors of the stairwell work." Fenway paced back and forth, a few steps in each direction. "He might have been able to turn off the door sensors to let himself onto different floors."

"More likely that security has a key to open the stairwell doors from the outside."

"And he'd have had access to everyone's hotel room with a master key, wouldn't he?" Fenway stopped pacing. "Stolen Christchurch's tennis bracelet, put it in Maggie's room, taken Annabel's sweatshirt from her hotel room—"

"That's something I've been meaning to ask you." Dez looked at Fenway. "You seem to think it's no big deal to break into Christchurch's room safe."

"When I interviewed her, I asked her what she used for the combination. She admitted it was something that the public could easily find out. If I had to guess, I'd bet it was her husband's birthday or their anniversary. Especially as she was using the safe to store a meaningful gift he gave her before he died."

"That's publicly available information?"

"Warren Christchurch has a Wikipedia page with his birthday. And a simple web search uncovers the date they married."

"So Ezekiel could have done it." Dez looked over Fenway's shoulder through the hotel's front windows. "He's got a possible motive for Levinson's murder. And he probably knows how to get into the ninth floor from the stairwell."

"But why kill Maggie?"

"I don't know yet."

Fenway closed her eyes and pinched the bridge of her nose,

thinking for a moment. "A lot of cars come with a valet key in addition to the two regular keys, right?"

"Some of them do."

"I asked Ezekiel if the team gave him a valet key to the Corolla. He said they didn't—but what if he was lying?"

"That would give Ezekiel access to the Corolla, too." Dez held up her index finger. "Means and opportunity to try to run Maggie over in front of the sheriff's office." She raised a second finger. "And he could've met her at Cypress Point Beach, too."

Fenway grimaced.

"No?"

"Maggie had to trust the person she met on the side of the highway. Maggie trusted Annabel. I'm not sure she even knew who Ezekiel was."

Dez thought for a moment. "Maggie and Ezekiel's daughter went to Shellmont at the same time. Maybe they were friends."

Fenway frowned. "I was friends with people in college. I wouldn't have trusted any of their fathers to meet me on the side of the highway at five in the morning."

"Then who? Who would Maggie trust enough to meet?"

Fenway put her hands on her hips and stared at the ground. Nothing fit together well enough. "Annabel. The coaches. The owner. Maybe another player—Darcy?"

"But none of them are on the security footage leaving the hotel. Or coming back."

"They left by the stairwell. And figured out a way back in." Fenway sucked in air through her teeth. "Or—maybe Ezekiel doctored the security footage. He could have been paid off even if he didn't kill Levinson."

"Now we're just throwing random ideas out." Dez walked toward her red Impala, parked on the street in front of the hotel. "Come on —we'll never find more evidence if we stand here yammering all day."

Fenway followed Dez to the car. "You know, we haven't talked much about the owner yet."

"Sandra Christchurch?"

"She was on the same floor as Levinson. My father says she's interested in selling the team—but with a coach who sexually coerces his players, that might lower the team's price significantly."

"More than the murder of the head coach and starting goalkeeper?" Dez took out her key fob and unlocked the car as she walked around to the driver's door. "And are you suggesting she stole her own jewelry and planted it in Maggie's room?"

Fenway was silent as she opened the passenger side door and sat. The card signed by "Lorraine," the shoe print, the missing Corolla key—she felt like she just needed one piece to fall into place and everything would click together.

"Congratulations," Dez said, "you've widened the list of suspects and made things more complicated." She clicked her tongue.

"We need more evidence," Fenway said.

"We need to find that Corolla," Dez said.

"The APB hasn't turned up anything?"

"Nope."

Fenway was quiet for a moment, then it dawned on her. "Everyone on the suspect list is either involved with the team or with the Broadmere."

"Right."

"That means the white Corolla is probably still here at the hotel." Fenway opened the car door. "I'll meet you back at the office."

CHAPTER TWENTY-THREE

In the driveway of the Broadmere Hotel, Fenway took her phone out of her purse and called Sarah Summerfield. Although it was a Sunday, she hoped Sarah would pick up. On the third ring, Sarah answered.

"Let me guess. You need me to get some information for you from IT."

"I hate to bother you on the weekend, Sarah—"

"—but I'm the only one from the office who can actually communicate with Patrick without pissing him off." She laughed. "Not that I mind the time and a half."

"Do you think you can have him run down financial information from the players and coaches over the last week?"

"I'll call Patrick and see what I can do."

"See if you can find anything suspicious about Lorraine Sunday's transactions. A note with her name signed to it—maybe one with romantic intentions—was slipped under Maggie's door on Thursday night or Friday. See if she ordered flowers, gift baskets, anything like that."

Sarah was quiet for a moment. "I heard about Maggie's death. I can't believe it—she was so young. I thought she'd be the national team's goalie for the next fifteen years." She clicked her tongue. "How are *you* holding up? I heard you're the one who found her body."

"I'm okay." Fenway cleared her throat. "I'm here at the Broadmere Hotel. I need to find that white Corolla you and I saw in the parking garage on Friday."

"What do the financials have to do with the Corolla—oh, of course. Gas stations, that kind of thing. I can ask Patrick to run the players' credit card charges over the last few days. Should I focus on anyone in particular?"

"Annabel is—well, let's just say we need to perform due diligence on her." Fenway rubbed her forehead. "I know she had the Corolla on Thursday night, and she didn't turn in the key. See if she's had any suspicious expenses over the last few days. Check out the other assistant coach, too. Rocky—wait, no—*Roger* Portello." Fenway paused, staring out to Broadway.

"That's a lot of information for Patrick to uncover," Sarah said. "I don't know how much of this we can get done today."

Fenway paused but decided not to press it. When Fenway needed information, Sarah almost always came through. "Maybe Patrick can start with the financials for Annabel."

The sound of a pen scratching on paper could be heard over the line. "Got it. We might have to bug a judge on the weekend too—"

"Dez is on her way to the office."

"You want me to meet her there?"

"If you don't mind."

Sarah hesitated. "I suppose I can come in for an hour or so."

"Thanks, Sarah, you're a lifesaver. Dez is already starting a couple of warrants, so work with her on adding these."

———

Instead of going into the hotel, Fenway turned left and walked into the parking garage. Her eyes adjusted to the dim light of the garage, and she heard the tapping of her flats on the asphalt as she strode toward the breezeway.

A minute later, she found herself on San Ysidro Street. It had only been two days ago when she had first seen this neighborhood. Now on Sunday afternoon, the block was alive. A few children were playing in their yards, and several cars were parked in front of one house, as well as jammed in the driveway, and the sound of upbeat music carried across the street to where Fenway stood. She looked up and down the street but saw no white Corolla.

Fenway gritted her teeth and blew air out. It had been a hunch, but Fenway had been sure she was right.

Wait.

About fifty yards to her left, on the other side of the street, a small sedan was parked with a new beige car cover over it—it still had creases in the fabric. Fenway began walking toward the covered sedan. It was the right shape for a Corolla, but with the cover on, she couldn't be sure.

She reached the car and knelt behind the rear bumper. Lifting a corner of the cover, she saw the white paint of the bumper and the bottom of the trunk hatch.

Pulling up the cover a bit more, she saw the Nevada license plate. She didn't have to pull out her notebook to recognize it was the team's Corolla.

She didn't know where the Corolla had been parked on Friday night, but Fenway strongly suspected that on Saturday morning, someone drove it to meet Maggie at the Cypress Point Beach trail off Highway 326.

And they had killed her.

She closed her eyes and imagined the scenario. Why would the Corolla driver leave the car parked behind the hotel?

The obvious answer was the killer was staying at the Broadmere. Or—perhaps they wanted to throw suspicion on someone staying there. Annabel had made a good suspect so far.

Fenway squeezed her eyes shut. No. If the killer had wanted to set up someone at the Broadmere, the Corolla would have been left in plain sight, not under a car cover. She opened her eyes and felt the cover's material between her fingers; it was a thin plastic, backed by what felt like polyester fleece, and it didn't fit snugly—it wasn't built for the exact make or model of the Corolla. When she first got her Accord, she'd looked at a few of these types of car covers online, but they seemed cheap.

Fenway took out her phone and called Dez.

"Roubideaux."

"Dez, it's Fenway. I've found the Corolla."

"What?"

"It's parked behind the Broadmere on San Ysidro Street."

"How did our people miss it?"

"It's under a car cover. Creases still in it—brand new." Fenway paused. "We need to get a fingerprint unit over here."

"Sure," Dez said, "but fingerprints aren't time stamps. We already know Annabel drove the car on Thursday, so if we find her fingerprints on the car, it won't help make a case against her." She paused. "Why didn't the killer get rid of the Corolla? Do you think they wiped it clean?"

"Maybe," Fenway said, "but I think they weren't planning on killing Maggie until yesterday morning. Maybe until Maggie called them. They hadn't yet planned how to cover their tracks." She stood, her knees cracking as she got up. "I think the more likely explanation is they didn't have time to get rid of the car."

"So they bought a car cover?"

"It would have done the trick if I hadn't been so nosy." Fenway smiled and rotated her neck. She saw the open door of the convenience store on the corner. "I'll go into the mini-mart next door to see if anyone inside saw who left the car here."

Dez typed for a few seconds. "Deputy Salvador will be there shortly—a couple of minutes."

Stuffing her notebook back in her purse, Fenway strode into the corner market. The door chimed as she walked across the threshold, and the man behind the counter turned his head to look at her.

Fenway pulled her badge out. "I'm with the coroner's office. How long has that car been out there covered with the sheet?"

"The car parked on the street?" The man stroked his wispy beard in thought. "It was here when I showed up for my shift this morning about ten thirty," he said. "I don't remember any covered car being around the shop yesterday, though."

"Did you see anyone hanging around the car?"

The man shook his head.

Fenway thanked the man and headed out the door.

She walked back to the Corolla and stared at the car for a moment, pacing back and forth on the sidewalk next to the passenger side. A sheriff's cruiser turned onto the street. Deputy Celeste Salvador rolled down her window.

"This the car in question?" Salvador motioned at the covered Corolla.

"Yep. Can you stick around until the fingerprint team shows up?"

"Sure." Salvador eyed Fenway thoughtfully. "You in a hurry?"

"No. Yes. Kind of. I want to canvass the neighborhood to find anyone who saw who left the car here."

Celeste turned her gaze to the busy front yards of the houses down San Ysidro, then back to the Corolla.

"The car cover looks new."

"I thought the same thing."

"Instead of talking to the neighbors, maybe the AutoQuest shop across Fourth Street would be a better idea."

Fenway stared across the street.

"Killer needs to get rid of the car but doesn't have time," Celeste Salvador continued. "Parks it behind the hotel on a residential street, but it's still out in the open. Looks up from their parking spot and sees an auto parts store. Thinks maybe they can get a car cover."

"Yeah," Fenway said. "I don't know why I didn't think of that."

"And it's a generic car cover too, not one made for that model of car." Salvador pointed to the bulge at the front of the driver's door. "See the bump over the side mirrors? It doesn't fit right. This is meant for late-model compact sedans, not specifically for a two-year-old Corolla."

Fenway nodded at Salvador, then walked past the convenience store, waited for a car to pass on the thoroughfare, and hurried across the street to the AutoQuest shop. In the parking lot, a burgundy Ford Mustang with one gray fender sat with its hood open, a man in a plaid shirt leaning over the engine.

Fenway walked across the parking lot and entered the front door, an electronic chime signaling her entry. The floor was a gold-and-cream linoleum tile, and a long counter ran down the right-hand side of the shop. Three point-of-sale stations sat behind flat black monitors perched on the high counter. The clicking of her flats on the linoleum seemed to echo loudly through the store, drowning out the low-volume classic rock on the speakers.

The store had about a dozen rows. Fenway walked down the main aisle until she saw a sign reading *Car Covers*.

The car covers were three-quarters of the way down the aisle. A generic beige cover, exactly like the one draped over the white Corolla, sat on the bottom shelf. The price label beneath it read $199.99. After seeing how cheap-looking it looked on the car itself, Fenway expected the cover to be about half that much.

But beggars can't be choosers. The killer couldn't get rid of the

Corolla and needed to stash it. The car cover was a necessary expense.

While it was possible the killer had two hundred dollars in cash, it wasn't likely. Fenway might be able to get a credit card receipt.

Fenway went back to the counter. Just as it had been when she walked in, no employees were behind the counter. She tapped the desk bell; the clear ding sounded high and strong throughout the store.

A woman in blue coveralls appeared, with a red paisley kerchief keeping her long black hair out of her face. "Hey, hon. Can I help you with something?"

"Were you working here yesterday morning?"

The woman narrowed her eyes. "Who's asking?"

Fenway pulled her badge out of her purse and showed it to the woman. "I'm with the coroner's office. I'm looking for someone who bought one of those beige car covers for a midsize sedan. They probably bought it yesterday. Might have walked in, or maybe drove up in a white Toyota Corolla."

The woman shook her head. "I was off yesterday. Jeff or Hassan, they were both here yesterday. One of them could tell you."

"Are either of them here?"

"Sorry, hon. They don't work Sundays."

Fenway thought for a moment. "Your point-of-sale system—can you go back to yesterday and see if you sold any of those?"

The woman frowned and shifted her weight. "Uh—I guess so. I'm kind of busy. It might take a minute."

Fenway resisted the urge to look dramatically around the empty store, reminding herself the woman might have been in the middle of inventory or stocking. Instead, she clasped her hands in front of her. "I'd really appreciate it."

The woman sighed but stepped to the computer and tapped on

the keyboard, murmuring to herself. Fenway willed herself to take a few steps back from the counter and wait, although she wanted to pace around the store and perhaps hover around the woman's workstation.

"Looks like it was a cash transaction," the woman finally said.

"Cash? Isn't that a two-hundred-dollar car cover?"

"Two fourteen forty-nine after tax," the woman replied.

Fenway scratched her head with both hands. Of course, it made sense. Whoever had killed Maggie would have tried to cover their tracks. If the killer had enough sense to purchase a car cover for the Corolla, they would have had enough sense to avoid a financial trail.

She put her arms back at her sides. "Where's the nearest ATM?"

The woman pointed to the back of the store.

Fenway nodded. "Great—do you have camera footage?"

She shook her head. "The ATM doesn't have a camera—it's one of those third-party systems."

"You have cameras in the shop?"

The woman shook her head. "My boss keeps talking about putting them in, but he hasn't done it yet."

Fenway frowned. "Maybe you can get Jeff or Hassan on the phone?"

The woman hesitated. "We aren't allowed to contact employees on their scheduled days off."

"This isn't about picking up a shift. This is a murder investigation."

The woman put her hands on the workstation and took a deep breath. "Company policy. Sorry."

Fenway took a step forward. "I—"

The woman's eyes widened slightly, but she tightened her jaw.

Fenway stopped and stepped back from the counter. "All right. Thank you."

She turned to face the door—and the plaque next to the door caught her eye.

Employee of the Month
> January: Jeffrey Matheson
> February: Hassan Anwar
> March: Hassan Anwar

Fenway strode out through the front, back toward Deputy Salvador, who was still waiting with the Corolla. Pulling out her phone as she crossed the street, Fenway called Sarah.

"Hi, Fenway," Sarah said. "I don't have any new information for you yet, but I'm working on it."

"I hate to do this to you, Sarah, but I have a couple more items to add to your to-do list."

Sarah caught herself mid-sigh. "Yeah, all right. Go ahead."

"I have a couple of employees from the AutoQuest who we need information from. Our killer might have made a cash purchase this morning, and I need them to describe the customer. If their memories are good enough, maybe even come to the station to look at a photo array."

"Got it," Sarah said, the sound of her pen audibly scratching on a notepad. "Do you have the names of the employees?"

"The first one is Jeffrey Matheson." Fenway spelled the last name. "The second one is Hassan Anwar—Hassan with two S's."

"Which AutoQuest?"

"The one on Fourth Street at the corner of San Ysidro."

"Got it. Oh—I gave all that information to Patrick. He came into the office a few minutes ago to work on it."

Fenway breathed out in relief. "Fantastic."

"But I had another idea."

Fenway blinked.

"I noticed that Sandra Christchurch announced that Levinson got fired, then he was found dead an hour later. Then the team let Maggie go—which I think was the owner's call—then *she* ended up murdered."

"Okay." Fenway remembered that Christchurch was tired and disheveled on Saturday morning—and had complained about a late night.

"So," Sarah continued, "I started to dig into Christchurch's investments and companies. A lot of stuff is hidden, but there's a fair number of public records out there, too."

"Did you find something?"

"Well—kind of. The first company she owned was XTL Events. They managed corporate trade shows. This was right at the same time more tech companies were going to Vegas for conferences. She made a small fortune off that and invested her way into bigger fortunes."

"She still owns the event management business, right?"

"That's correct. And I was digging around on their website and found—well, here, let me text you."

Fenway's phone dinged. She took the phone away from her face, put it on speaker, and looked at the picture Sarah had just sent.

The photo was of a silver-colored rod with a round ball at the end.

"What is this? Some kind of walking stick?"

"Look at the caption."

Fenway double-tapped the picture.

XTL Stainless Steel Banner Rod, 60 inch

· · ·

"I sent this picture to Dr. Yasuda," Sarah said. "Based on the width of the ball finial, she believes this fits the criteria for the weapon that killed Maggie."

"That doesn't prove anything," Fenway said.

"Except," Sarah said, "the Broadmere Hotel received two packages addressed to Sandra Christchurch on Wednesday—I have the dimensions listed in the shipment receipt. Long, thin boxes from XTL Events."

CHAPTER TWENTY-FOUR

Dez closed the door of the Impala. "I could have just stayed here, you know."

"I didn't know then what I know now." Fenway took a step down the sidewalk.

"Aren't you going the wrong way?"

"The shipping entrance is around the side."

"That's great, Fenway, but aren't they closed on Sunday?"

Fenway blinked, then stopped in her tracks. "That means we'll need to talk to Sandra Christchurch directly."

They walked to the front door of the hotel and crossed the lobby. Fenway reached out and pushed the button for the elevator.

Dez elbowed Fenway lightly in the ribs. "You think Christchurch is sick of talking to you yet?"

"I don't know." Fenway reached out and pushed the lit button again, and the elevator bank responded with a ding. "It seems like she'd—"

The doors opened, and Sandra Christchurch stood in the elevator.

"Excuse me, please, Miss Stevenson," she said coldly. "Unless you are here to escort me to the meeting with your father's lawyers, would you be so kind as to—"

"We need to speak with you, Ms. Christchurch." Fenway took a step back but didn't get out of the way.

"I'm afraid I'm on my way to an important meeting."

"And *I'm* afraid we need to have a conversation before you go anywhere."

Christchurch stepped out of the elevator. "Am I under arrest?"

Fenway sneaked a glance at Dez, who gave a slight shake of her head.

"I hope that won't be necessary," Fenway said, turning back to the Neons' owner. "But we've uncovered evidence, and we need an explanation."

"Evidence? What evidence?"

"Perhaps we can go somewhere to talk."

Christchurch sighed and looked at her watch. "Fine. I can give you fifteen minutes. Let's retire to the hotel restaurant. You can buy me a drink."

————

The server set down two iced teas and a glass of red wine on the square table between Dez, Fenway, and Sandra Christchurch in the empty hotel restaurant. Dez glared across the table at Christchurch, who pretended not to notice.

"On Wednesday afternoon," Fenway said, "you received two packages from XTL Events."

Christchurch frowned, reaching for the glass of wine. "I *what?*"

"Two long, narrow packages."

"In Las Vegas?"

"No—at the Broadmere."

Christchurch took a sip of wine. "I was in Las Vegas on Wednesday. I didn't arrive in Estancia until Thursday evening."

"Are you telling me that you never received those two packages?"

"Of course not. I—" Christchurch stopped talking, then sat back in her seat.

"What is it?"

"I can tell you with certainty that I didn't receive those packages." Christchurch took her phone out of her purse, then tapped the screen several times. "Wednesday, you said?"

"Yes."

"I'm usually notified when my company ships items to me. If you permit me a moment to go through my email..." She trailed off.

"Certainly." Fenway studied Christchurch's face as the Neons' owner searched her email. A slightly crooked vertical crease formed between her eyebrows, but no other signs of her emotions registered on her face. The woman must be tough to negotiate with.

After a minute ticked by, Christchurch's eyes relaxed, and she looked up. "5:21 P.M."

"What about 5:21 P.M.?"

"That's when the packages were picked up from the hotel's receiving department. Paul Levinson's signature is on the form." She turned the screen so Fenway could see.

Out of the corner of her eye, Fenway saw Dez shoot her a meaningful look—though she didn't get the meaning. "Can you tell us what was in the shipment?"

Christchurch took the phone back and tapped on the screen again. "Two banner rods." The vertical line between her eyes deepened, then cleared. "Oh, Coach Levinson asked me to order these."

"Why put your name on the mailing label?"

Christchurch smiled. "When you ship to the owner of the company, orders don't get lost."

Fenway scratched her chin. The Neons owner had answers—and

it seemed like the possible murder weapons may never have been in her possession. Still, there were unanswered questions.

"When I came to your hotel room door yesterday morning," Fenway said, "you were sleeping. You said you'd had two late nights in a row." She reached for her iced tea and pulled it in front of her, though she didn't pick it up. "We've talked about Thursday night. Can you tell me what you were doing Friday evening?"

Christchurch sighed. "I was on the phone with agents."

"Like FBI agents?"

A chuckle escaped Christchurch's lips. "No—sports agents. People who represent head coaching candidates. I have a fiduciary duty to the shareholders of the Las Vegas Neons. We are starting the season within two months, and I don't have a head coach." She took another sip of wine. "I cannot have a vacancy in the head coaching position after training camp starts for longer than a week. At the very least, I need to appoint an interim coach."

"And where were you this morning?" Fenway asked. "Let's say between three o'clock and seven."

"You want to know where *I* was?" Christchurch set down her glass. "You—you mean to tell me that Maggie was murdered, too?"

"Can you please answer the question?" Dez said.

"Hold on." Christchurch held her hands up, palms out. "Yesterday, I thought Coach Levinson died by suicide. Then I heard it was a murder investigation—and you had Miss Erskine at the sheriff's office for the whole day. The last thing I heard was that her body was found in a ravine below a cliff. And several members of the Neons received a suicide note from Maggie." She raised her eyebrows. "You're telling me—what, that someone pushed her off the cliff?"

Fenway shook her head. "That's not what hap—"

"Your whereabouts between three and seven this morning, Ms. Christchurch," Dez said.

"In my hotel room," Christchurch said, then turned to Fenway. "Where you found me yesterday morning."

"You were on the phone most of the night before that?"

Sandra's eyes flitted between Fenway and Dez. "It's important to me that I do this as quickly and smoothly as possible. I want to announce our new head coach here at our training facility. It won't do for me to hold the press conference at my corporate office. It doesn't send the right message."

"So you're holding a press conference to announce our murder victim's replacement?" Fenway asked.

Christchurch flinched. "I *certainly* wouldn't phrase it like that. We are announcing the next head coach of the Las Vegas Neons to carry us through the current season."

Fenway blinked a few times, rapidly. Then: "Did Coach Levinson's replacement know they were next in line?"

Christchurch frowned. "I've never discussed a succession plan before."

"Inside or outside the organization?"

Christchurch paused, then leaned back in her chair. "The name of our new coach is not yet to be released to the public."

"Might I remind you," Fenway said, "this is a murder investigation?"

"What does that have to do with naming a head coach?"

"Because whoever gets the coaching job now has a motive—or an additional motive—to get Coach Levinson out of the way."

Christchurch scoffed. "And with our starting goalkeeper dead? It's not exactly an ideal position our new coach finds herself in."

Fenway paused. "*Herself?*"

Christchurch closed her eyes, then opened them slowly. "All right. This cannot get out. We're still finalizing the contract with Lorraine Sunday."

Dez shifted her weight in her chair. "We're under no obligation to keep that information private."

Sandra Christchurch narrowed her eyes. "What is it you want, Detective Roubideaux?"

"You've provided precious little information to us," Dez said.

"I cannot contribute what I do not know."

Christchurch glared at Dez, and the sergeant returned her steely gaze.

Fenway tilted her head. Maybe there was a way past Christchurch's barriers. She took a deep breath, placing her hands at the edge of the table for support. "I find it odd, Ms. Christchurch, that as soon as you announce that someone is leaving the team, that person winds up dead."

Christchurch flinched.

"Do you find that odd, too?"

"I must say," Christchurch said carefully, "that I did notice the correlation."

"Do you have an explanation for it?"

Christchurch leaned back in her seat. "I don't have a clue. If you're looking to pin the crime on *me*, I'm afraid you'll need to look elsewhere. I have no reason to get rid of anyone after I fire them from the team or release them from their contract."

From their contract...

Fenway narrowed her eyes. "All AFF contracts have a gag order, do they not?"

"A privacy clause," Christchurch said icily.

"Coaches and players can't speak to the media—or they face fines that would pretty much bankrupt them."

Christchurch blinked. "'Bankrupt' is a strong word."

"In fact," Fenway said, leaning forward, "players and coaches can't even speak to the authorities without a subpoena."

"That's correct."

"But once you fired Coach Levinson, and once Maggie was let go, they were free to disclose anything about the inner workings of this team to the press or the police, isn't that right?"

Christchurch shifted uncomfortably in her seat. "Uh—I suppose so, although I don't have the contract language memorized."

"Annabel put in a formal complaint—and it was about Coach Levinson."

"I'm aware."

Fenway nodded. "I'm frankly surprised you've put up with it."

"We've been investigating for a while," Christchurch said. "We finally uncovered a troubling pattern of behavior at other organizations."

"Including Shellmont University," Fenway said, trying to keep her voice as even as possible. "When Maggie was a seventeen-year-old freshman. And yet Levinson continued to work for your organization. You were going to keep him here until the end of the season." Fenway picked up her iced tea, but her hand was shaking, so she set the glass down again.

"Players wished to speak off the record," Christchurch said. "Their stories were remarkably similar: Coach Levinson would take certain players under his wing, then provide—well, special treatment. Sometimes it was private training sessions. Sometimes it was verbal abuse in front of other team members. Sometimes it was—well, closed-door meetings with only the player and the coach. Sometimes those meetings were held at the coach's residence, often while his wife was in New York."

"Why not fire him immediately?"

"After speaking with our lawyers, we were prepared to buy out his contract at the end of the season. As I said, no one was willing to go on the record." Christchurch steepled her fingers and leaned forward. "Need I remind you, the team got to the finals last year. When a coach has a track record of success, it doesn't provide the owner much cover."

"But you left something out when I interviewed you on Friday," Fenway said. "Somebody changed your mind. Someone moved up your timeline to fire Coach Levinson—all the way to Friday morning."

Christchurch gave a curt nod. "You've spoken to Annabel."

"Yes." Fenway cocked her head. "Why didn't you tell me when I asked you before?"

"I suppose I didn't want to put Annabel in a situation where she'd have to violate the privacy clause in her contract."

Fenway raised her eyebrows.

Christchurch sighed. "And I didn't want to give you the idea that I had anything to do with his death. If I had told you that Annabel woke me up and took me down the hall to Coach Levinson's room, you might have accused me of something."

"What happened when Annabel took you to Levinson's room?"

"I clearly heard him and Maggie—together, as it were."

"And *that's* when you decided to fire him."

Christchurch took another sip of wine, then set it down on the table. Her voice was calm, but a vein in her neck stood out. "I had personally made him aware of the allegations against him. I told him he'd been captured on video, and we were considering our options. I told him that he had to cease all one-on-one meetings with players." She pursed her lips. "And yet he *still* has relations with Maggie in his hotel room—down the hall from me? No, no. That cannot stand."

"You felt personally offended," Dez said.

"Yes, of course," Christchurch said, then hesitated and spoke again quickly. "That Coach Levinson held player safety in such callous disregard."

"And after Annabel left?"

"I went back to my room. And—and I talked to my lawyers. And first thing the next morning, I sent a communication to the team, talked to some of them at six thirty, then fired him at the press conference."

"Annabel came to you because her agreement—in fact, all the employment agreements in the AFF—says she can't talk about it to anyone but you and league personnel."

"That's correct."

"The same goes for Levinson. He couldn't publicly defend himself against these accusations, or he'd have been fined, too."

"I suppose."

"But after Levinson was fired, *he* could talk about it, couldn't he? He could have gone to the press. Told his side of the story."

"I don't—" Christchurch leaned forward and rubbed her temples. "That never came into our thought process about his employment with the team."

"But he could have talked, yes?"

"I don't know. Perhaps." Christchurch shook her head. "Are you trying to pin a motive on me? Coach Levinson died *before* I held the press conference. So why would I kill him, *then* fire him?"

"You knew what he did to players would come out in the news, didn't you?"

Christchurch was silent.

"But you firing him? Now you look like the good guy. And because he's dead in a pool of his own blood nine stories up, you don't have to worry about him dragging this out, filing a lawsuit, alleging defamation—that would screw up your deal to sell the team, wouldn't it?"

"I don't know if you've noticed, but a murder investigation isn't helping much, either." Christchurch crossed her arms.

"Good point." Fenway picked up her iced tea; she took a long drink, then set the glass down. "Now, your second firing—Maggie Erskine."

Christchurch slumped her shoulders. "There's a morality clause in the contracts. She was accused of killing the head coach—we couldn't let her onto the field. And my tennis bracelet was found in her room. We might have stuck with her if the murder allegations fell by the wayside, but not when she steals from the owner."

"But then you realized *she* could talk to the police and the press, too."

"I never—" Sandra Christchurch leaned her elbows on the table and looked down.

The seconds ticked by.

"If you have further questions, I'll need to have my lawyer present."

Fenway's heart sank—but she had gotten Christchurch to reveal more than she expected. "I understand." She stood from the chair, Dez getting up too. "One more thing. When are you making the announcement about your new coach?"

"Tomorrow morning, nine o'clock, at the Nidever University soccer fields. We want the team to hear it firsthand."

"You don't think placing the media so close to the team will be a distraction?"

"A distraction for a single day, Miss Stevenson. The media will run out of steam after a few hours." Her eyes twinkled. "If you think it will be any more than that, I'm afraid you've seriously overestimated the interest in women's soccer in this country."

Christchurch continued to sit, sipping her wine, while Dez and Fenway left the restaurant.

As she walked back to Dez's car, Fenway glanced through the window at Christchurch. "We rattled her."

"You think?"

"She said she could give us fifteen minutes. We were talking for at least that long. And now she's just sitting there, trying to calm down before her business meeting."

Fenway's phone rang in her purse. She pulled it out and looked at the screen. It was McVie. She felt a pang of annoyance—at herself or at him?—because of the way they had talked that morning.

"Hi, Craig."

"Hey, listen, I just wanted to let you know that Amy said she had something important to tell me. I'm heading over there now."

Fenway was silent for a moment, then spoke. "Megan had something important to tell you, too. Maybe Amy wants to talk about her." She hesitated. "Why do you have to go over to her place?"

"I don't."

"Why go, then?"

"I didn't see Megan very long on Saturday. I thought we could talk. See if maybe she wants to spend part of spring break with me. Maybe go camping or something."

"Isn't she seventeen?"

"Okay, fine, maybe she wouldn't want to go camping with her dad, but it's important to offer, even if she doesn't take me up on it." He sighed. "Look, she's not doing great since the divorce. I want her to know I'd still like to spend time with her."

Fenway's stomach dropped. Why was her first reaction always one of mistrust?

"Anyway, I didn't want you trying to reach me tonight, not knowing I was at Amy's house. You've been kind of..." He trailed off.

Fenway bit her lip and waited.

"This case seems to bring a lot of stuff up for you." His words were halting, his tone careful.

Fenway nearly scoffed. Of course it did. Anyone who knew about Fenway and her Russian Lit professor would know—

Fenway stopped.

She still hadn't told McVie about her Russian Lit professor.

She had told Dez. She'd even had the uncomfortable conversation about it with her father. But she'd never told McVie.

He'd figured it out, though. She remembered how empty she felt a few months ago when she found out he knew, and Fenway hadn't been the one to tell him.

And she still hadn't told him. Not directly.

He had said—before they were officially dating—that if she ever needed to talk, he was there for her.

But he'd never mentioned it again.

And neither had she.

In fact, she still acted like she had to keep it from him. Like her Russian Lit professor was a dirty secret. Like their relationship wouldn't survive if she told him.

Fenway shook her head. She was being ridiculous. She *was* ridiculous.

She'd been dating McVie for less than six months, and it was already one of the longest romantic relationships she'd ever had. She was serious about McVie—more serious than she'd ever been about a guy before.

And if she wanted to trust him, she'd have to tell him—even if he'd already figured it out.

———

Fenway opened the door to the coroner's suite and walked in. Sarah looked up from her computer. She wore an oversized T-shirt, and her hair was back in a ponytail—Fenway had never seen her so casual.

"Hey, Fenway." She tilted her head. "You okay?"

"It's the case." And telling McVie. Fenway forced a smile. "How are you and Patrick coming along with uncovering the financial information?"

Sarah leaned forward in her chair, a little closer to the screen. "Judge Harada limited the scope of the warrant to financial transactions from the last week. We don't get access to any of their checking or savings accounts, but purchases from credit and debit cards are okay."

"What about ATM transactions?"

"Purchases only."

"How about the warrant for the coaches' office at Nidever?"

Sarah shook her head. "Private university property. Harada said the standards weren't met." She glanced behind Fenway. "Isn't Dez with you?"

"She stopped at Java Jim's. We had to refuel our caffeine tanks."

"What?" Sarah turned to Fenway, her eyes twinkling. "You didn't get me anything?"

"It's after four P.M. I thought you couldn't drink coffee—"

Sarah turned back to her screen. "I'm messing with you. Should I send Dez in when she gets here?"

"Yes." Fenway turned back to Sarah. "Whose financial information are you looking at now?"

"Annabel Shedd."

"Can you do me a favor and look at Lorraine Sunday first?"

"Why?"

"Because Dez and I talked to Sandra Christchurch. It seems Sunday will be the new head coach of the Neons."

"Oh. So you think that gives her a motive to kill Coach Levinson?"

"People have killed for less."

"Hang on—do you think she killed Maggie too? She was supposed to be the next big thing. Hard to have success without a decent goalie."

"The pieces haven't all fit together yet. Maybe Maggie wasn't nearly as good as everyone said. Lorraine Sunday is a World Cup-winning goalkeeper. She might have seen something—or *not* seen something—everyone else missed." She scratched her temple. "Or maybe she thought Maggie could identify her as the killer and risked starting over with a new goalkeeper over getting caught as Levinson's killer."

Sarah turned back to her keyboard. "I'll look at Coach Sunday's credit cards. I'll let you know if I find something."

Fenway went into her office, closing the door behind her, and took her laptop out of its case. She plugged it into the dock and woke the machine up, logging into the system and reviewing the first few pieces of evidence in the case.

Photographs of the hotel room where Coach Levinson was found. Fenway brought up the inventory list from the hotel room. Melissa was right: there'd been no keys found. So where did Levinson's Corolla key go?

The door to Fenway's office opened, and Dez came in, setting a large Java Jim's paper cup in front of Fenway. "Large latte."

"I thought for sure we'd have eliminated some suspects by now." Fenway reached for the coffee cup.

"You're not wrong."

"But no one has a solid alibi." Fenway took a sip of her coffee. "And while everyone had a motive to get rid of Coach Levinson, no one had anything against Maggie."

"Sandra Christchurch did."

Fenway paused, tapping her chin. "That's true. And Maggie would have trusted her enough to meet her at the beach."

Dez sat down in a guest chair on the other side of Fenway's desk. "I was standing in line at Java Jim's, and I started thinking about what you said about the owner's timing—firing people who wind up dead."

"I only did that to get her to start talking. She might have been angry at Maggie for stealing the bracelet, but she doesn't have a motive for Levinson. Not really. The murder inquiry has done more damage to the price of the team than an investigation into Paul Levinson sexually coercing players. And Christchurch would have known that."

"Only I wonder," Dez said quickly, "if there wasn't something to that."

Fenway took another drink from her latte, then set it down on the desk. "Like the gag order in the contracts?"

Dez nodded. "Once Maggie was let go, she could have talked about how Paul Levinson spent years grooming her—I mean, she was still a minor at Shellmont."

"If we were building a murder case against Paul Levinson for killing Maggie, I might agree with you. But last time I checked, Paul Levinson was murdered first."

"You don't think Maggie could point the finger at other people in the organization? For making sure Levinson had access to Maggie, to make sure that Maggie was convinced not to file complaints? If Maggie had evidence that someone in the Neons' organization enabled Levinson to keep coercing her, that could lead to serious consequences."

"Maybe Maggie's finger was about to point at the person who just got promoted to head coach," Fenway said. "We need to be at the press conference tomorrow."

PART 5

MONDAY

CHAPTER TWENTY-FIVE

ABOUT FIFTY REPORTERS, SEVERAL TELEVISION CAMERAS, AND A smattering of fans crowded around the temporary stage and lectern at the edge of the soccer field. The morning light was still filtering through the mist, and Fenway shivered in her thin coat, standing about thirty feet away from the stage.

"They're not here yet," McVie said, pulling a wool cap over his ears.

Fenway tried not to berate herself too much. She had asked McVie to pick her up and drive her to the press conference with the excuse that her car was still being held for evidence, and she'd intended to tell him, really tell him, about what happened to her in the Russian Lit professor's office. But he seemed strangely subdued and pensive, and Fenway remembered he'd talked to his ex the night before. She hadn't wanted to pile on with her problems—well, not exactly her problems, but if McVie was processing something Amy had told him, maybe her unburdening could wait.

Fenway ran a hand over her hair. "I'm sure the owner wants to make a grand entrance." Her phone buzzed, and she pulled it out of her purse.

Had to make a stop in San Miguelito
I will be at Nidever but I will be 15-20 min late

"Who's that?" McVie asked.

"Dez. She's running late. Had to run to San Miguelito."

McVie's eyebrows raised. "Think she and Dr. Yasuda are back together?"

"I do, yes."

"Good." McVie's eyes softened. "I'm rooting for them."

"Because Dez will be in a better mood?"

"That's not the *only* reason I'm rooting for them."

Fenway felt a rush of affection for McVie. She looked around, but there were too many reporters and cameras to get close to him and have him wrap his warm arms around her. She felt weird as it was, standing next to him and arriving with him. Everyone by now—at least, everyone at City Hall and at the local newspaper and television stations—knew Fenway and McVie were an item.

"Why did you want to attend the press conference?"

"Because," Fenway said, "all the main suspects are here in one place." She felt like a Texas Hold 'Em poker player, behind in the hand, but with many cards that could show up and give her the win. The report from Maggie's cell phone—whom did she call that morning? The shoe print—she needed to see just one person with the unique shoe. Or a hit on a purchase that would give her a clue which way to go.

Her phone buzzed. It was a text from Sarah.

Payment information

*Credit card purchase at Marks-the-Spot for hinge-mounted wedge
  door stops, stationery and sports drinks
Paid for with Vegas Neons company credit card*

Fenway waited, but no follow-up came. She texted back.

Whose name on the credit card?

Another moment, then Sarah's text came back.

*No name listed on transaction — Store will send signature imprint in 2-
  3 business days*

Fenway grimaced. That would be no help. Sarah sent another text; this one was a link to the same wedge-shaped hinge-mounted door stoppers she'd shown Fenway online. Fenway read the product description and clicked on a video—the stopper allowed the door to be invisibly propped open at any angle.

And the company credit card—that narrowed things down. Fenway assumed the owner—and maybe the coaches—had access to the Neons' card.

A rustling of jackets and a murmuring among the crowd. Fenway turned as Sandra Christchurch in a cream-colored peacoat, her short hair perfectly coiffed, emerged from the mist and strode up to the field.

She was followed by Lorraine Sunday, dressed in a Las Vegas Neons tracksuit. The two women walked onto the field and took their places on the stage: Christchurch behind the lectern, Sunday to her right.

"Where's the other guy?" McVie asked.

"They're announcing Lorraine Sunday as the new head coach. Rocky wouldn't be onstage for that."

"So—"

"Rocky Portello didn't get promoted." Fenway turned back to the stage and walked in place to keep her blood flowing, the gears in her head turning. "Before Coach Flash was fired, he thought he'd get the head coach job when Levinson left—I spoke to him a couple of days ago, and he told me a succession plan was already in place, though Christchurch denies it. And he said he thought his job would be in jeopardy after the news story broke, but I don't believe him. I think he expected to be promoted."

"There he is." McVie lifted his chin slightly in the direction of the front row, to the left of the stage. Rocky Portello, dressed in gray sweats with a Las Vegas Neons cap, stood, rocking back and forth on the balls of his feet. Portello watched Lorraine Sunday, his brow furrowed and his jaw clenched.

Fenway craned her neck to look at his shoes, but too many people were in the way.

"Fenway!"

She jumped slightly—it was her father, dressed in a black suit and a white dress shirt, a blue-and-gold scarf around his neck, leaning on his cane which sank slightly into the wet turf. "This weather reminds me of getting up early and overseeing construction at Ferris Energy."

"Mr. Ferris," McVie said, reaching over and shaking Nathaniel Ferris's hand.

"Craig—it's been a while. How are you?"

"Good."

"We'll have to get you and your girlfriend over to the house for dinner. That is, if she's not too busy dealing with her work."

"Dad," Fenway hissed, "what are you doing here?"

"Really? I'm surprised you haven't figured it out."

"You're buying the team?"

"I'm not—" Ferris sighed. "Sandra and I are having preliminary talks. We had a fruitful meeting yesterday. Being here at the press conference in person is part of the due diligence."

Fenway paused. "Are you okay being out here?"

"Relax. I'm going back to the walkway in a moment." He glanced around furtively, then lowered his voice. "The doctor changed my medication right after my meeting with you on Friday. My balance is much better today."

"Oh." Fenway pulled the strap of her purse up higher on her shoulder. "I'm glad to hear it."

He held up his cane. It was a shiny piano black with a jewel-encrusted top.

"I can't believe it," Fenway said. "You went with the British spy cane idea."

"The handle isn't a hidden dagger or anything, but I love it. Your stepmother has excellent taste." His eyes twinkled. "I'll leave you to it. Here on official business, I suppose."

"I am."

Nathaniel Ferris stepped away from Fenway and McVie. The crowd quieted as Sandra Christchurch stepped to the podium and tapped the microphone.

A slight hum of feedback came on but dropped almost immediately. The field was quiet. Christchurch took a step away from the microphone, and a man in a jacket with the Nidever logo jumped onto the stage and began talking with Christchurch.

The mist settled thickly over the pitch, and Fenway felt the dampness weigh on her skin. McVie took a small step to the side, toward Fenway, and their elbows touched. Fenway glanced up at Portello; the assistant coach was still glaring at the stage.

The seconds ticked by, each one dragging, as the man turned and swapped out the microphone on the podium. A click and a low hum, and Fenway flashed in her mind to the ride in the Uber with Maggie, then another flash of her hiding next to Fenway's car, then again of finding Maggie's dead body in the ravine next to the beach. She shuddered as Christchurch stepped back to the microphone.

"Thank you." Sandra Christchurch's voice was firm, perhaps a little louder than she'd intended. A small murmur ran through the audience, and Christchurch looked out over the small group of people gathered in front of the lectern.

"I'd like to thank everyone for showing up on short notice and in the chilly weather," Christchurch said. "We're certainly not used to this in Las Vegas."

Scattered nervous chuckles through the crowd.

"This week has been the most challenging in Las Vegas Neons history," Christchurch continued. "Today, we come together as a team, come together as a family, and we must heal. The road ahead, particularly the balance of training camp, will be difficult. Now, more than ever, we need the support of the fans, our adopted community here in Estancia, and each other. In that light, I am honored to announce the promotion of Lorraine Sunday to the position of head coach of the Las Vegas Neons, effective immediately."

The applause was mostly polite and reserved, but from the back, a chorus of cheers. Fenway craned her neck: the players on the team, and in front, Annabel Shedd, clapping enthusiastically.

"Do you think Lorraine Sunday knew Christchurch would promote her?" Fenway whispered to McVie as the new head coach stepped up to the lectern.

"What do you mean?"

"I think Rocky Portello believed he'd be next in line for the head coaching job when Levinson retired," Fenway answered. "But suddenly he gets passed over for the other assistant coach. Do you think Sunday knew?"

"Are you looking for a motive for Coach Sunday?"

Before Fenway could answer, Sunday began to speak, a sober reflection on recent events.

McVie bent down and spoke in a low voice next to Fenway's ear. "Sunday's got a World Cup resume, doesn't she? Doesn't that beat being an assistant coach in the European leagues?"

Fenway tapped her chin. "Sunday knew Levinson sexually coerced his players constantly." She pinched her lower lip in thought, staring at the ground in front of her. "Sunday knew it would be hard to get Levinson out, and Portello was still the heir apparent. But what if she figured out a way to bring Levinson's relationship with Maggie out in the open?"

McVie nodded. "I suppose Sunday might convince Sandra Christchurch that Portello was too close to Levinson to be trusted." He shoved his hands deeper into his pockets. "But why murder? Christchurch was ready to fire Levinson for cause."

"Maybe Sunday didn't know," Fenway mused.

"You'll have to pick a motive," McVie said. "Either you think she killed Levinson to get promoted into his position, or you think she went to his hotel room to confront him about his coercion of Maggie and things got out of control."

"It could be both."

"Confronting Levinson—taking the law into her own hands—that I could see. But the head coaching position? There are openings all the time in the league," McVie said. "A top assistant for a successful club like the Neons? They'd have to be considered for any open head coaching position, right?"

Fenway looked sideways at McVie. "Lorraine Sunday is a Black woman. I'm not sure she'd get a fair shake."

"What are you talking about?" McVie tilted his head. "This is a women's league. Sandra Christchurch—"

"Is one of the few female owners in the league," Fenway finished. "Sorry to burst your bubble, Craig, but it's not a level playing field."

"Sunday's won a World Cup."

"And has a decade of coaching experience at the professional level," Fenway said, "and she's never gotten so much as an interview for a head coaching position."

McVie shook his head. "If she did it, she didn't plan it. The murder weapon was one of Levinson's golf clubs. Crime of opportunity. Maybe she'd intended to confront him about his behavior, but knowing she could be head coach factored into her decision."

"I don't know," Fenway said. "I just found out someone purchased special hinge-fitted door stoppers. You can adjust them to make it look like a door is all the way closed when it isn't. Those probably facilitated the murder. Wouldn't that mean it had to have been premeditated?"

McVie paused. "Did we miss something?"

Considering McVie didn't have all the evidence at his fingertips, it was kind of him to throw in the "we"—when Fenway really knew that *she* had missed something. She was sure the murder hadn't been fully planned. "We can ask her after we arrest her." But her voice sounded hollow.

McVie grinned. "Okay, so now Sunday's head coach—she got everything she wanted. What doesn't fit?"

Fenway rubbed her chin in thought. "Maggie's murder fits. Coach Sunday gave her Corolla key to Annabel, making us think she didn't have a key. But she takes Levinson's key when she kills him. Second, she was the goalkeeping coach—Maggie would have trusted her enough to meet with her Saturday morning. Here's a theory: Lorraine Sunday bought those door stoppers so Coach Levinson and Maggie could be alone without detection."

"Didn't need the door stoppers for Thursday night. She went up in the elevator."

"But she would have needed to get back into her room without being detected. I theorize that Lorraine put the hinge stopper on the sixth-floor stairwell door—the floor Maggie was on."

McVie looked at the gray sky for a moment, then briefly nodded.

"So let's say that Lorraine Sunday ran interference for Levinson both now and last year. But when Maggie got released by the team, Sunday realized that Maggie could talk to the media about how Sunday enabled Levinson to sexually assault her, day after day, month after month. Sunday might find herself not only fired as head coach but blacklisted by the league."

"So how do you explain the tennis bracelet? And the card?"

Fenway blinked. "Sunday had the opportunity to take the bracelet. She was at the coaches' meeting in Christchurch's room."

"But shoving the card under the door?"

Fenway snapped her fingers. "She did that before Maggie got arrested. She was hoping to keep Maggie on her side, or maybe bribe her to keep her mouth shut. Then everything went sideways when Maggie was kept at the station all day."

McVie looked skeptical. "Giving Maggie the owner's beloved tennis bracelet? That doesn't make sense."

"It might have made sense to Sunday at the time. Besides, she doesn't have an alibi. Not for either of the times when the murders were committed."

McVie was quiet for a moment. Lorraine Sunday was speaking, but her tone was somber, and Fenway wasn't paying attention.

"You really think," McVie finally said, "Lorraine Sunday killed Levinson to have a shot at becoming head coach?"

Fenway pressed her lips together. "And then killed Maggie to keep her from going to the press with stories about how the whole organization covered up the sexual coercion."

Sunday's speech grew stronger and more forceful, then applause burst forth from the crowd. Fenway startled and began clapping along with them.

McVie leaned forward. "It's an interesting story, Fenway, but you don't have any proof."

Fenway blinked—and suddenly she was back on the Western

Washington campus walking as fast as she could away from her Russian Lit professor's office, and everything running through her head screamed *but you don't have any proof.* Her professor had been a powerful man in the department—on all of campus, in fact—and she was a community college transfer in her first semester.

She blinked again, and she was back on the Nidever campus, watching Lorraine Sunday speak.

Fenway looked up at McVie. "And that's why I'm here. Dez and I can talk to the team. We're uncovering more financial records every hour." The owner and assistant coaches, specifically—they might have all had access to the corporate card. Then she might have her proof.

"Right," McVie said as the crowd began to thin. He looked around. "I should get to the office—I've got some billing to take care of."

Fenway grinned. "What good is having a rich client if they don't pay you?"

"Exactly." He smiled, but his eyes were tired, almost sad. "So you'll wait here for Dez?"

Fenway nodded. "I've got to follow the team into the athletic offices. I need to ask about Sunday's alibi, at the very least."

McVie leaned forward and gave Fenway a quick peck on the lips.

"Can I see you tonight?" Fenway asked.

"Give me a call later."

———

Fenway walked into the mist, toward the university office buildings.

Her mind whirled. Lorraine Sunday hadn't been on her original list of suspects, but everything fit. With Paul Levinson out of the way, Sandra Christchurch on her side, and Maggie silenced, the head coaching position was hers.

Fenway shook her head. She was focused on Lorraine, but she still needed to keep an open mind.

She opened the door to the building where the coaches' offices were. She could hear Lorraine Sunday's strong, clear voice, enthusiastic but urgent—a focus on the prize, overcoming adversity. She opened the door next to the coaches' office and peered inside.

It was a conference room, and more than twenty people—mostly players—sat around a large table, with Sunday standing at the head. A few players turned to look at her.

"Excuse me a moment," Sunday said, walking over. "Good morning, Coroner. Can I help you?"

"Sorry—sorry," Fenway stammered. "I'll come back when you're done."

Lorraine motioned for her to come inside. "Actually, Coroner, this was a pretty short meeting—but I thought we could have a moment of silence for Maggie before we end. Would you like to join us?"

"Uh—sure." How could she say no? She stepped into the conference room, the door shutting loudly behind her. She looked around: Annabel Shedd, Lorraine Sunday, Rocky Portello, Darcy Nishimura, other players she had interviewed, sitting around a maple-topped conference table, all wearing their Neons' black-and-gold tracksuits.

Except Coach Portello—she realized she'd never seen him wear the Neons' tracksuit. He was in a Neons T-shirt and cap, as usual. Hmm—maybe the tracksuits were only for the women. No, that didn't make sense.

"Maggie was arguably the most fearless goalkeeper to play the game," Lorraine said to the room. "Her competitive spirit inspired everyone who played with her. Soccer has lost one of its greats, and we never even got a chance to know how great she could be." Sunday paused, swallowed hard, cleared her throat, and continued. "Let's take a moment to remember Maggie—and to dedicate this season to her."

Murmurs of assent quickly gave way to quiet, and Fenway set her purse on the chair next to her and bowed her head slightly.

The quiet of the room was almost eerie, and Fenway didn't dare call attention to herself in any way. The disconnected evidence whirled in her head—the car cover, the shoe print, the banner rods, the door stoppers...

And suddenly, the moment of silence was over. Sunday dismissed the players. "I'll see you on the field in twenty minutes."

"Actually, I've got some follow-up questions," Fenway said.

Sunday pursed her lips. "Make it half an hour," she shouted above the din of the players. Then, to Fenway, "Give me five minutes."

"I really can't—"

"Five minutes," Sunday said. "I'll meet you in the hallway." She turned to Coach Portello. "Rocky, can I see you for a moment?"

Fenway stood in the river of players for a moment before walking out with them. The hallway was noisy, a cacophony of overlapping conversations. Fenway grabbed the door handle of the coaches' office and stepped inside, closing the door behind her.

She took a deep breath and looked around. Not much had changed in the office from when she'd interviewed Lorraine Sunday—but something was different.

Coach Sunday's desk was on the right side of the room, Coach Portello's on the left, Levinson's in the middle.

She could rummage through Levinson's desk right now without the warrant the judge had declined. Five minutes—no one would know. If she found the key, she'd be sure Annabel was the better suspect—if not, she'd keep her focus on Sunday, maybe Christchurch, maybe even Ezekiel Washington. It wasn't ethical, and she'd never be able to use it in court, but it could help catch the killer.

She stepped in front of Coach Levinson's desk, debating with herself.

Then she blinked. Something was missing.

She looked all around the desk, but nothing seemed out of place. She raised her gaze to the wall behind his desk.

The banner. *Las Vegas Neons—AFF Western Conference Champions.* It was gone.

The banner rods. Metal finial-tipped dowels. XTL Stainless Steel Banner Rod. Sixty inches.

And Sarah's words rang in her mind: *Based on the width of the ball finial, Dr. Yasuda believes this fits the criteria for the weapon that killed Maggie Erskine.*

She stood and walked behind Levinson's desk. Had it fallen? No—it wasn't on the floor. She walked around the worktable. It was possible, of course, that Lorraine Sunday simply didn't think it was a good motivational tool like Levinson had.

Then she caught something out of the corner of her eye.

There, behind Coach Portello's desk.

She walked, almost trancelike, to his desk. A small hutch stood behind it, and in the space between the wall and the hutch was the banner.

Its banner rods—the stainless steel ones with the finials—were gone.

CHAPTER TWENTY-SIX

Fenway's mind raced. The coaches' office wasn't sacred ground—people were in and out of here all the time. Maybe there was a perfectly good explanation for the hidden banner and the missing rods.

She closed her eyes and saw the rug in her Russian Lit professor's office again—

She smacked her hand on the top of the hutch.

How could she not connect the dots? They were right in front of her.

Sunday hadn't been the one who'd arranged one-on-one player meetings with Levinson, who'd covered for the team, who'd smoothed things over with Maggie, week after week, month after month.

It was Coach Portello.

He'd been the one enabling Coach Levinson. Ever since Shellmont University.

The door opened, and Coach Portello walked in, looking shell-shocked, then almost jumped when he saw Fenway.

His voice was gruff. "What are you doing in here?"

Fenway cleared her throat and stepped away from the hutch, toward Coach Levinson's desk. "I wanted to speak with Coach Sunday, but it was too crowded in the hallway, so I came in here."

Portello narrowed his eyes. "Why are you behind my desk?"

"I—" Fenway's eyes darted around the room. Was there anything she could use for a weapon? Was there anything *he* could use for a weapon? "The last time I was in here, I saw the banner. I thought I'd get a similar one made for the coroner's office. I saw it behind the hutch and wanted to take a look." Fenway wasn't sure if she was a good liar, so something close to the truth would be the most believable, right? "Well, if you're done talking to Coach Sunday—"

"Oh, I'm done, all right." Portello strode to the closet, opened it, and pulled a cardboard box out.

Fenway blinked. During her interview with Lorraine Sunday, Annabel Shedd had put her gym bag in that closet—with her *Desert Treasure* sweatshirt. If Portello had access to that closet—

Still a lot of *ifs*. Lots of people could get into this room. Lots of people could have gone into the closet.

Portello was still talking. "Lorraine wants to take the Neons in a different direction, she says. So I have until the end of the day to pack my shit and get out of here."

Fenway looked down at Portello's shoes.

A large stylized eagle, the letter B embroidered on the side.

The shoe print from the hiking trail. The Bronson Eagle GTX4s.

Fenway swallowed hard.

"It's like last year's championship run meant nothing," Portello continued.

"That sucks. I'm sorry."

He smiled ruefully. "The good news is, the Neons are buying out my contract. The big fat check I'm getting eases the pain a little."

"Silver lining, then." Fenway felt herself break out into a sweat—

and immediately tried to slow down her breathing. She needed to keep him in the room until Dez arrived.

He scoffed. "Certainly not how I thought this would—well, never mind." He slammed the empty cardboard box down on his desk and started putting the pictures and knickknacks into the box.

Never mind, he'd said. His guard was down.

"You didn't tell me that Maggie called you the morning of her death," Fenway said. It was a guess—they wouldn't get the report for hours, if not days—but she thought she'd take the chance.

Portello looked up, his mouth agape. "I didn't—" Then he shut his mouth. "Oh, of course. Cell phone records."

"They do tell us a lot of information." Fenway couldn't keep the smile off her face; her bluff had worked.

Portello sighed and rubbed his forehead. "I didn't tell you earlier because of how it looked, all right? She calls me, wants her job back, wants me to talk to Christchurch. I said no."

"She must have been heartbroken." Fenway's shoulders were tight. At any moment, he might realize she had figured it out. Were the shoes enough proof? The cell phone records?

Maybe not.

A confession would be nice.

"Besides, it's not like you ever asked me directly if I'd spoken to her that morning."

"True." Fenway forced a smile onto her face. He was still making excuses about not telling the police about the phone call. It didn't fit, of course—with Maggie's email, he would have thought it was suicide, not murder, and therefore there'd be no reason to hide the phone call. But Fenway didn't push it. She needed a weapon, she needed handcuffs—she needed Dez.

Portello hesitated, then walked to the other side of his desk, pulled open a file drawer, and took files out, placing them on the desk. "Poor kid—but, you know, we can't employ killers on this team.

Real shame. Maybe she didn't think any other team would take a chance on her, either."

"But we never arrested her, Rocky." The words were out of her mouth before she could stop them.

"I think I speak for everyone on the team when I say we were expecting an arrest."

Fenway looked down. "Was it you who got her kicked off the team?"

"Me? Hell, no."

Quite a visceral reaction from the coach. Fenway cocked her head. "Why not?"

"Because—" Portello hesitated, and his eyes went to the ceiling briefly before settling back to the desk. "Without Maggie, we might get to the playoffs, but there's no way we'd win it all. Maybe it was a distraction, but it was distraction I was willing to live with."

Fenway tried to make eye contact with Portello, but he kept his head down. It was all a lie. He wanted her on the team because once her contract ended, so would the gag order. She'd be free to tell the police—or the media—that Rocky Portello had arranged her private meetings with Levinson. That Portello kept people away from Levinson's hotel room when he had female guests. That Levinson had threatened players with the Seven Summits, with a demotion in playing time, maybe even with getting blackballed in the league. Fenway would bet it had happened to others.

But if Portello had arranged for Levinson to meet with Maggie when she was a seventeen-year-old at Shellmont? That would be more than a fireable offense. That would mean jail time. The sex offenders' registry.

Portello couldn't risk that.

"If you felt so strongly about Maggie staying on the team, why tell her you wouldn't talk to Christchurch when she called you on Saturday morning?"

Portello stroked his mustache. "We—we'd already had the conversation with Sandra. She was *livid* about the theft of her bracelet. She couldn't let it go."

Of course. The stolen diamond tennis bracelet; that part of Portello's plan had backfired. Portello had stolen the jewelry, written the card—the stationery purchase from Marks-the-Spot. He'd put the bracelet in the card, signed it with Lorraine Sunday's name, and shoved it under Maggie's hotel room door—but never expected the card to get stuck.

So instead of Sunday getting blamed for the theft and fired, Maggie was let go.

And Coach Sunday had been promoted instead.

Fenway tried to clear her mind; she couldn't risk antagonizing Portello. He wasn't handcuffed to the table in the interview room at the sheriff's office. He was standing behind his own desk—and Fenway didn't have backup.

Portello knitted his brow and blinked at Fenway.

Shit. Did he just put two and two together? Could he tell she figured it out?

"You think someone framed Maggie," he said slowly.

"We're keeping all lines of inquiry open." She reached down into her purse and pulled out her cell phone. No message from Dez.

Portello nodded. "That makes sense." He stroked his chin. "You've been talking with Annabel Shedd a lot. You know, Annabel's always hated Levinson, ever since I got here. Maybe she'd had enough. I wouldn't be surprised if she killed him, framed Maggie, and then murdered her, too."

This was good. The longer he kept talking, the more likely it was that Dez would get there in time. "So, Rocky," she said, "what are your plans after this?"

He scoffed. "I got fired five minutes ago, and you want to know what my plans are?" He turned to the hutch, then got on his hands and knees. "I'll tell you something," he said from the floor, facing the wall. "If I had any sense, I'd take a nice, long vacation. Somewhere warm." He reached under the hutch and grunted. "You don't think it's Annabel either, do you?"

"I'm afraid I can't comment on an ongoing investigation."

Rocky stood.

And he held a metal-tipped banner rod in his right hand.

Levinson had ordered two banner rods.

Fenway stared at it for a moment, then looked into Portello's eyes. He knew.

"The tennis bracelet," he murmured. "I should have been more careful. But I figured the housekeeping staff would turn in the card, too." He shook his head. "Can't get good help these days, I guess."

Fenway took a tiny step back.

Portello turned the rod over in his hands. The metal rod looked heavy, but he lifted it easily. "Your phone. Put it on the desk."

Fenway looked down—she still had her phone in her hand. She reached out to lay it on the top of the desk—

BAM!

Fenway barely pulled her hand away in time—Portello brought the rod down on top of the phone.

The phone shattered, a hundred bits of electronics and plastic flying across the office. Fenway felt a small piece hit her elbow, hard enough to leave a mark.

"You've got to understand," he said, resting the rod up on his shoulder like a baseball bat, "that I was *expected* to run interference. Required, even. Levinson knew what he was doing. He knew the staff had to put up with it. He won divisions. He won championships. Shellmont got a fifty percent bump in alumni donations after he took us all the way. You think the athletic director wanted to stop that?"

Fenway stared at the banner rod in his hand, and the realization dawned on her. "You didn't buy the door stops so you could kill

Levinson. You bought them so Levinson could go down to the players' floor without being seen in the elevator."

"Close." Portello gave Fenway a sad, uneven smile. "It was much easier for Levinson just to get a player to come up to his room for a one-on-one strategy session."

"Levinson was doing this with more than just Maggie, then," Fenway said.

He shrugged. "Maggie was his favorite. Has been for years."

Fenway pursed her lips. "She was only seventeen at Shellmont. You were running interference so that your boss could have sex with a seventeen-year-old he was coaching?"

Portello shook his head. "You don't understand what the culture is like."

"I guess I don't," Fenway said. "I also don't understand why Maggie called you on Saturday morning."

He chuckled. "She *begged* me to take her back on the team, you know. I told her she'd have to prove to me how much she wanted it—she even said she'd run the Seven Summits."

"So you agreed to meet her at Cypress Point Beach." It snapped together in Fenway's mind. "You had her carry the banner rod. Did you bring buckets of rocks, too?"

His smile broadened. "Maggie thought she was doing penance, running up the trail to the ridge of the ravine, balancing those weights on the banner rod."

Little did she know she was carrying her own murder weapon. Fenway cleared her throat. "So what's next? You're going to smash my skull in just like you did to Maggie? You think you're going to kill me and get away with it?"

"Everyone saw you ask Lorraine—not me—to meet with you. I'll make sure to put your dead body on her desk. She'll be the prime suspect. By then, I'll have cashed my check and be long gone."

"It doesn't have to be like this," Fenway said. "The D.A. will take the circumstances into account. You hitting Levinson over the head? Heat of the moment. You were mad that Levinson kept coercing Maggie even after he was warned. You'd sacrificed everything for him, and he screwed you over."

"For a child," Portello said bitterly. "Maggie was a *child*."

"The D.A. can work with that, Rocky. We can recommend—"

Portello swung at Fenway.

With the desk between the two of them, she jumped back—and the rod missed her by less than an inch. She bumped against the worktable and scrambled on top of it.

Portello jumped over the desk, rod in hand. Unlike many coaches who got soft in the middle when their playing days were behind them, Portello was trim and in shape.

He swung at Fenway again.

She pushed herself back on the tabletop, and the rod glanced off her left shoulder.

A sharp pain shot down Fenway's arm.

She rolled off the table onto her feet.

Portello was still slightly off-balance, and Fenway aimed a kick right between his legs. He turned at the last second, and she connected with his thigh instead, still hard enough to make him drop to a knee.

The door flung open.

Annabel Shedd stood in the open doorway, holding a soccer ball, brows knitted as she tried to figure out what was happening.

"He killed Maggie!" Fenway shouted.

Annabel's face turned from confusion to rage.

She threw the ball at him with all her might, and he used the rod to knock it away easily—

But Annabel had launched herself at him.

Portello tried to sidestep her, but she knocked the rod out of his hand and they both hit the floor behind the worktable. Portello jumped to his feet and ran out the door.

Fenway took off at a sprint after him.

He tried to slam the door in Fenway's face, but she ran full speed, her left shoulder out, and braced for impact. She hit the door before it closed—pain shooting down her arm again—and the door flew open and bounced against the back wall.

Fenway looked down the hallway to her right—nothing. She looked to her left and saw Portello's foot, in the Bronson GTX4, disappear around the corner.

She took off running, the sound of the side door crashing open again behind her.

She didn't look back as she turned the corner. A door at the back of the hallway led outside and was slowly closing on its pneumatic hinges. Fenway pushed hard and sprinted, catching the door just before it closed.

She found herself behind the building on the other side of the quad and slowed to a stop. Where was Portello? She spun around—

—and Annabel Shedd, running faster than on her breakaway on her World Cup–winning goal, flew past her.

"You killed Maggie!" Shedd screamed, racing down the concrete path.

Fenway saw Portello, running hard, fifty feet ahead of Shedd, then making a hard right onto the field, past a hedge. She took a deep breath and began running.

There was no way Fenway could keep up with Portello.

She turned the corner around the hedge.

And saw that Portello was *much* slower than Annabel Shedd.

Shedd took a flying leap at Portello's feet, and the assistant coach tripped, falling to the earth. Shedd pounced on top of him and punched him in the jaw with all her weight behind it.

"You killed her!" Annabel repeated, her voice breaking.

"She would have ruined everything," Portello sobbed, blood running from his lip.

"She was *just a kid*!" Annabel screamed, rearing back to punch Portello again, but Fenway caught her arm before she threw another punch. "Let go of me! He murdered Maggie and he's—"

"Roger Portello," Fenway said firmly, above Annabel's voice, rolling Portello onto his stomach, "you are under arrest for the murders of Paul Levinson and Maggie Erskine. You have the right to remain silent—"

"Let go of me!" Annabel screeched.

"It's too bad Portello slipped and hit his face on a rock," Fenway shouted at Annabel. "I'm glad I won't have to arrest a superstar soccer player for assault."

Annabel glared at Fenway.

"I *won't* have to arrest a superstar soccer player for assault, will I?"

Annabel's breath hitched, but she sat back on her heels and shut her mouth.

Fenway pulled Portello's hands behind his back as she finished reading him his rights. Footsteps—Dez was there, shoving her handcuffs into Fenway's hand.

Fenway, sweating heavily in the misty air, stood and caught her breath. She looked up. All the Neons players—plus Lorraine Sunday and Sandra Christchurch—stood about ten yards back from the scene. McVie stood behind them with folded arms and a smile touching the corners of his mouth.

CHAPTER TWENTY-SEVEN

"I'm sorry I missed all the fun," Dez said.

"Don't worry, everything worked out," Fenway said, looking up from her laptop as she shifted her weight in the plastic chair. The break room at the sheriff's office was too hot, the heater overcompensating for the chilly day. Fenway had her left leg up on the chair in front of her, an ice pack on her knee and another on her shoulder.

"I expected the M.E. would have a big break in the case. That's why I was up in San Miguelito."

"Uh huh. You and Dr. Yasuda working together again."

Dez scratched her temple and looked down at the floor.

"And you seem more chipper than usual this morning."

Dez cleared her throat and looked away. "Maybe I am. But this whole case leaves a bad taste in my mouth." Dez pulled out another plastic chair across from Fenway and sat.

"Portello ran interference for Levinson, made sure he had privacy when he needed it." Fenway opened her email and clicked on the hardware store site link that Sarah had sent her. A picture of the hinge-mounted wedge-shaped door stop filled her browser window, and she turned her laptop so Dez could see the screen.

Dez leaned over. "That's the infamous door stop that Rocky used to get back into the hotel from the stairwell?"

"That's right," Fenway replied. "But he hadn't intended to use it to get away with murder. He used it to get players in and out of the stairwell, so they could go into Coach Levinson's room without being seen in the elevator."

Dez stared at Fenway's screen for a long moment, then glanced up. "It's hard to imagine that Maggie was under Levinson's thumb since her first year at Shellmont."

"I just saw an email from Patrick. He pulled years of electronic communication between the two of them—and it paints a very disturbing picture. She never had a chance."

Dez frowned. "Poor girl."

"Yeah." Fenway shifted positions, a fresh stab of pain going down her arm. "Is Portello talking?"

"He finally decided to clam up and ask for a lawyer. I think he realized he'd said far too much." Dez leaned back in the chair. "Patrick's also analyzing Maggie's email. He's working on how Portello could have faked the suicide note." She looked at Fenway, a smile playing at the corners of her mouth. "You knew the email was fake from the beginning."

"But I didn't know who wrote it."

"Even without that," Dez said, "I expect we'll get a mountain of evidence against Portello."

Fenway nodded. "The ATM transaction at the hardware store, the Corolla key, the signature on the Marks-the-Spot credit card transaction—it'll make for a very happy district attorney."

"And probably a plea instead of a trial." Dez grinned. "So now what?"

"After working the full weekend? I'll finish my paperwork, then maybe McVie and I will go out to dinner tonight." She chuckled. "He even agreed to Dos Milagros instead of some fancy schmancy place."

"Doesn't he have to close out with his very important client?"

"He's taking care of all that today. As far as McVie's concerned, Annabel isn't cheating. Mathilda Montague may not like it, but he's done."

Dez got to her feet. "I'll get you a couple new ice packs."

———

"Everything okay?"

Fenway turned in the passenger seat of the Highlander and looked at McVie. "Uh—I guess so." Was this the time to tell him about her Russian Lit professor? To leave it all on the table? He already knew, that was for sure, but if she could just *tell* him, maybe that would—

"I need to tell you something."

Fenway blinked at McVie. "What?"

"I mentioned before that Amy's selling the house." McVie set his jaw and turned into the parking lot of Fenway's apartment complex. "But that's not all. She's moving to Colorado."

"Oh." Fenway straightened up in her seat. "That's a big step."

McVie pulled into a parking space and turned off the engine. "Amy's already got a buyer for her business, too. She's just—leaving."

"Kind of sudden." Inside, Fenway was celebrating. McVie had never even hinted at going back to his gorgeous blonde ex-wife, but the prospect of her living a thousand miles away? That was great.

He took a deep breath. "Megan decided that she's going with her."

Fenway blinked. "And go to a brand-new school—in another state —her senior year? Why would she do that?"

"Apparently, her boyfriend not only broke up with her, he started dating her best friend. They've turned a bunch of Megan's friends against her—she feels like a pariah. Hates going to school. And her grades are showing it." McVie exhaled loudly. "Megan says she needs a fresh start. Amy agrees."

"Oh." Fenway was sad for McVie—she knew McVie loved his daughter. On the other hand, Megan was often surly to Fenway. It was understandable—Fenway *was* over a decade younger than Amy. Still, to only deal with Megan a few times a year rather than every other week? She forced a concerned frown onto her face and turned to McVie. "That must be tough. I'm sorry."

"I'm worried about my daughter."

"Yeah, it sounds like she's having a tough time. Maybe a fresh start will be good."

McVie hung his head, staring at the bottom of the steering wheel.

Fenway blinked, and her stomach dropped.

There was more.

"I've got to make sure Megan's okay, Fenway. She was on track to go to a good college, and now I don't even know if she'll graduate on time."

"Are you—" Fenway said, and she found she couldn't get the words out.

"I don't know what I'm going to do yet," McVie said softly. "I know Megan needs me. Amy doesn't care if Megan goes to college or even graduates. Someone has to make sure she does her homework. She needs a place to go when she can't handle her mother."

"But—Estancia is your home," Fenway whispered.

"There are cheap apartments near Amy's new house. I just got a big payout from Mathilda Montague—it'll keep me going for at least a year. I can have Piper run the business."

"A year? Then you'll be back?" They hadn't even *known* each other for a year. Could she even do long distance?

"I don't know."

"But—" Fenway choked on the words. *You're supposed to be with me, Craig. This may be your home, but it's my home now, too.*

McVie took a deep, shuddering breath. "I don't know what I'm going to do."

Fenway stared at McVie, a hot tear rolling down her cheek.

You told me you loved me.

But she knew what he would do. He'd already made up his mind. He just didn't know it yet.

CAST OF CHARACTERS

Fenway Stevenson: A former nurse practitioner with a master's degree in forensics, she moved to Estancia in April after her mother lost her battle with cancer. Fenway has a rocky relationship with her father. First appointed to fill out the coroner's term, she was re-elected four months ago.

Her family and friends

Nathaniel Ferris: The richest, most powerful man in the county, the oil magnate founded and owned Ferris Energy. Several months ago, he took a bullet for Fenway, was in a coma for two months, and was forced to sell his company.

Craig McVie: The former sheriff of Dominguez County, he lost the mayoral race in November. Recently divorced from Amy, he's now a private investigator. He and Fenway officially started dating after the election.

Piper Patten: Formerly in the county's IT department, this willowy redhead is a whiz at forensic accounting and data gathering. She likes the command line interface almost as much as she likes her boyfriend, Migs. She now works for McVie.

364 CAST OF CHARACTERS

Co-workers and law enforcement personnel

Sergeant Desirée "Dez" Roubideaux: A detective in the coroner's office, Dez has worked for the county for 25 years. She's a dedicated, determined investigator despite her wisecracks.

Melissa de la Garza: A CSI tech from neighboring San Miguelito County, de la Garza's team is a shared forensic resource with Dominguez County.

Sarah Summerfield: The newly hired coroner's assistant.

Deputy Celeste Salvador: A sheriff's deputy and friend of Fenway's.

Deputy Donald Huke: A rookie sheriff's deputy and Melissa's boyfriend.

Ezekiel Washington: A security specialist at the hotel where the Neons are staying.

Las Vegas Neons personnel

Paul "Flash" Levinson: The head coach of the Las Vegas Neons, his inappropriate behavior is catching up with him.

Sandra Christchurch: The owner of the Las Vegas Neons who has made her fortune in the hospitality business.

Rocky Portello and **Lorraine Sunday**: The two assistant coaches of the Las Vegas Neons, who have both spent over a decade of their careers coaching women's soccer.

Annabel Shedd: She kicked the winning goal in the latest World Cup championship match. Now nearing retirement, she mentors younger players.

Maggie Erskine: The new kid on the block who might be the greatest goalkeeper to ever play the game. The Neons are betting on her to be a superstar.

Mathilda Montague: Annabel's wife is the CEO of a Las Vegas-based gaming empire that happens to be the Neons' top sponsor—and she also happens to be McVie's top client.

MORE BY PAUL AUSTIN ARDOIN

The Fenway Stevenson Mysteries

Book One: The Reluctant Coroner

Book Two: The Incumbent Coroner

Book Three: The Candidate Coroner

Book Four: The Upstaged Coroner

Book Five: The Courtroom Coroner

Novella: The Christmas Coroner

Book Six: The Watchful Coroner

Book Seven: The Accused Coroner

Novella: The Clandestine Coroner

Book Eight: The Offside Coroner

Collections

Books 1–3 of The Fenway Stevenson Mysteries

Books 4-6 of The Fenway Stevenson Mysteries

The Woodhead & Becker Mysteries

Book One: The Winterstone Murder

Book Two: The Bridegroom Murder

Book Three: The Trailer Park Murder *(coming soon)*

Dez Roubideaux

Bad Weather

————

Sign up for *The Coroner's Report,*

Paul Austin Ardoin's fortnightly newsletter:

http://www.paulaustinardoin.com

Subscribe to Paul's Patreon, with several levels of members-only goodies:

https://www.patreon.com/paulaustinardoin

I hope you enjoyed reading this book as much as I enjoyed writing it. If you did, I'd sincerely appreciate a review on your favorite book retailer's website, Goodreads, and BookBub. Reviews are crucial for any author, and even just a line or two can make a huge difference.

ACKNOWLEDGMENTS

Many thanks to my editors Max Christian Hansen and Jess Reynolds, and to my cover designer Ziad Ezzat of Feral Creative. This book is much better because of you.

Thank you to all the early readers and reviewers. Special thanks to the Wordforge Novelists group in Sacramento, whose critical eyes and tough love were invaluable.

Thanks to my patrons, including J.W. Atkinson, Sandy D'Alene, Stan Peters, Janice Webber, and Donna White.

Special thanks to Cheryl Shoults, who has been invaluable creating, organizing, and maintaining my author newsletter, website, reader teams, promotions, and a million other items.

To my wife, my children, and my mother: I'm deeply grateful for your encouragement and support.